Mellen Chamberlain

John Adams

The Statesman of the American Revolution - with other essays and addresses,

historical and literary

Mellen Chamberlain

John Adams
The Statesman of the American Revolution - with other essays and addresses, historical and literary

ISBN/EAN: 9783337230951

Printed in Europe, USA, Canada, Australia, Japan

Cover: Foto ©Andreas Hilbeck / pixelio.de

More available books at **www.hansebooks.com**

JOHN ADAMS

THE STATESMAN OF THE AMERICAN REVOLUTION

*WITH OTHER ESSAYS AND ADDRESSES
HISTORICAL AND LITERARY*

BY

MELLEN CHAMBERLAIN, LL.D.

Formerly Librarian of the Boston Public Library

BOSTON AND NEW YORK
HOUGHTON, MIFFLIN AND COMPANY
The Riverside Press, Cambridge
1899

PREFACE

HAVING come to that time of life when one does not readily assume new cares, the author of these papers has asked me to arrange them, to make such slight modifications as seemed needful, and to answer for their safe conduct through the press.

Aside from the pleasure of serving Judge Chamberlain, if I may, it gives me great satisfaction to be instrumental in bringing this volume to the light. The least among many persistent friends, I have long thought that these scattered fragments should be sheaved in some permanent and accessible form. In this case the "solicitations of others" is no empty expression, behind which timorous authorship is often glad to protect itself. It would be easy, if it were desirable, to produce from letters, written by men of eminence, urgent requests that a larger public might be given the opportunity to become acquainted with material heretofore only available to the few through limited editions. Of one review, here reprinted, an historian of note, writing to an editor, says that it is the best piece of criticism made in this country "in our time;" and a well-known statesman, in expressing his regret that Judge Chamberlain had not earlier devoted himself to historical effort, announces his

belief that an adequate interpretation of the history
of New England would have been the sure result.

Without an exception the contents of this volume
were written by one who, up to his sixtieth year, had
been mainly engrossed in professional cares at the
bar and on the bench. He had, however, studied and
thought wholly for himself, where most men talk
and print the thoughts of other people. As a result,
when he came to express himself for the first time
in print in his full maturity, he had learned to dis-
card all irrelevancies, and to view men and events
without prejudice and violence. I do not readily
recall another instance of so long a reticence on the
part of one naturally inclined to forcible expression.

I especially desire to call attention to the unusual
substance of these essays — since essays they really
are ; for although most of them are nominally addresses, they are not the addresses of an orator who
merely graces an occasion. To have forced the recognition within a decade of a fresh hypothesis in American history, beset as our estimates of that history
are with reserves and mannerisms, is no slight achievement. To-day, however, historians, when they cast
up their balances, have to reckon in Judge Chamberlain's opinions on ecclesiasticism as a factor in
pre-revolutionary affairs. I cite this as one only of
several important contributions to historical thought.

Another side of Judge Chamberlain's life and
character is seen in the papers standing toward the
end of the volume, in which he has expressed his

views on literature and on the æsthetic and poetic considerations of life. His defense of imaginative literature is in gracious contrast to the severity of his attitude toward emotional and merely popular views of history.

It is quite possible that the literary reviewer will find in these pages repetitions of cherished theories; but that is almost inevitably incidental to papers of such a character, and it has not seemed necessary to bring everything to the gauge of consistency and perfect form.

My task has hardly been more than that of selecting these papers, presumably of greatest general interest, from among numerous others, and of grouping these efforts in what I have supposed to be the most effective way; but in doing this there has revived within me a sense of obligation to a man who insensibly steered me away from unsubstantial methods and showed me the value of moderation, candor, and entire independence of judgment.

No attempt is made to give citations to many recent articles and replies to some of the more controversial papers, as, for instance, the "Authentication of the Declaration of Independence."

Four of the articles have been printed, one each in the "Andover Review," the "Dartmouth Literary Monthly," the "Century Magazine" and the "Nation," and appear in this volume by the courtesy of the editors.

"The Revolution Impending," a paper of the first

importance, is here reluctantly omitted; but it may be found in vol. vi. of the "Narrative and Critical History of America." It has even been thought the strongest of Judge Chamberlain's writings. Charles Borgeaud, in his "Établissement et Révision des Constitutions en Amérique et en Europe," says of a passage which he quotes at length, "It would be difficult to indicate more clearly the real character of the American Revolution."

LINDSAY SWIFT.

CONTENTS

JOHN ADAMS

THE STATESMAN OF THE AMERICAN REVOLUTION

An Address before the Webster Historical Society
January 18, 1884

JOHN ADAMS

THE STATESMAN OF THE AMERICAN REVOLUTION

John Adams entered public life with the first session of the Continental Congress, which met at Philadelphia, September 5, 1774, and remained in the service of the country almost uninterruptedly until the close of his administration, March 4, 1801. Of this period, nine years were covered by the American Revolution, in which he took a leading part and held it with undiminished zeal and constancy until the Treaty of Peace in 1783. It is this part of his life of which I am to give some account.

His influence during this period of national history was mainly due to his ability; but he was fortunate in the time at which he intervened in public affairs, as also in the character of the colony from which he was a delegate to the Congress.

Of his great contemporaries, Franklin was not a member until the next spring, and after a little more than a year's service he went abroad on his French mission; neither was Jefferson, who in later years, as a political rival, drew the great body of the people to his way of thinking on national subjects; nor until eight years had passed away was Hamilton, of marvelous genius for statesmanship. Washington entered the Congress with John Adams, and on his suggestion a year later was transferred from civil life to the head of the army.

Of the Congress of 1774, Edward Rutledge and John Jay were younger than John Adams; but the greater part of the delegates were of an age which brings disqualifications for parliamentary leadership. John Adams was thirty-nine years old, and in the prime of his great powers. Peculiarities of temper, which in later years impaired his influence, at this time were a help rather than a hindrance. It must also be counted as his good fortune that he came from Massachusetts Bay; for though that colony was regarded with distrust and dislike by the middle and southern colonies, there were facts in her history, as well as something in the character of her people, which gave potency to her voice in the national councils and weight to John Adams as her leading representative.

Under such circumstances John Adams entered Congress, which he attended through the sessions of four years. During this period of revolution, which was also the period of necessary constitutional reconstruction, he rendered services such as no other statesman rendered, and more widely, more profoundly, and, unless present indications prove fallacious, more permanently impressed the political institutions of the country than any other man who has ever lived in it; and by reason of these services he became entitled to rank as the preëminent statesman of the Revolution.

My object is to show by what endowments, by what acquisitions, and by what use of his powers, can be justly claimed for John Adams the first place among such statesmen as Samuel Adams, John Jay, Thomas Jefferson, and even Benjamin Franklin.

There were no congressional reporters in those days. The members were pledged to secrecy. The journals are neither full nor accurate, and even John Adams's own diary fails us at some of the most critical and interesting points; yet his services in their results are historically clear and not difficult of estimation. It is more difficult, however, to estimate the character of the statesman who rendered these services; for though his purposes were single and his methods simple and direct, his character was complex. In certain aspects it seems to belong to no known type of the English race, nor can it be described in a phrase.

Here was a man born and bred in a narrow, provincial sphere, remote from the centres of liberal thought, untraveled, and separated by the ocean from those movements which so powerfully affected European society in the middle of the eighteenth century; and yet, in rare combination and large measure, he included in his character, and exhibited by his life and action, the best influences of the Reformation, in which those movements had their remote origin. Acknowledging the supremacy of conscience, and yielding implicit obedience to the claims of natural and revealed religion, he recognized its essential unity under all its varied forms of manifestation, and was free from the slightest trace of bigotry or sectarian narrowness. He believed in civil and religious liberty as inherent rights of the people, but under subjection, as are the forces of nature, to an intelligent and ever-active principle of law, which is Milton's idea of liberty. He was a provincial, with all the traditions of provincialism; and yet, undeniably, he was the foremost advocate and most efficient promoter of nationality. Before the colonies had declared themselves independent, and for the purpose of promoting that measure, he advocated the formation of state constitutions, and the severing of one tie which bound them to the mother country; and later, when the great Declaration had gone forth, he strove for a closer union and the semblance, at least, of a national government under the Articles of Confederation. Finally, when the war had closed and the terms of peace were under discussion, he, more than any other, secured to the nation the old colonial rights in the fisheries of Newfoundland, opened to navigation the mouth of the Mississippi when under doubtful jurisdiction, pushed the national boundaries from the Alleghanies to the great river, from the Ohio to the central line of the northern lakes, from the Kennebec to the St. Croix, and yielded the Canadas only to the necessities of peace.

It is an original, not an acquired, character we have to consider. His breadth of understanding and liberal views were not exhibited for the first time after he had left his native province for the wider theatre of national activity, nor when he had been in contact with speculative thought in Europe, but while yet a boy musing upon life and his possible relations to it.

John Adams possessed two faculties in a degree which distinguished him among his countrymen, and made him preëminently serviceable in a period of revolution, — the historic imagination which develops nationality from its germ, and clear intuitions of organic constitutional law. In these faculties he has never been surpassed by any American statesman, nor equaled save by him whose name needs no mention in this presence. There is evidence that from his youth

he was accustomed to trace the growth and development of nationality in the great epochs of Saxon and
English history and to project it under new conditions
in America; and that from the earliest days of the
Revolution he saw in the determining force of race
tendencies, united with free, independent government,
the inevitable greatness of his country. This gave
unity and consistency to his whole public career, in
which respect he stands nearly alone among public
men of equal rank. It also gave him faith when others doubted, courage when they quailed in the face
of danger, and constancy when they lost heart from
disasters. In the gloomy days which succeeded the
defeats at Brandywine and Germantown, when Washington and his army escaped destruction only by the
unaccountable remissness of Howe, John Adams said,
"These disasters will hurt us, but not ruin us." He
had unshaken confidence in the course of free empire.[1]

If we now look at some of those moral characteristics which marked him as a statesman, we shall find
certain race traits which he seems to have inherited
immediately from his British ancestry, rather than by
transmission through his colonial progenitors. He
possessed the pluck, courage, and bull-dog tenacity
which we ascribe to the English, and which all
through their history has stood them in such stead in
desperate civil and military encounters, often changing lost fields to fields of victory; and, on the other

---

[1] At a meeting of the American Academy in 1807, at the request of
Dr. Abiel Holmes, John Adams wrote on a slip of paper, now in my
possession, the following lines which he had seen inscribed in some
forgotten place : —

> "The eastern nations sink ; their glory ends,
> And Empire rises where the sun descends."

hand, there was no trace in his composition of the
craft, cunning, or selfishness which narrow circumstances and a hundred years of contest with a
treacherous and skulking foe are supposed, justly or
unjustly, to have engrafted on the New England
character of his day.

There was no strategy in his nature. His path led
straight to his object, and his movements in it were
simple and direct, though not always free from ostentation and self-assertion, not easily understood in so
great a man. In his victories we perceive no special
skill in plan or science of battle ; but his eye was
quick to detect the stress of the engagement, and
there his honest blows fell fast and heavy. How
clearly he saw the inevitableness of the issue, and
how pluckily for more than a twelvemonth, in Congress, he fought the fight of the Declaration ; and
against what odds — for nothing is now more clear
than this, that neither the Congress nor the people
as a whole were quite ripe for it. He carried the
measure by sheer force and persistence ; and he was
right. Yet it was one of those almost hopeless strug-
gles in which victory forms an epoch in the history of
human progress.

This directness of aim and impetuosity of movement were not the conventional methods, either in
the legislation or the diplomacy of his day, and they
subjected him to some animadversion from those
who respected his honesty and ability. While on his
Dutch mission, in 1781, to procure a recognition of
our independence and to effect a loan, he shocked the
old diplomatists by his memorial to their High Mightinesses and the Prince of Orange. This was issued
against the advice, and even remonstrance, of our

French allies.[1] But it led to ultimate success. I think it will be found that John Adams was always right in his well-considered judgments, and usually so in his measures; if any part of his conduct was open to criticism, it was his manner.[2]

When the cause of independence and nationality demanded an orator, — not brilliant declaimers like Henry, Lee, and Rutledge, but one who, with capacity for affairs, could bring powerful and intrepid advocacy into council and passionate appeals to patriotic sentiment, — such an orator was found in John Adams, the Colossus of debate.[3]

These special gifts were made effective by a vigorous and comprehensive intellect and high courage. All his powers were trained, and every opportunity for improvement embraced, with an assiduity not common in America at that day.

John Adams at his best was always a statesman; as a politician he made a very indifferent figure. In his country's ends he always succeeded — always; and in his own quite likely would always have failed,

[1] When copies of it reached America, Madison, writing to Pendleton, said, " I enclose a copy of Mr. Adams's memorial to the States General. I wish I could have informed you of its being lodged in the archives of their High Mightinesses, instead of presenting it to you in print." — Madison's *Letters*, i. 54.

[2] The memorial above referred to was not promulgated without mature consideration of the whole case. Writing a year later to Francis Dana, our then unaccredited minister to St. Petersburg, Adams said, " I see no objection against your attempt, as you propose, to find out the real disposition of the Empress, or her ministers. You cannot take any noisy measures like those I have taken here. The form of the government forbids it." — *Works*, vii. 544.

[3] The present estimate of Adams does not differ widely from Bancroft's ; but it was formed by a study of Adams's history and writings without reference to Bancroft, who has, it seems to me, overlooked Adams's most marked characteristic, — his historic imagination.

had he sought any that were merely personal. His much-derided administration, though conducted under great embarrassments, was useful to the country, and not without its period of national glory; and the measure which threw his cabinet into confusion was a bold stroke of statesmanship, conceived and persisted in without regard to party or personal interests. Ambitious, vain, egotistical, self-confident, and jealous, — for he was all these, as no one knew better or has oftener told us than himself, — these qualities, on a superficial view, detract from the perfection of his character, and have cruelly interfered with his just fame. But they were mere exaggerations of harmless qualities. Beneath them all we can perceive a complete and well-rounded character, — large, powerful, active, and full of humanities, — with more of individuality than that of any other public man of his day. His *forte* was action. " I never shall shine," he said, "till some animating occasion calls forth all my powers." When side-tracked in the vice-presidency, or finally ditched at Braintree, the engine puffed and snorted and let off steam in a very unedifying manner; but on a clear course, no matter what the load or what the grades, it moved with the swiftness and *verve* of the lightning-train — and, it may be added, with something of its racket.

In respect to a man endowed with such rich and varied gifts, we have a rational curiosity to know something of the processes of education and special training by which they were so supplemented that in due time this native of an obscure provincial town came to be regarded as the ablest constitutional lawyer of his day and the consummate orator and statesman of the Revolution. Nor are we without the means.

John Adams evidently was not unconscious of his powers, nor without ambition to make them servient to the interests of his country and Prepara-tion for public life. his own honorable fame. In his youth he divined the coming empire of America, and formed himself, I think not without prescience, for a distinguished part in its affairs. His self-examination was critical and unsparing. He carefully considered his life-work, as well as his own powers. To what had been given him he added much by reading, reflection, and conversation with those more mature than himself. Of his college life we know little ; but on his graduation he entered upon a wide course of study with commendable diligence. His diary tells us that he made himself acquainted with the great poets of antiquity : with Homer, Virgil, Horace, and Ovid. He knew Shakespeare, Milton, Baxter, and Pope, and apparently understood and enjoyed them. Before the adoption of the law as his profession, and for the purpose of determining his choice, he read with attention the works of the great divines, the political and philosophical writers then in vogue, and the authoritative treatises in medical science. When fairly engaged in the study of the law, he pursued it with such success that before the age of thirty he became one of the best-equipped lawyers in America.

" The study and practice of law, I am sure, does not dissolve the obligations of morality or of religion," so he wrote at the age of twenty, as he was entering on his course of study ; nor did he ever forget this conviction of his unhurt youth. His work was honest throughout, and he prepared himself honestly for it. He did not gauge his legal studies to the requirements of his native Braintree, where he began

to practice, nor by those of the metropolis in which he
was at one time settled. He aimed, he said, to dis-
tinguish himself among his fellow-students "by the
study of the civil law in its native tongues." With
Bracton, Britton, Fleta, Glanville, Coke, and Lord
Hale he became familiar, as also with Justinian and
the great commentators on the civil law. To these
must be added Montesquieu, Blackstone (then recently published), Voltaire's "Louis XIV.," and, in
fine, whatever was within his reach that could enlarge, enrich, or strengthen his understanding for
grasping the principles of law and constitutional government. Following the advice of Gridley, the Nes-
tor of the bar, "to pursue the study of the law rather
than the gain of it," he "labored to get distinct ideas
of law, right, wrong, justice, equity; to search for
them in his own mind, in Roman, Grecian, French,
English treatises of natural, civil, common, statute
law; to aim at an exact knowledge of the nature, end,
and means of government; to compare the different
forms of it with each other, and each of them with
their effects on public and private happiness for the
advancement of right; to assert and maintain liberty
and virtue ; to discourage and abolish tyranny and
vice." With these added extracts from his diary we
have the whole scheme of his life: "Let little objects be neglected and forgot, and great ones engross,
arouse, and exalt my soul." "I was born for business, for both activity and study. I have little appe-
tite or relish for anything else. I must double and
redouble my diligence." The recorded lives of great
statesmen have sometimes made us familiar with the
aspirations and purposes of their youth; but I recall
few instances where these were fixed so high, so unde-

viatingly pursued, and so fully attained by achievements which have indelibly impressed themselves on
the happy fortunes of a continent. These principles,
made efficient by an intellect of extraordinary power,
placed him foremost among the lawyers of his day;
and as we read the history of the country, we learn
without surprise that John Adams was also foremost
among those who established the freedom and nationality of America and laid the foundation of its government.[1] When he entered public life, in 1774, he
was probably well qualified to conduct causes and ar-
gue questions of public law before any tribunal sitting
at Westminster, and to represent with distinction any
English constituency in the House of Commons.

Such was the man to whom came his hour; and he
made it an epoch in history.

John Adams was too conspicuous to be overlooked
among the great men of the country, and the value of
his services was acknowledged by his contemporaries;
but I think they were not estimated at their true
value. We are in a far better position than they
were to do him complete justice. We understand the
Revolution itself in its causes and its progress much
more fully than those who were actors in it. The
century of the national existence just closed was to
them the dark, uncertain future; to us it has joined
the historic past. In it we see events in their relations and proportions which to them appeared incom-
plete and sometimes unrelated.

---

[1] John Adams's legal erudition does not, as is so often the case
among great lawyers, rest merely upon tradition. His dissertation
on the canon and feudal law, written at the age of twenty-nine, is still
extant, and may be read with profit even in the light of later studies.
It was erroneously attributed to Gridley, and pronounced by Hollis,
in England, where it was more than once reprinted, to be " one of the
very finest productions from North America."

But I venture to think that we shall not reach
these desirable results unless we unlearn
Character
of the
Revolu-
tion. some things we have been taught, and clear
away some prejudices which have proved so
fatal to successful historical research. We
seem now far enough removed from the Revolution to
study it historically, and not as partisans ; to be permitted to learn that then, as now, when people divide
into parties, not facts, nor right, nor conscience, are
wholly on one side.[1]   Nor does it seem longer necessary to conceal those facts which do not stand for
national honor, or to be compelled to guess them from
ambiguous and often disingenuous apologies.   It is
hardly exaggeration, however, to say that we can more
dispassionately discuss the causes of the late Civil
War, and lay bare the motives and conduct of the
men and parties engaged in it on either side, than the
motives and conduct of men and parties at the beginning of the Revolution, the intrigues in the Congress,
or the convention at Saratoga in 1777.

The result of this state of things, growing out of
undue solicitude for the reputation of individuals and
a patriotic disposition to exalt the successful party, is
that we have much history that is neither truthful nor
profitable for reproof, instruction, or guidance.

John Adams's fame as a statesman grew out of his
services during the American Revolution.   In the
endeavor to form a just estimate of those services, I
have been led to consider that event in its inception,
progress, and results, and to discover, if possible, the
exact relations of John Adams to it.   In the prosecution of this purpose I have observed some facts which
do not appear to me to be sufficiently emphasized, to

[1] See Dawson's *Handbook for the Dominion of Canada*, 103, 104.

say the least, in the histories of that period; and I have reached some conclusions which require a fuller statement of the grounds on which they rest than is ordinarily found in an address of this description.

It seems to me that we shall fail to appreciate the true character of the Revolution if we restrict its entirety to the events which transpired between the Stamp Act of 1765 and the Peace of 1783; for, thus limited, I am unable to find adequate causes in those events when regarded in their necessary political sequence, or when referred in historical parallelism to other movements of society which have resulted in the disruption of governments. The causes of revolution are usually remote from the event. No matter on what soil they are planted, the seeds of a new order of government germinate slowly, and only children's children are permitted to repose beneath its branches.[1] For the history of the Revolution we must go back to the planting of the seeds. John Adams is authority for this view of the subject. "The principles and feelings which contributed to produce the Revolution ought to be traced back for two hundred years, and sought in the history of the country from the first plantations in America." Seldom, if ever, are revolutions the spontaneous action of an entire community. Their interests may be the same, they may suffer from a common grievance, but people will not think alike. Divergences of opinions are sure to arise, and out of these parties are formed. A contest ensues with vicissitudes of fortune, but ultimately terminating in accordance with the movement of society out of which it springs. The American Revolution was no exception to this general rule,

[1] H. B. Adams's *Life and Writings of Jared Sparks*, i. 404.

though one might infer otherwise from much which passes for history.

To understand the services which John Adams rendered to the country in the Revolution, it is essential to understand the attitude of the parties which brought it on, and, with great exactness, the questions which divided them in their inception, progress, and urgency, at the time when he engaged in public affairs; and especially so in his case, since, to a profound knowledge of these questions, and the formative influence of this knowledge on his mind and character, was due in no small degree his success in giving direction and happy issue to the movement.

The commonly received notion is that the passage of the Stamp Act so clearly contravened the rights of the colonists as British subjects, that they with one accord rose in resistance, and after eight years of strife finally achieved their independence. I venture to think that this is the apparent, rather than the real, state of the case. I think that those who accept it fail to perceive the true nature of this demonstration, and wholly overlook the vital elements of genuine revolution which existed in the antecedent history of the two colonies whose hearts were earliest engaged in the cause — Virginia and Massachusetts — and made revolution possible; and that of these causes, perhaps the prime cause, without which the Revolution would never have begun when it did and where it did, was ecclesiastical rather than political, beginning with the settlement of the colony of Massachusetts Bay, and operating with unbroken succession and efficiency down to the commencement of hostilities.

It also overlooks the origin and continuity of that civil contest which began in Massachusetts with the

revocation of the first charter in 1684, between the
friends of the royal government and the champions of
popular rights, in which parties arrayed themselves
under the respective and successive lead of Randolph
and Danforth, Dudley and Cooke, Burnett and Wells,
on issues as sharply defined, involving the same general principles, and as hotly contested, as those which
divided Bernard and Hutchinson from James Otis
and Samuel Adams.

Another misconception which belittles the contest
and detracts from the merit of the patriotic party is
that which regards the Tories as a mere handful of
malignants, composed mainly of commercial adventurers and government officials having no stake in the
community, together with a few old families which, for
personal aggrandizement, set themselves in opposition
to the principles and measures of the patriots, and
sought to compass the subjugation and ruin of the
country in which they were born, and in which their
dearest interests centred.

The only remaining matter to which I shall allude
relates to the grounds on which the patriotic party
opposed the parliamentary claim of right to tax the
colonists. In reading the histories of those times, one
is likely to receive the impression that the outburst of
popular indignation which pervaded the colonies on
the news of the passage of the Stamp Act would not
have occurred had the colonists been represented in
Parliament; but there is no foundation for this impression. Their main objection was commercial, and
not political. It was to the tax, not to non-represen-
tation; still less to any merely theoretical claim of
parliamentary supremacy, as is evident from the quiet
which followed the repeal of the act, though accom-

panied by the express declaration of the right to tax
the colonists.   And we are to regard the resolutions
of the Congress of 1765, as well as those of the provincial assemblies in the early stages of the controversy, and perhaps as late as 1775, in the nature of
protests, like the Virginia and Kentucky resolutions
of a later day, designed, of course, to influence parliamentary legislation, but not as preliminaries of
forcible resistance.

But there came a time — earlier in Massachusetts
than elsewhere, for reasons to be given hereafter —
when all this was changed ; when the colonists came
to understand that there were colonial constitutions as
well as a British constitution, and that both were subject to like laws of growth and development; that by
the operation of these laws in the direction of natural
rights their own constitutions had come to be the basis
and measure of their rights and immunities ; that in
all cases, especially in internal affairs, where the imperial and colonial constitutional maxims conflicted,
the latter were the fundamental rule of right and action ; and finally, that if the validity of this construction involved a reference to the *ultima ratio*, it would
only be one more instance, of which English history
is full, of that mode of settling constitutional questions.   When the colonists came to this ground, they
had a good fighting position, not before.   Here John
Adams stood — stood nearly alone ; altogether alone
in the clearness with which he saw the strength of this
position, and in the courage and pertinacity with which
he maintained it.[1]   To this clear constitutional ground
he first led his own colony, and finally the representa-

---

[1] But see George W. Greene's *Historical View of the American Revolution*, 381.

tives of the thirteen colonies in Congress assembled, in a declaration of their rights in 1774, and of their independence in 1776. This was his greatest public service ; and it was the greatest feat of statesmanship during the revolutionary period. He had able coadjutors, but to him, more than to any other, the honor is due. This ground of rights under colonial constitution once taken, the strife was no longer rebellion, but maintenance of constitutional rights. "We are not exciting a rebellion," exclaimed John Adams. "Opposition, nay, open, avowed resistance by arms, against usurpation and lawless violence, is not rebellion by the law of God or the land." The colonists were no longer traitors, but patriots ; and those who undertook to force their position were justly deemed public enemies. Final success was no longer doubtful. The cause had aligned itself to the great movement of society, which began with the Reformation, in the direction of nationality, and in its support had secured the resources of a continent.

These positions must now be referred to their historic basis. It was by no accident that the Massachusetts in the Revolution. Revolution broke out in Massachusetts Bay. It could have happened, at that time, nowhere else upon the continent. Nowhere else had a succession of causes, civil and religious, operative through a hundred years, prepared the way for it. Hither the royal troops had been sent, because here they were needed to maintain the royal government ; and to these troops the first·armed resistance in which blood was shed was on the field of Lexington, April 19, 1775.[1]

[1] On this point it is scarcely necessary to quote authorities. One

Starting, then, from that place and hour, and running back on the line of colonial history in search of adequate causes not connected with antecedent causes, I find my progress arrested and my historic sense of cause and effect satisfied only by the events and motives which led to the settlement of the Bay in 1630. These motives were two : religious and civil liberty. And the greater of these was religious liberty. It was also the more efficient. And I find that these motives, regarded as causes, continued to exist and operate in clear religious and political sequence, with only insignificant interruptions and with scarcely impaired vitality, to the treaty of peace in that year of God of which the last was the happy centennial; and that the events which occurred between 1765 and 1783, though dramatically complete in themselves, yet historically are only the closing act of a drama which opened in 1630 with the coming of Winthrop and his Puritans.

Thus the American Revolution began in the colony of Massachusetts Bay, and in its vital and most potent force was religious rather than political. This character of the Revolution was impressed upon it by the circumstances which led to the Puritan hegira

will suffice. "In all the late American disturbances, and in every attempt against the authority of the British Parliament, the people of Massachusetts Bay have taken the lead. Every new move towards independence has been theirs ; and in every fresh mode of resistance against the law, they have first set the example, and then issued out admonitory letters to the other colonies to follow it." Mauduit's *Short View of the History of the New England Colonies*, 5. An address to the House, February 7, 1775, and before the events at Lexington, proposed by the minister, and carried after great debate, declared that a rebellion already existed in Massachusetts, countenanced and fomented by unlawful combinations in the other Colonies. Hildreth, *Hist. U. S.* iii. 61.

from England in 1630; and those circumstances, only
changed in form but remaining the same in
their essential character, continued to exist   Ecclesi-
until the events at Lexington in 1775 noti-   asticism
fied the Bishop of London, as well as the   the Rev-
King of England, that the descendants of   olution.[1]
the Puritans had referred both the polemics of the
hierarchy and the casuistry of parliamentary supremacy to the decision of war.   The motive which led to
the Puritan emigration was religious rather than civil.
It was from the crozier rather than the sceptre —
from Laud and the High Commission rather than
Charles the First — that the Puritans fled.[2]

[1] Notwithstanding what I say about "Ecclesiasticism as *a* cause
of the Revolution," some of my critics have hastily substituted *the*
for *a*. I wrote only after careful examination of original authorities
and much reflection. Many historical scholars have written me to
the effect that, while they were pleased to say that much in the
pamphlet was not only "new but also true," that part which treated
of ecclesiasticism was not only true, but had never before been
treated, so far as they had observed, with direct explicitness.

Since I wrote, I have found a large mass of authorities; but only
lately have I read the most remarkable letter of Roger Sherman in his
Life by L. H. Boutell, p. 64. I think it confirms all that I have said,
and places the subject where only one of his ability could place it.

[2] "Independence of English Church and State was the fundamental principle of the first colonization, has been its general principle
for two hundred years, and now, I hope, is past dispute. Who, then,
was the author, inventor, discoverer, of independence?   The only
true answer must be, the first emigrants. When we say that Otis,
Adams, Mayhew, Henry, Lee, Jefferson, etc., were authors of independence, we ought to say they were only awakeners and revivers of
the original fundamental principle of colonization." — John Adams's
Works, x. 359. "It is certain that civil dominion was but the secondary motive, religious the primary, with our ancestors in coming
hither and settling this land." — President Stiles, *American Pulpit*,
xxx. This view seems to be adopted by Harry A. Cushing in his
*Transition from Provincial to Commonwealth Government in Massa-
chusetts*, p. 14, as follows : —

"The time of reorganization in Massachusetts is marked by a

They came hither to escape the hierarchy of the Church of England and to set up one of their own. And it was in defense of this domestic hierarchy — though civil and religious liberty were indissolubly connected in their minds — that the clergy of New England, alone of all the professional or propertied classes, arrayed themselves on the popular side.

In the middle and southern colonies, as well as in New England, there had been political contests with the representatives of the Crown. All the colonies were dissatisfied with the Navigation Laws and Acts of Trade and the exercise of the royal prerogatives; but out of New England the colonists, who were mainly of the Church of England, — certainly not Puritans, — became quiet as the enforcement of these laws was relaxed or evaded. But in New England, and especially in Massachusetts, disquietude prevailed unceasingly, and the Revolutionary cause, when no other disturbing element was apparent, fluctuated with the efforts of the Bishop of London to establish Episcopacy in New England. For the accomplishment of this end there was the ever present, always active

variety of clear characteristics; it is, as well, divided into distinct periods. The underlying causes of the change appear in the strong difference in religious types between the home country and its colony, in the wholly different social surroundings and influences, in the increasing, if not even hostile, divergence of economic interests and activity, and in the almost antipodal political traditions nourished and acted upon by the more advanced colonists on the one hand, and, on the other, by the more conservative Englishmen."

Elias Boudinot, President of Congress, to Rev. James Caldwell, June 19, 1776: "Our Clergy have gone distracted, and have done us more injury than they will do us good in a great while . . . we have been quarreling with the Church of England these forty years past, about uniting Civil and Ecclesiastical Power; and now the moment we have the Power in our hands, we are running into the same extreme." — Leffingwell's *Catalogue*, No. 1170.

motive of sectarian zeal for the propagation of religious faith, and still more of ecclesiastical government. To this was added a special reason in the dissatisfaction of the Church of England people in Massachusetts, to whom Puritanic ways were displeasing. This class, consisting in the early days chiefly of crown officials and commercial sojourners, was not large, but increasing sufficiently, so as to excite the commiseration of the Bishop of London as sheep without a shepherd and wandering in unconsecrated pastures. His efforts for their relief kept the Puritans in hot water for more than seventy years, and gave rise to a mutual dislike which became hereditary. In their resistance to Episcopacy the Massachusetts people were regarded in England as bigoted religionists and refractory subjects. And so were they by the people of the colonies out of New England; a fact never to be lost sight of in tracing the progress of the Revolution. For the middle and southern colonies had been settled or become possessed by people in sympathy with the Church of England, or at least having no special cause of hostility to it, — as was the case with the Puritans, — under whose ministrations they were contented, with loyalty to the king, to worship God after the manner of their fathers.

To this grateful privilege of ecclesiastical relationship was added a pecuniary advantage, so long as the Society for the Propagation of the Gospel in Foreign Parts liberally expended the contributions of the piously disposed churchmen of the mother country in establishing parishes, erecting church edifices, and paying the salaries of missionaries in colonial territory. To this the other colonists saw no more objections than occur to the minds of our frontier settlers to the benevolent operations of the Home Missionary Society. But to the Puritans of Massachusetts, scattering the seeds of Episcopacy was sowing tares by the Evil One. To escape from soul-destroying conformity, their fathers had fled their pleasant homes in Lincolnshire and set up their altars in a bleak and sterile wilderness. They had come hither, not so much to erect a state as a church; and if after a time the two became one, that one was the church-state, not the state-church, between which there is an immense difference. They set it up for themselves, not for others. To the liberality of toleration they made no pretension, as is so often forgotten. To their new home came unwelcome intruders, and with them came trouble. I am now to trace this history.[1] Laud,

---

[1] Some years since, I noticed facts in ecclesiastical history apparently of more importance in the Revolutionary struggle than had been accorded to them by historians; and later, special study has confirmed this impression. This reticence on the part of those who wrote early on the war of the Revolution had been observed by Boucher, the Tory clergyman of Virginia, and by him attributed to some discreditable motive, such as a disposition to conceal the Puritan narrowness which would exclude Episcopalians from the privileges of church worship after their form. — *View of the Causes of the Revolution*, 148. Bancroft and Hildreth have treated the subject as fully, perhaps, as the necessary regard to proportions in a general history would permit; but neither, so as to apprise the reader how early and how continuously, nor, I think, how efficiently, ecclesiasticism operated as a cause of the Revolution. Hildreth, who treats the subject more fully and more directly than Bancroft, says, "The Congregational ministers of New England, an intelligent and very influential body, headed at this period by Chauncy and Cooper, of Boston, cherished a traditionary sentiment of opposition to British control, — a sentiment strengthened, of late years, by the attempts of the English Society for the Propagation of the Gospel to build up Episcopacy in New England by supporting there some thirty Episcopal missionaries. An unseasonable revival of the scheme for a bishop in the colonies had recently excited a bitter controversy, in which, since Mayhew's death, Chauncy had come forward as the Congregational champion;

at the head of the High Commission, began the
assault on the expatriated Puritans in 1634, but the

a controversy which could only tend to confirm the Congregational
body in hostility to the extension of English influence." — *History
of the United States*, iii. 55.

There is a very interesting letter written by John Adams to Dr.
Morse in 1815, the whole of which should be read by those who
would know the views of one most competent to speak on this subject. The following extract will serve to show some foundation at
least for the view I have taken in the text; and I may add, had
I met with it earlier in my reading, it would have saved me much
research, and the reader some pages of my own : —

"Where is the man to be found at this day, when we see Metho-
distical bishops, bishops of the Church of England, and bishops, arch-
bishops, and Jesuits of the Church of Rome, with indifference, who
will believe that the apprehension of Episcopacy contributed fifty
years ago, as much as any other cause, to arouse the attention, not
only of the inquiring mind, but of the common people, and urge them
to close thinking on the constitutional authority of Parliament over
the colonies ? This, nevertheless, was a fact as certain as any in
the history of North America. The objection was not merely to the
office of a bishop, though even that was dreaded, but to the authority
of Parliament, on which it must be founded. . . . If Parliament can
erect dioceses and appoint bishops, they may introduce the whole
hierarchy, establish tithes, forbid marriages and funerals, establish
religions, forbid dissenters." — *Works*, x. 185.

At an earlier date he had said, " It is true that the people of this
country in general, and of this province in special, have an hereditary apprehension of and aversion to lordships, temporal and spiritual. Their ancestors fled to this wilderness. to avoid them, — they
suffered sufficiently under them in England. And there are few of
the present generation who have not been warned of the danger of
them by their fathers and grandfathers, and enjoined to oppose
them." — *Novanglus*, February 13, 1775.

The bibliography of this subject is yet to be made. Here follow
some references to works which are incidentally or directly illus-
trative of ecclesiasticism in the Colonies, and which may be of service
to future students, though set down at random. Hutchinson's *History*,
iii. 15 ; W. Gordon's *Thanksgiving Discourse*, December 15, 1774, 24 n. ;
Gordon's *History*, i. ; Eddis's *Letters from America*, 50 ; Joseph Emerson's *Thanksgiving Sermon*, July 24, 1766, 12 ; W. Livingston's "Letter to John, Bishop of Landaff ;" *Historical Magazine*, ser. 2, v. 268 ;
Makemie's *Narrative of Imprisonment* (Force's Tracts, vol. iv.) ; *North*

civil wars prevented further efforts to set up Episcopacy until the Restoration. The contention, however,
did not cease when Presbyterianism became the state
religion under the Commonwealth, since the adherents
of that ecclesiastical polity sought to introduce it into
Massachusetts. This the Puritans resisted as strenuously as they had resisted prelacy. They had established independent churches, and determined they
should remain such. They agreed with John Milton, —

  " New Presbyter is but Old Priest writ large."

But the Restoration of Charles II. renewed the
strife under its old form — resistance to Anglicanism.
For as soon as the domestic affairs of the realm would
permit, royal commissioners were sent over to inquire
into the reports from Massachusetts Bay, " that his
subjects in those parts did not submit to his government, but looked upon themselves as independent upon

American Review, April, 1884, cxxxviii. 359; Waddington's *Congre-
gational History*, 1700–1800, 459; *Short Appeal·to the People of Great
Britain* (1776); F. Maseres's *Paraphrase on a Passage in a Sermon by
Dr. Markham* (1777); C. Chauncy's *Letter to a Friend* (1767); Sir J.
Johnson's *Orderly Book*, xii.; Bishop White's *Memoirs of the Protest-
ant Episcopal Church*, De Costa's ed.; J. L. Diman's *Orations and
Essays*, 223; T. B. Chandler's *Appeal to the Public in Behalf of the
Church of England in America* (1767); " Letter of Dr. Gibson, Bishop
of London," in Chalmers's *Opinions of Eminent Lawyers*; Franklin's
Works (Sparks's ed.), iv. 89; C. A. Briggs, " Puritanism in New York,"
Magazine of American History, xiii. 39; Otis's *Vindication of the Conduct of the House of Representatives*, 20 n.; Quincy's *Address*, September
17, 1830, 22 *et seq.;* Brooks Adams's *Emancipation of Massachusetts*, ch.
xi.; *Massachusetts Historical Collections*, iv. 4, 410 *et seq.; Life of Peter
Van Schaack; Votes and Proceedings of the Freeholders of the Town of
Boston*, November 20, 1772, 27; Perry's *Historical Collections relating
to the American Colonial Church*, iii., Massachusetts; Beardsley's *Life
and Correspondence of Samuel Johnson, D. D., Missionary of the Church
of England in Connecticut;* Tudor's *Life of Otis*; Ramsay's *History
Amer. Rev.* i. 199 (Phila., 1789).

him and his laws;" and with instructions "to take care that such orders were established there that the Act of Navigation should be punctually observed;" and to send home a detailed report of the frame and constitution of the local government in *church and state.*[1]

The significance of these directions was clear to the colonists when they found their old enemy, the Church of England Samuel Maverick, among the commissioners. This unfriendly scrutiny into their ecclesiastical and civil affairs was met by the colonists with infinite skill and patience, if not with entire candor; for nobody knew better than themselves that they had claimed and exercised substantial sovereignty in church and state, and that they were determined to yield it only in the direst extremity. In that extremity they soon found themselves; but neither they nor their descendants ceased to resist the introduction of prelacy, until armed resistance at the Revolution involved the thirteen colonies in a strife which had its origin in a question of parliamentary government.

In 1684 the enemies of the Puritan church overthrew the old charter under which the colonists had been allowed to manage civil and ecclesiastical affairs in a very free and independent way. What of disaster to civil and religious liberty, as the Puritans understood these terms, this change imported, soon became evident. It overthrew their constitution of government, it confiscated the title to their lands and all improvements on them, and it imperiled their cherished form of church government. The significance of the loss of their charter, in its influence upon the hundred years of controversy which ensued, will not

---

[1] Palfrey, *History*, ii. 584.

be fully appreciated unless we keep in mind that ecclesiastical as well as civil causes led to that result. It was not merely because the colonists had disobeyed the Navigation Laws, coined money, and performed other acts of civil sovereignty, that Charles's commissioners were sent on their errand of inquiry. In fact, the formation of the commission was instigated in the colony itself by those whose chief grievance was that they had suffered under the strictness of the Puritan hierarchy in not being permitted those consolations to be found by them only in the bosom of the Anglican church. "They discountenance the Church of England" was the constant complaint to the Privy Council by Randolph, the memory of whose malign influence as the evil genius of New England still survives in tradition as well as in recorded history.

The new order of things under the presidency of Dudley began May 25, 1686, and the day following the Rev. Mr. Ratcliffe, who had been sent over by the Bishop of London to institute Episcopal worship, waited upon the Council. Mason and Randolph, members of that body, proposed that he should be allowed one of the three Puritan meeting-houses to preach in; and in June the first Anglican church in New England was organized at Boston. The next year the Old South meeting-house was virtually seized by Andros, who had succeeded Dudley, and used for the Church of England service. "If," says Palfrey, "the demand had been for the use of the building for a mass, or for a carriage-house for Juggernaut, it could scarcely have been to the generality of people more offensive." [1] But the Revolution of 1689, of

---

[1] "The Quakers and other Dissenters were encouraged by Andros to refuse payment of the taxes levied by the towns for the support of

which the detestation of Episcopacy was one of the
chief causes, swept away Andros and his government,
and the Puritan Zion had comparative peace until
1699, when the Earl of Bellomont, the first Church
of England governor under the new charter, arrived.
He was attached to the communion of his church,
which he attempted to revive in Boston.   In this he
was encouraged by the Bishop of London, the dio-
cesan for America, and the Lords of Trade, who interested themselves to obtain for the colonists the
advantages of ecclesiastical supervision.[1]   And from
this time down to the breaking out of the war, Bishops
Tenison, Sherlock, and Secker were successively active
in promoting the establishment of an Anglican hierarchy, with resident bishops, in America;[2] and in 1761
there were in New England thirty missionaries who
had been sent over by the Propagation Society.[8]

For nearly a hundred years preceding the Revolu-

the ministers. . . . The celebrating of marriages, no longer exercised
by the magistrates, as had been the case under the old charter, was
confined to Episcopal clergymen, of whom there was but one in the
province.   It was necessary to come to Boston in order to be married."   Hildreth, *History of the United States*, ii. 84, 85.

[1] "The zeal of William's colonial governors on behalf of the
Church of England originated quite as much in political as in religious
motives.   Community of religion, it was thought, would be a security
for political obedience." — *Ibid.* ii. 214.

[2] *Massachusetts Historical Collections*, vii. 215 ; Palfrey, iv. 208.

[8] The Society for the Propagation of the Gospel in Foreign Parts
was established in 1701 ; but whether on the suggestion of the Rev.
Dr. Bray of the Church of England, who, as a commissary to supervise
the religious establishment of Maryland, embarked thither December
16, 1699, does not appear.

He was an intelligent gentleman, and established libraries in the
colonies ; but they were mainly theological, and of the Church of England.   As such they met with slight favor in New England, where only
a few were established.   See B. C. Steiner in *American Historical
Review*, ii. 59.

tiou, these efforts to establish Episcopacy in Massachusetts were causes of anxiety and alarm. On the anniversary of the death of Charles the First, January 30, 1750, and twenty-five years before war broke out, Dr. Jonathan Mayhew of Boston preached a discourse which became famous on both sides of the Atlantic, in which he attacked the doctrines of the divine right of kings, passive obedience, and the exclusive claims of the Episcopal hierarchy. A sentence from the preface to the published sermon will indicate its character and temper: " People have no security against being unmercifully priest-ridden but by keeping all imperious bishops, and other clergymen who love to lord it over God's heritage, from getting their feet into the stirrup at all." It breathed an intense spirit of religious and civil liberty, and did much to intensify the colonial hatred of the threatened Episcopal hierarchy.[1] In this it expressed — perhaps inspired — the sentiments of Samuel Adams, and was one of the most powerful influences which kept alive the spirit of revolution and finally prepared the minds of the Massachusetts colonists for open resistance. The following extracts will show how continuous was the hostility manifested to Episcopacy, — a feeling not confined to the ignorant, illiberal crowd, but shared by the most enlightened of the colonists.

Samuel Adams, as the voice of the House of Representatives, presumably expressing the sentiments of the people, in a letter to their agent in London in 1768 said: " The establishment of a Protestant Epis-

[1] " Say, at what period did they grudge
To send you Governor or Judge,
With all their Missionary crew,
To teach you law and gospel too ? "
TRUMBULL'S *McFingal.*

copate in America is also very zealously contended for; and it is very alarming to a people whose fathers, from the hardships they suffered under such an establishment, were obliged to fly their native country into a wilderness. . . . We hope in God such an establishment will never take place in America, and we desire you would strenuously oppose it. The revenue raised in America, for aught we can tell, may be as constitutionally applied towards the support of prelacy as of soldiers and pensioners." [1]

Dr. Andrew Eliot, the enlightened clergyman who declined the presidency of Harvard College, in one of a series of letters chiefly on this subject, written between 1768 and 1771, addressed to Thomas Hollis, in England, said: "The people of New England are greatly alarmed; the arrival of a bishop would raise them as much as any one thing." [2]

As late as 1772, the Boston Committee of Correspondence appointed to state the rights of the colonists, in their report made in Faneuil Hall, among other things declared that various attempts "have been made, and are now made, to establish an American Episcopate;" though "no power on earth can justly give temporal or spiritual jurisdiction within this province except the great and general court." [3]

It may be difficult for us who live under the mild and beneficent influence of Episcopacy to understand the alarm which its proposed introduction occasioned to the most liberal minds among our New England ancestors during the century which immediately pre-

[1] Wells's *Life of Samuel Adams*, i. 157.

[2] *Massachusetts Historical Collections*, xxiv. 422; Tudor's *Life of Otis*, 136.

[3] Thornton's *Pulpit of the American Revolution*, 102; and Adams's *Works*, ix. 287, 288.

ceded the Revolution. Making all due allowances for the exaggerated apprehensions of the common people (I mean those who were ready to mob a bishop), as well as for the personal pecuniary interest which the clergy of the ruling order had in resisting encroachments upon *their* establishment, there was at that time a real danger to civil liberty as it existed under democratic forms, in the attitude and claims of the Anglican hierarchy. Nor was New England alone in this state of alarm. There were many in Old England, some high in the church itself,[1] who deprecated the reactionary tendency towards an exercise of the temporal powers. In both countries the question was the same at the period of our Revolution, and had been for a hundred and fifty years. During this period the Puritans in Old England who abided the result of the contest on their native soil, and their descendants, finally threw off the excess of prelatical domination with its included doctrines of the divine right and passive obedience, and relegated Episcopacy in all but the name to the exercise of its spiritual functions, restrained the power of the nobles, extinguished that of the sovereign, and raised the people,

---

[1] English Dissenters, with some churchmen, were in full accord with their American brethren on this subject. Archdeacon Blackburne says, "They knew the hardships of those legal disabilities under which they themselves lay at home. They had good reason to believe that the influence of the established hierarchy contributed to continue this grievance. Their brethren in America were as yet free from it, and if bishops were let in among them, and particularly under the notion of presiding in established churches, there was the highest probability they would take their precedents of government and discipline from the establishment in the mother country and would probably never be at rest till they had established it on the basis of an exclusive test. They knew their American brethren thought on this subject just as they themselves did." — *Works*, ii. 73.

through the commons, to their true place in the body politic. To accomplish this cost one king his head, another his crown, and the people themselves untold treasures of blood and money.

Some of the Puritans sought quiet by flight into the New England wilderness; but in vain. They found no exemption in that way. The spirit of ecclesiastical domination followed them, and for a century and a half they strenuously resisted the re-imposition of that system which their brethren at home were endeavoring to throw off. The contest was essentially the same on both sides of the Atlantic, and continued down to the Revolution, of which it was one of the principal causes. During this long contest names often changed, and the evils experienced on one side of the water and feared on the other were mitigated by the lapse of time and the general progress of the age. But the principle contended for, — civil and religious liberty, — remained to the end.

The claim of the high churchmen was "that every country acts naturally and prudently in making the ecclesiastical polity conformable to its civil government." This was a proposition which neither the early nor the later Puritans would care to dispute, since they acted upon it themselves. Their contention was that, their civil government being essentially democratic, their ecclesiastical system should be the same. They opposed the engrafting of the prelatical system, which was monarchical, upon their system, which was republican, well knowing the tendency of ecclesiasticism to draw to itself the civil government. They saw Monarchy and Episcopacy as correlated facts, and in resisting the latter they resisted the former. Such was their view of the case; nor were the facts against them.

The Church of England, so far as it had a civil establishment, was the creature of Parliament. It looked up to the king as its head, and to the Parliament as its lawgiver. Its creed and book of prayer were established by statute. It could not reform its own abuses. Through Parliament the laity amended and regulated the church. The election of the bishops by the clergy was only nominal. The purity of spiritual influence was tarnished by this strict subordination to the temporal power.[1] This was the system. Its administration was still more objectionable to the Puritans. Its establishment in New England meant a return to that state of ecclesiastical and civil affairs from which they had suffered so much, and from which they fled to the privations and sufferings of an inhospitable wilderness.[2] So at least they regarded it, and the efforts of the Anglican hierarchy down to the Revolution never permitted this feeling to subside. Under the old charter, the churches, with the consent of the General Court, called their synods, which laid down or modified their platform of religious faith and ecclesiastical government according to the convictions of a body of professed Christians. But when the Congregational ministers of Massachusetts, as late as 1725, memorialized the General Court for permission to hold a synod, the Bishop of London, instigated by the Anglican clergy of Boston, brought the matter to

[1] Bancroft, *History*, ed. 1883, iii. 4
[2] The Episcopate would legitimately bring in the whole system of canon ecclesiastical courts, in contravention of the constitutional judicial powers of the provincial courts; the colonists would not, however, listen to the suggestion that the bishop's power would be merely spiritual, for they feared that, as Mayhew expressed it, if the bishop's foot was once in the stirrup the people would be effectually priest-ridden.

the attention of the home government; and Yorke, afterwards Lord Hardwicke, then attorney-general, and the solicitor-general, gave as their official opinion: 1. That synods cannot lawfully be held without the royal license. 2. That an application to the provincial legislature was a contempt of the sovereign; and, 3. That if notice of this should find them (the synod) in session, the lieutenant-governor should " signify to them . . . that they do forbear to meet any more;" and, if they persevere, " that the principal actors therein be prosecuted by information for misdemeanors."[1]   This incident of colonial history shows that the objection to Anglicanism was not merely theoretical, for it invaded the constitution of the civil government. Its adherents were generally on the side of prerogative; and John Adams has recorded in his diary, in 1765, that "the Church people are, many of them, favorers of the Stamp Act at present."[2]

However we of the present generation may choose to regard the apprehensions of the Massachusetts Puritans and their descendants late into the last century, in respect to the designs of the Anglican hierarchy, this fact — and it is the only fact of present interest — remains clear: that the series of events — and it is their continuity which should be particularly noticed — which stand to the Revolution in the relation of operative sequence, if not primarily of cause and effect, began in Massachusetts Bay with the coming of the Puritans; and that these events were religious as well as civil, unless the true expression would be, religious rather than civil.

[1] Palfrey, iv. 454, and the admirable *Memoir of John Checkley*, by Rev. E. F. Slafter, i. 86 (Prince Society).

[2] *Works*, ii. 168, 348.

Nor was the ecclesiastical element as a cause of the Revolution restricted to Massachusetts. It entered into the controversy — was one of the causes of the Revolution — in Virginia as well as in Massachusetts, but with a difference. The Puritans fled to Massachusetts because they hated Anglicanism ; the cavaliers fled to Virginia because

Ecclesias-ticism in Virginia.[1]

[1] When this address was delivered in 1884, it was, so far as I had noticed, the earliest historical presentation of ecclesiasticism (associated with political liberty) as one of those causes which brought on the Revolution. I restricted the influence to Massachusetts and Virginia ; not that I did not suspect that it was far more general, but that I then lacked authorities for a positive statement. I now add one of the most remarkable, showing how effective ecclesiasticism was in New York as leading to revolt. It is in a letter of Ambrose Serle from New York, November 8, 1776, to Earl Dartmouth of the British Ministry, and is in Stevens's *Facsimiles of Manuscripts*, vol. xxiv. No. 2045.

By some inadvertence at the time when this paper was preparing, I failed to consult Foote's *Annals of King's Chapel.* Had I then read this work I should have seen that I had been anticipated in my views, and have acknowledged the industrious research, candor, good judgment, and literary ability which, as I think, have been combined in an equal degree in no historical work by an American since Belknap's *History of New Hampshire.*

Grounding myself as I did on original authorities rather than on later views, it was thus that I failed to read Foote. Had I done so, it would have saved me vast labor and much thought, which I do not however now regret, for I was enabled to form an independent judgment which happens to accord with that of Mr. Foote.

One reason for the opposition in New York (where one would least expect it) to Secker's plan of setting up Episcopacy in the colonies is found in a paper by Charles H. Levermore, in *The American Historical Review*, vol. i. p. 238. It is to the effect that the Livingstons and several of their Whig associates, warm asserters of civil and ecclesiastical liberty, were graduates at Yale, where, at that time, Calvinism and hatred of prelatical authority were no less violent than at Harvard. The whole paper should be read, and especially pp. 240, 241, and 248.

See regarding New York, Grahame's *History*, ii. 305 ; H. A. Cushing's *King's College in the American Revolution* (Columbia University Bulletin, March, 1898).

they hated Puritanism. The Puritan hostility to Anglicanism was based upon the profoundest religious conviction. It was transmitted to their children, and ever associated with the trials and sufferings of the first generation. It was kept alive by the unintermitting efforts of the English hierarchy to establish its ecclesiastical system in the Puritan colonies. Whatever may have been the feelings of the Virginia churchmen in the days of the Revolution towards the Congregationalists of New England, owing to circumstances which will be presently narrated, they came together on the ground of hostility to Anglicanism, which, as has already been said, was a cause of the Revolution.

It was one cause;[1] no one claims that it was the sole cause. And it has been dwelt upon at some length, not only because it seems to have failed of due recognition in the historical accounts of that event, but also since a clear understanding of the matter is essential to a correct view of the position of Samuel Adams the Puritan, one of the prime movers of the Revolution, as well as somewhat by way of contrast of John Adams, its great statesman.[2]

[1] Jonathan Boucher, writing from the extreme High Church view, puts this matter in an interesting light. "That the American opposition to Episcopacy was at all connected with that still more serious one so soon afterwards set up against civil government was not indeed generally apparent *at the time* [in Virginia]; but it is now [1797] indisputable, as it also is that the former contributed not a little to render the latter successful. As therefore this controversy was clearly one great cause that led to the Revolution, the view of it here given, it is hoped, will not be deemed wholly uninteresting." — *View*, 150.

[2] The difference was this: Samuel Adams was a Puritan and Calvinist of the strictest sect. John Adams strenuously dissented from Calvinism, but firmly adhered to the doctrines of the Puritans concerning civil and religious liberty, and regarded with equal aversion the designs of the Anglican hierarchy. His dissertation on the Canon and Feudal Law, already alluded to, was a "Tract for the Times."

The union between Massachusetts and Virginia in
the Revolution has been alluded to ; a union which,
considering the respective origin and history of the
two colonies, was incongruous and almost grotesque ;
a union of the descendants of the fanatical Puritans
and of the High Church loyalists, of the roundhead
and of the cavalier.   And yet these two colonies entered the contest earlier than any other, — Virginia
the earlier, if it is regarded as merely civil, — and
were mutually helpful and steadfast to the end.   This
phenomenal embrace requires explanation to the by-
standers from both parties.

The religion of Virginia was Anglican ; and it was
the established religion, with the canons, the liturgy,
and the catechism.   The anniversary of the execution
of Charles I. was a legal fast, and the restoration of
Charles II. was a holiday.   Besides their glebes and
parsonages, a maintenance was secured to the parish
ministers in valuable and current commodities of the
country ; and the New England laws against Quakers,

It was printed in the year of the Stamp Act, 1765, when he was
twenty-nine years old, and shows how inseparably ecclesiastical and
political tyranny were associated in his mind as things of present
dread, and also how thoroughly he had studied the questions on which
in later years he exercised a commanding influence.   He was fully in
accord with Mayhew, Chauncy, Eliot, and Samuel Adams in their hostility to the Anglican pretensions and endeavors to establish an Episcopate in the colonies.   At the age of twenty he asked, "Where do
we find a precept in the Gospel requiring ecclesiastical synods, convo-
cations, councils, decrees, creeds, confessions, oaths, subscriptions, and
whole cart-loads of other trumpery that we find religion encumbered
with in these days ? " — *Works*, ii. 5, 6.   " Honesty, sincerity, and open-
ness I esteem essential marks of a good mind.   I am, therefore, of
opinion that men ought (after they have examined with unbiased judgments every system of religion, and chosen one system on their own
authority for themselves) to avow their opinions and defend them
with boldness." — *Works*, ii. 8.

says Hildreth, to whom I am indebted for this paragraph, were in full force.[1]

Devotion to the church was a test of devotion to the king as its head and defender, and non-conformity was identified with republicanism and disloyalty.[2]

The following extract will serve not only to show the views of a Virginia Anglican, but it also throws much light upon the attitude of the New England Congregationalists in relation to the introduction of Episcopacy : " The constitution of the Church of England is approved, confirmed, and adopted by our laws, and interwoven with them. No other form of church government than that of the Church of England would be compatible with the form of our civil government. No other colony has retained so large a portion of the monarchical part of the British Constitution as Virginia ; and between that attachment to monarchy and the government of the Church of England there is a strong connection." [3]

The aspect in which the New Englanders appeared to the people of Virginia, and the obstacles to be surmounted in securing their cordial coöperation in the Revolution, may be seen in the same author : " That a people [Virginians] in full possession and enjoyment of all the peace and all the security which the best government in the world can give, should, at the instigation of another people [New Englanders], for whom they entertained an hereditary national disesteem, confirmed by their own personal dislike, suddenly and unprovoked, and in contradiction to all the opinions they had heretofore professed to hold on the

---

[1] *History*, i. 512.

[2] Thompson's *Church and State*, 34, 35.

[3] Boucher's *View*, 103.

subject of government, rush into a civil war against a nation they loved . . . . is one of those instances of inconsistency in human conduct which are often met with in real life, but which, set down in a book, seem marvelous, romantic, and incredible. This, however, is an unexaggerated description of the general temper of mind which prevailed in the people of Virginia and Maryland towards those of New England." [1]

One more extract from the same writer will show the approach of Virginia and Massachusetts to the same ground : " When it is recollected that till now [1771] the opposition to an American Episcopate has been confined chiefly to the demagogues and independents of the New England provinces, but that it is now espoused with much warmth by the people of Virginia, it requires no great depth of political sagacity to see what the motives and views of the former have been, or what will be the consequences of the defection of the latter." [2]

It is now desirable to understand by what circumstances two provinces so dissimilar in their form of government, religion, social life, and general habits of thought were brought together on the common ground of hostility to Episcopacy, which was so considerable a cause of the Revolution.

There were Puritans in Virginia, though but a handful, who in the early days of the colony had established relations with their New England brethren. Commercial relations also existed between these col-

---

[1] Boucher, xxxiv. This writer suggests in a note that the New Englanders endeavored to overcome these prejudices by pitching on Mr. Randolph, a Virginian, to be the first president of Congress, and on Mr. Washington, who was also a Virginian, to command the American army.

[2] *Ibid.* 103.

onies, and some points in their civil history were not dissimilar. Both had suffered from the repeal of their charters, and both had lived in chronic dissatisfaction with the mother country ; and if at any time and for any cause the Revolution had failed in Massachusetts, it would not have been hopeless until it had also failed in Virginia. But on these two colonies it rested. The constitution of Virginia, when compared with that of Massachusetts, was monarchical, and, as has been said, her religion was Anglican, and it was the established religion.

In 1740 there was not, so far as is known, a single Dissenting congregation in Virginia ; but in 1770 there were eleven Dissenting ministers regularly settled, who had each from two to four congregations under his care.[1]

Ecclesias- ticism in Virginia politics.

At the Revolution, and for thirty years before, Virginia had been making strenuous efforts to throw off the Anglican system, so far at least as related to its temporal powers; and during the same period, as always, Massachusetts was as strenuously resisting its imposition. In this respect they were alike. But the resemblance ends here. In the latter colony it was essentially a question of civil and religious liberty ; in the former it was essentially a question of taxation.

Every one is familiar with the case between the clergy of the Established Church in Virginia and the planters, known as the "Parsons' Case," which gave first occasion to Patrick Henry for the display of his unrivaled eloquence. It arose out of a question of tithes, in substance, and has a twofold significance in Revolutionary history. In the first place, it served to undermine the influence of the Anglican hierarchy ;

[1] Boucher, 100.

and secondly, it drew into question the right of the king to set aside a Virginia law respecting a matter essentially domestic, this very matter of tithes. Singularly enough, it united ecclesiastical and civil questions as causes of the Revolution in Virginia as they had been united, yet with a difference, in Massachusetts from the beginning of her settlement.

If we desire to know the attitude of some of the Virginians, — how many is only matter of conjecture, — near the time when the war broke out, we have the most authentic intelligence. Madison, writing to Bradford in Pennsylvania, in April, 1774, says, " Our Assembly is to meet the 1st of May, when it is expected something will be done in behalf of the Dissenters. Petitions, I hear, are already forming among the persecuted Baptists, and I fancy it is in the thoughts of the Presbyterians also, to intercede for greater liberty in matters of religion. . . . The sentiments of our people of fortune and fashion in this respect are vastly different from what you have been used to. That liberal, catholic, and equitable way of thinking, as to the rights of conscience, which is one of the characteristics of a free people, and so strongly marks the people of your province, is but little known among the zealous adherents of our hierarchy. . . . Besides, the clergy are a numerous and powerful body, have great influence at home by reason of their connection with and dependence on the bishops and crown, and will naturally employ all their arts and interest to depress their rising adversaries, for such they must consider Dissenters who rob them of the good-will of the people, and may in time endanger their livings and security." In the previous January he wrote to the same, " I want again to breathe your free air. . . . Poverty and luxury prevail among all sorts ; pride, ignorance, and knavery among the priesthood. . . . This is bad enough, but it is not the worst I have to tell you. . . . There are at this time in the adjacent county not less than five or six well-meaning men in close jail for publishing their religious sentiments, which in the main are very orthodox." In another letter to the same he says what is much to the point, " If the Church of England had been the established and general religion in all the northern colonies, as it has been among us here, and uninterrupted tranquillity had prevailed throughout the continent, it is clear to me that slavery and subjection might and would have been gradually insinuated among us." [1]

It is obvious from the preceding extracts how Madison regarded the efforts of the New England Puritans in their resistance to the imposition of Episcopacy ; but that he was not pleased with all their conduct appears from the following : " I congratulate you on your heroic proceedings in Philadelphia with regard to the tea. I wish Boston may conduct matters with as much discretion as they seem to do with boldness." This is also relevant to the Revolution : " I verily believe the frequent assaults that have been made on America (Boston especially) will in the end prove of real advantage." [2]

---

[1] *Letters of Madison*, i. 10 *et seq.*

[2] *Ibid.* 10. In stating the motives which drew the people into the Revolution, it ought not to be concealed that there were some not altogether creditable. Madison gives this: "As to the sentiments of the people of this Colony with respect to the Bostonians [in regard to the Port Bill], I can assure you I find them very warm in their favor. . . . It must not be denied, though, that the Europeans, especially the Scotch, and some interested merchants among the natives, discountenance such proceedings as far as they dare, alleging the injustice and

From the foregoing outline of a phase of ecclesiastical history in the Massachusetts Colony may be seen how early, as well as continuously, the religious element operated as a cause of the Revolution ; and how — and yet with what difference — Virginia came to stand on the same ground with the former colony.

.Although ecclesiasticism stands first among the causes which prepared the Massachusetts colonists for the Revolution, and was influential in precipitating that event, yet the event itself was a disruption of the civil and political relations between the contending parties, and as such should be traced to its origin.

Origin of the political revolution in Massachusetts.

Soon after the restoration of Charles II., the colonies came to have a common grievance in the operation of the Navigation Laws and Acts of Trade,[1] which were designed to pour the wealth of commerce into the lap of England, and by the prohibition of certain manufactures in the colonies to create a market for English productions; but previous to the Stamp Act there was no British regulation which

perfidy of refusing to pay our debts to our generous creditors at home." *Ibid.* 16. Boucher is more explicit on this subject. He says, " Among other circumstances favorable to a revolt of America, that of the immense debt owing by the colonists to the merchants of Great Britain deserves to be reckoned as not the least. It was estimated at three millions sterling ; and such is the spirit of adventure of British merchants, and of such extent are their capitals and their credit, that not many years ago I remember to have heard the amount of their debts to this country calculated at double that sum : it is probably now trebled." — *View*, xl.

[1] " If any man wishes to investigate thoroughly the causes, feelings, and principles of the Revolution, he must study this Act of Navigation and the Acts of Trade." And of those who wrote in favor of their enforcement, " All I can say is, that I read them all in my youth, and that I never read them without being set on fire." — Adams's *Works*, x. 320, 336.

produced the same practical results in all the colonies. Most of the manufactures were in New England, while her lumber and the tobacco of Virginia — for cotton was not yet, and rice and indigo were grown only on a limited territory of the Carolinas — constituted the bulk of American commerce. These circumstances served to bring Massachusetts and Virginia to the same platform in the Revolution. They also explain in some degree the backwardness of some other colonies whose interests were less severely affected by the British commercial policy. But these resemblances in certain facts of Massachusetts and Virginia affairs in their relation to the common cause should not lead us to overlook the essential differences in their civil and ecclesiastical history.

Massachusetts history more immediately concerns us. Whatever rights the king may have intended to confer upon the members of the Massachusetts Company by their charter of March 4, 1629, two things are clear. First, it is clear that the charter is susceptible of a legal interpretation which makes it the basis of a government proper with very large powers, having little more than a formal dependence upon the crown;[1] and it is equally clear that the colonists themselves were disposed to give, and did give, the most liberal construction to their charter powers. Hutchinson says of them, "Upon their removal they supposed their relations both to civil and ecclesiastical government of England, except so far as a special reserve was made by their charter, was at an end, and that they had right to form such new model of both

---

[1] See the discussion of this subject by the late Prof. Joel Parker in *Lectures before the Lowell Institute on Early History of Massachusetts*, 357.

as pleased them." [1]   On this construction of their powers they acted.

But the home government took an entirely different view of their powers, as well as of the conduct of the colonists in the exercise of them.   As early as April 28, 1634, a commission for regulating plantations was issued to the Archbishop of Canterbury, the Lord Keeper, and others, to inquire, besides other matters, whether any privileges or liberties granted to the colonists by their charter were hurtful to the king, his crown, or prerogative royal, and if so, to cause the same to be revoked.[2]

Here began the long contest which raged with changing fortunes until the treaty of peace in 1783. It was an endeavor, on one side, to set up and maintain a free and essentially independent government; and, on the other side, to overthrow such a government, reduce the colonists to monarchical subjection, and regulate their affairs agreeably to the imperial policy.   To such a contest there could be only one result: the colonists were sure to win.   Growth, development, a boundless continent, remoteness, the inherited fierce spirit of liberty which neither fire nor steel had been able to subdue, and invincible courage, in time would settle the question.   It was a question of time, and this they seem to have felt all through their history until the final consummation of their expectations.   In any other view of the subject their conduct was neither consistent nor entirely to their credit.

Chalmers, an accurate though unfriendly historian, has sketched the progress of the colony towards independency for the first fifty years in the following

---

[1] *History of Massachusetts Bay*, i. 368.   [2] Parker, *ut sup.* 375.

words : " Massachusetts, in conformity with its accustomed principles, acted, during the civil wars, almost altogether as an independent state. It formed leagues, not only with the neighboring colonies, but with foreign nations, without the consent or knowledge of the government of England. It permitted no appeals from its courts to the judicatories of the sovereign State, without which a dependence cannot be preserved or enforced. And it refused to exercise its jurisdiction in the name of the Commonwealth of England. It assumed the government of that part of New England which is now called New Hampshire, and even extended its powers farther eastward, over the province of Maine. And by force of arms it compelled those who had fled from its persecution beyond its boundaries into the wilderness to submit to its authority. It erected a mint at Boston, impressing the year 1652 on the coin as the era of independence . . . thus evincing to all, what had been foreseen by the wise, that a people of such principles, religious and political, settling so great a distance from control, would necessarily form an independent State." [1]

Chalmers's statement is not exaggerated. It matters little with what intent respecting their future political relations the colonists embarked for Massachusetts Bay. Their ecclesiastical independence was an avowed purpose from the beginning; and circumstances of which they promptly availed themselves favored the formation of an independent civil state. Nor should their actual condition at the time of the Restoration be overlooked in reading their subsequent history down to the Revolution.

[1] *Political Annals,* 181.

This state of affairs in the Puritan colony, the
refuge of the Regicides, could hardly have been other
than displeasing to Charles II. and his advisers.
They determined to change it, but their success was
partial and temporary. Undoubtedly the loss of their
charter was a serious blow to the colonists. It was
their first fall, but they soon regained their feet. The
substituted government under the presidencies of
Dudley and Andros was resisted by all prudent
means, and by violence even, before a knowledge of
the progress of the Revolution of 1689 had opened a
fair prospect of success. The charter of 1692 was
forced upon the colonists in derogation of their acquired constitutional rights; and had they then, or at
any time down to the Revolution of 1775, quietly submitted, the result would have been serious to their
liberties. But they did not submit, though then, as at
the later period, there were those who counseled submission; and during the succeeding century there were
infractions of their constitutional rights, in which
from prudential considerations they silently acquiesced.

The king, by his Court of Chancery, abrogated the
first charter, and imposed upon the colony one less
favorable to popular rights. Here is the answer of
the colonists in their Declaration of Rights of the
same year, entitled an act setting forth general privileges: " No aid, tax, tallage, assessment, custom, loan,
benevolence, or imposition whatsoever shall be laid,
assessed, imposed, or levied on any of their Majes-
ties' subjects or their estates, on any color or pretence
whatsoever, but by the act and consent of the governor, council, and representatives of the people, assembled in general court." [1]

[1] *Acts and Resolves Province Massachusetts Bay*, i. 40. This is an

It is not easy to overestimate the importance of this Declaration of Colonial Rights. In the very first year of the new charter the General Court opened the contest on the grounds on which, eighty years later, after sóme preliminary skirmishing on less tenable positions, the battle was fought and independence won. It is also interesting to know that in 1765, at which time John Adams intervened in public affairs, in his first public address before the governor and council, on the question of opening the courts which had been closed for lack of stamps, he took the identical position of the General Court in 1692; and again, in the general Congress of 1774, in the Declaration of Rights of the colonies.

Resistance was not confined to mere declarations. The obstruction by the colonies of the Navigation Laws and Acts of Trade,[1] their assumption of powers not

early expression of the later political maxim, "No representation, no taxation;" but the meaning of "representation," in England at least, seems to have been different from that in the colonies. In England, "the idea was that representation in Parliament was constituted, not by the fact of a man's having a vote for a member of Parliament, but by the fact of his belonging to one of the three great divisions of the nation which were represented by the three orders of Parliament, — that is, royalty, nobility, commonalty." — Moses Coit Tyler in *American Historical Review*, i. 34, 36. Palfrey says, "If this had been confirmed, the cause of dispute which brought about the independence of the United States would have been taken away. But such proved not to be the will of the Privy Council of King William." — *History*, iv. 139. This statement is misleading. It is quite true that the Council disallowed the whole act, but fortunately they specified the grounds of their objections. These objections relate to section 8, respecting the allowance of bail, and section 9, which relates to escheat and forfeitures. To the sections which declare general rights — the colonial Magna Charta — no objections were made, and they consequently retained the political significance which inheres in all unchallenged claims of right.

[1] In 1698, when the General Court was asked to pass laws enforcing the Acts of Trade, even the conservative councilors insisted

granted by charter, their refusal to transmit their laws
for examination or to allow appeals from their judicial
decisions, at length produced legitimate results in England; and in 1701, as oftentimes later, called forth
impatient notes of warning from the Board of Trade :
" The denial of appeals is a humor which prevails so
much in proprietary and charter plantations, and the
independency they thirst after is now so notorious,
that it has been thought fit those considerations and
other objections should be laid before the Parliament." [1]   But these warnings and threats were disregarded until the patience of the home government
was exhausted and a bill for the repeal of the charter
was introduced,[2] which failed in the exigencies of
more pressing concerns.

Under the first charter all officers were elected

"that they were too much cramped in their liberties already, and
they would be great fools to abridge, by law of their own, the little
that was left them. "— Hildreth, ii. 202. This spirit became hereditary. John Adams has said, "These acts never had been executed,
and there never had been a time when they would have been or could
have been obeyed." — Letter to Tudor, March 29, 1818, *Novanglus*,
245.

In 1728, when Governor Burnett, under royal instructions insisted
that the General Court should fix by law the governor's salary instead
of leaving it to depend upon the temper of that body from year to
year, they persistently refused, "because it is an untrodden path,
which neither we nor our predecessors have gone in; . . . because it
seems necessary to form, maintain, and uphold our constitution; . . .
because it is our undoubted right to raise and dispose of moneys for
the public service of our free accord, without any compulsion; and
because, if we should now give up this right, we shall open a door to
many other inconveniences." — See *Journal of the General Court.*

To these maxims of policy and government they and their successors adhered to the end, notwithstanding royal menaces. This was
revolution as clearly as any declaration which more immediately preceded the war.

[1] *Palfrey*, iv. 200.

[2] *Massachusetts Historical Collections*, vii. 220.

directly or indirectly by the people; under the second charter the governor was appointed by the crown, with a negative upon the election of the speaker and councilors chosen by the House. To this invasion of their old constitution the people lacked the power of forcible resistance ; but the popular party, under the consummate leadership of Cooke, neutralized the governor's power and held him in thrall by exercising their constitutional right of determining his salary. And this they continued to do with exasperating persistency and disregard of the royal instructions quite down to the Revolution.[1]

[1] Palfrey has graphically described the chronic contests between the royal governors and the representatives, as also between the latter and the more conservative council, all of which is more fully seen in the journal of the House, which, from 1715 to 1730, he does not appear to have consulted. " The House of Representatives began to print its journal just before the beginning of Belcher's administration, the first publication being of the proceedings of May 27, 1730." —*History*, iv. 532 n. This is erroneous. The printed journals of the House — and I am informed that they exist in no other form — begin with 25th May, 1715, and were continued without interruption till the Revolution. In his concluding chapter he has deemed it necessary to excuse the conduct of the popular branch towards the crown and its representatives. But this depends. If the people of Massachusetts, between 1692 and 1774, their original charter having been taken away and another forced upon them, regarded themselves as within the realm, entitled to all the rights and immunities of British subjects, and bound to bear their share of the burdens imposed by the imperial policy, it is not difficult to understand why, in the eyes of the government and people of Great Britain, and even those of the neighboring colonies, their conduct was regarded as captious and rebellious. Compared with the burdens borne by their fellow-subjects within the three kingdoms, their own were light, and their condition prosperous. People understand the operations of governmental policy. They know how unequally tariffs and navigation laws affect different sections, classes, and interests; and yet they submit to them for reasons satisfactory to the majority. Our ancestors neither liked nor submitted to this policy ; they obstructed, disobeyed, and evaded its operation so far as was consistent with their safety. Nor could they

This view of the beginning and progress of the
contest which ended in the Revolution might be supported by much additional evidence; but I trust that,
even in the foregoing imperfect sketch, it fairly
appears that the Massachusetts Puritans came to the
Bay that they might be free and independent in their
civil and ecclesiastical affairs; that with the first
monition of danger in the days of Charles the First
they determined to maintain their independence at all
hazards; that the contest thus begun continued with
varying fortunes until the final decision of the questions involved was referred to arms; and, finally, that
during these hundred and fifty years of contention

endure with patience or treat with decent respect the governors sent
to rule over them, and still less the natives raised to that high but
most uncomfortable position. From one point of view it is difficult
to see why; for these representatives of the crown, in ability, learning, character, and good dispositions, would compare favorably with
those chosen by themselves under the Constitution, and were angels
of light compared with those we have inflicted on our territories.
Except that they were royal governors, it is not easy to find any in-
superable objection to Bellomont, Shute, Burnett, Shirley, or even
Bernard.

But, on the other hand, if we find, as I think the colonists found,
in the repeal of the first charter and the imposition of a royal government upon a people essentially free and independent, the justify-
ing cause of irreconcilable hostility, and an invincible determination
to throw it off on favorable occasion, then their ninety years of strife,
obstruction, and hostility towards the crown and its representatives,
and final appeal to arms, become clear, reasonable, patriotic, and
worthy of perpetual remembrance and benediction — and, least of
all, demand apology.

The people out of New England, except the Virginians, had no
similar experience, and but little knowledge of the real situation of
the Massachusetts Puritans. Hence it is not strange that they, in common with those of the British Islands, had come to regard the Yankees with prejudice and dislike; or that with reluctance they finally
placed themselves on the Massachusetts grounds, as they did under the
lead of John Adams.

the colonial constitution was growing and developing itself into a free republican constitution as the basis, measure, and protection of all their rights.

Against this background of civil and ecclesiastical history John Adams appeared on the Revolutionary stage. He had studied this history carefully, and its significance in relation to coming events he fully appreciated. It was revolution, and had been revolution from the overthrow of the first charter. That he so regarded it he has expressly told us. From the outset, with his first public utterance, he placed himself squarely on this basis of the provincial constitution ; and there he stood, constant, consistent, to the end. This is his great distinction. From it he overthrew Hutchinson and Leonard, otherwise unassailable. Any other position was full of logical pitfalls ; this was sound, clear, tenable, and on it the contest was decided in Massachusetts. *John Adams's attitude to the Revolution.*

Had the history of the other colonies been the same as that of Massachusetts, with its formative influence upon the people and their leaders, the decision of the question would have been the same as hers, and the consummation of the Revolution would have been comparatively easy. Had Massachusetts with New England finally stood alone, the day of her deliverance must have been postponed. But with Virginia and Massachusetts in alliance — and notwithstanding a general dissimilarity there were facts common to their history which brought them shoulder to shoulder — the Revolution, though difficult, was not impossible.

It was this difficulty which John Adams encountered and overcame at the head of the national party which he, more than any other man, gathered, inspired, and led.

For the American Revolution, like all epochal movements in the direction of nationality and freedom,
depended upon the movement of parties.   These now
demand our notice.

When the Revolutionary struggle in Massachusetts,

The Rev-
olution in-
evitable.

which had been suspended during the events
which culminated in the destruction of the
French power in America, broke out anew
with the Stamp Act of 1765, there seems to have been
a feeling common to all the colonies that growth,
situation, and conflicting interests would in time sever
the political relations which existed between the mother
country and her colonies ; and this opinion, if such
that may be called which so vaguely existed in their
minds, was the opinion of Hutchinson and Oliver no
less than of James Otis and Samuel Adams.   It is
true they disclaimed this, sometimes with vehemence.
John Adams did so.[1]

He said that at no time before the Declaration of
Independence was he averse to reconciliation, and that
he had no desire to see the relations with England
severed.   There is abundant similar testimony.   The
talk of the warmest of the patriots was full of loyalty
to the king and of affection for the mother country.
Nor were they insincere.   They gloried in the name
of Britons.   Ties of blood and attachment to the old
home were strong, and their pulse quickened with
memories of Pepperell before the bastions of Louisburg and of Wolfe on the Plains of Abraham.

But beliefs are not necessarily desires, and we re-

---

[1] And yet he has told us that long before the war broke out he and
Jonathan Sewall, the loyalist, agreed in their sentiments respecting
public affairs, and both were of the opinion that the British ministry
and Parliament would force the colonists to appeal to arms. — *Works,*
ii. 78.

cognize as inevitable many things which we deprecate. Could the colonists have been blind to facts and tendencies which all the world saw ? The testimony on this point is clear and decisive. The following are only a few of the observations which have been collected by writers on this period of our history. In his notes upon England, which were probably written about 1750, Montesquieu had dilated upon the restrictive character of the English commercial code, and had expressed his belief that England would be the first nation abandoned by her colonies. A few years later, Argenson, who has left some of the most striking political predictions upon record, foretold in his memoirs that the English colonies in America would one day rise against their mother country, that they would form themselves into a republic, and that they would astonish the world by their prosperity. In a discourse delivered before the Sorbonne in 1750, Turgot compared the colonies to fruits which only remain on the stem till they have reached the period of maturity, and he prophesied that America would some day detach herself from the parent tree. Still earlier than Turgot's prophecy, Kalm, the Swedish traveler, contended that the presence of the French in Canada, by making the English colonists depend for their security on the support of the mother country, was the main cause of the submission.[1]

But more decisive as to the prevalence of this belief among the colonists are some of their own words. Dr. Andrew Eliot, writing to Hollis in England, December, 1767, says, " We are not ripe for a disunion ; but

---

[1] See Lecky's *History of the Eighteenth Century*, iii. 200. Bancroft has also treated this question in his *History of the United States;* and see Frothingham's *Rise of the Republic*, 245.

our growth is so great that in a few years Great Britain will not be able to compel our submission ; " [1] and in 1772 Dr. Charles Chauncy said " that in twenty-five years there would be more people here than in the three kingdoms, the greatest empire on earth." [2]

But no one save John Adams expressed this undercurrent of thought so clearly as William Livingston in 1768 : " Americans, the finger of God points out a mighty empire to your sons. . . . The day dawns in which this mighty empire is to be laid by the establishment of a regular American Constitution. . . . Peace or war, famine or plenty, poverty or affluence, — in a word, no circumstance, whether prosperous or adverse, can happen to our parent ; nay, no conduct of hers, whether wise or imprudent — no possible temper of •hers, whether kind or cross-grained — will put a stop to this building. There is no contending with omnipotence ; and the predispositions are so numerous and well adapted to the rise of America that our success is indubitable." [3]

No one can read the history of the colony in its original sources without meeting evidence of the existence of the belief that the time would come when the colonies would grow into a great and independent empire. Not that they wished to set up for themselves at once. On the contrary, quite apart from any sentiment of loyalty, it is not improbable that they were too fully sensible of the advantages of their position as appendages of the crown, with the privilege of drawing upon the imperial resources in warding off

---

[1] *Massachusetts Historical Collections*, xxxiv. 420.

[2] Adams's *Works*, ii. 304.

[3] *The American Whig*, quoted with variations by Boucher, *View*, xxvi., and by Frothingham, *Rise of the Republic*, 244.

the attacks of the French, which as independent colonies they would be obliged to meet with their own men and money. Nor did they look forward to any definite time when it would be for their advantage to terminate these relations, nor to any specific course of action which would hasten that event. Nevertheless, their political action tended to render that result inevitable, nor was the feeling which inspired this action allowed to subside ; for, from the earliest days down to the war, whenever they showed restiveness under the British rule they were charged with aiming at independence.[1]

The Massachusetts colonists may not, as they said, have aimed at an independence, yet they steadily, and seemingly not unconsciously, pursued a course which would inevitably lead to it.

From the first it seems to have been inevitable that the political relations between Great Britain and her colonies in America should be finally severed ; but when and how — whether by the silent influence of growth or as the result of violence — were questions in abeyance, and subject to chance. The lots were cast, and it was war.

But war was not resorted to merely as the solution of difficulties which arose from the growth and development of the colonies. They had not reached that stage — in time sure to come — when union made subjugation impossible. Undertaken solely on that ground, the war, as we now see, was premature. The colonies were not ripe for it. Nor were they strong enough for it. Unaided, they would have failed, as fail they did until

The Revolution precipitated by party action.

---

[1] See Evelyn's *Diary*, May 26, 1671, *et seq.* Also a letter from Dummer to the House, quoted in Palfrey, iv. 407 n.

aided. The war was precipitated by party action in Massachusetts. The opposite view, which has led to infinite misconception of the Revolutionary struggle, finds countenance only in the general and apparently spontaneous uprising of the continent in resistance to the Stamp Act. But that demonstration was utterly deceptive, as afterwards appeared, so far as it seemed to indicate any settled conviction and determination. It was a commercial protest, backed by no ulterior purpose of forcible resistance. The repeal of the act, notwithstanding the reaffirmance of the principle in the Declaratory Act, apparently satisfied the public mind everywhere out of New England — perhaps out of Massachusetts. It seems to have been so even in Virginia. Jefferson's statement on this point is clear, and it is decisive. In Virginia, between 1769 and 1773, he says, " Nothing of particular excitement occurring for a considerable time, our countrymen seemed to fall into a state of insensibility to our situation ; the duty on tea not yet repealed, and the Declaratory Act of a right in the British Parliament to bind us by their laws in all cases whatsoever still suspended over us." And John Adams, as late as 1772 writes, " Still quiet at the southward ; and at New York they laugh at us."

This doubtless correctly represents the apathy everywhere prevailing out of Massachusetts. The real state of the case seems to have been, if the colonies are regarded as a whole, that the opposition to the British acts was based on pecuniary interests rather than on deeply seated political convictions ; and when the immediate danger of taxation passed away, the popular hostility subsided, as Jefferson says. But the situation in Massachusetts was peculiar. In the first place, the ecclesiastical question, instead of being one of tithes and of yesterday, as in Virginia, was as old as the colony, and laid hold on the deepest and most sacred convictions of the people ; and, as we have seen, it was a burning question, entirely independent of any question of parliamentary taxation, and wholly un-affected by the repeal of the Stamp Act or the modi-fications of the other revenue measures. And in the next place, as we have also seen, there had always existed in Massachusetts as in no other colony two distinctly arrayed parties divided on questions directly leading up to colonial independence. And in these circumstances rather than in any exclusive virtue or intelligence of this colony — I speak this with bated breath — is to be found the reason why Massachusetts was earliest and most persistent in the war to which she furnished nearly one third of the troops brought into the field, although her territory before the close of the first year was freed from the foot of the in-vader.

The war began in Massachusetts. It was brought on by the action of parties. These parties, the radi-cals and the conservatives,[1] were as old as the race, and will survive with it. They came over with Win-throp. At first these graduates of old Cambridge were sufficiently though somewhat incongruously oc-cupied in framing ordinances respecting yoking and

---

[1] Adams to Jefferson: " You say our divisions began with Federal-ism and anti-Federalism. Alas! they began with human nature ; they have existed in America from its first plantation. . . . A Court and Country party have always contended. Whig and Tory disputed very sharply before the Revolution and in every step during the Revolu-tion. Every measure of Congress from 1774 to 1787 inclusively was disputed with acrimony, and decided by as small majorities as any question is decided in these days " [1812]. — *Works*, x. 23.

ringing of swine, party fences, and the laying out of
townways and highways; but these affairs with some
others of more importance attended to, and interstate
affairs after the subsidence of Laud's demonstrations
being in abeyance, they divided on theological polemics, and thus preserved the civilization which was
imperiled in a frozen, savage wilderness. But the
arrival of Charles's commissioners in 1664 made hot
work for both parties; and the historian of New England has recorded " that before the close of the first
century political parties had arrayed themselves not
only upon local questions, but also upon questions *of
the relation of the Colonies to the Empire."*

With the inauguration of the new government in
1692 party strife was renewed, and continued with
intervals of repose through the entire provincial
period. Party questions were somewhat in abeyance
through the French wars to the treaty of peace in
1763, but became grave during the period of commercial torpidity which ensued, and rancorous upon the
passage of the Stamp Act in 1765. Nor are we permitted to believe that the magnitude of the interests
involved or the serious consequences likely to flow
from erroneous action preserved the discussion from
intemperance, or that conclusions were reached with
sole reference to the public weal. Contemporaneous
newspapers and pamphlets and the published proceedings of the people in town meeting assembled, and of
their representatives in the General Court, contain
ample evidence that the party heats, personal interests,
and mob violence, to which many of those now living
were witnesses in the late civil war, had their prototypes in the Revolutionary era.

At both epochs and in both parties were found rad-

icals and conservatives, statesmen and politicians, patriots and self-seekers, intelligent adherents and blind
party devotees.   At both epochs and in both parties,
in the name of liberty and under the guise of patriotism, against persons whose only offense was a silent
adherence to their own convictions, were committed
acts of violence instigated in the frenzy of party by
those whose names and character should constitute
denial, and recorded without disapprobation by historical partisans.

In the Revolution parties were outlined by the general principles of their respective adherents, but were
by no means homogeneous.   There were those in the
governmental or Tory party, as it then began to be
called, who doubted neither the omnipotence of Parliament over the colonies nor the wisdom of its exercise in levying a tax, while others were satisfied with
the affirmation of the right.   And in the patriotic
party many deprecated a resort to forcible resistance
who strenuously denied the British pretensions.   Of
these Franklin and Dickinson were the most eminent; and as late as 1776 their opinions were the
opinions of the majority out of New England.[1]

Adams writes to Plumer: " You inquire whether
every member of Congress did, on the 4th of July,
1776, in fact cordially approve of the Declaration of
Independence.   I then believed, and have not since
altered my opinion, that there were several who signed
with regret and several others with many doubts and
much lukewarmness." [2]

---

[1] See Franklin's letters in Tudor's *Otis*, 302 n., and *Magazine of
American History*, September, 1883, article " Dickinson ; " also Hildreth, iii. 45, 57, 77.

[2] *Works*, x. 35.   See Frothingham, *Rise of the Republic*, 514 *et seq.*

With the exception of the clergy, the party affiliations of no class could be accurately predicted. Parents and children, brothers and sisters, and lifelong friends found themselves arrayed in hostile ranks as religious and political convictions, marriage, social relations, interest,[1] or even accident, dictated.

The number of the people in each of these parties is not susceptible of precise determination, and varied somewhat with the changing fortunes of the contest. Many of those who finally adhered to the crown were among the most earnest denunciators of the Stamp Act. John Adams has recorded it as his opinion that "in 1765 the colonies were more unanimous than they have been since, either as colonies or states." From 1760 to 1766 was the purest period of patriotism, from 1766 to 1776 was the period of corruption. This agrees with the opinion of Jefferson, so far as he refers to the same period. Nor is there anything unusual in this phase of parties. So long as dissatisfaction was expressed by declarations of rights, or even mob violence, patriotism was cheap; but when it became apparent that affairs were drifting to armed resistance, uncertain in its issue, many who had been conspicuous as patriots drew back, and finally entrusted their fortunes to the government as the stronger party.

Of the barristers in Boston and its immediate vicinity, Thacher died in 1765, Otis became incapacited in 1771. Five were loyalists, and John Adams alone

---

[1] "The managers of our public affairs, like those on your side of the Atlantic," writes Dr. Eliot to Thomas Hollis, December 10, 1767, "are governed by private views and the spirit of a party. Few have any regard to the good of the public. Men are patriots till they get in place, and then they are ! ! ! anything." — *Massachusetts Historical Collections*, xxxiv. 414.

lived through the Revolution as the advocate of American independence. Twenty-four of the principal barristers and attorneys in the colony and one hundred and twenty-three merchants and traders, including a few others in Boston, signed the address to Governor Hutchinson, May 30, 1774; and similar addresses to Governor Gage, as late as October 14, 1775, were signed by the same class of people, and in still larger proportion to the population, in Salem and Marblehead. Plymouth County was the stronghold of the loyalists. On the evacuation of Boston, March 17, 1776, Sir William Howe was accompanied by fifteen hundred of these people; and in September, 1778, the General Court specified, in an act forbidding their return, the names of more than three hundred citizens in the several counties. These numbers include only those who were conspicuous as landed proprietors or in the mercantile and professional classes. The Tories were in possession of the principal offices in the gift either of the crown or the people. As the conservative party and having something to lose,[1] they were sat-

The Party of the Loyalists.

---

[1] John Adams gives the impressions which the wealthy delegates from the other colonies to the Congress of 1774 had received in respect to those of Massachusetts. It had been represented to them that Hancock was fortunately sick, and Mr. Bowdoin's relations thought that his large estate ought not to be put to hazard. So they sent Mr. Cushing, who was a harmless kind of man, but poor and wholly dependent on his popularity for his subsistence; Mr. Samuel Adams, who was a very artful, designing man, but desperately poor, and wholly dependent on his popularity with the lowest vulgar for his living; and John Adams and Robert Treat Paine, who were two young lawyers of no great talents, reputation, or weight, who had no other means of raising themselves into consequence than by courting popularity. And they were all suspected of having independence in view. — *Works*, ii. 512. This, of course, is John Adams's statement, and it contains so much of truth and significance as to enhance our estimate of his candor.

isfied with the existing order of things, and in that
state of mind found it easy to indulge the sentiment
of loyalty which inheres in the British subject in all
lands so long as he is allowed to do as he pleases.
Not that the Tories were fonder of paying taxes than
were the patriots, but they were content when the obnoxious tax was repealed, and were disinclined to make
an issue on the Declaratory Act which proclaimed the
parliamentary right to tax.   To these political sentiments was united the profoundest conviction that the
colonists, unaided, could never withstand the power of
the empire when put forth in its might, and that the
hope of friendly intervention by the continental powers
of Europe was a dream sure to be interrupted by a
rude awakening.   As the event showed, this was their
fatal mistake.

Such was the party of the goverment, or the Loyalists.   Such was the formidable party, intrenched in
wealth, office, and social influence, which confronted
John Adams and his associates; and it is his and
their glory to have overthrown it.

The patriotic party is less easily described, since it
contained many heterogeneous elements.   As
The Patriotic Party.   a whole it was the party of the opposition,
such as is always found under all forms of
government.   In Massachusetts, its formation on well-
defined issues antedates by more than a hundred years
the resistance to the Stamp Act, and was coeval with
the inauguration by Charles II. of those measures designed to reduce the colonies to subjection.   The real
purpose of this party, though seldom avowed, was
from the first substantial independence of the crown
of England.   At no time was it troubled with scru-
ples.   It hoped immunity from the chastisement

threatened by the king in his embroilment in foreign wars.[1] It resisted the abrogation of the old charter; it imprisoned Andros and Dudley; and when resistance proved unavailing, it sought to save the liberties of the people by neutralizing the anti-democratic elements in the new charter of 1692. The struggle thus begun never changed its character, and, as we have already seen, never ceased until the peace of 1783. Two things must never be lost sight of. First, that this resistance was the resistance of a party. From the first stage of the contest to the last there was a Tory party which counseled submission; and this party was proportionally more numerous in its early than in its later stage. Secondly, that from first to last the action of the patriotic party was resistance and obstruction. It was not the attitude of slaves seeking their freedom, but of freemen resisting subjugation. The difference is immense, and on its perception depends a knowledge of the real character of the American Revolution, which was the final victory in a hundred years of party strife, with unbroken continuity of unvaried purpose, — the maintenance of independence rather than its acquirement, — originating in a province, but at length, and mainly through the influence of John Adams, enkindling the heart of a continent.

Besides reasons of state which embittered the colonists were some of a personal nature, affecting those especially who suffered under the usurpation of Andros or were displaced by Dudley. This personal

[1] "They say," writes a commissioner in 1665, "they can easily spin out seven years by writing, and before that time a change may come; nay, some have dared to say, who knows what the event of this Dutch war may be?" *Calendar of State Papers*, quoted by Professor Seeley, *Expansion of England*, 68 n.

element was never absent from the contest in any of
its stages, and finally became one of the most potent
forces in arraying the Massachusetts colonists in
armed hostility to British authority.

The lull of political excitement during the French
war was only temporary. With the restoration of
peace the people, no longer distressed by the anxieties
occasioned by war and irritated by the operations of
the Anglican hierarchy, were ready to give ear to the
whisperings concerning the ministerial purpose to
raise a revenue in America. The passage of the
Stamp Act in 1765 left no doubt on that subject.
This was the occasion for the reopening of old party
questions, and party strife ensued, which continued
with scarcely any mitigation until the war.

But this was true chiefly of Massachusetts. In the
colonies to the southward the repeal of the act was
followed by the general apathy which so much alarmed
and disgusted Jefferson. The facts verified the conjecture of Franklin. In his examination before the
Commons in 1766, he was asked if the Americans
would be satisfied with the repeal of the Stamp Act,
notwithstanding the resolutions of Parliament as to
the right; and his answer was, "I think the resolutions of Right will give them very little concern if
they are never attempted to be carried into practice."

Additional reasons for the apparent change in public sentiment may be conjectured. At first it seems
not to have been generally understood that all sums
raised in America by taxation were to be expended
there in the defense and government of the country.
To this there doubtless were good practical and constitutional objections; but these would not be likely
to strike the common mind with the same force as a

project to replenish the British exchequer from the
pockets of the colonists. Nor was it unlikely that the
acts of violence which everywhere accompanied the
popular expression of disapprobation of the measure
should on second thought cause some apprehension
in the minds of those friendly to law and order.
Property also became alarmed.

But whatever may have been the reasons for the
popular falling off, there can be no question as to the
fact; and if it had been true in the same degree in
Massachusetts as in the other colonies, it is doubtful
whether the conflict would have occurred when it
did.

In Massachusetts, however, there was to be no
peace. The Stamp Act was repealed, but the Declaratory Act remained, and the Bishop of London did
not stay his hand. The Puritan pulpit rang with
unceasing alarm until its voice was drowned in the
clangor of arms. Not one of the causes which had
kept the royal governors in contention for sixty years
was settled or in abeyance. New causes were constantly arising, — often made; and it was the evident
determination of the patriotic party that they should
be settled only in one way — with substantial independence of British authority in all matters of domestic
policy. To these causes must be added the personal
hostility, which had become deadly, between Bernard
and Hutchinson on one side and James Otis, Jr., and
Samuel Adams on the other.

The last-mentioned causes kept the contest alive in
Massachusetts, which seemed to be in a state of col-
lapse in other colonies, until the arrival of the East
India Company's teas revived colonial interest in public affairs.

In the early stages of the controversy, international
Samuel as well as local, James Otis, Jr., was the
Adams leader; but after a while his light began to
the great flicker, and in 1771 went out and was seen
party
leader. no more. Thacher, less to be pitied than
Otis, had found an early grave. Joseph Hawley and
Samuel Adams remained; but Hawley's residence
was remote from the scene of immediate conflict, and
occasional fits of despondency rendered untrustworthy
for sudden exigencies one of the most able and interesting but little known patriots of the Revolution.
Samuel Adams remained, and in all local, religious,
political, and personal relations the Revolution in
Massachusetts found in him its greatest leader.[1]

If his colony was not quite ripe for armed resistance, nor all of them strong enough, unaided, to
carry through the contest if entered upon; or if, as
was the judgment of Hawley,[2] and as later events
seemed to indicate, there was danger, on one hand,
that the conflict would be precipitated without adequate preparation, and on the other, that the people
would grow weary of the strife, — it was Samuel
Adams who kept alive the spirit of resistance, and
with infallible sagacity piloted the bark of liberty

[1] " Adams, I believe, has the most thorough understanding of liberty and her resources in the temper and character of the people
though not in the law and constitution, as well as the most habitual,
radical love of it of any of them, as well as the most correct, genteel,
and artful pen. He is a man of refined policy, steadfast integrity,
exquisite humanity, genteel erudition, obliging, engaging manners,
real as well as professed piety, and a universal good character, unless
it should be admitted that he is too attentive to the public, and not
enough so to himself and his family." — John Adams in 1765: *Works*,
ii. 163.

[2] See a remarkable letter on this point, written from Northampton, February 22, 1775, to Thomas Cushing, in *Massachusetts Historical Collections*, xxxiv. 393.

through these dangerous seas. Apathy might prevail elsewhere, but in Massachusetts it was not allowed to prevail. At one time there seemed to be danger; but never was an exigency in human affairs more clearly discerned nor more resolutely met. Never was opposition more thoroughly organized nor led with more consummate skill. To this work Samuel Adams gave his time without stint, his whole heart, and his admirable ability. His convictions of the justice of the cause were founded on the rock. His faith in its ultimate triumph was as the faith of the martyrs. He was the last of the Puritans, with the zeal of the first of the Puritans.[1] He hated kings, but most of all popes and bishops. The crown and the crozier were alike detested symbols of tyranny. The king was an offense far away; Hutchinson was an offense near at hand. He gathered, united, and led the patriotic party of his day. Into it he infused his own courage, zeal, and constancy. He was the unrivaled politician of the Revolution. Without him it would never have occurred when it did nor as it did. In this work Samuel Adams was the foremost and greatest man.

But the Revolution needed a statesman. Beginning in a colony, it was provincial. It required to be nationalized. It began on a party basis of local politics; it needed a constitutional basis. It had enlisted the sympathies and resources of a colony. It needed the sentiment of nationality and the resources of a continent. To supply these needs was the work of John Adams.

Nationalization of the Revolution.

[1] Adams to Morse : "If James Otis was Martin Luther, Samuel Adams was John Calvin . . . cool, abstemious, polished, and refined, though more inflexible, uniform, and consistent."

The country needed — and, as the ill-starred campaigns of 1776 showed, it was one of its sorest needs — one who could enlist the sympathies of continental Europe in behalf of the hard-pressed colonists, shield them from hostile intervention, and secure for them material assistance. For this work, no less by the happy constitution of his mind than by the varied experiences of his life, of all men Franklin was best fitted.

Finally, the Revolution needed a leader for its armies: it needed Washington.

Of these men, all required for the initiation and successful issue of the Revolution, each could do his own work supremely well, but neither that of the others. In completeness and grandeur of character Washington stands alone. In mass of intellect Franklin is accounted first and John Adams second; but if amount and variety as well as importance of service as statesmen be taken into the account, Franklin and Adams might change places.

Under such circumstances of colonial history John Adams appeared on the theatre of public affairs. Before we can rightly estimate his career we must know in what character he appeared. Of course he was not a Tory, nor was he a Son of Liberty, though elected as such. He neither represented nor did he ally himself to any merely political party. He put himself at the head of that great movement of the race in America towards nationality, visible to the discerning, as we have seen, everywhere except to those who were in it. John Adams himself was only vaguely conscious of it, or of his relations to it. In this he was like the monk of Erfurth and the son of the brewer of Huntingdon. But, no less than Luther or

Cromwell, he was elected to lead and direct the movement of an age.

At the age of twenty he said, "Soon after the Reformation a few people came into this new world for conscience's sake. Perhaps this apparently trivial incident may transfer the great empire of Europe into America. It looks likely to me; for if we can remove the turbulent Gallics, our people, according to exactest computation, will in another century become more numerous than England itself. The way to keep us from setting up for ourselves is to divide us." This was in 1755, four years before Wolfe's victory on the Plains of Abraham and five years before James Otis argued against the Writs of Assistance.

This divination of nationality in the future empire of America was not, as it has been regarded, the work of a meditative mind turned politician, but an intuition of that historic imagination already spoken of which led him in later years to head the movement that realized the prophetic vision of his youth. No two characters in our revolutionary period are more strongly contrasted than Benjamin Franklin and John Adams. Natives of the same colony and in some respects representative of the spirit of its people, in others they differed as widely from it as they did from each other. Franklin's intellect was of the first order, under the supreme control of common sense, of which he was the incarnation. This determined his attitude to the Revolution. He was opposed to it so far as its promoters contemplated armed resistance to Great Britain. Always averse to war, he would have patiently waited until time and growth should sever the colonies from the mother country. He did not believe the colonies were strong enough to fight the king; but when Samuel Adams forced the hand of the minister and war became inevitable, Franklin threw his great influence with the patriotic party. As matter of judgment, he was right. The colonists were not strong enough to withstand even the feeble generals of the king. At the time of French intervention the game of war had gone against them, and the last two years were fought largely with French troops and French money. Franklin's judgment was controlled by his great reason. He had no imagination. This is where he differed from John Adams. As Adams said of himself, " It had always been his destiny to mount breaches and lead the forlorn hope." He had faith in it. He had seen it through all the ages in the victorious van, and his imagination was kindled by the historic review. It was just this sublime intuition of nationality which distinguished him among his contemporaries; and this united with great abilities and high courage made him the first statesman of the Revolution.

The value of this gift to the cause which John Adams came to represent, or to himself personally, can hardly be overestimated. He had said that " by looking into history we can settle in our minds a clear and comprehensive view of the earth at its creation; of its various changes and revolutions; of the growth of several kingdoms and empires; and that nature and truth, or rather truth and right, are invariably the same in all times and in all places." This intuition enabled him to discern in race tendencies, situation, and growth the inevitable result of the approaching contest; and when the hour for choice came he cast his fortunes not with the governmental party as might have been expected from his constitutional and professional conservatism, but with those ready to battle for freedom and nationality. And this faith in the prophetic movements of events left no room for doubt as to the justice of the cause or of its ultimate success. And so he never quailed in the face of danger, never was disheartened by disaster, and his every step was a step forward.

Besides the faculty by which John Adams divined the end and every intermediate step from the beginning, in the logical order of events, he possessed another of scarcely less value to the cause. By constitution of mind as well as by special education he was constructive; and in this order: before he tore down, he planned reconstruction. Governments were not the results of accident, but growths from germs maturing as the oak from the acorn by laws of race, situation, and the facts of national life. His reconstruction, therefore, as we shall see, was in accordance with these laws. Familiar as he was with the theories of government from the republic of Plato to those of his own times, and not unwilling to adopt whatever would incorporate itself into that system which his race had found most serviceable, he had no faith in systems which lacked the sanction of proved utility. His work was new. To disrupt an empire was not new. It was not new to overthrow governments. But to overturn thirteen royal provinces, and without intervening anarchy to set up in their stead thirteen independent governments ; to loose the bands of an empire and reform the contiguous parts into an united whole with such coherence as enabled it to maintain itself against formidable odds, — this was something new in history, and to many seemed impossible.

Samuel Adams represented the Puritan element in the contest in Massachusetts. To him the Revolution was the last in a series of events reaching back through a hundred years to resist the imposition of the Anglican hierarchy on the descendants of the Puritans. Civil and religious liberty were indissolubly united in his affections, but his inspiration was religion. This fervor, which gave him power among his own people, detracted from his influence in those colonies in which the people regarded the Massachusetts Puritans as bigoted fanatics.

John Adams was also a believer in religion, but he had read Shaftesbury, Bolingbroke,[1] and Hume. To him religion had its place, — the first place in natural order in every well-regulated mind. But he was no bigot and had no invincible repugnance to any form of religious belief.

And so in civil government he believed in orderly, constitutional subordination. But in his scheme it was a subordination to laws, not men. He believed in laws. As a lawyer he admitted the supremacy of law; but as a statesman he recognized the distinction between those rules which in judicial tribunals determine the rights of persons and those general maxims applicable only to legislation. In construing the British Constitution or that of his own colony, it was not with him a question of original theory, but of present fact. " When Massachusettensis says that the king's dominions *must* have an uncontrollable power, I ask whether they *have* such a power or not," is his way of reasoning. What by growth, development, and actual oper-

---

[1] Adams to Jefferson : "I have read him [Bolingbroke] through more than fifty years ago, and more than five times in my life, and once within five years past."— *Works*, x. 82.

ative force have these several constitutions come to
be as matter of fact to-day? Parliamentary supremacy is doubtless a constitutional maxim in England,
and the supremacy of the Great and General Court
in all internal affairs, civil as well as ecclesiastical, is
and always has been a constitutional maxim in the
province of Massachusetts Bay. And in both cases
the validity of these maxims is to be determined, not
by the declarations or admissions of past ages, but by
the potentiality of a present declaration. To the assumed right of Parliament to tax the colonies, as a
corollary of parliamentary omnipotence, he offered no
theory of constitutional construction, but answered,
" Our provincial legislatures are the only supreme
authorities in our colonies." Colonial constitutions,
like the British Constitution, he assumed were flexi-
ble, readily adapting themselves to changed circumstances, subject to growth and development, and the
sole measure of the rights of the people, whenever as
matter of fact they had come to rely upon them as
such. Nor did he fail to perceive nor shrink from the
conclusion that, when time and circumstances brought
on the inevitable conflict, force would be the final
arbiter. To the acceptance of this doctrine he led the
national mind, as represented in the Declaration of
Rights by the Congress of 1774, and inspired it at a
later date with the audacity to defy a power greater
than its own.

Such seems to have been John Adams's theory of
the provincial constitutions, though nowhere expressly
formulated in words and perhaps not even in his own
mind ; but everywhere evinced by his conduct, not
otherwise consistent or intelligible. He frequently
met his antagonists, such as Hutchinson and Leonard,

on their own ground, and sometimes overthrew them by skillful fence; but his strength and his power were in his practical recognition of the American constitutions. And if, as has been suggested, he has nowhere given us a complete statement of his constitutional views during the controversial period, but left them to be inferred, as in the Declaration of Rights, he is not peculiar in this respect. Great leaders, especially if like John Adams they are men of action, are seldom the formulators of their own principles of conduct, and are not always conscious of them. They are men of intuitions; and their chief distinction is that they are the first to feel the movement of the age, recognize its significance, and give it beneficent direction.

Excepting the year 1770, when John Adams was a member of the General Court, he had no official relation to public affairs. In the vulgar strife between those who had place and those who wanted place he felt no interest. Poor, ambitious, conscious of great powers, he doubtless desired opportunities for their exercise. He saw positions of power and emolument in his profession engrossed by the old historic families which adhered to the crown. Into this charmed circle he gazed, he tells us, not without envy. But he was a man of principle, with a just sense of honor, and no demagogue. Poorly adapted for the game of politics, and lacking the faculty which moulds the sentiments of numbers into some definite form of action, he made a poor figure as a politician. By the constitution of his mind, by taste and education, he was fitted for statesmanship; and when that career was open to him, he entered upon it with such success that he soon became recognized as the most commanding statesman of the country.

The Revolution encountered difficulties apart from the evident determination of the ministry to sustain the parliamentary authority. As a domestic question, it was to be rescued from party squabbles and placed on such constitutional grounds as would satisfy the sound judgment of those on whom it depended for support, as well as the fervid patriotism of those whose obstreperous demonstrations were silenced by the first call to less noisy duty. It also required to be nationalized; for unless Massachusetts was to stand alone, and standing alone to fail, it was essential that all the colonies, of diverse nationalities, histories, and religions, and without special good-will to Massachusetts, should nevertheless unite with her on common ground, make her cause their cause, and count the work done only when a free, independent empire should rise out of the ruins of thirteen royal governments. The cause in Massachusetts did not stand exactly on the right basis. It was too local and personal. It was too largely a question between the ins and the outs to excite interest in the other colonies, and in the ecclesiastical contention they had no sympathy with the Massachusetts Puritans.

To one of less abundant resources or less confidence in them, to one with less faith in the future empire of America, grounded on the historical development of nationality and constitutional government by the Anglo-Saxon race, the magnitude and difficulties would have been appalling. But John Adams brought ability, courage, and devotion to the cause, and he gained it. When he entered Congress in 1774 he found the representatives of the thirteen colonies brought together chiefly by commercial considerations, having no principle of cohesion and no purpose of united action,

except peaceful resistance to parliamentary taxation.[1]   But before he left Congress in 1777, and more
through his instrumentality than any other, these colonies had become *independent* states, some with constitutions for which he constructed the plan, and *united*
states, with the germ of a constitution which took
shape under the Constitution of the United States, in
which were embraced the essential features of the
Constitution of Massachusetts, the work of his own
hands.   Such an opportunity has seldom presented
itself to a statesman in any age or country; seldom
has such opportunity been so successfully improved.

The period between 1765 and 1775 was prolific of
party pamphlets, in which the parliamentary
pretensions and colonial rights were discussed with zeal and often with great ability.   Massachusetts contributed her full share of this
literature to the common cause, and added a series of
state papers comprising messages from the royal governors and answers from the two houses, together
with resolutions from conventions and popular assemblies, probably unsurpassed in volume by similar productions emanating from any other colony.   Owing
to her peculiar situation and the frequent occasion
she gave for interference in her affairs by the king or
his representatives, few constitutional questions of
colonial import failed of exhaustive discussion.   John
Adams's contribution to this revolutionary literature
was considerable in amount, and the direction he gave

*Constitu-
tional
questions.*

---

[1] In the Congress of 1774, "after the first flush of confidence was
over, suspicions and jealousies began to revive.   There were in all the
colonies many wealthy and influential men who had joined, indeed, in
protesting against the usurpations of the mother country, but who
were greatly disinclined to anything like a decided rupture." — Hildreth, iii. 45.

to it was followed by consequences of importance to the patriotic party in Massachusetts, and later to the national party in Congress.

The Stamp Act and other colonial measures which proceeded from the British ministry became party questions on both sides of the water, and were discussed in Parliament with the heat which characterizes party declamation at all times. In those days as well as in later days, and in grave histories, these declamatory utterances were regarded and cited as statesmanlike determinations of constitutional questions. Nothing can be more misleading. They were mainly party cries of the opposition, similar to those with which we became familiar in the congressional debates which preceded the late Civil War. Chatham's splendid eloquence gave currency to declarations which had no foundation in constitutional law, and Camden, from whose judicial mind more caution might have been expected, conceded and not long after denied the American position; nor was either utterance without suspicion of political or personal motive. Their object was not to support the rights of the colonists, but to overthrow their opponents. There were those among the colonists at the time who held these partisan declarations at their just estimate. John Adams said, " I know very well that the opposition to ministry was the only valid ground on which the friendship for America that was professed in England rested." Camden, who had asserted with the colonists that taxation and representation were inseparable, later, in 1767, declared that his doubts were removed by the declaration of Parliament itself, and that its authority must be maintained. But this attitude of the opposition in England, though not generally understood in America, was of great advantage to her cause. It encouraged the colonists in their resistance and led to a feeble and vacillating policy in the ministry, which showed itself in the inefficient conduct of the war.[1]

The questions of constitutional law raised by the parliamentary revenue measures affecting the colonies neither at the time nor since have received a satisfactory solution. Regarded as questions of law determinable in courts of justice, or of the legislative power under the British Constitution, in which aspect a lawyer would at first be likely to regard them, John Adams might well have hesitated in forming an opinion. Otis at the outset took the ground that Acts of Parliament were not binding on the colonies; but on fuller consideration of the subject, in his work on the " Rights of the Colonies," he conceded the claim of parliamentary supremacy. This was Chatham's doctrine coupled with a distinction between external and internal taxes; and Franklin had incautiously admitted " that an adequate representation in Parliament would probably be acceptable to the colonists." John Quincy Adams quotes Jefferson's statement, " that in the ground which he took, that the British Parliament never had any authority over the colonies any more than the Danes and Saxons of his own age had over the people of England, he never could get anybody to agree with him but Mr. Wythe. It was too absurd." He then adds, " In truth, the question of right as between Parliament and the colonies was one of those upon which it is much easier to say who was wrong than who was right. The pretension that they had the right to bind the colonies in all cases

[1] See *Quarterly Review*, January, 1884, p. 7.

whatever, and that which denied them the right to bind in any case whatever, were the two extremes equally unfounded ;. and yet it is extremely difficult to draw the line where the authority of Parliament commenced and where it closed." [1]

John Adams drew the line against the authority of Parliament in any case whatever except by the colonial consent; and this position, taken in the earliest stages of the controversy, he consistently maintained to the end. And this was the only tenable ground. Once admit the supremacy of the British Constitution in regulating the internal affairs of the colonies, and there was no ground for constitutional resistance to any acts affecting them as distinguished from the people within the three kingdoms. On that ground neither Hutchinson nor Leonard was answered.[2] It was a question of fact, and chiefly as to time. When the colonial charters were the evidence of corporate existence within the realm for extra-territorial purposes, they like all domestic charters were subject to alteration or repeal; but when by lapse of time, growth, and usage they had become governments proper, regulating their own internal affairs, they then became colonial constitutions which excluded all other authority. This I understand the position of John Adams to have been. Burke recognized the

[1] *Life and Works*, viii. 282.

[2] General political maxims never have had, and probably never will have, practical force either in courts or legislative bodies. To quote the maxim that taxation and representation were inseparable as a guide to legislation or as a ground for legal resistance to a law already passed, while five sixths of the people of England, whole counties, large towns, and many of the Channel Islands were, or had been, wholly unrepresented though fully taxed, was practically as absurd as for a fugitive slave to quote the Declaration of Independence or the preamble to the Constitution in a court of law.

effect of usage in determining constitutional rights. " Do not burden them with taxes; you were not used to do so from the beginning. Let this be your reason for not taxing." Of course the British Parliament were quite at liberty to take an entirely different view of the question, as they did, and its practical solution depended on the relative strength of the parties.

John Adams was brought face to face with this question, and took his position in regard to it before the Governor and Council in 1765, on the petition of the town of Boston for reopening the courts, which had been closed for the want of stamps required by the act. A few days before he had written in his diary, " It is my opinion that by this inactivity we discover cowardice and too much respect for the act. This rest appears to be, by implication at least, an acknowledgment of the authority of Parliament to tax us. And if this authority is once acknowledged and established, the ruin of America will be inevitable." This was on the 18th of December. On the 20th is the following : " I grounded my argument on the invalidity of the Stamp Act, it not being in any sense our act, having never consented to it."

On the validity of this position John Adams staked his legal reputation, his hopes, his fortunes, and the welfare of his people.

It is one of the highest claims of Washington to the gratitude of mankind that he carried the country through a long war in strict subordination to the civil authority ; and it raises our respect for John Adams that, his position once taken on the fundamental law of his colony, he maintained it with courage and fidelity, without swerving from principle and without recourse to the arts of a demagogue. ·He began his career as a statesman, and such he remained to the end.

After the death of Thacher and the retirement of James Otis, Jr., John Adams became the trusted adviser of the patriot leaders on all legal and constitutional questions. They had need of him, for the party which adhered to the crown was led by very able men, who carried with them the influence of wealth, social position, and official station. A cause supported by such men as Hutchinson, Sewall, and Leonard could be overthrown only by powerful assailants. Better than any man of affairs save Hutchinson, John Adams understood the history, legislation, and constitutional law of his colony ; and probably no man of his day, on either side of the Atlantic, had more carefully considered the foundations of government, or the formative process by which constitutions adapt themselves to the changing circumstances of national life. He recognized their present validity only so far as they conformed to the laws of national growth ; and he saw that they retained their identity only as the oak is identical with the acorn from which it sprung.

In the legal and constitutional controversies which preceded hostilities, the dialectical force was by no means wholly on the side of the patriotic party. Hutchinson was a formidable antagonist, and more than once caused anxiety in the camp of the Whigs. And he was surpassed by Daniel Leonard, whose weekly papers, published in the winter of 1774–75 under the signature of " Massachusettensis," raised this anxiety to positive alarm. These celebrated letters, — if such can be called celebrated which no one reads ; a classic lost to literature amid the ruins of the cause which brought it forth, — written with evident sincerity of purpose and almost pathetic tenderness of feeling, were likely to affect the popular mind very powerfully [1] at a time when the colony seemed to be drifting into war. His constitutional argument was strong, perhaps unanswerable on the ground on which he put it; and his appeals to the judgment, good sense, and right feeling of the community required an answer. The eyes of the Whigs were turned to John Adams. He had just returned from the Congress at Philadelphia, in which, with infinite difficulty, he had brought the delegates to the true fighting ground of the Revolution. With the constitutional argument he was perfectly familiar. The answers of the House of Representatives, in January and March, 1773, to Hutchinson's messages, were indebted to him for their legal astuteness, which was adopted by Samuel Adams and used with the skill which characterizes his acknowledged compositions. I refer to these controversial papers only for the purpose of showing the attitude of John Adams to the main question. The Tory writers, assuming that the colonists were British subjects within the realm, and with rights and duties determinable by the construction ordinarily given to the British Constitution in practical legislation, had little difficulty in making plain that no line could be drawn between absolute parliamentary supremacy in all cases whatever and total independence. This was forcing the controversy to an issue for which the colonists as a whole were not ripe, as John Adams had sorrowfully learned in the recent Congress at Philadelphia. As a Massachusetts issue he could accept it with prompt decision; but

---

[1] " Did not our Massachusettensis
For your conviction strain his senses ? "
TRUMBULL's *McFingal.*

there were other parties to be conciliated, and he
necessarily wrote with a view to the state of feeling in
the other colonies and in England as well, where the
contest was regarded with intense interest. In discussing the question as one arising on the construction of
the British Constitution, he showed both power and
learning in attack as well as in defense ; but he was
in close quarters with an antagonist worthy of his
steel, and as is usual in such cases he experienced the
varying fortunes of war.

But on his own ground — the position taken before
the Governor and Council in 1765, on the petition
for opening the courts ; and later, in the fourth article
of the Declaration of Rights by the Congress at Philadelphia — he was on firm, constitutional ground, and
historically correct, if the general course of colonial
history rather than isolated facts is regarded. Some
of these positions have been already referred to ; but
as he is about to pass from the provincial to the national stage, and as the replies to " Massachusettensis "
were the latest and most authentic expression of his
views on the colonial constitution, I refer to them
again.

On the parliamentary modification of the charter
contemporaneous with the Boston Port Bill he says,
" America will never allow that Parliament has any
authority to alter their constitution. She is wholly
penetrated with a sense of the necessity of resisting it
at all hazards. And she would resist it if the constitution of Massachusetts had been altered as much
for the better as it is for the worse." The inviolability
of the colonial constitution, and that constitution as
the basis and measure of colonial rights, was his doctrine.

This bold position was the true position. No sounder doctrine ever emanated from any American constitutionalist; and when John Adams assumed it, defended it, and brought his colony to stand upon it and fight the war upon it, he rendered her a service of statesmanship such as has never been surpassed. It changed the nature of the contest. Acts which would have been rebellion to the British Constitution, and made all participators in them traitors, were no longer such, but justifiable and patriotic defense of their own constitutional liberty.

The Whigs were no longer fighting against Great Britain, but for the protection of their own rights. The difference was immense, and so were the consequences. This new feeling nerved the arm and fired the hearts of many whom the idea of treason inspired with something of its old terror. Every act of ministerial power designed to coerce the colonists was usurpation, and the ministerial troops became an organized mob which might be lawfully resisted.

Important as were the consequences of John Adams's doctrine of the inviolability of colonial constitutions in affording a good fighting position, other and even more important consequences flowed from it. If the people of the several colonies were living under constitutional governments of their own, and not merely royal charters revocable at the pleasure of the imperial government, it followed that they had a right to change their constitutions at will and mould them to their changed circumstances. This was what John Adams incessantly urged in the Congress of 1775, and what was as strenuously resisted by a large party not yet ripe for independence, which, they claimed, and with truth, such a measure would promote more than

any other conceivable. Finally Adams prevailed ; and
while the war was going on, several of the colonies
adopted State governments on models furnished by
him, and notably his own State, the constitution of
which he drafted, and from which was adopted the
frame of government in the Constitution of the United
States. Fifty millions of people to-day live under a
constitution the essential features of which are after
his model. Thirty-eight States now have constitutions
in no essential respect differing from that which he
drafted. Thus widely is his influence felt. How permanently, God only knows. But until constitutional
government is overthrown on this continent, the work
of the GREAT CONSTITUTIONALIST will endure.

As an example of his insight and grasp of constitutional principles may be cited his action in respect to
the impeachment of the judges who accepted salaries
from the crown instead of the province, in contravention of the provincial constitution. Peter Oliver was
chief justice. His brother, the stamp distributor, had
been compelled to renounce his office under the Liberty
Tree. But the chief justice was understood to be of
sterner stuff, and probably would have yielded his
life sooner than his office at the dictation of the mob.
The Whigs — and most of all the Whig lawyers —
were in doubt. But John Adams had no doubt. The
provincial constitution, he claimed, contained the germ
of every power which had been developed in the British Constitution in the centuries of its growth ; and
now that the exigency had arisen which called forth
the latent resources of the provincial constitution,
with that promptness, decision, and sound judgment
which always characterized his action when there was
anything to call forth his powers, he proposed the

impeachment of the chief justice by the House before
the Council.   After his professional brethren had recovered from their astonishment at the audacity of
this proposal, and come more fully to understand the
constitutional basis on which it rested, they fell in with
the idea, and proceedings were inaugurated, which
were brought to a summary end by the war and the
flight of Oliver to England on the evacuation of Boston by the king's troops.

When John Adams was transferred from a provincial to a national stage as one of the delegates from
Massachusetts to the Continental Congress, which met
at Philadelphia in September, 1774, he became associated with a body of very able men, among whom he
at once assumed a leading position, as he had done in
his own colony.   He was by considerable the ablest
man in the body, and in his line of constitutional
statesmanship by far the best equipped.

But his position was one of great difficulty.   It is
only after a careful study of the proceedings of this
Congress and the subsequent history of some of its
members that we come at its real character.   It was
a Peace Congress.[1]   Some of the colonies had been
compromised by their attitude in respect to the East
India Company's teas ; and the extreme measures of
the British government in closing the port of Boston
and altering the charter of the contumacious people
of Massachusetts excited the apprehension of other

---

[1] That such was its character is evident from the final resolutions
adopted : —

"We have for the present only resolved to pursue the following
peaceable measures : 1, to enter into a non-importation, non-consump-
tion, and non-exportation agreement or association. 2 and 3, to address
the people of Great Britain, the inhabitants of British America, and
to prepare a loyal address to his Majesty."

colonies as to the ulterior purposes of the ministry. While it was the patriotic desire of the Congress to express their sympathies and to stand by the people of Boston in the hour of their sufferings, it was hoped and expected that some conciliatory course would be followed which would allow the ministry and the Massachusetts people to extricate themselves from their difficulties without recourse to war.

John Adams had no faith in the efficacy of the petition to the king, nor in the addresses to the people of Great Britain and the Canadas. Matters had gone so far in New England that they would be satisfied with no terms short of the withdrawal of the royal troops, the reopening the port of Boston, and the total repeal of all measures designed to reduce them to obedience. At the same time, not only the British ministry, but the British people also, were demanding the complete submission of the Bostonians or the infliction of condign punishment. So far as Massachusetts was concerned, the war was inevitable. John Adams saw it to be so, and prepared himself for it.

He endeavored to prepare the Congress for it, and not without valuable results. The great work effected by this Congress was the bringing the colonies on to common ground by a declaration of their rights. Opinions were divided. A compromise ensued, and the famous fourth article was the result. It was drawn by John Adams, and carried mainly by his influence, and reads as follows : —

" That the foundation of English liberty and of all free government is a right in the people to participate in their legislative council ; and as the English colonists are not represented, and from their local and other circumstances cannot be properly represented in the British Parliament, they are entitled to a free and exclusive power of legislation in their several provincial legislatures, where their rights of representation can alone be preserved in all cases of taxation and internal polity, subject only to the negative of their sovereign in such manner as has been heretofore used and accustomed. But from the necessity of the case and a regard to the mutual interest of both countries we cheerfully consent to the operation of such acts of the British Parliament as are *bona fide* restrained to the regulation of our external commerce, for the purpose of securing the commercial advantages of the whole empire to the mother country and the commercial benefits of its respective members, excluding every idea of taxation, internal or external, for raising a revenue on the subjects in America without their consent."

This was not precisely what John Adams wanted, but it was much. When this declaration went forth, the cause of Massachusetts, in whatever it might eventuate, was the cause of the colonies. IT WAS NATIONALIZED. This was John Adams's greatest feat of statesmanship. On it the success of the impending war and the Declaration of Independence rested.[1]

Congress, having completed its work, adjourned

---

[1] It is interesting to learn that John Adams regarded the declaration of the Congress on the subject of parliamentary power over the colonies merely as the reaffirmance of the old colonial doctrine. "Thus it appears," he says in *Novanglus*, "that the ancient Massachusettsians and Virginians had precisely the same sense of the authority of Parliament, viz., that it had none at all; and the same sense of the necessity, that by the voluntary act of the colonies, their free, cheerful consent, it should be allowed the power of regulating trade; and this is precisely the idea of the late Congress at Philadelphia, expressed in the fourth proposition of their Bill of Rights."—*Works,* iv. 112.

October 26, 1774. This body has been much commended for its moderation and ability. Chatham eulogized the remarkable series of addresses it sent forth ; but neither Samuel Adams nor John Adams nor some of the Virginians were satisfied with the results of the Congress. As Bancroft says, " Congress did not as yet desire independence. Had that been their object, they would have strained every nerve to increase their exports and fill the country with the manufactures and munitions which they required." On the contrary, they agreed upon certain commercial restrictions upon the trade of the mother country and those colonies which should side with her, hoping thereby to coerce the king's government, by the influence of the manufacturing and trading classes at home, to desist from that commercial policy which was the chief ground of their displeasure. As matter of fact the Revolution had not cast off its commercial phase. It had, however, made one capital declaration of colonial rights.

The value of this stroke of statesmanship became apparent in the next session of Congress in May, 1775. The events at Lexington and Concord had precipitated the contest which the majority of the people of the colonies wished to avoid. But the die was cast, and one of the delegates at least had measured the magnitude of the struggle that had begun, the necessity of nationalizing it, and of bringing to its support the full powers and resources of a continental government. This sagacity and statesmanship were evinced by the completeness of his plans; and his practical force, by his final success in carrying them into operation in spite of innumerable obstacles thrown in his way. " We ought," wrote John

Adams to General Warren, July 24, " to have had in our hands a month ago the whole legislative, executive, and judicial of the whole continent, and have completely modeled a constitution; to have raised a naval power, and opened all our ports wide." When the intercepted letter which contained the above extract was published at Philadelphia, it "displayed him as drawing the outlines of an independent state, the great bugbear in the eyes of members who still cling to the hope that the last resort might be avoided." These views subjected him to animadversion, and even cold treatment, to the extent that he "was avoided in the streets by many as if it were a contamination to speak with such a traitor."

We see the magnificence of his plan to create the empire which he foresaw in his youth. We see the sagacity of the measures by which it was to be accomplished. We also see, what those who opposed him were soon to see, the vast resources, the untiring labors, and indomitable courage which he brought to the execution of these plans.[1]

His plan was to sever at once every political tie which bound the separate colonies to Great Britain in

[1] " Her (Massachusetts) government passed out of royal hands before the Continental Congress had been in session a month. After a partially successful appeal for the advice of the Continental Congress, hers was the first government to be placed on a new although confessedly temporary foundation; and from one of her leaders went forth to the other colonies one of the strongest single lines of influence toward the speedy erection of commonwealth governments. Massachusetts endorsed heartily, even if for the time incompletely, the principal feature of John Adams's plan of political campaign; and it was toward the full realization of his policy in the complete establishment of commonwealth governments that the leaders aimed consistently during the few years of the distinctly transitional period." — Harry A. Cushing's *Transition from Provincial to Commonwealth Government*, 13, 14.

their royal governments, and to lay the basis of their independence by the erection of state governments in their stead; to nationalize these state governments by confederation, and to give this new government the substance as well as the form of nationality by adopting the army before Boston and putting it under national commanders; by constructing a navy; by issuing bills of credit; by sending embassadors to foreign nations; and finally, by declaring the thirteen colonies the free, independent United States of America.

To the accomplishment of this work of building a nation, no one of all the great men with whom he was associated addressed himself with a clearer comprehension of what it involved, or more ably or more assiduously devoted himself to it, than John Adams.

This was his great work. Before its substantial completion I do not think he could have been spared. I see no one who could have filled his place between 1774 and 1777. But after that period, the Revolution in successful progress, independence declared, and the work of constitutional reconstruction well advanced, he might have retired to well-merited repose. The Congress thought otherwise; and John Adams, who always heeded the call of his country, embarked for Europe charged with diplomatic duties. He was well informed in matters of public and international law, but was not, I think, specially adapted for a diplomatic career. He rendered some excellent service, but none which might not have been as well performed by his able associates, unless we may still question whether their zeal for the preservation of the old colonial rights to the fisheries and for extending the boundaries of the country to their furthest limits was equal to his own. He certainly had always before his eyes the vision of his youth — the Empire of America. Not even in a later day was Webster's view wider, more national, or more patriotic; nor in the largeness and liberality of his commercial policy has he ever been surpassed by any of our public men.

Doubtless there is a tendency to over-estimation when our eyes are fixed somewhat exclusively upon a single actor in a cause which enlists the abilities of other eminent men. But I think we may safely add our own to the according voices of those patriots who were personally cognizant of the services of John Adams, in assigning to him the preëminent place among the statesmen of the Revolution. He did not bring to the Revolution so large an understanding as Franklin's. But Franklin lacked some things essential to the cause which John Adams possessed. He lacked youth. At the critical period which was forming an epoch in history, he was an old man, with great interests depending on the existing order of things, averse to extreme measures, especially war, and without special training for constitutional questions. Jay, Jefferson, Wythe, Henry, Lee, Gadsden — not to mention others — were able men, and rendered great services. But, save Franklin, no man in the colonies was so largely endowed as John Adams. His understanding was extraordinary. He planned well, and he executed his plans. There was no other man of so much weight in action as he. There were wise men — some, estimated by conventional standards, much wiser than John Adams; but none whose judgments on Revolutionary affairs have proved more solid or enduring. There were younger men of genius and older men of great experience in affairs; but John Adams was just at that period of life when genius becomes chastened by experience without being over-powered by adversity.

But whatever may have been the value of his ser-vices when compared with those of his great compa-triots, it is sufficient title to lasting honor and the unceasing benedictions of his countrymen that John Adams had a conspicuous place among those who builded a great nation, made it free, and formed gov-ernments for it which seem destined to endure for ages and affect the political condition of no inconsid-erable part of the human race.

While living John Adams had no strong hold on the people, and at one time, as he said, an immense unpopularity, like the tower of Siloam, fell upon him; and now that he is dead, even the remembrance of his great services seems to be growing indistinct. He probably lacked many of those qualities which attract popular favor, and those which he possessed, such as courage and steadfastness, were exhibited on no theatre of public action, but in the secret sessions of the Con-tinental Congress. Passionate eloquence on great themes touches the heart to finer issues; but no sylla-ble of those powerful utterances which, as Jefferson tells us, took men off their feet, was heard beyond the walls of Independence Hall; and even the glory of the transaction which made the old hall immortal rests upon the hand which wrote, not upon that which achieved, the Great Declaration. This ought not to be altogether so. It matters little to the stout old patriot with what measure of fame he descends to remote age, for he will never wholly die; but to us and to those who come after us it is of more than passing consequence that we and they withhold no tribute of just praise from those unpopular men who deserve the respectful remembrance of their country-men.

In the public squares of the city have been erected statues of those great men, save John Adams, whose services were indispensable to the initiation and successful issue of the Revolution — Samuel Adams, Benjamin Franklin, and George Washington ; but our eyes seek in vain for any adequate memorial of him whose life, public and private, was without blemish, whose essential character is worthy of all admiration, and whose services·ought never to be forgotten so long as free, united, constitutional government holds its just place in the estimation of the people.

THE
AUTHENTICATION OF THE DECLARA-
TION OF INDEPENDENCE

JULY 4, 1776

Reprinted from the Proceedings of the Massachusetts
Historical Society, November, 1884

AUTHENTICATION OF THE DECLARATION

FEW historical events which have occasioned controversy are referred to definite time and place by such overwhelming weight of authority, personal and documentary, as that which assigns the authentication of the Declaration of Independence, by the signatures of the members of Congress, to Independence Hall in Philadelphia, July 4, 1776. After it had been called in question, this was distinctly affirmed by two of the most eminent of the persons then present, one of whom was the author of the Declaration, and the other the most powerful advocate of the resolution on which it was based ; and their concurring statements appear to be corroborated by memoranda claimed to have been written at the time, as well as by the printed official Journal of the Congress of which both were members; and yet it is more than probable that both eye-witnesses were mistaken and the memoranda untrustworthy, while the printed Journal is demonstrably misleading. This is all the more extraordinary since the error relates to an event in respect to which error is hardly predicable. It is not a question as to what took place on some widely extended battlefield crowded with struggling combatants, but as to what passed directly under the eyes of fifty intelligent gentlemen in the quiet and secret session of the Continental Congress.

The question is this: Was the draft of the Declaration of Independence, which after various amendments was finally agreed to on the afternoon of July 4, forthwith engrossed on paper and thereupon subscribed by all the members then present except Dickinson? This is affirmed by Adams and Jefferson, and in this the printed Journal seems to sustain them. But this, Thomas McKean, himself a signer, present on the 4th, and voting for the Declaration, has explicitly denied; and so have Force,[1] Bancroft,[2] and Winthrop.[3] With some variation in phrase, these writers agree with Mr. Webster,[4] who says that on the 4th " it was ordered that copies be sent to the several States, and that it be proclaimed at the head of the army. The Declaration thus published did not bear the names of the members, for as yet it had not been signed by them. It was authenticated, like other papers of the Congress, by the signatures of the president and secretary."

Of the more recent writers, Frothingham [5] and Randall,[6] unable to see their way in this conflict of authority, have left the matter in doubt; while Dr. Lossing, who had said that " the Declaration of Independence was signed by John Hancock, the President of Congress, only, on the day of its adoption, and thus it went forth to the world,"[7] having reëxamined the

---

[1] *The Declaration of Independence*, 63.

[2] *History of the United States*, viii. 475.

[3] *Fourth of July Oration*, 1876, 28.

[4] *Works*, i. 129; see T. F. Bayard's oration in *Proceedings on Unveiling Monument to Cæsar Rodney*, 47, and Roberdeau Buchanan's *Life of McKean*, 37.

[5] *Rise of the Republic*, 545 n.

[6] *Life of Jefferson*, i. 171 n.

[7] *Field Book of the Revolution*, ii. 79.

question, or convinced by the statements of Mrs.
Nellie Hess Morris, [1] has changed his opinion, and
now affirms that it was engrossed on paper and signed
on the 4th by all the members who voted for it, and
subsequently on parchment, and again signed on August 2 in the form well known in facsimile.[2]

The first to challenge the commonly received opinion that the Declaration of Independence was engrossed and then signed by the members of Congress
on July 4 was Thomas McKean. Shortly after Governor McKean's death in 1817, John Adams sent to
Hezekiah Niles eight letters written to him by McKean between June 8, 1812, and June 17, 1817.
These letters were published in Niles's "Weekly
Register" for July 12, 1817 (xii. 305 *et seq.*). In
one of them, dated January 7, 1814, which is too
long to be given in full, but which may be found *ut
supra*, and also in the "Collections of the Massachusetts Historical Society" (xliv. 505), Governor
McKean says : —

"On the 1st of July, 1776, the question [on the Declaration] was taken in committee of the whole of Congress,
when Pennsylvania, represented by seven members then
present, voted against it, four to three. Among the majority were Robert Morris and John Dickinson. Delaware
(having only two present, namely, myself and Mr. Read)
was divided. All the other States voted in favor of it.
The report was delayed until the 4th ; and in the mean
time I sent an express for Cæsar Rodney to Dover, in the
county of Kent in Delaware, at my private expense, whom
I met at the State House door on the 4th of July in his
boots. He resided eighty miles from the city, and just

---

[1] *Potter's American Monthly*, iv.-v. 498.
[2] *Ibid.* 754.

arrived as Congress met. The question was taken. Delaware voted in favor of Independence. Pennsylvania (there being only five members present, Messrs. Dickinson and Morris absent) voted also for it. Messrs. Willing and Humphries were against it. Thus the thirteen States were unanimous in favor of Independence. Notwithstanding this, in the printed Public Journal of Congress for 1776 (vol. ii.) it appears that the Declaration of Independence was declared on the 4th of July, 1776, by the gentlemen whose names are there inserted, whereas no person signed it on that day ; and among the names there inserted one gentleman, namely, George Read, Esq., was not in favor of it; and seven were not in Congress on that day, namely, Messrs. Morris, Rush, Clymer, Smith, Taylor, and Ross, all of Pennsylvania, and Mr. Thornton, of New Hampshire ; nor were the six gentlemen last named members of Congress on the 4th of July. The five for Pennsylvania were appointed delegates by the convention of that State on the 20th July, and Thornton took his seat in Congress for the first time on the 4th November following ; when the names of Henry Wisner, of New York, and Thomas McKean, of Delaware, are not printed as subscribers, though both were present in Congress on the 4th of July and voted for Independence. . . . After the 4th of July I was not in Congress for several months, having marched with a regiment of Associators, as Colonel, to support General Washington, until the flying camp of ten thousand men was completed. When the Associators were discharged I returned to Philadelphia, took my seat in Congress, and signed my name to the Declaration on parchment."

In transmitting this letter to Mercy Warren for her reading, John Adams said : —

" I send you a curiosity. Mr. McKean is mistaken in a day or two. The final vote of independence, after the last debate, was passed on the 2d or 3d of July, and the Declaration prepared and signed on the 4th.

"What are we to think of history, when in less than forty years such diversities appear in the memories of living persons who were witnesses?

"After noting what you please, I pray you to return the letter. I should like to communicate it to Gerry, Paine, and Jefferson, to stir up their pure minds." [1]

Governor McKean's recollection was certainly at fault in one or two particulars. His patriotic and successful endeavor to bring Rodney up from Delaware was that he might vote on the main question, — the Resolution of Independence, which passed the 2d of July. It is doubtful, also, whether he was correct in saying that Wisner of New York voted either for the Resolution or for the Declaration; for, though he may have been in favor of independence, the delegates from that State were not authorized so to vote until July 9, nor was their authority communicated to Congress before July 15.[2] McKean was in error on some collateral points; but was John Adams right and McKean wrong on the main question, — the signing of the Declaration on the 4th? It is premature to decide until all the evidence is produced; but there is a noticeable letter written by John Adams to Samuel Chase from Philadelphia, July 9, in which he says: "As soon as an American seal is prepared, I conjecture the Declaration will be subscribed by all the members, which will give you the opportunity you wish for of transmiting your name among the votaries of independence." [3] From this it is clear that Chase, whose name appears on the printed Journal

---

[1] *Massachusetts Historical Collections*, ser. 5, iv. 505.
[2] *Journal of Congress*, ii. 265.
[3] *Works*, ix. 421.

of the 4th as a signer, was not in Philadelphia on that day, nor until after the 9th; and a question arises, why Chase, on his return to Philadelphia, should not have signed that Declaration which John Adams says he and others signed on the 4th, instead of waiting for the general subscription, which he conjectured would take place after the preparation of an American seal. The following entry in the Journal shows that Carroll was not in Congress until after that date, though his name is entered on the same Journal, when printed, under July 4, as then present and signing the Declaration : —

July 18. " The delegates from Maryland laid before Congress the credentials of a new appointment made by their convention, which were read as follows : —

" In CONVENTION, ANNAPOLIS, July 4, 1776.

" *Resolved,* That the honorable Matthew Tilghman, Esq.; and Thomas Johnson., Jun., William Paca, Samuel Chase, Thomas Stone, Charles Carroll of Carrollton, and Robert Alexander, Esqrs.; or a majority of them, or any three or more of them, be deputies to represent this colony in Congress, etc. etc. . . . Extract from the minutes : G. DUVALL, *Clerk.*" [1]

---

[1] *Journal of Congress,* ii. 273. The addition to the name of Charles Carroll, in the above resolve, of the words " of Carrollton," shows that such was his common designation before he signed the Declaration of Independence. Carroll, though he had a large property at stake, was one of the most ardent of the patriots, and as impatient as any of his associates at the delay of his colony to take the ground of independence ; and on the very day on which the printed Journal represents him as at Philadelphia and signing the Declaration he was at Annapolis, where he had been for some time engaged in the finally successful effort to bring the recalcitrant Assembly to the point of voting the resolve quoted in the text. Due consideration of the significance of the foregoing facts begets doubt respecting the story which has been widely circulated and has gained some

But the most particular and apparently the most irrefragable statement in favor of the popular belief that the Declaration was signed on the 4th by the members then present, except Dickinson, is found in Jefferson's memoranda, and also in his letter of May 12, 1819, to Samuel Adams Wells.[1] And first the memoranda. At the end of the Declaration, on page 21, Jefferson has appended the following : —

" The Declaration, thus signed on the 4th on paper, was engrossed on parchment and signed again on the 2d of August."

And in brackets : —

"Some erroneous statements of the proceedings on the Declaration of Independence having got before the public in latter times, Mr. Samuel A. Wells asked explanations of me, which are given in my letter to him of May 12, '19, before and now again referred to. I took notes in my place while these things were going on, and at their close wrote them out in form and with correctness ; and from one to seven of the two preceding sheets are the originals then written."

credence. It is to the effect that when the members were signing the engrossed copy of the Declaration on August 2, Hancock, with some implied allusion to his own large fortune supposed to be imperiled by his signing, asked Carroll, who also was rich, " if *he* intended to sign." Perhaps there was nothing in the character of Hancock which would have prevented his asking such a question ; but certain facts stand in the way. Carroll took his seat July 18. The next day Congress voted that the Declaration, when engrossed, *should be signed by every member of that body.* So that if Carroll's patriotic efforts at Annapolis, which secured to himself and his delegation the right to vote, left any doubt as to his intention in that regard, the above vote of Congress renders the insolent question attributed to Hancock altogether improbable. The same may be said as to the alleged addition to Carroll's signature of the words " of Carrollton " in consequence of the taunt of a by-stander that their omission might save him his estate.

[1] Jefferson's *Writings*, Boston ed., 1830, i. 20, 94.

In the margin the editor informs us that the above note is on a slip of paper pasted in at the end of the Declaration. There is also, he tells us, sewed into the manuscript a slip of newspaper containing McKean's letter, from which it appears that Jefferson intended to make an issue of fact with Governor McKean.

Jefferson, in his letter to Wells, says : —

" It was not till the 2d of July that the Declaration itself was taken up, nor till the 4th that it was decided ; and it was signed by every member present except Mr. Dickinson.[1] The subsequent signatures of members who were not then present, and some of them not yet in office, is easily explained if we observe who they were ; to wit, that they were of New York and Pennsylvania. . . . Why the signature of Thornton of New Hampshire was permitted so late as the 4th of November, I cannot now say."

It is important to notice that when Jefferson speaks of a " Declaration thus signed," he must have had before him one that bore the signatures of the New York and Pennsylvania delegates, as well as that of Thornton of New Hampshire, as he mentions them.

The letter to Wells bore date May 12, 1819. On August 6, 1822, more than three years later, he added the following postscript to a copy which he had preserved : —

" Since the date of this letter, to wit, this day, August 6, '22, I have received the new publication of the Secret Journals of Congress, wherein is stated a resolution of July 19, 1776, that the Declaration passed on the 4th be fairly engrossed on parchment, and when engrossed be signed by every

---

[1] If the Declaration was signed on July 4, it is fair to ask why R. R. Livingston's name was not in it ; for he was on the committee to draft it and he is represented in Trumbull's picture as present on its presentation.

member ; and another of August 2d that, being engrossed and compared at the table, it was signed by the members."

As neither the resolution of July 19 nor the signing on parchment of August 2 appear except as hereafter given in his memoranda of matters he "took notes of in his place while these things were going on," and as he was certainly in his place August 2, when he signed the parchment Declaration, it is not surprising that he was disturbed when they came to his notice nearly fifty years later, since he had apparently forgotten them.

It is true he says, " The Declaration thus signed on the 4th, on paper, was engrossed on parchment and signed again on the 2d August." The latter date shows that the entry was made a month after the first alleged signing. " The Declaration thus signed," to which he refers and which he had before him, contained the signature of Thornton, which carries the date forward as late as November 4. There is no evidence of the existence of a printed copy of the Declaration, with the signatures of the members attached, before that issued under a resolution of Congress, January 18, 1777; and the imprint of the official journal which contains the names of the signers is of the same year. From these facts it seems to follow that Mr. Jefferson's memoranda were made later than that date.

We now proceed to a more careful examination of these memoranda. If they were made by Jefferson at the close of each day, or within a few days after the transactions they record, they would settle the question against any amount of opposing testimony of less authoritative character. But it is evident, on critical consideration, that such of these memoranda as relate to the signing of the Declaration on the 4th of July were made up with the printed Public Journal before him; and as that did not appear until the next year his notes lose the authority of contemporaneous entries. Indeed, he tells us himself that the statement of facts as we have it was made up " at their close."

It is not a little remarkable that, with the printed Journal of July 4, which bore Thornton's signature of November 4, before him, Jefferson should not have asked himself how that name should be found, not upon the *Declaration*, but upon the *Journal* of that day. When Thornton came down from New Hampshire in November, he doubtless signed the parchment Declaration in compliance with the order of July 19, " that the same, when engrossed, be signed by every member of Congress." Though coming late, Thornton was a member of that Congress. In order to make Jefferson's assumption effective, the clerk must then have produced the paper Declaration and requested Thornton to sign *that*. But neither of those signings would put Thornton's name on the *Journal* of the 4th. It could have come *there* only by the clerk's false entry that Thornton was present and signed on the 4th; for the entries of July 4, July 19, and August 2 are in the handwriting of Charles Thomson. To state this supposition is to contradict it. Nor is Jefferson's way out of the difficulty more clear if we accept Mr. Randall's [1] solution, which seems to be adopted by Dr. Lossing,[2] that the non-appearance of the paper Declaration to-day is to be accounted for by the presumption that it was destroyed as useless when the parchment was signed on August 2; for had that been

---

[1] Randall's *Jefferson*, i. 173.
[2] *Potter's American Monthly*, iv.-v. 755.

the case Thornton's name would not have appeared on an instrument destroyed three months before he entered Congress.

The real state of the case begins to appear: *the printed Public Journal for July* 4, 1776, *varies from the original.* There are three publications which purport to give the proceedings of the Old Congress, in whole or in part. The first is entitled "Journals of Congress. Containing the Proceedings in the year 1776." The proceedings for July, 1776, were not officially published until more than six months after their occurrence. The last entry in the Journal for that year is December 31; and the preparation of the copy, with a full index, would probably delay its publication until the spring of 1777. For more than forty years this was the only Journal known to the public. It was that which Adams and Jefferson had before them when they so explicitly stated that the Declaration of Independence was signed by the members present on July 4. This printed Journal appears to sustain them in that statement.

The second of these Journals is entitled the "Secret Journals of the Acts and Proceedings of Congress," and was first published in 1821, in four volumes, agreeably to Congressional Resolves. These volumes contain those records of domestic and foreign affairs which Congress thought it wise to keep from the public eye, and are found in manuscript volumes distinct from those which contain the Public Journals.

The wisdom, secrecy, or timidity of Congress is clear from the fact that the three resolutions, one of them relating to independence, which Richard Henry Lee moved on June 7, 1776, are referred to in the Journal of that day only as " certain resolutions respecting independency; " nor were they ever extended on the records, and only became known in the manner presently to be explained. On the 10th one of these resolutions was set out by way of recital.

The third of these Journals is to be found in Force's " American Archives," and is not the Journal kept by Charles Thomson, the secretary of the Old Congress, but an account of the proceedings of Congress made up from the Journals above described, and the minutes, documents, and letters preserved in files by the secretary. It lacks the authority which appertains to a journal extended by a sworn secretary of the body whose proceedings it records ; but, nevertheless, it is doubtless the most authentic account of the transactions of Congress which we possess. From the files Force printed the original paper which contained Lee's famous resolutions.[1]

With this account of these several Journals I now propose to bring them together, so far as relates to the Declaration of Independence. It will be understood that in speaking of the Public Journals of Congress I refer in all cases, unless otherwise specified, to the *printed* Journals.

Proceedings according to the Public Journal.

July 4, 1776. Agreeable to the order of the day, the Congress resolved itself into a committee of the whole, to take into their farther consideration the declaration ; and after some time the president resumed the chair, and Mr. Harrison reported that the committee have agreed to a declaration, which they desired him to report.

The declaration being read was agreed to, as follows : —

---

[1] See facsimile in *American Archives*, 4th ser. vi. 1700.

A DECLARATION *by the Representatives of the* UNITED STATES *of* AMERICA *in Congress assembled.*

[*Here follows the Declaration in the form we have it.*]

The foregoing declaration was, by order of Congress, engrossed, and signed by the following members : —

John Hancock.

New Hampshire.
Josiah Bartlett.
William Whipple.
Matthew Thornton.
Massachusetts-Bay.
Samuel Adams.
John Adams.
Robert Treat Paine.
Elbridge Gerry.
Rhode Island.
Stephen Hopkins.
William Ellery.
Connecticut.
Roger Sherman.
Samuel Huntington.
William Williams.
Oliver Wolcott.
New York.
William Floyd.
Philip Livingston.
Francis Lewis.
Lewis Morris.
New Jersey.
Richard Stockton.
John Witherspoon.
Francis Hopkinson.
John Hart.
Abraham Clark.

Pennsylvania.
Robert Morris.
Benjamin Rush.
Benjamin Franklin.
John Morton.
George Clymer.
James Smith.
George Taylor.
James Wilson.
George Ross.
Delaware.
Cæsar Rodney.
George Read.
Maryland.
Samuel Chase.
William Paca.
Thomas Stone.
Charles Carroll, of Carrollton.
Virginia.
George Wythe.
Richard Henry Lee.
Thomas Jefferson.
Benjamin Harrison.
Thomas Nelson, Jun.
Francis Lightfoot Lee.
Carter Braxton.
North Carolina.
William Hooper.
Joseph Hewes.
John Penn.

South Carolina.	*Georgia.*
Edward Rutledge.	Button Gwinnett.
Thomas Heyward, Jun.	Lyman Hall.
Thomas Lynch, Jun.	George Walton.
Arthur Middleton.	

Resolved, That copies of the declaration be sent to the several assemblies, conventions and committees, or councils of safety, and to the several commanding officers of the continental troops; that it be proclaimed in each of the United States, and at the head of the army.

In the Secret Journal there is no entry under the 4th of July, 1776.

Proceedings in Congress 4th July, 1776, as given in Force's "Archives." [1]

Agreeable to the Order of the Day, the Congress resolved itself into a Committee of the Whole, to take into their further consideration the Declaration; and after some time the President resumed the chair, and Mr. *Harrison* reported that the Committee have agreed to a Declaration, which they desired him to report.

The Declaration being read, was agreed to, as follows:—

[Here follows the Declaration, as in the Public Journal, *but without any signatures.*]

Ordered, That the Declaration be authenticated and printed. That the committee appointed to prepare the Declaration superintend and correct the press. *Resolved,* That copies of the Declaration be sent to the several assemblies [etc., as in the Public Journal].

The Secret Journal.

July 19, 1776. Resolved, That the Declaration passed on the 4th be fairly engrossed on parchment, with the title and style of " The Unanimous Declaration of the Thir-

---

[1] 4th ser. vi. 1729.

TEEN UNITED STATES of AMERICA ;" and that the same, when engrossed, be signed by every member of Congress.[1]

The Public Journal has no entry on this day respecting the Declaration; but the Proceedings in Force's " Archives " contain the resolve as above.[2]

The Secret Journal.

August 2, 1776. The Declaration of Independence being engrossed, and compared at the table, was signed by the members.[3]

The same is found in Force's " Archives," [4] but not in the Public Journal.

The Public Journal.

January 18, 1777. *Ordered*, That an authenticated copy of the declaration of independency, with the names of the members of Congress subscribing the same, be sent to each of the United States, and they be desired to have the same put upon record.[5]

Assuming that the entry in the Public Journal of July 4 is genuine, the above order is superfluous, since as such it merely repeats the former order, and couples with it the expression of a desire that the several States would record it. The operative clause is to print the Declaration with the *names of the members signing* it. This was accordingly done, and for the *first time*. From the copy thus printed was made up the Journal of the 4th July, *as printed* more than six months antecedent.[6]

---

[1] *Secret Journal, Domestic Affairs*, ii. 48.
[2] Force's *Archives*, 5th ser. i. 1584.
[3] *Secret Journal, Domestic Affairs*, ii. 49.
[4] Force's *Archives*, 5th ser. i. 1597.
[5] *Journals of Congress*, iii. 28.
[6] See *New Hampshire Historical Society Collections*, ii. 139, for

With these extracts from the Journals and Proceedings before us, and assisted by certain well-known and indisputable facts, it ought not to be difficult to discover the truth respecting the apparent signing of the Declaration of Independence on the 4th of July, 1776.

It will be observed that the statements of these Journals are inconsistent, if not contradictory.   The Public Journal says, under date of July 4 : —

" The foregoing declaration was, by order of Congress, engrossed, and signed by the following members."

In the Proceedings the corresponding entry is as follows : —

" *Ordered*, That the Declaration be authenticated and printed.   That the committee appointed to prepare the Declaration superintend and correct the press."

" *Resolved*, That copies of the Declaration be sent to the several assemblies," etc.

Now, it is hardly conceivable that these inconsistent orders could have passed at the same time and in relation to the same subject-matter.   One or the other of them must be incorrect.   It is noticeable that what seems to be an order in the Public Journal is only a narrative of an alleged fact, namely, that " the foregoing declaration was, by order of Congress, engrossed and signed by the following members."   It is pertinent to ask, By what order, and where is it recorded ? The Journal contains no such order, nor do the files. Nothing exists independently of the above recital to show that any such order was ever passed ; nor is the narrative a correct recital of facts.   That is, it

Hancock's letter, January 31, 1777, sending a copy to New Hampshire.

states what is known to be untrue, — in part, from subsequent entries in the Journal itself. The New York members, whose names are recorded as present and signing the Declaration on July 4, were not authorized to sign until the 9th, nor was that authority laid before Congress until the 15th.[1] Of course they did not sign before that date. As we have already seen, Chase was not present on the 4th, nor was Carroll, who did not take his seat until the 18th.[2] Rush, Clymer, Taylor, and Ross, of Pennsylvania, whose names are recorded as signing on the 4th, were not chosen delegates until July 20;[3] nor did Thornton appear in Congress until November 4.[4] So far as these delegates are concerned, the Public Journal, which represents them as present in Congress on the 4th of July and signing the Declaration, is clearly spurious.

In the next place, the record of the Public Journal as printed is at variance with known facts. If, as it asserts, the Declaration was signed on the 4th, it should be found in the files of that day; but search has repeatedly been made for it without success, nor has it ever been seen or heard of. It may have been lost; but there are facts making it by far more probable that it never existed. If the signatures of the delegates were affixed, in whole or in part, to the Declaration on the 4th, they formed an important part of the instrument, since they constituted its sole authorized and required authentication, when it was

---

[1] See Sparks's *Life of Gouverneur Morris*, i. 109, 110; *Life of Sparks*, i. 524, 525; as to the Connecticut members, see *Massachusetts Historical Society Proceedings*, ser. 2, iii. 373 *et seq.*

[2] *Journals of Congress*, ii. 273.

[3] *Ibid.* 277.

[4] *Ibid.* 441.

printed and sent to the several assemblies and read at the head of the army. We have the copies which were so sent and read. But these copies contain only the signatures of John Hancock, as president, and Charles Thomson, as secretary, of the Congress, who claim to have signed it *in behalf and by order of* that body.[1] So that, if the order of Congress, as is asserted by the Public Journal, was that the Declaration should be signed by the members, and so sent forth, then Hancock and Thomson must have caused it to be printed without these signatures, and falsely claimed that their own were added by authority. For not only cannot this original Declaration, which Jefferson says was signed by the delegates on the 4th, be found, but not even one of the printed copies which were ordered by Congress. This fact points to an inevitable conclusion. Such a paper never existed save on the false Journal as printed by Congress.

On the other hand, the proceedings and orders, as set forth in the "American Archives," strictly conform to congressional precedents. All its proclamations and similar public documents went forth under the authentication of the president and secretary, unless otherwise ordered, as was the case with the Address to the King and other like addresses of the Congress of 1774. Any other method, save by express vote, would have been illegal. Since the Declaration, though of the nature of a legislative act, was in some respects out of the ordinary course, the president and secretary might well seek instruction. Congress forthwith gave them directions to authenticate it and print it under direction of the committee that drafted

---

[1] The same authentication is given in the *Annual Register*, 1776, 161.

it, and then send it to the assemblies and to the army. This was done immediately. Lossing has stated that the Declaration was agreed to about two o'clock in the afternoon. It was printed during that afternoon and evening, and the next day was sent forth to the world.[1] Copies of the Declaration are not rare. There is one in the library of the Historical Society; and a copy was printed at Salem, doubtless within a few days after the receipt of that distributed by order of Congress. Its authentication is as follows : —

Signed by order and in behalf of the Congress,
> JOHN HANCOCK, *President.*

Attest, CHARLES THOMSON, *Secretary.*

The ordinary authentication was by the signatures of the president and secretary, followed by their official title; and the peculiarity of the authentication of the Declaration in the use of the uncommon words, "Signed by order and in behalf of the Congress," shows that it was so authenticated by the express vote of that body.

In a word, the proceedings of Congress with respect to the Declaration, as contained in the "American Archives," and given above, conform to and account for all known facts; while the record of the same transaction, as found in the Public Journal, is contradicted by other entries in the same Journal, and is at variance with all the external circumstances attending and following the transaction.

But the case does not rest wholly upon the reasons given above. Thus far in this analysis I have confined myself to the printed Journals of Congress and

---

[1] See note in Frothingham's *Rise of the Republic*, 544, from which one might infer that the Declaration was published on the 4th.

to such facts as are of public notoriety; and if the
case were allowed to rest here, I trust it has been
made to appear that the Public Journal of July 4,
reciting that the Declaration of Independence was
signed by the members of Congress on that day, is
erroneous. But the error requires explanation as
well as demonstration. The error is in the printed
Journal which does not conform to the original manuscripts. Of these there are three which are more
fully described in the subjoined note.[1]   Two of them

[1] For the interesting facts given above I am indebted to the courtesy of S. M. Hamilton, Esq., of the State Department, Washington,
who, in the absence of Theodore F. Dwight, Esq., to whom I had
addressed some inquiries, had written the following letter and its
enclosures.

DEPARTMENT OF STATE, WASHINGTON, November 5, 1884.

DEAR SIR, — . . . I fail to discover any printed half-sheet of
paper, with the names of the members afterwards in the printed
Journals stitched in.   I have found, however, a printed copy of the
Declaration inserted in one of the manuscript Journals covering the
period in question, and have, by the enclosures, endeavored to give
an accurate idea of the same.

Three of the manuscript Journals of the Continental Congress
cover July, 1776.   One begins, or rather the first entry in it is under
date of, May 25, 1776, and ends July 24.   In this appears the printed
copy of the Declaration.   The next begins with entry under date of
May 14 (continuing the record of that day, begun in the preceding
volume), and the last August 6, 1776.   In that the Declaration appears as a regular and continuous entry, and is in the same handwriting as the rest of the Journal.   The third Journal is the *Secret
Domestic Journal,* which contains no entry between June 24 and
July 8, 1776.

Taking your queries as they come in your letter, I may say, —

1st.   The enclosure gives an idea of the only printed copy of the
Declaration inserted in any manuscript Journal.

2d.   As will be seen, the printed names of Hancock and of Thomson are the only names appearing attached to it in *any* form.

3d.   It will be seen, also, that the names of the States do not
appear.

4th.   The words, " The foregoing declaration," etc. (*vide* printed relate to the events of July 4, and all include the Declaration of Independence in some one or more of

Journal, ii. 245), have not been found in the Journals, neither in the manuscript copy of the Declaration nor in the printed half-sheet. They (the words above quoted) appear in the printed Journals only.

5th. Neither of the Public Journals nor the Secret Journal contains any written names to the Declaration.

Enclosure marked No. 1 is to represent the printed half-sheet. That marked No. 2 is in a manner a comparison of the entries in the two Public Journals of so much of the minutes under the 4th of July as relates to the Declaration, with the exception of that part relating to copies being sent to the several States, etc. The copying ink denotes the entries as in the Journal containing the printed half-sheet; the red ink shows them as appearing in the Journal containing the Declaration in manuscript: that is, the words in red ink appear in the Journal containing the Declaration in manuscript in addition to those in the former, while words in red brackets do not appear therein.

I am, sir, very obediently yours,

S. M. HAMILTON.

MELLEN CHAMBERLAIN, Esq., etc.

The printed page not conveniently allowing the exhibition by type or photography of Mr. Hamilton's enclosures, they may be described as follows: No. 1 is a folded sheet of paper designed to represent the size and form of the manuscript Journal which contains a printed copy of the Declaration attached by wafers. The size of the sheet, when folded, is 8 by 12½ inches. On the *verso* of the first leaf the writing covers the upper half of the page, the lower half being left blank, apparently to receive by attachment the printed broadside of the Declaration now found there. This copy is twice folded so as to adapt it to the page of the Journal. The printed matter measures 11½ by 17¾ inches. Its authentication is in print and as follows: —

Signed by ORDER and in BEHALF *of the* CONGRESS

JOHN HANCOCK, *President*

Attest

CHARLES THOMSON, *Secretary*

The imprint is: "PHILADELPHIA: PRINTED BY JOHN DUNLAP." Above this printed copy of the Declaration, and forming part of the manuscript Journal which begins with May 25 and ends July 24, 1776, are the following entries, under date of July 4, 1776: —

.   .   .   .

its stages.   They are all at variance with the printed
Public Journal, though agreeing with each other in all

"Agreeable to the order of the day the Congress resolved itself
into a committee of the whole to take into their further consideration
the declaration

"The president resumed the chair

"Mr. Harrison reported that the committee of the whole Congress
have agreed to a Declaration which he delivered in

"The Declaration being again read was agreed to as follows"

[*Here the printed Declaration is attached by wafers.*]

On the next page is the following : —

"Ordered That the declaration be authenticated & printed

"That the committee appointed to prepare the declaration superintend & correct the press."

This is the true Journal of Congress for July 4, omitting the order
respecting its transmission, etc.

Now compare this with the spurious printed Journal, and the fals-
ity of the latter clearly appears.   The printed Journal reads : —

"The foregoing declaration was by order of Congress, engrossed,
and signed by the following members."

Then follow fifty-five names of gentlemen, many of whom were not
members of Congress at that time.

The other copy of the manuscript Journal is as follows, *so far as it
differs from the first copy;* and, as will be seen, the differences are
merely verbal.   This is found in enclosure No. 2.

[*Journal entirely in manuscript, with the Declaration in the same handwriting, from May 14 to August 6, 1776.*

So much of the minutes under 4th July as relates to the Declaration.]

·   ·   ·   ·   ·   ·   ·   ·   ·   ·   ·   ·   ·

Agreeable to the order of the day the Congress resolved itself into a
committee of the whole to take into their further consideration the
declaration *and after some time*

The president resumed the chair &

Mr. Harrison reported that the committee have agreed to a declaration, which *they desired him to report*

The declaration being read was agreed to as follows.

A Declaration by the Representatives of the United States of America
in Congress assembled

[The italicized words do not appear in the Journal to which is attached the printed copy of the Declaration.]

essential particulars. In neither of them is found an order for the subscription of the Declaration July 4,

Mr. Dwight has placed me under additional obligations by the following letter, which throws much light upon the Journals of the Old Congress; and it is matter of regret that I am unable to present in connection with this subject several valuable enclosures which he caused to be prepared.

DEPARTMENT OF STATE, WASHINGTON, December 23, 1884.

. . . .

As to the several Journals : Charles Thomson, as you know, was the "perpetual Secretary" of the Continental Congress; and, from all I can gather, he was a man of the strictest probity, and was most conscientious in the discharge of his important trusts. It would be interesting to discover how much influence he exerted in the first councils. I am confident it was considerable. To him we owe the preservation of all the records of the Continental Congress, — not only the Journals, but all those fragments now so precious, *e. g.*, the original motions, the reports of committees, the small odds and ends, which are the small bones of history. They are all in this room, and at my elbow as I write. One of them, for instance, is the original of Lee's motion reproduced, but without proper explanation, by Force, in the *American Archives.* You allude to it.

The Journals of Congress are, with some very few exceptions, entirely in the handwriting of Thomson. He seems to have been present at every session. The series of the archives of the Congress very properly begins with what he termed the "Rough Journal," beginning with the proceedings of September 5, 1774, and ended with the entry of March 2, 1789, and was probably written while Congress was sitting, the entries being made directly after each vote was taken. It is contained in thirty-nine small foolscap folio volumes. The second of the series is a fair copy of the "Rough Journal," from September 5, 1775, to January 20, 1779, — in ten volumes folio. From this copy, it is stated in a record in the Bureau, "the Journals were printed; and such portions as were deemed secret were marked or crossed by a committee of Congress, — not to be transcribed." In this he has amplified some entries, and given more care to the style and composition of his sentences.

This explanation will account for the "two Public Journals." The "Rough Journal" should be regarded as the standard. No. 3 of the series of archives is the "Secret Domestic Journal," comprising entries from May 10, 1775, to October 26, 1787; the fourth number is a Secret Journal, foreign and domestic, comprising entries from October 18, 1780, to March 29, 1786 (the foregoing two numbers form two vol-

nor any copy or account of a declaration so signed,
nor any reference to such a paper.   On the other

umes).   No. 5 is in three volumes, and is called "Secret Journal of
Foreign Affairs," November 29, 1775, to September 16, 1788.   No. 6
is in three volumes, and is designated " An imperfect Secret Journal; "
it contains entries made from the *Journal of Congress*, September 17,
1776, to September 16, 1788.   No. 7 is a small quarto volume, containing but few entries, called the "More Secret Journal."   No. 8 is a
folio, Secret Journal A, 1776–1783: the contents of this volume appear
to be merely minutes of proceedings, which were afterwards entered
on the Public Journals.   (This volume does not contain any record of
July 4, 1776, or any reference to the signing of the Declaration.)   The
foregoing will afford you, I trust, a sufficiently just idea of these in-
valuable records.

The copy for the first edition of the Journals was probably prepared
by Charles Thomson; but he was not responsible for the matter
printed therein, as he distinctly states on the fly-leaf of the first volume of the fair copy (No. 2 of the series) that the selection was made
by a committee of Congress.   The responsibility for the introduction
of the names of the signers at the close of the Declaration cannot now
be determined.   It is entirely reasonable to suppose, however, that
there was no intention to mislead; but that, as the names appeared in
no other printed form, they were inserted for the information of the
public.   The Secret Journals were naturally not then suited to publication.   To be sure, we must acknowledge that the entry of the record
of engrossing and signing on the Secret rather than on the Public
Journal indicates that there existed some reason for considering these
acts as of a confidential character.

The Journals, it must be remembered, were not the accounts of an
individual, but were the accepted records of Congress; that then, as
now, each day's proceedings were read to that body before they obtained the authority necessary for their preservation.   I dwell upon
this in order that you may not attribute the discrepancies between the
originals and the printed journals to the carelessness of a clerk or of
the secretary.   In my opinion, the responsibility rests with Congress
alone.

That part of the Journal of 1776 as printed by Peter Force in the
American Archives appears to me, from a hasty comparison, to be a
mongrel, made up primarily from the first printed edition of 1777,
corrected in some few particulars by the copy from which that edition
was printed (No. 2 of the series described above), and punctuated and
capitalized to suit his own fancy.   He has in the punctuation and cap-
italization altered both the manuscript and printed versions.   The
matter he appended as notes, and which seems as much a part of the

hand, in one of them, which is the same as is given in the Proceedings in Force's "Archives," is pasted a

original record as the caption and names of the signers in the printed Journal of 1777, was taken from a variety of sources in the archives, to which he, of course, had access. Mr. Sparks offended also, and was summarily criticised, for similar changes of the originals he printed.

. . . .

With the original of Madison's *Journal of the Debates in the Constitutional Convention* we have the autograph notes written out by Jefferson for Madison, concerning the debates on the Declaration, which Mr. Gilpin has carefully printed in the *Papers of James Madison* (i. 9–39). It might be profitable to compare that version with the portions of the same printed in vol. i. of the *Writings* of Jefferson, and in vol. i. of Elliot's *Debates.*

In view of the fact that the Secret Journal containing the record of July 19 and August 2 was published in 1821, it seems to me very strange that the recollections of Jefferson and others should have been preferred to that veritable official account of the signing.

I am very incredulous as to the existence of a signed copy of the Declaration prior to the engrossed copy. We have the veritable first draft in the writing of Jefferson, and the remains of the copy engrossed and signed on parchment alluded to in the Secret Journal entry of July 19. Had there been another bearing the signatures of the delegates, it is fair to suppose that the same care for its preservation would have been exercised as that to which we owe the other records and documents. It would not have invalidated the second copy. The actual signing of such a preliminary copy would have added no more strength to the action of Congress in adopting the Declaration than the entry on the Journal of that action, which was and is now a conclusive and binding record. It was not signed on the Journal; such a signing would have been a very irregular proceeding. It seems to me that a special direction to the president of Congress and to the secretary to authenticate the copies sent out by order of Congress was not deemed necessary; such an authentication was incident to the duties of their respective offices. The copies so sent out bear, not written, but printed signatures.

Of that first printed broadside we have the copy wafered in the Journal, and another among the papers of Washington, which he read, or caused to be read, to the army, as mentioned in General Orders of July 9, 1776.

As you have clearly demonstrated, but for the insertion of the names in the first printed Journal so as to appear a part of the record of the 4th July, all this mystification could not have occurred. But I repeat that the insertion is not to be regarded as an intention to mislead, but printed copy of the Declaration, authenticated by the signatures of Hancock and Thomson, agreeably to the order of Congress, and is doubtless one of the copies printed on the night of the 4th or morning of the 5th of July. Had the printed Public Journal followed this manuscript, which conforms to and explains all extrinsic facts appertaining to the Declaration, all subsequent misapprehension would have been avoided. Governor McKean had special reasons for investigating the matter at an early date. He was present on the 4th and voted for the Declaration ; but inasmuch as it was not signed on that day, as he asserted, his name did not appear on the Journal, nor on the copy engrossed on parchment and signed August 2, since at that time he was away from Philadelphia with the army. Some time later — Bancroft says, in 1781 — he was allowed to affix his signature to the engrossed copy, where it now appears. His signing in 1781 did not affect the *Journal* of July 4, 1776, as Jefferson seems to have supposed would be the case with Thornton and the New York and several Pennsylvania members, who were likewise absent on July 4 or not then authorized to sign. McKean's name does not appear among the signers of the Declaration of Independence in the Journal printed in 1777, nor in the edition of 1800. It is given in that of 1823, and possibly in some of an earlier date, which I have not seen. Now, at any time after 1781, if the Declaration

to enlighten, the public ; and that it is so printed is due to inadvertence.

. . . .

  Believe me to be, my dear sir,
             Very sincerely yours, `
                  THEODORE F. DWIGHT,
               Chief of Bureau of Rolls and Library.

were printed from the engrossed copy, it would include McKean's signature; but if from the printed Journal of July 4, his signature would not be found. It was just this discrepancy between copies that led to an investigation. In the letter already quoted from, Governor McKean says: " In the manuscript Journal Mr. Pickering, then Secretary of State, and myself saw a *printed half-sheet* of paper, with the names of the members afterwards in the printed Journals stitched in; " and in another letter,[1] June 17, 1817, he says that neither the manuscript of the Public Journal nor that of the Secret Journal has any written names annexed to the Declaration. In this statement he is undoubtedly correct; but apparently he has confounded, in the lapse of years and by the loss of memory, the printed copy authenticated by Hancock and Thomson, which is wafered to the manuscript Journal, with a copy bearing signatures, which does not now appear. Trusting to this statement of Governor McKean respecting the copy of the Declaration with the signatures of the signers stitched into the manuscript Journal, I had supposed, until I received Mr. Hamilton's letter, that the falsification was in the record; but it now appears that it is in the printed Journal.

As has been said, had the Public Journal as we have it been printed from the manuscript Journal as it stands to-day, with the printed Declaration omitting the authenticating signatures of Hancock and Thomson, we should have a narrative of the proceedings on the 4th precisely as they occurred. But, unfortunately, it was not so printed. Published as it was, and as we have it, the Journal is doubtless erroneous and

---

[1] Portfolio, September, 1817, 246.

misleading; and though, at this late day, we may be unable to divine all the reasons which prompted the course that was pursued, there is no evidence of a design to falsify the record. When " the committee appointed to superintend the publication of the Journals " were empowered and instructed, by a resolve of September 26, 1776, to employ Robert Aitkin " to reprint the said Journals from the beginning, with all possible expedition, and *continue to print the same*,"[1] Charles Thomson probably furnished him with a copy of the proceedings of July 4, and their authority did not extend to the Secret Journal, in which alone was entered the resolution of July 19 for the engrossment of the Declaration on parchment and the subsequent signing thereof, August 2. But when they furnished copy for July 4, they appended to the Declaration the following statement : " The foregoing declaration was, by order of Congress, engrossed, and signed by the following members." We infer, and have a right to infer, that the engrossment and signing were on July 4; but the printed Journal so affirms only by implication. All the facts stated were true at the time of their statement, some time subsequent to September 26. The error consists in throwing back to July 4 the order for engrossment of July 19, and the signing of August 2. Any more specific statement of these later matters would have been a breach of the resolution of secrecy which was repealed, and then only virtually, by a resolve fifty years afterwards to print these Secret Journals. The veil of secrecy which rested on the transactions of July 19 and August 2 undoubtedly had a tendency to refer the events of those days to July 4. Evidently Mr. Jefferson,

---

[1] *Journal*, ii. 391.

one of the most intelligent and active participators in those events of July 19 and August 2, was surprised when they were recalled to his notice in 1822 by the Secret Journal, which had then been published for the first time.[1] Apparently, and not without reason, under these circumstances of secrecy, every transaction relating to the Declaration of Independence had been referred, both by Jefferson and John Adams, to July 4. For more than six months Congress had withheld the names of those signing the Declaration. This may have been from prudential considerations. Unless the Declaration was made good by arms, every party signing it might have been held personally responsible for an overt act of treason. Whether this would have been the case in respect to Hancock and Thomson, who were not acting in any personal capacity, and possibly even in opposition to their own convictions, in accordance with an express direction of Congress, may be a matter of question. But whatever may have been their reasons, there is no doubt as to the fact that Congress not only sat with closed doors, and pledged the members to secrecy,[2] but withheld even from its Secret Journals some of its most important proceedings. The fact has already been stated in regard to this very matter of independence that Congress had deemed it imprudent to extend on its Journals Lee's resolutions on which the battle was fought ; and had they not been preserved on the files, we should never have known their authentic form from any public record.[3]

---

[1] *American Historical Review*, i. 168.

[2] A facsimile of the Resolution of Secrecy of November 9, 1775, may be found in *American Archives*, 4th ser. iii. 1916.

[3] See facsimile of these resolutions. *Ibid.* 4th ser. vi. 1700.

Such are the facts respecting the signing of the Declaration of Independence and the errors in the printed Journals recording the same.[1]

It is to be regretted that doubt should rest upon transactions, and the records of transactions, which are connected with an event so important in the history of a nation as the declaration of its independence. The printed Journal, so far as relates to what

---

[1] In the foregoing paper it has been my purpose to discuss a single question : Was the Declaration of Independence signed July 4 by the members of Congress ? Had my aim been more popular, I should have drawn, for more interesting particulars, on the authorities cited in Winsor's *Handbook of the American Revolution*, 103 *et seq.*, and Poole's *Index*, 339, title "Declaration of Independence."

The reader who has followed me in the foregoing paper may ask why Force, Webster, Bancroft, and Winthrop have not explained the matter, instead of each resting on his own authority in opposition to the express statements of Jefferson and Adams who have the support of the Journal. The answer, except so far as Force is concerned, is obvious : that neither the observance of proportion in a general history nor the limits of a Fourth of July oration will allow of minute and tedious explanations. But with respect to Force the case is different. The limits of his monograph on the Declaration were not restricted. He was brought face to face with the question. He understood it better than any other man, and better than any other he could have explained the difficulty had he chosen to do so. He did not so choose. The trouble with him was that his pamphlet was controversial. It was an attack on that part of Lord Mahon's *History of England*, in which he gives an account of the Declaration of Independence. Following Jefferson and the printed Journals of Congress, Lord Mahon had said : "The Declaration of Independence, appearing the act of the people, was finally adopted and signed by every member present at the time, except only Dickinson. This was on the 4th of July." — *History of England*, vi. 98. Force's curt answer to this is as follows: "The Declaration was not 'signed by every member present on the 4th of July,' except Mr. Dickinson." — Force's *Declaration of Independence*, 63. Thus he made a point against Lord Mahon on the score of accuracy. True, Force knew how, and by what authority, his lordship was misled. He could have given the explanation which would have relieved the historian; but that was not his purpose.

took place on the 4th of July, 1776, is clearly untrustworthy; and one of the original manuscript Journals is not altogether accurate. When the record was extended on that Journal, by wafering to a page, apparently left blank for the purpose, the printed copy of the Declaration of Independence authenticated by the signatures of Hancock and Thomson, it was made to assert facts as of the 4th of July which actually occurred on the 5th. The authentication and the printing of the Declaration were ordered on the 4th as something to be done later; and should not have been entered as something done on that day, as the Journal affirms. Nor is this unfortunate error confined to the records. The engrossed copy of the Declaration which was signed on August 2 is made to say, in substance, that all the names attached to it were there subscribed on July 4; and there is nothing on the instrument to indicate that any signatures were added on August 2, and even of a date so late as 1781, when McKean signed it.

These errors are the more to be regretted, since they are irremediable. They must stand on record for all time. The Journals in no new edition will be changed so as to conform to the truth; and should they be so changed they would lose their authority as the Journals of Congress. But though the record must stand, and the engrossed copy and all its facsimiles continue to assert that it was signed July 4, there can be no objection to the reconstruction of these documents, as matters of history, so that they shall conform to the truth.

The several entries on the Journal which relate to the Declaration of Independence should read as follows: —

"July 4, 1776.   The Declaration being read was agreed to, as follows: [Here should appear the Declaration without any signatures or authentication, as is the case with one of the manuscript Journals.]

" *Ordered*, That the Declaration be authenticated and printed.   That the committee appointed to prepare the Declaration superintend and correct the press, etc.

" July 19.   *Resolved*, That the Declaration passed on the 4th be fairly engrossed on parchment, with the title, etc.; and that the same, when engrossed, be signed by every member of Congress.

" August 2.   The Declaration agreed to on July 4, being engrossed and compared at the table, was signed by the members, agreeably to the resolution of July 19.

" November 4.   The Hon. Matthew Thornton, Esq., a delegate from New Hampshire, attended, and produced his credentials.

" *Ordered*, That Mr. Thornton be directed, agreeably to the resolve passed July 19, to affix his signature to the engrossed copy of the Declaration, *with the date of his subscription*.

" January 18, 1777.   *Ordered*, That an authentic copy of the Declaration of Independence, with the names of the members of Congress subscribing the same, be sent to each of the United States, and they be desired to have the same put upon record.

" ——, 1781.   Whereas it has been made to appear to this present Congress that the Hon. Thomas McKean was a member of Congress from Delaware in the year 1776, and that, on July 4 of that year he was present and voted for the Declaration of Independence, but being absent with the army at the time of the general subscription of that instrument on August 2: therefore,

" *Resolved*, That the said Hon. Thomas McKean be allowed to affix his signature to the aforesaid Declaration, he adding thereto the date of such subscription."

Such was the course pursued by McKean and other post-signers of the Articles of Confederation, which were agreed to by Congress, July 9, 1778. McKean's name is signed as follows : " Tho. M'Kean, Feb. 12, 1779."

With the foregoing changes and additions the Journal of Congress would conform to the real transactions respecting the Declaration of Independence.

The engrossed copy reads as follows: " In Congress, July 4, 1776. The UNANIMOUS DECLARATION of the thirteen united STATES OF AMERICA." After the Declaration follow the signatures. They should have been preceded by some such recital as the following : " The foregoing Declaration having been agreed to on July 4, by the delegates of the thirteen united colonies, in Congress assembled, and the same having been engrossed, is now subscribed, agreeably to a resolution passed July 19, by the members of Congress present this 2d day of August, 1776."

Independence was announced to the world July 4, 1776. That is glory enough for the most insatiate of days. It needs not the honors of July 2, nor those of August 2. On the former of these days when Lee's resolution, " that these United Colonies are, and of right ought to be, free and independent States; and that all political connection between them and the State of Great Britain is, and ought to be, dissolved," — when this resolution was agreed to by the Congress on July 2, the battle had been fought and the victory won. Two days later came the 4th, which, like all its successors, was less the occasion of a battle than of a triumph. What was done on July 2 realized the ardent wishes of the patriotic party in thirteen colonies. Its consummated act was a notable achievement of advocacy; and the great patriot fondly hoped that it would be celebrated to the remotest times.[1]   But it is

[1] John Adams, writing to Mrs. Adams from Philadelphia, July 3, 1776, said: "Yesterday the greatest question was decided which ever was debated in America, and a greater, perhaps, never was nor will be decided among men. A resolution was passed without one dissenting colony, 'that these United Colonies are, and of right ought to be, free and independent States,' etc. You will see in a few days a Declaration setting forth the causes which have impelled us to this mighty revolution. . . . The second day of July, 1776, will be the most memorable epocha in the history of America. . . . It ought to be commemorated as the day of deliverance, by solemn acts of devotion to God Almighty," etc. — *Works*, ix. 417. But it was to be otherwise. The second day of July has altogether passed from the memory of men. In fifty years from that time the editor of Niles's *Weekly Register*, shortly after the death of Adams and Jefferson in 1826, quoting the above letter, changed its date from the 3d to the 5th of July, and printed the passage, "the second day of July, 1776," as follows: "The Fourth of July, 1776, will be a memorable epoch in this history of America!"

Even so careful a writer as Mr. Webster fell, in his later life, into the same error. From the accuracy of his account of the authentication of the Declaration of Independence, it is evident that he had examined all that had been published on that subject before 1826. Nothing of value has since been added to his statement, while some of the later glosses could well be spared. — *Works*, i. 129. But he did not undertake to explain how the confusion arose: perhaps he did not even know, because, when he wrote the eulogy on Adams and Jefferson, he was far away from the original Journals, an inspection of which alone discloses the source of the error. In this eulogy he has given two supposititious speeches on the resolution of July 2. That these speeches were on the resolution, and not on the Declaration, is evident from the opening sentence, "Let us pause! This step, once taken, cannot be retraced. This *resolution*, once passed, will cut off all hope of reconciliation." — *Works*, i. 132. Notwithstanding this, Mr. Webster, writing in 1846, to one who had inquired respecting the authenticity of the speech attributed to John Adams, said: "The day after the *Declaration* was made, Mr. Adams, in writing to a friend, declared the event to be one which 'ought to be commemorated as the day of deliverance, by solemn acts of devotion to God Almighty.'" — *Works*, i. 150. It is needless to add that Adams's letter was written the day before the Declaration instead of the day after, and referred to the Resolution of Independence of July 2, and not to the otherwise. The glory of the act is overshadowed by the glory of its annunciation.

Declaration of July 4. For some account of the origin of the change of the date of John Adams's letter, see *Letters Addressed to his Wife*, i. 128, n.

THE CONSTITUTIONAL RELATIONS

OF THE

AMERICAN COLONIES TO THE ENGLISH GOVERNMENT AT THE COMMENCEMENT OF THE AMERICAN REVOLUTION

A Paper read before the American Historical Association, in Boston, May 23, 1887

THE CONSTITUTIONAL RELATIONS

OF THE

AMERICAN COLONIES TO THE ENGLISH GOVERN-
MENT AT THE COMMENCEMENT OF THE
AMERICAN REVOLUTION

No thoughtful reader closes a volume of American history, or perhaps of any history, without the conviction that the author's conclusions drawn from the included facts depend very much upon his point of view, as well as upon the forum to which he refers them for adjudication; and that in estimating the value of his work we must likewise take into account his nationality, political and ecclesiastical associations, constitution of mind, and temperament, as influences which, unconsciously it may be, have affected his judgment.

There is high authority for something like this. In the preface to Chalmers's "Introduction to the History of the Revolt of the Colonies," Jared Sparks, to whom that preface is attributed, says "the author was a lawyer, and he has discussed the subject before him in the spirit of his profession, adhering to legal interpretations and distinctions. It is possible that any American lawyer, taking the same premises, would come to the same conclusions; and it may be admitted that the premises are correct, since they are drawn from state papers and legal records of the highest authority. The error lies in the mode of viewing the subject."

I quote this passage for the immunity it affords one who wishes to present some old subjects from a new point of view; and because nowhere else in Sparks's writings have I noticed a better illustration of two of his eminent qualities as an historian, — perfect candor and critical sagacity.[1]

[1] Sparks was a careful investigator, as any one finds who enters fields which he has reaped with expectation of profitable gleaning; but if to learn his methods and to catch his spirit, no time so spent ought to be regarded as time lost.

An American in every fibre of his constitution, Sparks believed in the justice of the Revolutionary cause, and was loyal to the memory of those whose lives he wrote; but he never exalted his heroes by belittling their associates or by maligning their opponents.

He placed the American cause in the most favorable light, and did not indulge in that urbane condescension towards opponents which sometimes marks the meritorious work of Lord Mahon, and he never imperiled his case as Lecky, an abler writer than Lord Mahon, sometimes has done by inattention to facts essential to its support.

Nor, on the other hand, did Sparks conceal ugly facts,* or change their import by artful and disingenuous arrangement of them. He arrayed all the forces, friendly or hostile, although, as it sometimes

* Lord Mahon charged him with doing so, but I think Sparks's vindication of his integrity is complete. The strongest case against him is that of suppressing Washington's reiteration of an opinion unfavorable to New England. There is no doubt that Washington entertained such an opinion. That constitutes an historical fact: but if he has recorded that opinion in a letter to Brown, does it make it any more a fact in that he has also recorded it in letters to Jones and Robinson? Sparks gives the first record, but to save space omits the paragraphs in which similar opinions are given in letters to two other correspondents. That, I think, states the case fairly. It may be said that Sparks should have given all such passages or indicated their omission by stars or otherwise. Why those opinions more than others? To have given a résumé of all omitted passages would have swelled his volumes unduly. If proper editing would require such notice of repetitious passages, why not, on the same grounds, the omission of all repetitious or unimportant letters? It may be admitted, however, that Sparks's editorial rules are not those now in vogue; but in fairness it ought not to be forgotten that in dealing with such a mass as the Washington papers, Sparks was confronted with a new and very difficult problem. See also H. B. Adams in *Magazine of American History*, July, 1888.

Between the peace of 1763 and the Declaration of Independence the political relations of the American colonies to the crown, and to Parliament, and the degree of their subordination to imperial authority, were questions of practical import which gave rise to discussions sometimes profound and always earnest; but after April 19, 1775, the clamor which they had occasioned was, for a time, silenced by the greater din of arms. During the period of constitution-making which ensued, they were often referred to in the debates of the Convention of 1787 and in the pages of the "Federalist;" but not long after they, with other causes of the Revolution, were relegated to the closet of the historian.

My purpose in this paper is to suggest that the questions rife at that stage of the Revolution were not new questions — only newly important; — that they were coeval with the first political organizations in the British-American colonies, and had vexed them at every

The questions of the Revolution not new.

happened, his flank was turned, or his front disordered by mutinous auxiliaries which he had brought into the field.*

History was regarded by Sparks, as it ought to be by every one, as the record of impartial judgment concerning the motives and conduct of men, of parties, and of nations, set forth in their best light; and he was incapable of attempting to pervert that judgment by doubtful testimony or by unscrupulous advocacy, which represents one party as altogether wise and patriotic and the other as altogether unwise and malignant, — an attempt which must ultimately fail, since it finds no support in the nature of man, in intelligent observation, or

* An instance is found in Sparks's *Franklin* (iv. 450), where he seems to justify the use made of Hutchinson's private letters, on the ground that Hutchinson had secretly used Franklin's in the same way; but from Hutchinson's letter to the Earl of Dartmouth, which Sparks prints, it is evident that Franklin's letter, instead of being private, was his official letter, as agent, to the Speaker of the House, and therefore public property; and, as may be conjectured, Hutchinson sent it to the Earl of Dartmouth unofficially lest, upon a "call for papers," it should find its way to the House of Commons, and thence, as had Bernard's and Gage's letters, back to Boston. See R. Frothingham's *Warren*, 225 n.

stage of their development down to the Revolution;
and, instead of being settled by that event, that they
are still vital — and are not unlikely once more to
become absorbing questions, as more than once in the
mean time they have been.   Their settlement on a
just basis depends, as Dr. Sparks seemed to think,
upon the selection of the right point of view.   And
since discordant opinions have arisen in respect to the
same facts and circumstances when submitted to similar apprehensive intelligences, history should serve
as a lens which gathers up all the rays colored by passion, prejudice, interest, or unwarranted judgments,
and recomposes them into the white light of truth.[1]

If the controversy at the time of the Revolution
respected the political relations of the colonies to Great Britain, and the degree of subordination due from remote dependencies to
some central authority, what tribunal had
jurisdiction of such questions, and by what principles
were they to be determined?   Were they determinable solely, as the Tories in both countries claimed,
by the British constitution? or, as the Whigs finally
claimed, had the colonial constitutions acquired that
degree of consistency, and the people living under
them such numbers and weight in the empire, as warranted them in determining their inter-state relations

Of the competent tribunal.

in common sense. He had a healthy contempt for demagogues, —
historical demagogues in particular — as corruptors of youth.*

[1] The following paper was prepared with no view to its publication, but merely to be read before the Historical Association.   Nor is
it the result of any exhaustive study of the precise questions of which
it treats; and the writer, although he believes in the essential validity of the historical propositions which it undertakes to set forth,
desires, nevertheless, that they should be regarded as theses for discussion rather than as his final judgments.

* *Life of Sparks*, i. 571, ii. 180 n.

in accordance with these constitutions? Or if we
say, as there is some reason for saying, that the real
difficulty was practical rather than political, and related principally to the degree in which the interests
of agricultural states ought to be subsidiary to the
mercantile policy of British merchants, then perhaps
an appeal would lie to the economic system which
Adam Smith was just bringing into prominence, with
promise of free trade to the colonies agreeably to the
policy since adopted by the British government. Or,
finally, was the question one concerning the rights of
man, as Jefferson claimed; and in that case, what
rights: those which are natural, positive, and inalienable, or such as are qualified by public law, constitutions, and municipal organizations? On the question
in this form the opinions of authoritative writers
on government would be entitled to great weight.
Clearly much depends upon the forum, as well as
upon the point of view. Sparks suggested the error
of Chalmers, which was also that of the king and his
ministers, and of Parliament, and of the Tories on
both sides of the water. Their facts might be well
authenticated and their logic valid, but they looked
at the subjects in controversy " from the wrong point
of view," unless we agree with Goldwin Smith, who,
it is reported, regards the Revolution as a calamity
to both parties, by which America was deprived of
her history, and a great schism was caused in the
Anglo-Saxon race.

The Whigs conducted the controversy with infinite
tact, changing ground as the exigencies of
their situation required. At first, as a party, The Patriotic party.
they argued the question as one arising under the British constitution ; and finally, as Jefferson
declared, by their inalienable rights as men.

At no time before or since the period between 1763 and 1776 has the Anglo-American shown greater intellectual activity or a firmer grasp of political philosophy or more aptness in adapting it to practical politics. Sprung from the parent stock at the time of its greatest vigor and of its most splendid achievement, as if by natural selection for his work in the New World, he was less endued with the spirit which sought expression in the imaginative literature of the great dramatists than with those principles meditated by Sir John Eliot in his lonely cell, and for which Hampden died on the field, — principles which moulded the constitution, so that it restrained the power of the crown, enlarged that of the people, and gave free play to that genius which made Great Britain, after Rome, the greatest power for civilization the world has ever known. Of such origin and with such associations the men of the Revolution, adopting the conclusions of Sidney, Harrington, and Locke, — the principles of nature and eternal reason, as John Adams called them, — applied them to public affairs in a body of political literature unsurpassed in amount or quality by anything which preceded or which has followed. Had their writings been of the closet merely, such encomium would be extravagant; but what justifies it is that profound speculations on the nature and purpose of government were united with a practical sagacity which adapted means to ends and secured the result desired.

This period of discussion was followed by seven years of war, in which, by a series of victories some of which were military and others only moral, they made good the declaration that " these united colonies are, and of right

What the war settled.

ought to be, free and independent states." The war
settled that, if it settled nothing more. Then followed
the Confederation. The states were jealous of their
rights, and some of them insisted on monopolizing for
their own use advantages which the Confederacy
should have shared. The government fell into de-
crepitude, and the people narrowly escaped anarchy.
In due time the colonies, by their representatives,
met in Philadelphia and formed a general constitution. Presumably the result of their labors would
embody the principles which they had adopted in
their controversy with Great Britain, at least as
modified by the vicissitudes of war and by their application to practical affairs. But how far this was
the case will appear if we examine the questions one
by one. Things do not change by changing their
name.

If the quarrel between Great Britain and her colonies was respecting the king's prerogatives, Some
and the colonial contention was that such things
which it
large and varied powers could not wisely, did not
nor consistently with the spirit of the con- settle.
stitution since 1688, be intrusted to a single person,
however exalted, or wise or well-disposed, they did
not long continue of that opinion ; for in forming the
Constitution of the United States they clothed their
President with prerogatives such as no British sovereign since the English Revolution had exercised.[1]

Was it the question of the right of Parliament to
enact commercial laws which injuriously affected the
colonies whose chief interest was agricultural? Our
tonnage act, passed in the first session of Congress,
was similar in principle and design to the acts of

[1] See *Massachusetts Historical Society Proceedings*, ser. 2, v. 156.

Charles II., and with some modifications is still in force, and has operated, and now operates, unfavorably to the agricultural States of the seaboard which stand in similar relations to the commercial and manufacturing States of the North as the colonies stood to Great Britain; nor need I say that our trade laws produced similar disquiet, and at one time threatened serious consequences.

Or was it a question of taxation by a body in which they neither had, nor could have, adequate representation? That has been the complaint in our Territories and sparsely populated States, as it was in the days of the Stamp Act; and though not yet loud or serious, it may become so, and with the difference that instead of being a hardship feared it will be a hardship felt.

If the appointment and pay of the judiciary without efficient control of it by the people or their assemblies caused rational discontent, the grievance remains under the new government as it was under the old, and is aggravated by the adoption of the English system of Equity, Prize, and Admiralty jurisdiction to an extent unknown to the colonies.

Finally, was it the theoretical question of the universal, inalienable rights of man to life, liberty, and the pursuit of happiness? After how many years and at what cost of life and treasure was the Great Declaration made good!

No one who reads the debates of the Convention of 1787 can fail to notice that the friends and the opponents of the proposed Constitution divided on questions involving the same principles as those which divided the Revolutionary parties; nor can one read the Constitution itself without perceiving that its acceptance

The failure to settle these questions.

by the Convention was a triumph of the legitimate successors of the Anti-Revolutionary party of 1775. "It was not even proposed," says Hildreth,[1] "to curtail the appointing power, the veto, or the extensive authority vested generally in the President, nor seriously to limit the powers of Congress or the jurisdiction of the Federal Courts." The Constitution failed to receive the signatures of some of the ablest members of the Convention; and "it was exceedingly doubtful whether, upon a fair canvass, a majority of the people, even in the ratifying States, were in favor of it."[2] So dissatisfied were the people, not only with the Constitution, but also, and even more, with what was omitted, that its adoption was accompanied by numerous proposed amendments; only two, however, of those relating to matters mooted at the Revolution became parts of the Constitution — those prohibiting the quartering of troops in private houses and the issue of general warrants. And so far were the Revolutionary questions from being settled in accordance with the results of that event, it has been said that from 1789 to 1860 they caused nearly as much dissatisfaction with the general government in the States south of the Potomac as the policy of the British government caused in the colonies between 1763 and 1775; and that evidence of this is found in the Virginia and Kentucky resolution,[3] in the assault on the judiciary

[1] *History of the United States*, iv. 118. In November, 1787, Elbridge Gerry wrote to John Wendell, "I think (the Constitution) neither consistent with the principles of the Revolution or of the constitutions of the several States."

[2] Hildreth, *ibid.* 28.

[3] These resolutions expressed the sentiments of the Republicans, who claimed to represent the states-rights party, or the old revolutionary party of Jefferson, Samuel Adams, and George Clinton, as op-

in Jefferson's administration, and in the dissatisfaction of South Carolina with the tariff in 1832, to say nothing of the extent to which such problems entered into the conflict which led to civil war.

The war, then, did not settle these questions; it merely disposed of them under a new order of things, and left their settlement to us or to those who may come after us; and it may be that the late Civil War merely placed them in abeyance for the second time, and that nothing but their final settlement on just economic grounds will cause them to disappear from American politics.

I therefore regard the period between 1763 and 1776 as one of the most significant in our history; for the questions then rife reach back to and are inextricably interwoven with the history of each colony from its first planting; and, reaching forward also, how fully they have entered into our later history is known to every intelligent reader.

A clear understanding of the constitutional questions which perplexed the colonists of the Revolution depends somewhat upon a knowledge of their antecedent history. American history before the Revolution is neither romantic nor picturesque, nor, as a whole, is it striking. It is barren of incidents, lacks great characters,

The character of our history.

posed to the Federalists, who were charged with entertaining the monarchical principles of the old Tories and, by the forced construction of the Constitution, with having perverted the government, and with having administered it on principles adverse to those of the Declaration of Independence. The tendency of the general government from the beginning undoubtedly has been towards consolidation; and if the results of the late Civil War may be regarded as an expression of the final judgment of the people as to the constitutional questions involved, it is an interesting commentary on those mooted between 1763 and 1776 — though in no respect affecting the main question of independence.

contributes little or nothing to statesmanship, war, or policy, and still less, if less be possible, to literature or art. The glory of Wolfe is not our glory. The foot of no colonial soldier climbed the steeps or trod the heights behind Quebec, and none but the veteran troops of England heard the triumphant cry, "They run!" or caught the hero's parting words, "I die content." And if we have nothing to show save the results of conflicts with miserable Indian tribes, or the not very creditable military and naval expeditions against the Canadians, a foe vastly inferior in number and resources; or of civil history save the Antinomian controversy, or the hanging of a few Quakers and of a more considerable number of witches — or those accounted such, — acts which had no essential relation to the soil or climate of the country, and in no respect differentiated its people or their history from those of any other people, I think we might close the volume without loss of instruction or delight.

But, on the other hand, our history is unique in its origin, isolated in its progress, and is the best exponent of the new order inaugurated by the revival of learning and the Reformation, because it rests upon a broader human basis and clearer recognition of individual rights. More than any other history it gives promise to the hopes of man, and records development under exemplary constitutional forms and methods which other nations appear to regard with interest.

The history of America, unlike that of most nations, is not shrouded in the mists of mythology nor in the darkness of barbaric ages. From the beginning it stands, for the most part, in the clear light of authentic facts. It traces its origin, as no other nation can, from public documents, such as land patents, incorporative charters, proprietary grants, or royal commissions, in the interpretation and construction of which, with the included facts, may be found all, or nearly all, that is of value. In these documents the beginning of our essential history is to be sought, rather than in the forests of Germany or in the fens of Lincolnshire; and with them and the records of the Board of Trade, royal instructions, assembly journals, and Chalmers's Opinions, and with little other aid, any one of historical insight and general culture, observant of the logic of events and well acquainted with men, their motives, and modes of bringing to pass their purposes, — not necessarily a jurist, but like Hutchinson, Ramsay, Trumbull, and Belknap, with clear conceptions of organic and municipal law, — could write the history of the thirteen colonies in his closet.

Another characteristic circumstance of our history is its isolation. Before the war of 1755 it had, so far as I can perceive, no essential dependence upon European affairs — not even those of England; certainly none which changed the direction or rate of progress which the people were making under influences purely American. This is not the view taken by the historian of the United States or by the historian of New England; and I am aware how much their histories gain in interest by being projected on a background in which we see the movements of armies and the pageantry of kings and courts.[1]

Original tendencies of the race and acquired habits

[1] Without doubt, the colonies were a factor in European politics; but how far the converse is true is not so clear. The essential history of the colonies is that of their development; and the historian may disregard, or pass lightly over, whatever did not materially affect that development. Perhaps the French war of 1755, which resulted in the overthrow of the French power in America, presents the strongest case

and impulses were transmitted in both of its branches, and doubtless influenced the emigrants in their new

of a colonial war growing out of European complications; and yet, with regard even to this war, it is a question how far it affected the development of the colonies — that is, in consequence of that war and its result, how was their subsequent history different from what it would have been had the war never taken place or had the result been different? But see *Massachusetts Historical Collections*, ser. 4, iv. 370. The answer must be uncertain, yet there are facts which lead to the conjecture that the result made, or had it been different would have made, no essential difference.

Wolfe's success at Quebec is often spoken of as having changed the history of the French and English colonies. It was indeed a splendid achievement of British arms; but Creasy wisely counted the battle of Saratoga, not that at Quebec, among the " Fifteen Decisive Battles of the World."

Nor was the immediate effect upon Canada itself very great. Eleven years later, the Quebec Act of 1774 was a politic, if not a necessary, recognition of the *status quo;* and it is worth considering how far, even to this day, those circumstances and conditions which accelerate or retard the prosperity of a people were changed by the war. (See an instructive paper, by John George Bourinot, LL. D., of Ottawa, in the *Scottish Review* for April, 1887.)

It may be conceded that the reduction of Canada precipitated the American Revolution. It is not claimed, I think, that it caused that event. How, and to what degree, then, did it hasten it? It is usually said that after the peace of 1763 the British colonies, no longer exposed to hostile inroads of the French and Indian allies, were better able to resist the unpropitious legislation of Great Britain.

This aspect of the case was fully discussed by English and colonial statesmen, among whom was Franklin; and the English negotiators of the treaty of 1763 were in doubt whether they ought to retain Canada as one of the results of the war or give it up for Guadeloupe; and it would seem that they made a great political mistake in their decision, unless we overestimate the effect of the reduction of Canada upon our subsequent history.

Let us suppose that the French had retained Canada. Would that fact have wiped out the enormous debt incurred by its conquest or have prevented its increase for the defense of the colonies; or would the colonies, thwarted in their wishes, have become enamored of stamp acts, navigation laws, or Townshend's revenue measures?

Wolfe's victory did not precipitate, or make more exigent than his defeat would have done, any of those questions which had been open home under unwonted circumstances ; but the colonists were far from the complications of European politics, and when histories so dissimilar are treated in relation, and with due regard to historical perspective, American history loses its distinctive characteristics and much of its value. I prefer, therefore, to regard it, as I believe it to be, the history of Englishmen more or less imbued with the principles of the Reformation and of the Petition of Right, who cut themselves loose from Europe, with its old institutions and associations, and without pattern, or assistance, or very effective interference — though that was often threatened — undertook on bare creation, to develop

for more than a hundred years, and finally brought on the war. The debt, as has been said, remained to be paid; nor could it be paid, or even remain stationary, except by subjecting the colonies to an imperial policy, involving the adoption of essentially the same measures as those which led to rebellion.

Why, under such circumstances, would they have been less willing to seek relief in independence, or the French less willing to incite them to rebellion, on occasion ; and when the colonists were brought to the contemplation of that, as in time they must have been, could they have been blind to the consideration how much more effective French assistance would be (than it really was under other circumstances) when that power held the St. Lawrence and the northern approaches to Lake Champlain ? The northern campaigns of 1775-6 and 1777, to say nothing of Sullivan's expedition of 1778, would have been eliminated, and the concentration of colonial energies and resources in the middle and southern colonies have thus been permitted. In regard to this matter, see Franklin's *Familiar Letters*, Sparks's edition, 247, 266.

The real contest between England and France in which the colonies, as a whole, were interested, was for the Ohio and the Mississippi, not the St. Lawrence ; and had the attack on the left flank of the French at Quebec failed, it would by no means have prevented, or more than temporarily delayed, one on the French centre, from a base of the Atlantic, protected by the naval power of England. A war for the great watercourses and the fertile lands on their banks would have followed, and with the result usual in the contests for empire between England and France. The French centre once broken, New Orleans and Quebec would have been untenable.

thirteen autonomous states out of as many land companies. No doubt when America was discovered she
parted company with the undetermined ages in their
sluggish movement and cast off into the rapid stream
of historic time ; but she was far from the centre of
the current, and in a new world soon formed one for
herself.

Such, as it appears to me, has been the isolation and
direct development of the independent governments of
America from colonial charters or their equivalents.
It was self-development, — in New England primarily
on the basis of ecclesiastical independency closely interwoven with economic independency, which out of
New England was the leading motive ; and its history
gains in interest and value as it reaches that point
when acts of incorporation and royal commissions
ceased to be such, and became potentially the basis of
governments proper, agreeably to the laws of growth,
usage, and necessity in a land remote from the old
world and having little connection with it.[1]

With this conception of the origin and historical
and political significance of the questions *Some*
which were rife between 1763 and 1776, I *consti-*
pass to their relation to the American Revo- *tutional*
lution. *ques-*
tions
exam-
Jefferson, in his declaration to the world *ined.*
of the causes which justified the assertion of colonial
independence, has given singular prominence to the

---

[1] A signal interference by the home government with the colonies
was the revocation of the Massachusetts charter in 1684, followed by
the Dudley-Andros interregnum, and that by the second charter ; but
the affair, neither in detail nor in mass, deflected the history of that
colony by a hair's breadth from the old line of *development ;* and we
look in vain for the scar of the wound which Charles II. in his anger
inflicted on the body politic.

exercise of the king's prerogatives; and his arraignment of him at the bar of public opinion seems like a personal assault.   Jefferson knew, and no one knew better, that some of the real causes which warranted the Declaration, such as the Navigation Acts and the ecclesiastical laws in Virginia, had existed a hundred years before George III. began to reign; and that for the later revenue measures he had only a divided responsibility, such as arose from his assent to parliamentary acts the veto of which might have cost him dear.[1]   In Mr. Webster's " Eulogy on Adams and Jefferson " will be found the reasons which probably influenced Jefferson in making the king the chief offender.   "The best of kings," as James Otis and Samuel Adams somewhat profusely, and perhaps not

---

[1] As to the king's constitutional responsibility nothing need be said, for he, like the sovereign people, can do no wrong; but with this difference, that if he *does*, he can be decapitated: with the other, it is not so!   As to his moral responsibility for acts done in his name, it should be considered that his connection with them was often merely nominal.   An appeal from the decision of a colonial court to the king in his bench was an appeal to the judges of the highest English court. And so an appeal to the king in his council was an appeal to the ministry.   We read that the king settled the boundaries between provinces, or vetoed their laws, or gave instructions to governors, or issued his royal commission; but so far were these acts from being the personal acts of the king, that the probability is that he knew little about them, except as he was informed by the secretary for the colonies of what had been settled by the ministers; and that both he and they, in these cases, acted on the advice of the great law officers, and followed precedents from which neither could safely depart.

The impersonal nature of the prerogative is shown by the fact that though the government of New Hampshire between 1679 and 1774 with a short interregnum was based on the king's commission, apparently the written evidence of his personal will and revocable at his pleasure, yet I doubt if any instance can be found where, on account of royal dissatisfaction — which means the dissatisfaction of the ministry — the tenor of his commission was changed.   Though theoretically otherwise, it was as permanent as a royal charter.

with entire sincerity, were in the habit of calling him, was in no respect the worst of kings ; and when free from the cruel malady which made hapless his later years, he was tyrannical neither in his political nor in his personal conduct; [1] nor was he without solicitous regard for the welfare of his American subjects. It was his paramount purpose, as it was Jackson's and Lincoln's under circumstances not dissimilar, to preserve the integrity of his empire; and in this he exhibited two qualities — courage and decision — which stood for so much with the most popular president of the United States when, in 1832, their unity was threatened by a dissatisfied State.

Though Jefferson regarded with disfavor those who exercised autocratic powers — especially if hereditary — until he came to exercise them himself, he probably had no personal animosity towards the king, but spoke harshly of him as he did, and regardless of facts, from political necessity. *The act which he undertook to justify before the world was renunciation of allegiance to the king to whom, if to any one, it was due, — not to the ministry, nor to Parliament, nor to the British people.* [2] Therefore he sought something in his conduct which would warrant the

---

[1] So thought John Adams. See his *Letter to Timothy Pickering,* 1822.

[2] The operative act which severed the colonies from the crown was Lee's resolution of June 7, 1776, passed by Congress on July 2, and was in these words: " *Resolved,* That these United Colonies are, and of right ought to be, free and independent States, that they are absolved from all *allegiance to the British Crown,* and that all political connection between them and the State of Great Britain is, and ought to be, totally dissolved." And as the Declaration was merely an announcement to the world, on the 4th of July, of what had been enacted on the 2d, Jefferson was obliged to follow Lee's resolution. Jefferson, in his *Autobiography* (p. 12), gives a résumé of the opinions of such

rupture of the empire.   None of the real grievances, such as the enforcement of the Navigation Laws,[1] the revenue measures, or the Boston Port Bill, would serve his purpose, because, apart from the constitutional maxim that all the king's public acts were done under the advice of his ministers, who were alone responsible for them, the king, as a matter of fact, instigated none of those measures, and, as the veto power was then regarded, he could not have withheld his assent to them without endangering his crown.

But every exercise of the prerogative, however far from the fact, ostensibly as well as constitutionally, was the sole act of the king, for which he was re-

men as John Adams, Lee and Wythe, who favored the passage of the Resolution of Independence, to the effect that, " as to the people or Parliament of England, *we had always been independent of them,* their restraints on our trade deriving efficacy from our *acquiescence only,* and not from any rights they possessed of impairing them, and so far, our connection with them had been federal only, and was now dissolved by the commencement of hostilities :

" That, as to the king, we had been bound to him by allegiance, but that this bond was now dissolved" by certain acts more fully set forth by Jefferson in the Declaration of Independence, and also in the preamble to the new constitution of Virginia which Jefferson had drawn.—Randall's *Jefferson,* i. 195.

The Declaration, as drafted by Jefferson, was no sudden, no novel product.   He had been over the whole subject, and was thoroughly master of it, as appears from the draft of instructions which he prepared for the delegates to the Congress of 1774 (*Autobiography,* i. 122), which, though not fully accepted, afterwards appeared in *A Summary View of the Rights of British America.*

[1] " I think it [the act of navigation], if uncompensated, to be a condition of as rigorous servitude as man can be subject to."   " They found, under the construction and execution then used, the act no longer tying but actually strangling them." — Burke's *Speech on American Taxation.*

" I judge so from the system of monopoly and exclusion which governs all your political writers upon commerce, except Mr. Adam Smith and Dean Tucker — *a system which is the true prime cause of your separation from your colonies.*" — Turgot to Dr. Price, 1778.

sponsible. Therefore Jefferson attacked him in an indictment consisting, as originally drawn, of twenty articles, several of which contained two or more specifications. In nineteen of these he is made sole culprit; and in one, the thirteenth in order, he is associated with the two Houses of Parliament; seven relate to the exercise of the veto power in one form or another; two, to the appointment, tenure, and pay of the judges; one, to the increase of revenue officers, and seven, to the abuse of his powers as commander-in-chief of the army and navy.

Had the king been arraigned on these charges before a court of justice, undoubtedly by advice of counsel he would have demurred to the bill, which, I hardly need say, means that admitting the facts to be as set forth, still he ought not to answer, since the acts complained of were done in the exercise of his constitutional prerogatives.

The charge, for example, that " he has refused his assent to laws the most wholesome and necessary for the public good," is, on constitutional grounds, without support; for it was not only his prerogative right so to refuse, but it was a right expressly reserved, with two or three exceptions, in the very instruments to which the colonies owed their existence, and which they had assented to by accepting them. Jefferson would not have helped his case, as matter of law, by insisting that it was the abuse, not the exercise, of the powers of which he complained; for of that the king was sole judge.

Looking at the case, therefore, from the constitutional point of view, as Chalmers and the Tories looked at it, judgment must have been for the king. That is, by the British constitution the king stood on the same ground as that on which the President of the United States, the governors of most of the states, and the mayors of many cities stand when they veto legislative acts ; and no more than they are was the king justly liable to impeachment therefor.

By fiction of the British constitution the king sat in person in his colonial courts, as well as in those within the realm; and when he required substitutes, as well he might, to perform this ubiquitous and exacting service, he claimed the right accorded by the constitution, to say by whom, and on what tenure, and with what pay these vicarious services should be rendered. The pay of the judges by the king was the feature most obnoxious to the colonists. They cared less who was judge, or how long he held the office, so long as they could bring him to terms, as they often did, or even drive him from the bench, by diminishing or withholding his salary. The result was that when the king sued in his own courts for his revenues or for trespasses on the timber land of the crown he was generally cast in his suit. This question the Revolution temporarily adjusted without settling. It was left to us, and we are in doubt ; for there are intelligent people who take the Revolutionary ground, as opposed to the Tory ground of that period which we have generally adopted, that the judiciary, not less than other departments of the government, ought to depend upon the popular voice for their election, pay, and tenure of office.

The king, like the president of the United States, by his prerogative was commander-in-chief of military and naval forces of his empire, and in peace as well as in war determined their movements, posts, and quarters. Regarded then as a constitutional question,

Jefferson's complaint on this head amounts to no more than this: that George III., though he probably had little to do with it, directed the forces in the colonies for purposes and in a manner which was not approved of by the colonists. But that is seldom the case with those whom the government undertakes to reduce to subjection. Certainly it was not so in the late Civil War, in which both combatants made loud and doubtless just complaints against each other of inhumanity and disregard of the laws of war; and Congress and the press and many very wise people were more willing to take command of the army than to allow the constitutional authorities the exercise of that function.

Tory writers both at home and abroad sneered at Jefferson's constitutional notions. Not that Jefferson did not know the constitution; few knew it better. His difficulty was that in armed rebellion he was obliged to fight the battle before the world, not as a rebel, but as one contending for the rights of the colonists under the constitution, which, as he claimed, had been invaded by the sovereign. On that ground his task was severe — perhaps beyond his strength.

If his situation had allowed, Jefferson doubtless would have said what certainly was true, that the king, by advice of his ministers and by virtue of his prerogatives and as a coördinate branch of the legislature, had exercised his constitutional powers adversely to the economic interests of his colonial subjects; and that they, having petitioned and remonstrated without redress, were compelled to sever those relations which formed the basis of their allegiance to him and of his power over the colonies. But that was revolution!

The real position of the colonies.

This was the real position of the colonists, and in it was the justice and strength of their cause; and we may speculate whether they might not have better taken it at the outset, since to that position have gradually come the wise and dispassionate thinkers of both countries in the present generation.

They followed English precedents, however, in the course they adopted; for I believe the opinion is gaining ground, adversely to Hallam and some other English constitutionalists, that in many, perhaps most cases, and notably in the case of ship-money, Charles I. was within his strict constitutional prerogatives.[1] Nevertheless, the people rebelled and slew him as a tyrant who claimed and exercised unconstitutional powers, when his real offense was the exercise of constitutional powers without any warranting necessity.[2]

Jefferson was right in his main purpose; but his indictment of George III. is perhaps the only one ever drawn in which the real offense is not even mentioned, and where an innocent party was vicariously substituted for the real offender!

Nevertheless, Jefferson's arraignment of the prerogatives in the person of the king did little or nothing for their settlement, since they remain, even with augmented force, under the new order as under the old. Prerogatives in a monarchy are the divine rights

---

[1] Hall's *Customs of England*, i. 141, 145.

[2] Where great principles or even great interests are at stake, constitutional guaranties or restrictions are of little avail. How little some of us know, who had no doubt in respect to the guaranties of chattel slavery, but, nevertheless, deliberately disregarded them, and gloried in doing so; while many attested their sincerity by the sacrifice of their lives. And so, as we look at it, and as I think the world, including Great Britain, now looks at it, Jefferson was right in his main purpose; and if, on strictly constitutional grounds, he was wrong, like Cæsar, "he was wrong in just cause."

of the sovereign king; under a democracy, the divine rights of the sovereign people. This is the theory. Practically, under both forms of government, they are grants of power by the people to their rulers; and if the king's prerogatives were justly obnoxious to the colonists, why did they, not many years after, invest the President with power to appoint cabinet officers, foreign ambassadors, judges, and the whole civil and military service for a people since become sixty millions? [1] This is one of the questions which the Revolution did not settle, and it has been reopened again and again, with a persistency which causes solicitude in some quarters as to the result, especially in respect to the judiciary.

Unsatisfactory results of the controversy.

Jefferson smote the claim of parliamentary supremacy squarely in the face. He denied that Parliament had any rightful authority over the colonies; and asserted that the exercise of such jurisdiction was foreign to our constitution, unacknowledged by our laws, and that all its acts were usurpations. This opinion he had expressed before the Revolution, and Wythe agreed with him; but as he said, he could find no one else who did. No wonder; for the facts were against them. In several instances and on various subjects Parliament had legislated for the colonies with their assent, and even at their request. If Jefferson accepted the original doctrine that the colonies were the king's colonies, subject to his direction to the exclusion of all other, his position is intelligible. Franklin had expressed similar opinions; but both regarded monarchical power when opposed to popular

[1] See Letter of John Adams to Roger Sherman in Boutell's *Life of Sherman*, 315.

rights with aversion, and it is difficult to resist the conviction that their utterances were merely political.

Jefferson's theory of the relations of the colonists to the crown was as old as the colonies themselves, and grew out of the public law of Europe in the fifteenth century; by that theory the king made laws for them, if royal provinces, by the terms of his commissions to their governors, and he regulated all of them by the exercise of his prerogatives. Nevertheless, from an early period the prerogatives had been invaded by Parliament, so that at the time of the Revolution they were in such doubt that statesmen might well differ as to the rights of Parliament to tax the colonies. They claimed exemption by arguments to which Chatham and Camden gave assent, and sometimes for reasons which illustrated the self-complacency of the true Briton and all of his descendants, especially in Massachusetts. [1]

[1] That people, says Mauduit (Hutchinson's *Letters*, 59, 2d ed., 1774), pleaded the charter of 1691, in which it was provided that they should have and enjoy all liberties and immunities of free and natural subjects, within any of the king's dominions, his heirs, and successors, to all intents, constructions, and purposes whatsoever, as if they and every of them were born within his realm of England. The English subjects within the realm, they said, "have a right to choose representatives for themselves, and are governed only by acts of Parliament; under our charter, therefore, we have the same rights as the people of England have to choose our representatives, and to be governed only by the laws made by our assemblies in which alone we are represented; and the Parliament of England has nothing to do with us." This is ingenious. It is also very English and very American. Both peoples seem to think that there are certain rights which Englishmen and their descendants as such, distinguished from Frenchmen, Spaniards, or Dutchmen, for example, carry with them into all parts of the world, to be pleaded there against local jurisdiction. "I am a Roman citizen," exclaimed Paul in a country remote from Rome, but subject to its laws. "I am an Englishman," exclaims one who travels in foreign parts where English law does *not* prevail, and

The dispute was mainly one of point of view. If the colonists were without the realm, and merely the king's subjects, as was their relation by constitutional theory at least, parliamentary legislation affecting them was usurpation; but if they were within the empire, which was questioned argumentatively by the colonists, though that was the opinion in England, and if they were entitled to the privileges of the British constitution, and subject to its burdens with all the exceptions to its general provisions and frequent departures from its principles, then the rights and duties of the colonists, as of those within the four seas, were determined by precedents, judicial decisions, and opinions of the high officers of the law. This, of course, was the legal and constitutional view of the matter; and had it prevailed, the colonists were as much bound by the king's prerogatives and parliamentary proceedings as were the home subjects, five sixths of whom, notwithstanding the general maxim that representation and taxation are correlative rights and burdens, had no effectual participation in their own government, and least of all in the power by which they were taxed.

The British and Tory point of view.

This was the opinion of Mansfield, and finally of Camden, and it was supported by arguments of such

expects his claim to be allowed. The real meaning of the charter was, that any citizen of Massachusetts going to England or Jamaica, or to any other of the king's dominions, should have the same rights as though he were born in England; but it did not mean that in Massachusetts or Jamaica he should have the rights, general or local, which he might have and enjoy in England. Such has been the interpretation given to a provision in the fourth article of the Articles of Confederation similar to that in the Massachusetts charter.

weight that some of the British liberals [1] were forced
implicitly to acknowledge its legal validity.[2]

[1] Burke's *Conciliation with the Colonies.* (*Works*, Little & Brown
ed., 1839, ii. 48.)

[2] In 1765 Camden said that Parliament had no right to tax the
colonies; in 1767 he affirmed that right, and accounted for his change
of opinion by the Declaratory Act which accompanied the repeal of
the Stamp Act. We who live under a written constitution which
divides and apportions the powers of government, and defines rights
and duties with exactness of phrase, have difficulty in understanding
how the British constitution can be changed in an hour without reference to the will of the people. But a glance at our own history
makes it quite clear. For example : Nothing is more certain than
that the framers of the Constitution designed, by the machinery of an
electoral college, to remove the election of the President and Vice-
President as far as possible from popular influence; and yet the
exercise of the power lodged in the college, according to constitutional
provision and intent, would at any time since the adoption of the Constitution have produced a revolution !

Again: more than half of the present territory of the United
States was acquired by a purchase not authorized by the Constitution,
as Jefferson, who consummated it, admitted; but the precedent once
set, not even by the representatives of the people in Congress, but by
an usurpation of power by the executive, it virtually became part of
the Constitution, and without scruple has been followed by other acquisitions by purchase, by conquest, by treaty, and by joint resolution.

I say nothing of the extension and modification of the Constitution
by judicial construction which so alarmed and disgusted Jefferson,
and only allude to the high authority (Lodge's *Webster*, 176),
which admits that the validity of Mr. Webster's opinions in 1830
respecting nullification rests upon what the Constitution had become
at that time rather than upon the intent of its framers in 1787. Seeing then the potency of precedent under a democracy as well as
under a monarchy, and in the case of a written constitution by its
terms changeable only by formal amendments, I can listen with respect, even if I do not assent, to the powerful reasoning of Mansfield
that the colonies, especially after the Declaratory Act of 1766, were
subject to parliamentary authority in all cases whatsoever.

" Constitutional difficulties never will stand in the way of a majority. . . . Even in so select a body as the Senate of the United States,
a mere variation of phrase will contrive a loop-hole to escape from
the most bare-faced usurpation of power." John Quincy Adams's
Diary, i. 417.

Nevertheless, this is the British view. There was also an American view which the Whigs had a clear right to take, as they did when they questioned whether the British construction, with the Declaratory Act of 1766, had been acquiesced in by the colonists so as to give to it the force of constitutional law binding on them in their relations to the mother country. The Whig point of view.

There is also an entirely different view which acknowledges the force of precedent and usage, and which seems to me conclusive so far as relates to the right of Parliament directly to tax the colonies. It is that presented in the fourth article of the Declaration of Rights by the Congress of 1774, drawn by John Adams, and claims in substance the existence of colonial constitutions as well as of the British constitution, and that the former as well as the latter were the results of growth, development, usage, and precedent; and that by these constitutions the power of Parliament did not extend to direct taxation for revenue,[1] but was limited by the countervailing colonial constitutions, which in that respect had become part of the general constitution, to taxes imposed by the navigation laws and some others, to which the colonists had given their implied assent, and from which they had received equivalent commercial protection. But direct taxation was another matter. For a hundred and fifty years the power, if it ever existed, had been in abeyance, and the colonies had been allowed to grow John Adams's view.

---

[1] In a notable passage in Burke's "Speech on American Taxation" (*Works*, Little & Brown ed., 1839, i. 492), he distinguishes the constitution of Britain from the constitution of the British empire, conceding to the latter the power of taxing in Parliament as an instrument of empire *and not as a means of supply.*

and shape their governments and their policy and manage their affairs without direct contribution to the imperial exchequer even for their own government and defense.

I have said that the war settled none of the constitutional questions for which it was waged; nor did the new Constitution itself settle them except by returning to the British construction. This, it is true, was brought about only with great difficulty; for there was a large minority led by such men as George Mason, Elbridge Gerry, and Samuel Adams, who strenuously contended that in adopting the Constitution of 1787 the people surrendered everything, except independence, for which they had fought seven years. If the present Constitution is evidence of such surrender, it is one more example of the tenacity with which the race clings to the principles and essential forms of government, no matter by what name they are called, to which they have been attached, and with which are associated their progress and their glory and even their misfortunes.

The con-
stitu-
tional
questions
remain
unsettled.

If I have any difficulty in determining the validity of the American position within the Constitution, either imperial or colonial, I have none whatever in this: that the navigation laws and acts of trade, taxation without representation, the attempts to force an episcopate on the colonies, and the exercise of the royal prerogatives, were so clearly at variance with the natural and acquired rights of the colonists, that at the time when they chose to assert and rely upon them they were clearly justified in armed resistance;

The true
position
taken in
the pre-
amble of
the Decla-
ration of
Independ-
ence —
the natu-
ral right
of men to
settle
their own
form of
govern-
ment.

and so were they if the British connection contravened the sentiments of three millions of people as to what constituted the pursuit of happiness. This, however, is not in the light of constitutional law, but is an appeal to the rights of man. Here Jefferson was strong, unassailable — in the preamble, if not in the body of the Declaration. Jefferson is a great character and needs a great stage around which may gather all the races of men to hear what he has to say. He requires no interpreter. For six thousand years the world had been waiting for the words which he so spake that all men heard.

REMARKS ON THE NEW HISTORICAL SCHOOL

REPRINTED FROM THE PROCEEDINGS OF THE MASSACHUSETTS
HISTORICAL SOCIETY, JANUARY, 1890

THE NEW HISTORICAL SCHOOL

WITHIN the last decade there has grown up among us a new school of history which has its principal seats at the higher universities. It is now so well known by its leading characteristics that a minute description of it would seem like pretending to a new discovery. Its promise is high, and even thus early its work is more than respectable as that of young men mainly of scholastic training, unacquainted with affairs, and without opportunities for observing how the elementary facts which make history are colored and even transformed in legislative assemblies, by judicial decisions, and .in the tumultuous proceedings of the crowd. Gibbon has recorded that his captainship in the Hampshire grenadiers had not been useless to the historian of the Roman Empire ; and every one knows how much the historical insight of Clarendon, Hume, and Macaulay was quickened, and how much their narratives gain in closeness and verisimilitude by their participation in government, diplomacy, and parliamentary affairs. And so will it be with the new school of American historians. Years and experience will add greatly to the value of their future work.

Their methods are the comparative of Bopp and the critical of the later scientists ; and these are something more than new names for old processes. Hutchinson, Belknap, Trumbull, and Ramsay were diligent seekers and close observers. They did good work ; of its kind none better has been since done. But their field of observation was no wider than the subject in . hand, of which they gave the facts very exactly, but not their relative values ; nor were they curious about remote causes or the origin of institutions.

The new methods have produced surprising results in history as well as in science. The historian of the new school, distrusting second-hand authorities, resorts to original documents ; and if these are legal, which is more than likely to be the case in American history, as our English colonies were based on legal instruments, and their constitutional history is mainly to be found in the legal interpretation of those instruments, he acquaints himself with the rules of interpreting such documents. The neglect of this obvious duty has often led to deplorable mistakes. At the same time he considers how often, and how justly, legal arguments and conclusions are overruled by considerations of public policy. This is especially necessary in the history of the period just before the Revolutionary War, when the weight of purely legal argument was mostly on one side, and on the other a weightier colonial policy. Deeper than legal principles, deeper even than questions of public policy, and more potent, were the instincts and traditions of the race, though voiced as they often were by wild cries of the mob, unthinking and sometimes cruel, but generally right in their main purpose. It was by his recognition of these and by his appeal to them that Pitt, with vague notions of constitutional law and sometimes mistaken in his views of public policy, made his first administration the most glorious in British annals ; and that Macaulay, gathering their varied expressions from recondite sources, added to his narrative much which

will be more valued than its brilliancy and picturesqueness.

The methods of the new school are adapted to their
subjects of research ; and these, judiciously chosen as
yet, are those which require neither a large canvas nor
imaginative treatment, but rather, patient investigation and thoughtfulness, — such as the origin and
growth of local institutions, municipal governments,
constitutions, and social science. Nor is this history of
our institutions limited to their beginnings and growth
on American soil, but the inquiry is pushed into the
remote *habitats* and ages of our Anglo-Saxon race.

Nothing could be better than this, though not without its perils in treatment. In a large view the human
race is one ; its thoughts, desires, necessities, and
modes of action are similar ; and so, to that extent, is
its essential history. But such generalizations are
more safely used by the anthropologist than by the
historian. Nevertheless, there is a certain fascination
in tracing the unity of history. It pleases the reader
not less than the historian. There are few more effective paragraphs in any history than those in which
Guizot affirms that " neither the English revolution
nor the French revolution ever said, wished, or did
anything that had not been said, wished, done, or attempted a hundred times before they burst forth ; . . .
and that nothing will be found of which the invention
originated with them, nothing which is not equally
met with, or which at all events did not come into
existence in periods which are called regular." [1]

I have spoken of this school as new, — new in its
methods and new in its purposes ; and so, doubtless,
it is in this country, but not in Europe. Its prototype

---

[1] *English Revolution*, preface.

is to be found there, and there its most distinguished master, Dr. Edward A. Freeman. His view of our history may be gathered from a paragraph in which he says that " the early institutions of Massachusetts are part of the general institutions of the English people, as those are again part of the general institutions of the Teutonic race, and those are again part of the general institutions of the whole Aryan family." And there he says he stops; but he adds that his friends do him no wrong who make such institutions common to all mankind.[1]

The new American school inclines to go no farther than Freeman goes. But there is danger even in this. It is frequently said that our emigrant ancestors brought British institutions to Massachusetts; and with this notion we seek in English towns the prototypes of our own, and so back to those communities in the German forests vaguely described by Tacitus and Cæsar. I think there are reasons for caution in accepting the conclusions of some of our recent historical writers based on the theory of Dr. Freeman.

Analogies do not constitute identities. Instincts are not institutions; nor does similarity of design or adaptation of institutions indicate heredity or even relationship. When Englishmen sought new homes on American soil, they doubtless came with the purpose of organizing society and government; but they would have done so without such antecedent purpose. With forethought they brought many things. But there is no evidence that they brought institutions, or had even meditated the form which they would give them. They certainly brought with them the instincts,

---

[1] *Introduction to American Institutional History* (Johns Hopkins University Studies), 13.

traditions, and habits of their race, and these determined their action in unwonted situations and gave
shape to their institutions. We know with some exactness what they brought with them. We have the
lading of the ships in which they came. Besides themselves, their wives, their children and servants, they
brought clergymen, physicians, surveyors, mechanics,
with food to serve until the soil should yield it. They
brought clothing, furniture, tools, utensils, weapons
offensive and defensive, and animals. They brought
" Ministers, Men skilfull in making of pitch, of salt,
vine Planters, Patent Under Seal, a Seal, wheat, rye,
barley, oats, a head of each in the ear, beans, peas,
stones of all sorts of fruits, as peaches, plums, filberts,
cherries, pears, apples, quince kernels, pomegranates,
woad seed, saffron heads, liquorice seed, roots sent and
madder roots, potatoes, hop roots, hemp seed, flax seed
against winter, connys, currant plants, tame turkeys,
and madder seed." But we nowhere find mention of
Magna Charta, the British Constitution, the Petition
of Right, or English institutions. Nor is much said
about them in their books, sermons, diaries, or correspondence. But when they needed, they found them
directly enough in the traditions and instincts of their
race.

While their general purposes were clear, there is no
evidence that they had any definite and fixed plans as
to their government or institutions. The evidence is
all the other way. Their charter, the expression and
measure of their rights, gave them no power to set up
a government save for managing a land company. If
they intended to bring an English town with them, as
is so often said they did, they were singularly lacking
in care; for when they had organized their common-

wealth government, and arranged themselves in separate communities for which corporate town powers were necessary, no warrant was found in their charter, and to meet the necessity they were obliged to usurp the power of forming corporations, for which they were afterwards called to account, and greatly to their cost.

So our English ancestors did not bring English towns with them, nor English churches, nor vestries, nor British institutions. But on occasion they builded for themselves, as Englishmen always and everywhere had done and still do, according to the exigencies of their situation and after the manner of their race, just as the seeds they brought with them produced, each after its kind, but modified by differences of soil, climate, and situation. And so doubtless was it with their ancestors and ours, who came from the forests of Germany to England; but it is questionable whether they brought German towns into England. We must not be misled by analogies or resemblances, nor assign to nationality what belongs to all races. Wherever people are gathered in stationary communities, their communal wants will be essentially the same, and will be provided for essentially in the same manner. But it is quite probable that a fully organized New England town differed in as many particulars and as widely from an English town as that from a German town, or as that from one in the heart of Africa.

It is not to be inferred from what has been said that the new historical school has generally fallen into the mistake indicated, though perhaps there is a tendency to do so.

One of those who adopted the extreme view as to

the origin and powers of New England towns was the late Professor Alexander Johnston. His opinions took shape in a monograph entitled "The Genesis of a New England State," published in 1883, which was substantially incorporated into his history of "Connecticut: A Study of Commonwealth Democracy," published in 1887. On the appearance of this work I read it with interest; but finding some statements and opinions, presently to be referred to, which seemed to me questionable at least, I made memoranda which form the substance of what I am now saying. Professor Johnston possessed many qualifications for writing history. He readily apprehended and swiftly methodized the facts appertaining to his subject, and presented them in an attractive style. His views of the origin and development of our institutions were those of the new school pushed beyond their extreme limits; but his way of handling facts and drawing inferences from them was his own, and in my judgment not to be commended.

His views are best set forth in his own words, as follows : —

1. "Connecticut's town system was, by a fortunate concurrence of circumstances, even more independent of outside control than that of Massachusetts; the principle of local government had here a more complete recognition; and in the form in which it has done best service, its beginning was in Connecticut.

2. "The first conscious and deliberate effort on this continent to establish the democratic principle in control of government was the settlement of Connecticut; and her Constitution of 1639, the first written and democratic constitution on record, was the starting-point for the democratic development which has since gained control of all

our Commonwealths, and now makes the essential feature of our commonwealth government.

3. "Democratic institutions enabled the people of Connecticut to maintain throughout their colonial history a form of government so free from crown control that it became really the exemplar of the rights at which all the colonies finally aimed.

4. "Connecticut, being mainly a federation of towns, with neither so much of the centrifugal force as in Rhode Island nor so much of the centripetal force as in other colonies, maintained for a century and a half that union of the democratic and federative ideas which has at last come to mark the whole United States.

5. "The Connecticut delegates, in the Convention of 1787, by another happy concurrence of circumstances, held a position of unusual influence. The frame of their commonwealth government, with its equal representation of towns in one branch and its general popular representation in the other, had given them a training which enabled them to bend the form of our national Constitution into a corresponding shape; and the peculiar constitution of our Congress, in the different bases of the Senate and House of Representatives, was thus the result of Connecticut's long maintenance of a federative democracy."

The foregoing propositions contain several matters in respect to which I find myself not in accord with Professor Johnston, but I shall advert to two only; and these are, first, his ideas of the origin of Connecticut towns, the functions assigned to them in the formation of that Commonwealth, and their subsequent relation to it; and second, the alleged influence in the Convention of 1787 of the Connecticut system in giving shape to the Constitution of the United States.

Before giving further extracts from Professor Johnston's history, I will notice briefly the circumstances of the settlement of the valley of the Connecticut, detailed more fully by Palfrey.[1]

The most considerable emigration to Massachusetts Bay which followed the coming of Winthrop in the summer of 1630 was a party of East England people who landed at Boston, September 4, 1633. Of these the most conspicuous were John Cotton, Thomas Hooker, Samuel Stone, and John Haynes, of whom all except the last were clergymen, and all except the first were prominent in bringing about three years later the exodus to Connecticut, and in setting up a new commonwealth there in 1639. Hooker and Stone were settled at Newtown, now Cambridge, as pastor and teacher of the church there; and in the summer of 1636 they led many of their congregation as well as the church to what is now Hartford, where Haynes joined them the next year. Warham, the Dorchester clergyman, also carried his church and part of the congregation to Windsor. These churches emigrated as organized bodies, thus creating vacancies in these several towns, which were filled by the formation of new churches at Cambridge, under the charge of Shepard, and at Dorchester, under the charge of Richard Mather, the famous progenitor of the more famous Increase and Cotton Mather. But the emigrants from Watertown, Boston, and Roxbury, accompanied by several eminent men, went as groups of people unorganized either as church or community.

Thus, after three years' residence in the Bay, these people went away to Connecticut. Indeed, they had been settled only a few months before they conceived and made known their dissatisfaction with things as

[1] *History of New England*, i. 444, *et seq.*

they found them, and began to form plans for removal. The reasons they assigned for this desire were as follows : —

1. " Their want of accommodation for their cattle, so as they were not able to maintain their ministers, nor could receive any more of their friends to help them ; and here it was alleged by Mr. Hooker, as a fundamental error, that towns were so near to each other.

2. " The fruitfulness and commodiousness of Connecticut, and the danger of having it possessed by others, Dutch or English.

3. " The strong bent of their spirits to remove thither." [1]

In the two years before the emigrants led by Hooker had reached Connecticut, a considerable number of people must have gathered there; for the General Court, September 3, 1635, ordered " That every town upon the Connecticut shall have liberty to choose their own constable, who shall be sworn by some magistrate of this Court ; " and on March 4 of the next year appointed a commission to order provisionally for one year the affairs of the people there, and to call a court of the inhabitants to execute the authority granted. When the powers of the Massachusetts commissioners expired, the people of the several

---

[1] Palfrey, *History of New England*, i. 445. Dr. Palfrey finds other reasons than those assigned for their desire to remove to Connecticut; and his views are adopted by Charles M. Andrews, Fellow in History, 1889–1890, Johns Hopkins University, in his monograph entitled *The River Towns of Connecticut*. It seems to me, however, that much which has not been said may with good reason be said on the other side. Under three heads, Mr. Andrews has admirably treated the Early Settlement, the Land System, and the Towns and the People of Connecticut. Mr. Andrews does not accept Professor Johnston's peculiar theory in respect to the Connecticut towns, and quotes judicial decisions on the subject.

towns chose their successors, and held courts until the adoption of a constitution, January 14, 1639. A material fact to be noted is that in all of the proceedings of the General Court of Massachusetts relating to the Connecticut settlers, they are spoken of as "our loving friends, neighbors, freemen, and members of Newtown, Dorchester, Watertown, and other places, who are resolved to transport themselves and their estates unto the River of Connecticut, and there to reside and inhabit." No mention is made of any " migrating towns."

I now return to Professor Johnston's narrative. He says : —

" The independence of the town was a political fact which has colored the whole history of the Commonwealth, and, through it, of the United States. Even in Massachusetts, after the real beginning of the government, the town was subordinate to the colony ; and though the independence of the churches forced a considerable local freedom there, it was not so fundamental a fact as in Connecticut. Here the three original towns had in the beginning left commonwealth control behind them when they left the parent colony. They had gone into the wilderness, each the only organized political power within its jurisdiction. Since their prototypes, the little *tuns* of the primeval German forest, there had been no such examples of the perfect capacity of the political cell — the 'town ' — for self-government. In Connecticut it was the towns that created the Commonwealth; and the consequent federative idea has steadily influenced the colony and State alike. In Connecticut the governing principle, due to the original constitution of things rather than to the policy of the Commonwealth, has been that the town is the residuary legatee of political power ; that it is the State which is called upon to make out a clear case for powers to which it lays claim ;

and that the towns have a *prima facie* case in their favor wherever a doubt arises " (p. 61).

With these extracts before us we can state more succinctly Professor Johnston's theory. He says, though somewhat vaguely, that towns came from the forests of Germany to England, and from England to Massachusetts Bay ; and, more distinctly, that three of them — Watertown, Newtown, and Dorchester, — as organized towns, migrated to Connecticut, and there in 1639 set up a commonwealth as the result of their joint corporate action : — that these towns, having created a commonwealth, became the pattern for towns in other commonwealths ; and so happily had their system of confederated towns worked, and especially in relation to the commonwealth, that the Connecticut delegation in the Convention of 1787 were able to persuade that body to form the Constitution of the United States on the same basis, — the Senate, with its equal and unalterable representation of sovereign States answering to the independent Connecticut towns ; and the House of Representatives, elected by popular vote, answering to the Connecticut Council, elected in the same manner. Professor Johnston says : —

" And this is so like the standard theory of the relations of the States to the federal government that it is necessary to notice the peculiar exactness with which the relations of Connecticut towns to the Commonwealth are proportioned to the relations of the Commonwealth to the United States. In other States, power runs from the State upwards and from the State downwards ; in Connecticut, the towns have always been to the Commonwealth as the Commonwealth to the Union. . . . In this respect the life principle of the American Union may be traced straight back to the primitive union of the three little settlements on the bank of the Connecticut River. . . . It is hardly too much to say that the birth of the Constitution [of the United States] was merely the grafting of the Connecticut system on the stock of the confederation, where it has grown into richer luxuriance than Hooker could ever have dreamed of " (pp. 62, 322).

The fallacy of this scheme lies in his theory respecting towns, — their existence independent of some sovereign power.

This leads, then, to an examination of the nature of towns. Three things seem necessary to constitute a town, — territory, population, and corporate existence.

It must have definite territory with a certain permanency of tenure. A military company, a camp-meeting, or a tourist party — frequently more numerous than the inhabitants of some towns — occupying territory for an indefinite time and, it may be, observing many regulations which govern towns, nevertheless does not constitute a town. Nor does a migratory body of people such as is found in pastoral regions; for when the inhabitants of a town remove to another locality they do not take their town with them, though no town remains behind. Whether they go to a place within the same jurisdiction or to one outside of it, in either case on removal their corporate powers revert to the state, and they become a voluntary organization unknown to the law and without rights before it. They are relegated to their natural rights. Again, the inhabitants of a town constitute a legal unit which, for certain purposes at least, absorbs the individuality of its members. It is a corporation by express creation of the state, or has become such by prescription; and one of the tests of such a body-corporate is its power to sue and its liability to be sued in its

corporate name. When, therefore, certain inhabitants
of Watertown, Cambridge, and Dorchester migrated
to Connecticut, even though they constituted the major part of the inhabitants of those towns, and even
though they had carried the town records and other
evidences of their corporate existence along with them,
which they did not, they went simply as a body of unorganized people voluntarily associated for seeking a
new residence. They did not take the towns along
with them. After the migration the map showed no
vacancies with asterisks referring to the margin,
" Gone to Connecticut." They went, according to the
act authorizing their going, as " divers of our loving
friends, neighbors, freemen, and members of Newtown,
Dorchester, Watertown, and other places ; " and they
went under the government of commissioners authorized, not to create towns, but to exercise certain
powers of state over them for the space of a year. So
little is the foundation for Professor Johnston's assumption " that three fully organized Massachusetts
towns passed out of the jurisdiction of any commonwealth, and proceeded to build up a commonwealth
of their own " (p. 12).

But were it possible and were it true that the
three Massachusetts towns migrated as such, it is
neither true nor is it possible that they could have
set up a commonwealth, though their people might
have done so, and in fact did.

Professor Johnston calls the town the political
cell from which the commonwealth was evolved.
But a town can be the germ of nothing but a
greater town ; never of a commonwealth. The rights
and duties of towns are communal, and for such
rights and duties they may provide ; but even then

these powers are delegated, not inherent. The state may, and often does, attend to these matters. But the rights and duties of the state primarily concern sovereignty, external relations, and general laws affecting the inhabitants of all the state. Some of these powers the state, for convenience, may delegate to the inhabitants of towns, such as the election of constables, who are officers of the state not of the town, and whose legal relations are to the state not to the town.

On the other hand, it need not be denied that a town may be something more, and like the Hanse Towns become qualifiedly independent. But this is not in consequence of the development or extension of communal functions so as to include national functions. It is by taking on new functions. Where these are exercised, it is not because they belong to the town or city in its corporate capacity, but because they are assumed by the people, and their assumption is allowed by neighboring states; and even then they owe a qualified allegiance to some sovereign, which is inconsistent with the idea of an absolutely independent commonwealth.

If we look at the natural order of towns and commonwealths, it will appear that the latter is first. The primary question of government which concerns every community is that of sovereignty. When this is not denied, the question is in abeyance; nor does it practically arise where communities, under a previously settled order of relations to the sovereign power, proceed at once to provide for their communal relations.

And so we find that the first act of legislative bodies is to provide for the safety of the body politic, and later for communal affairs. They first establish the state, and then erect towns. Nor is this order ever reversed. The genesis of the state is not from its parts, — confederated districts, towns, or counties,— but from the sovereign people, who arrange themselves into towns and counties.

The same is true of a confederacy of independent states, whether monarchical or democratic; for behind the resultant form of confederation are the people, who assent to the proposed relation.

The genesis of American commonwealths is historically clear. (1) They originated with mere adventurers for fishing, hunting, or trading, who without territorial ownership or by state authority established themselves on the coast. Among these, though with other views, must be included the Pilgrims driven out of their course by adverse circumstances, as well as the first settlers of Rhode Island and Connecticut. (2) They originated with those who had purchased lands and obtained charters. (3) They were founded under proprietary governments. (4) They were founded as royal governments. In all these cases we find that people first addressed themselves to their foreign relations and to the perfecting of their autonomy. Neither towns nor town records appear until much later. Nor does it change the order of these relations that the state simultaneously took upon itself the direction of communal as well as of general affairs. The town was not the primordial cell which developed into a state, but the state was the mother of her towns. Development is along the lines of original constitutions, and seldom or never passes over into a different genus.

In accordance with this order, while the three Massachusetts towns of Watertown, Cambridge, and Dorchester, with their records and corporate powers and muniments, remain where they were first settled, it is true that a large number of their inhabitants, between 1634 and 1637, migrated to Connecticut and settled as communities in places now known as Hartford, Windsor, and Wethersfield. They went as unorganized bodies of people, by permission of the Bay Colony, which, for reasons stated in their commission, had assumed jurisdiction over that part of Connecticut — a fact recognized by the migrating parties. It is further true that these same people, — not in any corporate capacity, for that they lacked, — on the expiration of the Bay Colony commission, chose commissioners for themselves ; and in 1639, in the language of their own constitution, "We the Inhabitants and Residents of Windsor, Hartford, and Wethersfield . . . do associate and conform ourselves to be as one Public State or Commonwealth." Such was the genesis of Connecticut. Towns had absolutely nothing to do with it. They did not even exist ; and it was not before 1639 that the unorganized communities which went from the Bay Colony were set up as corporations. Instead of being the creators of the commonwealth they were its offspring. From the commonwealth they derived all of their powers. Nor is their character in any essential respect changed — they are neither more nor less than towns — by the fact that the state, for the convenience of towns more widely separated from one another and removed from a common centre than were those in the Bay, chose to delegate a larger share of her authority to them than Massachusetts did to her towns. In both cases they derived all their power from the state and conferred none upon it. Nor were they any more " little republics," or more independent of state control than other towns in New

England, because in apportioning representation to the General Court town lines were used to express the territorial unit of representation.

It would seem that Professor Johnston's theory of town sovereignty was adopted to lay the foundation for his fifth proposition, that in the Convention of 1787 the equal and unchangeable representation of the States in the Senate of the United States was based upon the Connecticut system of town representation. So far from this being probable, the fact is that while the representation in the Senate of the United States was state or corporate representation, the representation in the General Assembly was not corporate representation, but essentially the representation of the people determined, not by corporate powers, but by town lines.

We find nothing in the debates of the Convention of 1787 which warrants the view of Professor Johnston. Theories of government were discussed, constitutions of the several States were referred to, and some of their provisions, notably those of Massachusetts, were adopted; but the main features of the Constitution were determined by the necessities of the situation and the interests of sections and of States, — as large or small, agricultural or commercial, slaveholding or non-slaveholding.

The Connecticut delegation had great influence in the Convention, first, because Sherman, Johnson, and Ellsworth were very able men, and the only three very able men from any State who worked together; and secondly, because Connecticut, being neither one of the largest nor one of the smallest States, held a position of great influence as mediator between the two classes of States.

THE

GENESIS OF THE MASSACHUSETTS TOWN

TAKEN FROM A DISCUSSION HELD BY CHARLES
FRANCIS ADAMS, ABNER C. GOODELL, Jr.,
MELLEN CHAMBERLAIN, AND
EDWARD CHANNING

REPRINTED FROM THE PROCEEDINGS OF THE MASSACHUSETTS
HISTORICAL SOCIETY, JANUARY, 1892

THE GENESIS OF THE MASSACHU-
SETTS TOWN

Mr. Adams, in presenting his paper on the " Genesis of the Massachusetts Town and the Development
of Town-meeting Government," has told us that it was
written as a chapter of his forthcoming History of
Quincy ; and that he had sent copies of it to several
gentlemen of the Society — to myself among others —
with the request that at this meeting they would express their opinions respecting the conclusions which
he had reached.

This treatment of historical questions is a new departure which, so far as it tends to bring about a consensus of opinions, might be followed with advantage ;
but in the present instance, inasmuch as the matters
contained in Mr. Adams's paper, as well as those in
an earlier one to which he has referred, have been subjects of correspondence between us, and as my general
views have been presented to the Society in a paper
entitled " The New Historical School," [1] there may be
no good reason for my saying more than this, — that I
regard Mr. Adams's paper as a valuable contribution
to the literature of the subject, and in general that it
accords with my own views. Nevertheless, before I
sit down I may advert to the few points on which we
appear to differ.

[1] *Massachusetts Historical Society Proceedings*, series 2, v. 264.

In the mean time I wish to say something about the parochial theory, which, though not new, is newly interesting from the prominence given to it by the distinction of its recent advocates, among whom was Mr. Adams ; but as he has relieved the ship by throwing overboard the parish system as the most cumbersome and least valuable part of the cargo, advised and assisted therein somewhat, as he frankly tells us, by one or two of the passengers who had made the voyage, some explanation of the reasons which influenced them seems due at this time.

The origin of the New England towns is not a new question. It has been discussed at home and abroad by those whose training and predilection for historical questions qualified them for such investigations. I propose, therefore, to mention those which have come under my eye, and have aided me in forming the conclusion that these towns were of domestic and secular origin, owing little to English models, and least of all to English parishes.

In 1845 Richard Frothingham,[1] as the result of his investigations, said that " England did not furnish an example of New England town government ; " and this seems to have remained his opinion twenty-five years later.[2]

In 1857 Mr. Justice Gray of the Supreme Court of the United States, then reporter of the decisions of the Supreme Court of Massachusetts, in notes to the case of Commonwealth *vs.* Roxbury [3] treated one phase of the question with great thoroughness and ability.

In 1865 Joel Parker, formerly Chief Justice of New

---

[1] *History of Charlestown*, 49.

[2] *Proceedings of the American Antiquarian Society*, October, 1870.

[3] 9 Gray's *Reports*, 451.

Hampshire, then professor in the Law School at Cambridge, with wider scope inquired into "The Origin, Organization, and Influence of the Towns of New England." [1] Having myself some years ago and again quite recently gone over the same ground in original authorities, and without reference to his work, I find that I am in accord with Professor Parker's views; and were it otherwise, I should venture dissent only on the clearest grounds, and with the consensus of those on whose judgment I could safely rely. For his paper in substance, though not in form, is the judicial opinion of one whose practice as a leading lawyer at an able bar or as judge in the highest legal tribunal of his State led him to explore the origin of New England towns with the thoroughness and accuracy required by his great responsibility.

I have also read Mr. Melville Egleston's "The Land System of the New England Colonies," which seems to me an admirable piece of work; and not less admirable and with wider range are the papers of Mr. Charles M. Andrews, now professor in Bryn Mawr College, on "The River Towns of Connecticut," [2] "The Beginning of the Connecticut Towns," [3] and "The Theory of the Village Community." [4] Mr. William E. Foster, of Providence, an accomplished writer on historical subjects, has published a valuable paper on "Town Government in Rhode Island." [5] Either

---

[1] *Massachusetts Historical Society Proceedings*, ix. 14.

[2] *Johns Hopkins University Studies in Historical and Political Science*, 1889.

[3] *Annals of the American Academy of Political and Social Science*, October, 1890.

[4] *Papers of the American Historical Association*, v. 47.

[5] *Johns Hopkins University Studies in Historical and Political Science*, 1886.

to mention or to commend in this presence " The Origin of Towns in Massachusetts," by our learned associate Mr. Goodell,[1] would be equally superfluous.

The opinion of Professor Parker, that New England towns were essentially indigenous, has been questioned, sometimes directly and sometimes indirectly, by the New Historical School, in which Professor H. B. Adams, the late Professor Johnston, Professor John Fiske, and our associate Professor Edward Channing, are leaders; and therefore after some hesitation I have concluded to review, though not exhaustively, the origin of New England towns. Mr. Adams's thoroughgoing paper makes it unnecessary for me to go over the whole ground. There are at least three theories in respect to them.

First, that they were native to the soil, and planted by English emigrants with the instincts, traditions, and methods of their race, but controlled, nevertheless, by their charters, patents, or royal commissions, and the conditions of situation utterly unlike those which surrounded them in England.

Second, that they were copies of English prototypes, as those were of German, and these, again, of those in remote regions inhabited by the Aryan race; and that certain resemblances common to all are specific and conscious imitations rather than those forms and modes of action which arise spontaneously in all ages and everywhere when men gather in permanent bodies as village communities or as organized municipalities. One of the most distinguished of those who have adopted this theory and pushed it to its extreme limits was Professor Johnston, who claimed that towns — not companies of men merely,

---

[1] *Massachusetts Historical Society Proceedings*, series 2, v. 320.

but organized towns — migrated from England to Massachusetts Bay and thence to Connecticut.[1]

[1] In the paper on " The New Historical School " above referred to, I said that in the cargoes shipped by our ancestors to Massachusetts Bay no such thing as a town was to be found; and this I hear has been regarded as a denial of what no one ever thought of asserting. I had in mind the following paragraph in Professor Johnston's *The United States : Its History and Constitution*, 10: " In New England local organization was quite different. A good example is the town of Dorchester. Organized (March 20, 1630) in Plymouth, England, when its people were on the point of embarkation for America, it took the shape of a distinct town and church before they went on shipboard. Its civil and ecclesiastical organizations were complete before they landed in Massachusetts Bay, and came under the jurisdiction of a chartered company. Its people governed themselves in all but a few points, in which the colony asserted its superiority. As the colony's claims increased, the town's dissatisfaction increased. In 1635 the town migrated in a body, with its civil and ecclesiastical organizations still intact, into the vacant territory of Connecticut, and there became the town of Windsor." This is what had been asserted, and this is what I denied, — that a town came over with Winthrop's fleet in 1630. The sole foundation for the assertion, so far as I am aware, is the following passage from Blake's *Annals of Dorchester*, 7, amplified somewhat from a similar passage in Clap's Memoirs in Young's *Chronicles of Massachusetts Bay*, 347: " These good People [those who came to Dorchester with Maverick and Warham] met together at Plymouth, a Sea-port Town in ye S^d County of Devon, in order to Ship themselves & Families for New-England; and because they designed to live together after they should arrive here, they met together in the New Hospital in Plymouth and Associated into Church Fellowship, and Chose ye S^d Mr. Maverick and Mr. Warham to be their Ministers and Officers, keeping ye Day as a Day of Solemn Fasting & Prayer, and ye S^d Ministers accepted of ye Call & Expressed ye same." From this it seems to have been inferred that certain persons who met at Plymouth, in England, with the intention of going to Massachusetts Bay, by forming a church and choosing church officers and expressing their purpose to live together on reaching New England, thereby became a body politic, civil and ecclesiastical, at Dorchester, Massachusetts, without having acquired that character by prescription or by incorporation under the charter. So far as this assumption applies to the town, it does not require serious refutation; nor am I sure that it is better founded in respect to the church. The simplest idea of a church is that of a body of people

Third, is the theory which, while it denies or is silent in respect to the Germanic origin of New England towns, claims that they are essentially reproductions of the English parish, and their procedure that of the English vestry. The late Rev. Mr. Barry, if not to the fullest extent of this theory, goes very far when he says: "The idea of the formation of such

associated together with a common belief, having power to admit and reject members, and to discipline them on charges which if not proven might be actionable with damages, except for the immunity accorded such bodies by the law of the place. That such a body can exist *proprio vigore* without the permission, expressed or implied, of the civil power, is, I confess, utterly at variance with my ideas on the subject. Had it been so, what would have prevented any like number of Baptists, Church of England men, or Roman Catholics having right to allotments of lands under the Company, from forming themselves into churches and transporting themselves to Massachusetts Bay, with ecclesiastical rights and privileges in spite of the Puritan church? How the far less pretentious claims of the Episcopal Brownes were met by Endicott and his Council is matter of history; and how the General Court regarded such voluntary associations even by those whose theological tenets and church forms were unexceptionable, may be learned from the following order of the General Court, March 3, 1636: "Forasmuch as it hath been found by sad experience, that much trouble and disturbance hath happened both to the church and civil state by the officers and members of some churches, which have been gathered within the limits of this jurisdiction in an undue manner, and not with such public approbation as were meet, it is therefore ordered that all persons are to take notice that this Court doth not, nor will hereafter, approve of any such companies of men as shall henceforth join in any pretended way of church fellowship, without they shall first acquaint the magistrates, and the elders of the greater part of the churches in this jurisdiction, with their intentions, and have their approbation herein" upon pain of being excluded from admission as freemen. — 1 *Colonial Records*, 168.

I do not propose to discuss this theory further than I have already done in "The New Historical School," chiefly because, if not given up, it has at least been greatly shaken in late years; but partly because its critical examination leads me into fields with which I am not altogether familiar, and from which those who are, bring back widely different and inconsistent reports.

communities [towns] was probably derived from the parishes of England; for each town was a parish, and each as it was incorporated was required to contribute to the maintenance of the ministry, as the basis of its grants of municipal rights."[1]

Professor Fiske puts it unequivocally that the town government in New England "was simply the English parish government brought into a new country and adapted to the new situation."[2]

If there be any doubt how far our learned associate Dr. Edward Channing accepts this theory in his "Town and County Government," he is here to resolve it if he so chooses.

I have read these authorities with the attention due to the subject, and with the respect commanded by the learning and ability of the writers; but if they mean more than this, that the aptitude of the English race for government is greater than that of the Latin and Celtic races, chiefly by reason of its experience in legislative bodies, among which may be reckoned English town-meetings and parish vestries, then I must dissent for reasons which I now proceed to give. But first let us confront these theories with the phenomena of admitted facts in regard to the origin of New England towns.

The sporadic settlements in New England which ultimately became colonies, or towns within them, were not made on territory under the acknowledged jurisdiction of any sovereign authority capable of instant and effective protection in case of assault; but

[1] *History of Massachusetts*, i. 215.
[2] *Civil Government in the United States*, 30, 41, 42. And see other references by Mr. Adams to the *Memorial History of Boston*, i. 405, 427, and Brooks Adams's *Emancipation of Massachusetts*, 20.

on the contrary, proprietorship and jurisdiction were claimed, on the one hand, by Indian tribes, and on the other, by the French with whom the English were chronically at war. This fact lay at the foundation of origins, and had a formative influence upon de-.velopments from them, since it forced the settlers, whether families like those of Maverick at Winnisimmet, Blackstone at Boston, and Walford at Charlestown, or groups like those at Falmouth and Saco in Maine, and Portsmouth, Exeter, and Dover in New Hampshire, and Plymouth, Salem, Boston, Groton, Haverhill, Deerfield, Springfield, and Northfield in Massachusetts, and Providence, Portsmouth, Newport, and Warwick in Rhode Island, and Hartford, Wethersfield, and Windsor in Connecticut, to postpone communal affairs, such as roads, local police, care of the poor and schools, to affairs of state, such as war and peace, limits of territory, jurisdiction and defence. Each of these towns was the possible centre of an independent colony; and five of them (Exeter, Boston, Plymouth, Providence, and Hartford) became such.

This phenomenon in the origin of New England towns may not be unique; but to find anything like it in the Old World, we must run back into the remote past until we meet a case where people leaving the protection of a settled government sought a region foreign and remote; and there, first asserting and maintaining independent statehood,[1] finally rele-

---

[1] To this fact of statehood common in the history of so many of the early towns, I think is largely due that spirit of independence, as little republics, which sometimes asserted itself even against the paramount government, but was always finally reduced to due subordination. The mistake has been made of regarding this spirit of independence — a survival from earlier days — as an ultimate fact of political inde-

gated themselves or were relegated into subordinate communities, from which they developed into corporate bodies having essential resemblance to those New England towns which have attracted attention on both sides of the water, as something the precise like of which does not appear in recorded history.

The next phenomenon, though not peculiar to New England towns, is this, — that between their coming together either subject to some paramount government or living independent of any such government and their final incorporation as bodies politic, these village communities exercised certain rights and performed certain duties not unlike those which afterward appertained to them as incorporated towns. By common consent, it would seem, they divided some lands among themselves and held other lands for common use, either for wood or pasturage, and in both cases assuming corporate ownership so far at least as to make good title in the allottees. They also provided in respect to those communal necessities which, few and simple at first, increase with the growth of village communities. Nor is it unlikely, but on the contrary it is most likely, that for better understanding of their common interests they came together in assemblies, chose a chairman, appointed committees, and delegated certain powers to a select number of their body, just as they had done in their

pendence in later days. Nothing can be further from the truth. Towns were sometimes obliged to assume the duties of the state, and on the other hand, the state not infrequently discharged communal offices ; but when their character as state or town was ultimately determined, each was relegated to its own proper functions. All the powers and the very existence of towns are derived from the state. At any time it may unite or divide them, enlarge or diminish their powers, or even take them away altogether.

English parish vestries, and for that matter as reasonable people in all nations and in all ages have done and must still continue to do. In the absence of records, the facts of this stage of communal life are conjectural rather than determinate. From their later records, however, we learn some things which they did, but little as to the precise mode of doing them. This experience doubtless had great influence in shaping the form, determining the character, and regulating the conduct of towns after they became incorporated bodies; and indeed, I think that the later definition of their powers and duties by the state was mainly in confirmation of what had come to pass from the nature of things and their circumstances.

The third phenomenon is the erection of these communities into bodies politic by incorporation, not as units of the sovereign state,[1] but as dependent bodies owing their corporate existence and exercising all their delegated functions in strict subordination to the paramount power.

The last phenomenon presented by New England towns to which I shall advert is the promulgation by Massachusetts as early as 1636 of their rights, powers, and duties, with a completeness and precision to which the advanced civilization of two and a half centuries has found little to add. Of course new in-

---

[1] I cannot regard towns as units of the state, as some do. I do not see that the mere aggregation of like things produces an unlike thing, as that several hundreds of towns of derived and limited powers constitute a state of sovereign powers, or that a hundred copper cents can be constituent units of a gold dollar, or, in fine, that species by combination can form a new genus. I prefer to regard the state as an aggregation in a body politic of those units capable of forming a state, — the duly qualified inhabitants thereof, upon whom, in the last analysis, monarchies and even despotisms, as well as republics, rest.

stances and new applications of communal powers and duties have arisen, and others doubtless will arise in the future; but the principle — that of incorporation for communal purposes — remains the same as it was in the beginning.

I now proceed to consider the attempt to affiliate New England towns upon the English parish.

We all know what a New England town is to-day, — its organization, the source of its powers and privileges, and under what sanction it performs its duties. But what an English town or an English parish is, — what their several jurisdictions, powers, rights, duties, and relations to each other and to the sovereign authority are, — it is not easy to say with precision. Their origins reach back to a remote and clouded antiquity, and they are what they are, not by written laws, but by growth, prescription, and specially granted privileges, so varied and anomalous that any definition of them has almost as many exceptions as there are cases included in it.

There is another impediment to the successful investigation of English institutional origins. With us, in respect to our own, such questions excite no feeling more poignant than a rational curiosity as to the truth of history; but with our English brethren similar questions are burning questions, involving in their settlement either way not only the sacrifice of deeply seated political and ecclesiastical prejudices, but also important political and pecuniary interests. Hence in the discussion of them, as in a lawyer's brief, authorities which make for one side are set forth with fullness, while those which make for the other side are too frequently suppressed or slurred over.[1]

---

[1] In his *History of Representative Government*, Guizot has no-

In England, time out of mind, there has been contention between those who, on the one hand, would retain within parish control not only the prudentials of the church, but also the maintenance of roads, the care of the poor, etc. ; and those, on the other hand, who would withdraw from an essentially ecclesiastical body like the parish the care of matters purely secular, and intrust the direction of them to that civil corporate body known as the town.   This contention arrays people into parties : one claiming that since, in the order of institution, the towns antedate the church and include the great body of qualified inhabitants, by fair right they should control those secular interests which belong to municipal bodies ; and the other, denying the premises, and asserting that the parish is not only the older institution but that it is and always has been a secular institution, demand that its control of secular affairs be continued.

And so this historical question becomes an economic question upon the settlement of which depends the patronage of office and the disbursement of the large sums annually expended in municipal affairs, — whether they should be open to the whole body of qualified inhabitants of the town, or continue as they have been, in the management of the parish, which, though composed mainly of the same persons as the town, is nevertheless by its possession of machinery essentially ecclesiastical, and, under the influence of ecclesiastics beyond popular control, confines to a few persons rights and duties which belong to all.

tice the influence of political predilection in shaping the argument and determining the conclusion both of Whigs and Tories, — the former in support of popularizing parliamentary representation, claiming for it a remote antiquity ; and the Tories, always willing to restrict popular privileges, asserting that everything which sustains these privileges was a late innovation.

On any question of English local history fairly treated, I defer to the English decision of it, however at variance with any opinion I have drawn of original authorities; for I am aware that an American must mainly read those authorities along the lines, and that only a native is privileged to read between the lines, where the truest part of history is always to be found.

But I am not willing to accept any history, foreign or domestic, written to serve a party or an interest; and such, after careful examination, I think is Toulmin Smith's "The Parish," greatly relied on by those who find the origin of New England towns in the English parish of the seventeenth century.

Toulmin Smith claims that the parish antedates the town; that its origin and functions were secular, not ecclesiastical, but that this secular body had drawn to itself certain ecclesiastical functions; to all this is opposed authority equally high, at least, and the manifest tendency of ecclesiastical power everywhere and in all ages to usurp secular powers.

Brande[1] says that "in the earliest ages of the church, the parochia was the district placed under the superintendence of the bishop, and was equivalent to the diocese; . . . But although parishes were originally ecclesiastical divisions, they may now be more properly considered as coming under the class of civil divisions." A late writer whose work[2] is commended by our associate Dr. Channing, as "the best description of the English parish at the present day," says: "Though in its origin the parish was probably framed upon the old township, it soon became a purely eccle-

---

[1] *Dictionary of Science, Literature, and Art,* title "Parish."
[2] Elliot's *The State and the Church*, p. 55.

siastical division, and the permanent officers were ecclesiastics also. The church-wardens, with the parishioners in vestry assembled, presided over by the clergyman, managed the affairs and administered the parochial funds. Gradually the tendency increased to treat the parish, for purposes of local administration, as a unit as well as an ecclesiastical division; and it in particular acquired statutory authority to impose rates to provide for its poor and to elect officers to collect and administer the funds belonging to it; whilst on the parish from the earliest times the old common law had always imposed the duty of maintaining and repairing the public roads."

But against all this Toulmin Smith contends,[1] that the parish is an essential part of the fabric of the state; that its original and main work and functions were secular; that those who seek to represent these as being ecclesiastical are truly, though without always intending it, enemies both to the religious and civil institutions of the country;[2] that the parish was made for the administration of justice, keeping the peace, collection of taxes, and the other purposes incidental to civil government and local well-being; that ecclesiastical authorities are very anxious to make it appear that parishes took their rise from ecclesiastical arrangements; that ecclesiastics no sooner became established in parishes than they endeavored to make their authority paramount; that the old meaning of the word *town* was simply what we now call parish, and that in country churchyards, in parishes where there has never been any *town* in the modern

---

[1] *The Parish*, pp. 11, 12, 15, 23, 26, 33.

[2] This and similar passages, I think, justify me in calling his work a partisan affair.

sense, inscriptions will be found, both of old and recent date, naming the parish, township, or otherwise, as the *town*.[1]

Now, whatever may be the truth in this conflict of authorities respecting the nature of towns and parishes before 1600 or after 1630, it would be much to our purpose if we could learn what the parish was between those dates; for then the education, character, and prejudices of those who were to make New England towns were mainly formed by their participation in English parish affairs. What, then, during these formative years was there in the conduct of English parishes that would predispose our towns to accept or to reject them with their vestry system of administration, as models of their town organizations and the conduct of their town-meetings?

This question may be answered in part by a quotation from Toulmin Smith's book : " One of the most daring and insidious of ecclesiastical encroachments has been the attempt to interfere with the election of

[1] It is by such argument as this that Toulmin Smith endeavors to prove the legal identity of the corporations in England known as towns and parishes; and to the same effect I have found, under some mislaid reference, the following : " Memorandum that this year 1581, by the consent of the parish of Stowmarket there was grant made to two persons of the ground commonly called the town ground of Stowmarket for the term of three years paying to the church-warden . . . and the town further do condition, etc. ; " from which another writer infers that the town and parish were interchangeable names of the same body. In that case we should have the parish (that is, the town) consenting to a lease made by the town (that is, the parish); or, in other words, the town makes a lease, and then the town consents to its own act, which is absurd. The real transaction seems to have been this : the town, one corporation and owner in fee, makes a lease of the " town ground ; " and the parish, another corporation, having some interest in that ground, for a valuable consideration paid to the church-wardens, the parish representatives, consents to the lease, thereby giving a clear title.

church-wardens, and to take the election of one of
them out of the hands of the 'temporal estate,' and
make the office the donative of the parson.   This
attempt was made by certain ecclesiastical canons
adopted by Convocation in 1603." [1]   This was one of
the one hundred and forty-one articles of the Book of
Canons which passed both houses of Convocation in
May, 1603, and was ratified by the king, but was
afterward declared by the courts to bind only the
clergy, not having been confirmed by act of Parliament; [2] but long before this it had done its intended
repressive work upon the Puritans, against whom it
was chiefly aimed.   Besides the article already quoted,
designed to enlarge the power of the established
clergy in parish affairs, were others respecting parish
clerks.   Among the duties of the parish were the
repairs of the church edifice ; and under cover of this,
Laud, some years later, caused the restoration of those
paintings and relics of superstition and idolatry, as
the Puritans thought them, which had been destroyed
after the Reformation. [3]   And in general, the parish
vestry, sometimes legally and sometimes otherwise,
and always by the power and influence of its officers,
became an effective instrument in the enforcement of
those cruel measures which caused so much suffering
to the Puritans, and finally drove them into exile in
New England.   This, surely, was not precisely the
education, training, and personal experience which
would cause them to become so enamored of the parish system as to make it the model of their Massachusetts towns.

---

[1] *The Parish*, 201.
[2] Neal's *History of the Puritans*, ii. 57.
[3] *Ibid.* 240.

After the Reformation an English church with its parish vestry performed a function of the English government, and its foundation was in the constitution. A local church was part of a system co-extensive with England, recognizing no superior, no equal, no other.

The creed, ritual, liturgy, and discipline of one church were those of every other established church; and all were ordained or sanctioned by Parliament, — a secular, not a spiritual body.

Its ministers, each of whom was a corporation, were not chosen by the local church or parish, but on presentation of the patron in whom that right was private property subject to sale or mortgage, and who was not infrequently influenced by most unworthy motives, were instituted by the bishops of the diocese; and their support was not by voluntary contributions of the people, but mainly by tithes exacted from them under parliamentary laws.

Its secular or prudential affairs were managed by the vestry, whose powers, enlarged sometimes by law and sometimes by ecclesiastical usurpations, had come to include matters having no relation to religion.

That the high-churchmen who settled Virginia should adopt this system, as they did, would accord with the fitness of things; but that Puritans should do so was not likely nor in accordance with the facts.

For the Puritans who came to Massachusetts Bay were in revolt against both sides of the system; and no sooner had they reached Salem than they swept away every vestige of it. And not long after Endicott, as has been said, shipped the Brownes back to England for openly expressing what non-conformists had professed, — loyalty and love for the Church of England. So wide and profound was the change they had undergone since leaving their native shores, that those who had been non-conforming Puritans in England became independents in Massachusetts Bay, and ever after, in creed, discipline, and church order, were in no essential respect distinguishable from the Separatists at Plymouth.

What, then, was the independency which Winthrop and his people set up, and whence came it? The Puritan church system established on New England soil, regarded either as a protest against the Arminian tendencies of the English Church, or as a mode of ecclesiastical government having relations to civil society, was an exotic brought from Geneva to England, and thence to New England. The Church of England, at the time of the great emigration, was led by the Arminian Laud; the Puritan Church of New England embraced the creed of Calvin as interpreted and enforced by the Synod of Dort. The Church of England was dominated by a hierarchy to which the churches in every parish in England were in subjection. A Genevan church chose its own creed, established its own discipline and order of worship, called its own pastor and supported him by voluntary contributions.

It was this simple Genevan system which the refugees from persecution in the days of Mary brought back on their return from the Continent in the days of Elizabeth and James; and it was this Genevan system, theological and ecclesiastical, which Elizabeth and James and Charles sought to crush by all the powers of government, civil and ecclesiastical; and it was from the persecution brought on by the conflict between the two systems that they fled to New England; nor did it cease even there.[1]

They fled from the Arminian Laud; what likelihood of their bringing Arminianism to Boston? They fled from ecclesiastical exactions countenanced, and in some particulars enforced, by the Church of England vestry and parish authorities; what greater likelihood of their choosing an English parish as the model of a New England town?

Of course, in both systems — that which they left behind and that which they built up in their new homes — there was one common factor, an Englishman; an Englishman with the instincts, traditions, and habits of his race, — a race averse indeed to new methods and inclined to old methods, but, nevertheless, never allowing them to stand long in the way of needed reforms or to impede the course of essential justice, as Strafford with the law on his side found, and Charles I. with the constitution on his side, and as did James II. when a convention assumed the powers of Parliament and changed the succession to the crown against the claim of divine right and established order. The Puritans were Englishmen in England; they were no more and no less than Englishmen in Boston Bay. We need not be surprised, therefore, nor draw any unwarranted conclusions

---

[1] The influences which prompted the movement of Laud in 1634 to overthrow the Massachusetts charter may be gathered from Thomas Morton's letter written from England, in May, 1634, to William Jeffreys in Massachusetts; "which shows what opinion is held amongst them [their lordships] of King Winthrop with all his inventions and his Amsterdam fantastical ordinances, his preachings, marriages, and other abusive ceremonies, which do exemplify his detestation to the Church of England and the contempt of his Majesty's authority and wholesome laws, which are and will be established in these parts, *invitâ Minervâ.*" (*New English Canaan*, Prince Society ed. 63.)

from the fact that in their new homes they did some things after the old fashion.

And because New England towns issued warrants and posted notices for town-meetings, and chose chairmen and conducted business precisely as they had done in English towns or vestries, and as civilized people everywhere do, it does not follow that they modeled their towns to the pattern of an English parish.

What are the essentials of the two systems respectively? In the English system the Church of England, with its associated parish, was a constituent part of the English government, and its bishops were an estate in the realm. In Massachusetts, on the contrary, neither religion nor ecclesiasticism was a constituent in the constitution, — the charter of a land company. Both were functions assumed by the General Court, and were ultimately lopped off with no remaining scar. However influential the clergy may have been, — and their influence can hardly be overestimated, — they had neither place in government, nor summons to the General Court, nor voice there unless asked, and no more political power in the affairs of state, town, or church than other freemen. Nor was their loss of comparative influence in later days by reason of their elimination from the constitution: they were never in it.

What has been said of the clergy may also be said of the church. It had no part in the government, general or local. It sent no delegates to either house, and even its own synods were held only by express permission of the General Court.

Of the forces formative of a constitution, that is the most original and dominating which longest survives.

The potent has permanence; the non-essential falls away. And so in New England towns to-day the full current of their democratic life-blood flows without a strain from the veins of that composite ecclesiastical, hierarchical, and civil body known as the English parish. Even its name must have been distasteful; for it was sedulously avoided by people and legislators for fifty years or more, and then came into use with precinct and district, chiefly to describe a part of a town set off to form another religious society.[1]

For the foregoing reasons I am not in accord with those who trace the origin of New England towns to English parishes or find essential resemblances between them.[2]

[1] The relation of the town to the church within it came to be, outside of Boston, the same as that of the modern religious society to the church with which it is connected; that is, it built and kept in repair the church edifice, and its consent was necessary to the settlement of a minister nominated by the church, and it determined the amount of his salary to be levied on the taxable persons and estates within the town. All these matters were transacted in town-meeting duly called, and record thereof entered by the town clerk. When a town was found too large, or its inhabitants too numerous to be accommodated in a single church, or for other sufficient reason, it was divided territorially to form a second church. This second church, like the first, in its secular affairs was based on the taxable persons and estates within its limits; and the new religious society was called the second parish, district, or precinct, — precinct being, I think, its legal designation. This new precinct was a *quasi* corporation for religious purposes, and, like the town, required a clerk to keep its records, and assessors and collectors. Its powers and duties were defined by statute; and we then begin to hear the word "parish," — a survival, and the only survival I find of the English parish, — in common use as the most convenient designation of the new division.

[2] In this investigation I have not been unmindful of the danger which lurks in general statements of facts, or in conclusions from them in respect to the complicated and anomalous nature of English towns and parishes at different times and in different parts of England. Though I believe I have good authority for every statement I have made, yet when I see that English specialists on the subject differ so

In the development of the autonomy of the New England colonies there were three distinct forces aside from soil, climate, and situation, all acting toward a common end and dominated in a sense before unusual by a common public sentiment, which formed the atmosphere out of which neither could have lived and done its appointed work. These were the state, the town, and the church; and these three, though in some sense distinct, were not three states, but one state, since the fundamental idea of a state implies its unity, however its powers are distributed or by whatever agencies its functions are executed. Yet they were distinct in this sense : they were organizations, not merely several collections of individuals performing certain functions of government. They were corporate bodies, each having a life of its own, but all working together for the common welfare. The powers of neither were inherent. The state derived its powers from the crown ; and the town and church theirs severally from the state.

I find, as I think, that the Puritan state and town on New England soil were essentially indigenous, and their development the outcome of life under the new conditions. The charter of Massachusetts, it is true, was of English origin and with English definition of its powers ; but from its start on Massachusetts soil it swiftly developed from a land company into a gov-

widely among themselves, notwithstanding their opportunities for local study, and aided as they are by traditions and other sources of information not accessible to non-residents, I cannot hope to have avoided errors. It may be observed, however, that if any historical question is to be settled on general facts, — by the trend of the stream rather than by its occasional windings and retrogressions, — it is the one before us, in respect to which strong probabilities have a determinative force when the facts are disputed.

ernment proper, exercising the powers and functions of sovereignty with only nominal subjection to the parent state; and New England towns in like manner developed their autonomies with slight reference to their English analogues, but mainly under the influence of the new government, and entirely in its spirit, — that of a new departure in a new world.

The very settlement and permanence of New England were due to influences not at all in accord with the economic or political motives which before had led to the formation of colonies with the permission of the parent state. It was religion, but not the church, — religion in the life of individuals, not religion as a corporate power. To it, as such, the colonists accorded no independent place in their system, but held it in strict subordination to the civil power.

Thus Massachusetts, in some respects unique in the motives which led to its settlement and original in transforming its land-company charter into a frame of general government, ordered the founding and character of its towns, churches, and other institutions on the basis of an independent commonwealth. But it is the origin of her towns with which I am mainly concerned.

It is not always easy to fix the beginning or the end of an institution. We may observe, indeed, when its sun rises and when it sets; but where begins its dawn or when its twilight ends is quite another matter, and not amenable to exact definition. And so is it in respect to Massachusetts towns. If we refer their origin to the first enumeration of their powers, our search ends with the often quoted ordinance of the General Court, March 3, 1636;[1] if to their

---

[1] *Massachusetts Records*, i. 172.

power and liability to sue and be sued, then with the statute of 1694; or if to their formal incorporation as bodies politic, then only with a search for nearly two hundred and fifty years, ending with the statute of 1785.

The period of uncertain twilight, therefore, is between the possible unrecorded action of Endicott and his Council after the arrival of the charter at Salem in 1628 and the ordinance of 1636 above referred to; and this period I shall now attempt to explore with such lights as are afforded.

Of the several attempts to form settlements along the New England coast prior to 1628 apart from Plymouth, that at Sagadahoc, in 1607, was a total failure; those of Weston, Gorges, Morton, and Wollaston, in or about Weymouth and Quincy, between 1622 and 1625, came to naught; and those in New Hampshire, by Thompson at Little Harbor and the Hiltons at Dover, in 1623, after a sickly existence for some years, were brought under the Massachusetts jurisdiction in 1641, and so remained until their formation into a royal government, July 10, 1679. These enterprises did not stand the strain of labor, want, and sacrifice.

A few individuals with their families, as Maverick at Winnisimmet, Blackstone at Boston, and Walford at Charlestown, — probably survivals of wrecked companies, — maintained isolated plantations; but the largest company of Englishmen north of Plymouth were the remnants of those who, under the direction of English capitalists, between 1623 and 1626 had undertaken to form a plantation in connection with the fisheries at Cape Ann, from which they removed to Salem.

This settlement, for some time under the care of Roger Conant, became the basis of the Massachusetts Bay Colony ; and those interested in it — chiefly West England people, — reinforced by London capitalists in 1627, obtained from the Council of New England a grant of land, March 19, 1628, which included the greater part of Massachusetts as now bounded, and, June 20 of the same year, sent over John Endicott as governor, who reached Salem on September 6 following. The next year, March 4, 1629, the king granted them a charter.

This, it is to be remembered, was a land company formed as a business enterprise, whose policy determined the nature of the first settlement, and finally the character of the Massachusetts towns. Their plan contemplated the building of one central town capable of defense against foreign foes, and so regulated that while it allowed the planting of other towns in due time, it would nevertheless present an unbroken front to Indian hostilities such as had devastated Virginia,[1] and threatened the sporadic settlers at Winnisimmet.

This also ought to be remembered, — that when Winthrop and the East England Puritans, in the autumn of 1629, embarked their fortunes in the enterprise, it assumed a more distinctively religious character which did much to shape the character of New England. For while the Company from the first — greatly influenced, doubtless, by the very reverend and truly pious John White of Dorchester, by

[1] "Be not too confident of the fidelity of the salvages . . . Our countrymen have suffered by their too much confidence in Virginia." — Cradock to Endicott, February 16, 1829, Young's *Chronicles of Massachusetts Bay*, 136.

some regarded as the real father of New England — provided for the conversion of the Indians,[1] Winthrop and his associates seem to have contemplated the grander scheme of a commonwealth in church as well as in state.

As I have said, Endicott arrived at Salem early in September, 1628, and as governor immediately took charge of the plantation. Before setting sail for his government he was doubtless instructed as to his powers and duties; but these instructions, if ever reduced to writing, have not been preserved. We may assume, however, that they were in accord with those sent over to him in letters under date of February 16, April 17, and May 28 of the next year, 1629, and the accompanying ordinances.

A résumé of these powers and duties in respect to matters now in hand will give some idea of the influences which Endicott brought to bear in forming the character of towns and churches before the coming of Winthrop, and throw light upon proceedings after that event, where the records are silent.

On April 30, 1629, the General Court in England declared its intention " to settle and establish an absolute government at our plantation " in Massachusetts Bay, and in pursuance thereof elected Endicott (who had been at Salem nearly eight months) governor ; and he received a duplicate of the charter, and the seal of the Company. With his council he had full legislative and executive powers consistent with the ' charter and not contrary to the laws of England ; could seize and hold the lands claimed by Oldham

---

[1] " And we trust you will not be unmindful of the main end of your plantation, by endeavoring to bring the Indians to the knowledge of the Gospel." — Cradock to Endicott, *ut supra*, 133.

under the Gorges patent and expel intruders thereon; could set up a government there and build a town and choose a minister for it; arrange with the old planters in respect to the lands they occupied, allot lands and convey them by the Company's deed under seal, build a house for the ministers at the public charge, and build one chief town and determine location of all others.

In the execution of these large and varied powers, it is not altogether likely that a man of Endicott's positive views and character, exemplified by his excision of the cross from the banner of England and the expulsion of the Church of England Brownes, would find models for his towns in an English parish, thus engrafting an anomalous and highly artificial system on bare creation.

The population of Salem, including those who came with Endicott in September, 1628, was not above sixty persons,[1] to whom Higginson added two hundred the next year; and all, " by common consent of the old planters, were combined into one body politic under the same governor."[2] By sending Endicott and Higginson with their companies to Salem, the Company determined where " the town " should be built, houses erected, and all to be fortified, as Higginson informs us, with " great ordnance ; " and thither came the greater part of Winthrop's fleet in June, 1630. So the location of the principal town was designated by the Company in England; and yet it shows the nature of this determining power, that when the Company was transferred to Massachusetts Bay and had examined the situation more carefully,

---

[1] Young's *Chronicles of Massachusetts Bay*, 13 and note.
[2] *Ibid.* 259.

Cambridge, not Salem, was made the capital town. Plans formed in England gave way to the exigencies of the new situation; and this was the case all through their history.

Thus Salem was the first town established under the Massachusetts patent. The next was Charlestown, and in this wise. Walford had been there some years when Graves and Bright, probably with the Spragues, were sent by Endicott in 1629, agreeably to the instructions of the Company, to forestall the intrusion of Oldham under the Gorges patent. Graves was the Company's engineer, and went to Charlestown to build the town ; and Bright was the minister sent to preach to the people and presumably to gather a church.

Such was the origin of the first two permanent towns set up on Massachusetts Bay soil; and whatever else may be in doubt, such as the precise time of the separation of communal affairs from the more general charter government and their commitment to the town as an organized body politic, it seems to be clear that the choice of their sites, their laying out, the building of their houses, their municipal and religious organizations, whatever they may have been, were by the authority and express order of the General Court, and without the slightest reference, so far as can be detected, to English towns or parishes. And I think the sequel shows that this was also true in respect to all later towns.

I have called these settlements at Salem and Charlestown towns, and such they finally became; but at what time they assumed these communal functions does not clearly appear. They were never incorporated even by giving them names, as was the case with some other towns; and if such naming was equivalent to incorporation, as Professor Parker holds, the omission perhaps implies that they were regarded as already municipal corporations in 1630. The emigrants to both places were entitled to lands by allotment and conveyance thereof under the Company's seal; but no evidence of such deeds, if any were ever made, has survived, nor are there records of such allotments until some years later, though there is ample evidence of private ownership and cultivation as early as 1629, when Higginson came. It is not improbable that Endicott allotted to each party the land to which he was entitled, or for lack of such allotment that each chose for himself, as had been agreed that he might.

But neither the people gathered at Salem under Conant nor the governments set up there and at Charlestown by the Company constituted a town in the modern sense of that word, and least of all in the sense which has made New England towns famous in history. For a time they were something more than towns, and something less, — something more, since they were centres of the charter government in whose affairs they participated; something less, because they were denied the exclusive privilege of developing their local autonomy. Circumstances determined their final character.

We must therefore widen the basis for generalization, and I now recall the circumstances which attended the settlements in and about Boston Bay.

The first emigration under the Company was led by Endicott in 1628, the second by Higginson in 1629, and the third by Winthrop in 1630. This last landed at Salem, June 12, and found Endicott's plantation

— or colony, as Dudley called it — "in a sad and un-expected condition, above eighty of them being dead the winter before, and many of those alive weak and sick; all the corn and bread amongst them all hardly sufficient to feed them a fortnight." [1]   No marvel that Salem "pleased them not as a place for sitting down;" and five days later (June 17) Winthrop with a party came over to Boston Bay to explore the country. They sailed up the Mystic, and on their return to Salem reported in favor of Medford, as is supposed, for the site of "the town."   A later party preferred Cambridge; and accordingly their people and goods were brought around and landed at Charles-town, because from sickness they were too weak to carry their baggage and ordnance up the river; and from August 23 to September 28 Charlestown was the seat of government.

While in this deplorable condition — fifteen hun-dred people all weakened by the long voyage and many sick of fevers and scurvy, without houses or adequate shelter from the sultry heat of August, more trying to Englishmen than the winter cold — news came that the French were preparing to attack them. There are few sadder stories than theirs. In this complication of disasters, not less than a hundred of their number, discouraged at the prospect before them, returned to England in the same ships that had brought them over.

In this exigency of their affairs, too weak to fortify Cambridge against the enemy, they changed their plans, and sought safety by "planting dispersedly," — some at Charlestown, some at Boston, some at

---

[1] Letter to the Countess of Lincoln in Young's *Chronicles of Massachusetts Bay*, 311.

Medford, some at Watertown, some at Roxbury, some at Saugus, and some at Dorchester.[1]

This was in August, 1630, less than a month from their coming into Boston Bay. A month later, September 7, the Court of Assistants " ordered that Trimountaine shalbe called Boston ; Mattapan, Dorchester; & the towne upon Charles Ryver, Waterton," [2] and this has ever since been regarded as equivalent to their incorporation. And thus we see that within three months after coming to shore in a wilderness the Company, contrary to their intention of building only a single town at first, were compelled by circumstances to lay the foundations of five towns, and permit the settlement of three others. And this, I think, is the origin of all later towns, — in the paramount power of the General Court, modified by the circum-

---

[1] Dudley, in Young's *Chronicles of Massachusetts Bay*, 313.

[2] *Massachusetts Records*, i. 75. This order suggests two inquiries. If intended as an act of incorporation, as it ever since has been regarded, why was Boston included, and Newtown, or Cambridge, omitted ? It may have been that the Court deemed the establishment of the government at Cambridge as an act of incorporation. And it is noticeable that some years after the capital had been transferred to Boston the Court, in 1638, ordered " that Newetowne shall henceforward be called Cambrige," thus following the precedent in the text. —*Ibid.* i. 228.

If the order was intended as an act of incorporation, why was it not expressed in terms, that the inhabitants of the places named should be bodies politic, with all the powers and subject to all the duties of like corporations in England so far as applicable to their situation ? As a lawyer, Winthrop knew that a corporation — which the Company was — could not create corporations, that being the prerogative of the crown ; and were this prerogative assumed, that it might be an awkward fact, if explanation were demanded, as it was in respect to so many things a few years later. In 1639 Winthrop told what his policy had been, — as little positive legislation as possible ; but " to raise up laws by practice and custom," as involving no transgression of the limitations in the charter. Was this an instance of the application of his good policy ?

stances of each particular case. As further evidence
of this, on the same day of the foregoing incorporation of Boston, Dorchester, and Watertown, it was
ordered " that no person shall plant in any place
within the limits of this patent, without leave from
the Governor and Assistants, or the major part of
them. Also, that a warrant shall presently be sent to
Aggawam, to command those that are planted there
forthwith to come away." [1]

What has been said accounts for the origin of Massachusetts towns so far as relates to their planting.
If we now look forward six years to the Act of the
General Court of March, 1635, we shall learn how
their powers were recognized by implication, and
what they were.[2]

But I admit that we must go deeper into the matter; for it may be fairly said that the Act of 1636 [3]
was essentially a recognition of the powers, rights, and
privileges already acquired and exercised by towns
at that date; and if so, the question still remains,
What were the origin and development of towns in
the form in which they now exist?

What we desire to learn, however, is not by what
principle of human nature, everywhere and at all
times apparent, it is, that every body of men who
find themselves associated with a view to permanent
residence in a particular place, after sufficient assurances of not being molested from without, forthwith

---

[1] *Massachusetts Records*, i. 76.

[2] *Ibid*. i. 172.

[3] It will be observed that this order confers upon towns no powers;
it is restrictive. The language is that the freemen of any town or
the major part of them shall *only* have power, and so forth. In the
Revision of 1660 (p. 195) the law is made positive by striking out
"only."

prepare to meet those communal necessities which arise in all communities; but rather what there was in the inherited or acquired character or training of Englishmen which differentiated the modes of development and results of their work from that of any other people. If they had kept records of their proceedings from the outset, we should be in a fair way to learn what we desire to know; but it was otherwise, for the earliest, those of Dorchester, began some time in 1631, though with only a single entry for that year, — a year after its settlement, — and those of Boston not until September, 1634, — four years after its settlement. But the records from what may be called the historic period, though meagre, throw some light upon the antecedent period, and indicate that the first subject which engaged their attention was, as naturally would be the case with all incipient communities, the distribution of their lands and assurance of boundaries and title. Then would follow simple police regulations, and regulations as to roads, churches, and schools. The matters must have been few and simple, for so they remained after they found it desirable to keep records of them.

Now, in respect to the first and most important of these matters, they were not relegated, as all settlers on territory not under a general government are, to mutual agreement, certainly not as to the quantity of land to which each was entitled, for that had been definitely fixed beforehand; nor would the question of quality arise until all desirable lands were taken up. And so we find, after these records begin, that party fences and use of common lands are subjects of most frequent attention.[1]

[1] It would be most interesting to learn precisely how they arranged

As has been said, the sites of the town within which allotments were to be made were fixed by the General Court, and the quantity of land to which each party was entitled, by ordinances in the nature of agreements between the Company and the settlers; and all that remained would be for each to receive his allotment by the proper authorities, or, that failing, to select for himself within certain prescribed limits, as he was entitled. And neither in these nor in any subsequent proceedings, whatever difficulties might come, would they find guidance in their experience in the affairs of an English town or parish. The Dorchester records, which seem to be typical, are instructive on this point. For the first three years there are hardly a dozen entries, and these chiefly of the character above described. At the end of their third year they seem to have developed their autonomy so far as to feel the necessity of bringing their action into regular and prescribed methods of procedure. But it is a little remarkable that if they came over as a fully organized English town and church, as some have thought they did, or with only lively recollections of their experience in the working machinery of an English parish vestry, they did not at once put it in operation; or if it be said that for aught we know they may have done so, then it is still more remarkable that after three years' trial of it, a dozen more years of tentative efforts were needed, as is indicated by their votes in 1633, 1636, 1642, and

with regard to these allotments; but the records, if any ever existed, — which is not likely, — have not been preserved. Probably they did the business in a very informal, but apparently mutually satisfactory way; for nothing is said about allotments (and the fact is noticeable) for some years after the first settlements, — in Dorchester for more than two years after, and in Boston for more than four.

1645, before they found that the requirements of their situation were met. No; as their situation and the exigencies of their unwonted life were entirely new to them, so they found it necessary to invent and develop new methods for a satisfactory adjustment. The records of other towns show a similar state of affairs, and the adoption of similar tentative efforts in the development of their autonomies.

But lack of space forbids the present consideration of the many interesting questions connected with the general subject of the origin of towns; and this especially, — how far the conditions of development of towns and town-meeting government in other New England colonies differed — and I think they did not essentially — from those imposed upon them in Massachusetts.

In the foregoing observations I have not attempted to traverse the whole ground covered by Mr. Adams, nor, indeed, have I confined myself to it; but have spoken chiefly of some matters which appear to me to require a more critical examination than they have yet received, so far as I am aware.

It now remains to say a few words on some points in Mr. Adams's paper; and in order to make clear the matters on which we appear to differ, I will begin with those on which we are agreed. We seem to agree : —

1. That the development of the Massachusetts government, under its charter, was on purely secular lines, and mainly without reference to English precedents or influence ; [1]

---

[1] I have heard it said, for example, that the Massachusetts Senate and House of Representatives, as two distinct houses, trace their

2. That the Massachusetts towns, neither in their origin nor in their development, have any essential relations to English towns, parishes, or vestries, but were planted by the authority and under the direction of the General Court; and that they regulated their communal affairs and modes of procedure therein agreeably to the requirements of novel subjects and unwonted conditions;

3. That the Massachusetts church, though modeled on the Genevan system in creed, discipline, and mode of worship, rested on a civil and not on an ecclesiastical basis, without independent powers or privileges, but holding all in due subordination to the General Court;[1] and

4. That the Massachusetts land system, or rather titles and assurances of estates, was anomalous, and is not easily to be understood at this day.[2]

origin back through the two colonial houses of the Magistrates and the Deputies, to the Houses of the Lords and of the Commons. The truth is, that the division of the General Court into two houses, sitting apart from each other, in 1643, was owing to a strictly local and even ludicrous circumstance.

[1] Ralph Smith was not permitted to go out to Massachusetts Bay unless he would bind himself "not to exercise the ministrey within the lymitts of our plantation, neither publique nor private, without the consent and approbation of the government there established by us," and "to submit to such orders as shall be there established." *Massachusetts Records*, 37 f., 390, as quoted in 9 Gray's *Reports*, 505.

[2] I yield to no one in admiration for Mr. Doyle's *English in America*, but I should not select as an example of his best treatment of colonial subjects the following passage quoted with approval by Mr. Adams: "In New England the soil was granted by the government of the colony, not to an individual, but to a corporation. It was from the corporation that each occupant claimed his right. . . . The New England township was a landholder." This statement overlooks, first, the quite numerous and very large grants of land to leading men in the colony, either as dividends on their stock or for eminent services rendered. Secondly, it overlooks the orders of the Company in Eng-

Now for the matters in respect to which we appear to differ.

The distinction between "inhabitants" and "proprietors," about which Mr. Adams and Mr. Goodell seem to be at variance, raises a somewhat difficult question which I am not quite sure that I fully understand; but as far as I do, I think there are grounds for Mr. Goodell's *caveat*. Mr. Adams's views respecting the origin, development, and autonomy of Massachusetts towns differ so widely — and in my judgment, for the better — from much that passes for history,

land to Endicott at Salem for the conveyance to individuals, as they were entitled, of lands by the Company's deeds under seal; and, as I think, that all titles, whether by deed or allotment by the Company, or by its agents, — which, as I conceive, were the towns *pro hac vice*, — were holdings from the Company and not from the town. In no just sense were the towns landholders; that is, they neither bought nor sold nor leased lands; nor, save some common lands, did the towns hold them for community use. In strictness of law, the towns not being legally incorporated bodies politic, — for then, as now, one corporation cannot create another corporation; that being a prerogative of sovereignty, — they could not take, and therefore could not make, title. Those proceedings were, as I have said, anomalous, and hard to understand. Nevertheless, whatever they wished to do they found a way of doing in sublime disregard of English law and usages. Doubtless the General Court said from time to time that certain towns should "have enlargement," or that lands should "belong" to them; and it is also true that the towns held such lands, some of which they distributed by allotment, and others held for common use, and that these titles are now good, but on what theory, unless that of long possession, as the colonists claimed in Andros's time, it is difficult to understand. It would seem, however, that all land-titles to-day within the limits of Massachusetts Bay rest upon conveyances in some way from that Company; but there can be no question that the control which the towns, whether owners in fee or implied agents of the great Land Company, exercised in their distribution, had great influence in developing and forming the character of their autonomy. And in this aspect of the matter, Mr. Doyle undoubtedly well says, that "of the various rights of the New England township the most important, perhaps, was the territorial."

that I am inclined to accept them not only as a valuable contribution to the studies of the subject, but as generally sound; and yet, if I may dissent from some of his positions, — and that, I suppose, is what I am here for, — I should put some things a little differently, or at least use a different nomenclature.   For example, I do not perceive the analogy which he perceives between the General Court and Court of Assistants on the one hand, and the "inhabitants" and "selectmen" on the other, in respect to the subjects or to the modes of their action severally, — certainly it was not institutional; nor do I think that "freemen or inhabitants" are interchangeable terms equally descriptive of the same class of people; nor that "the inhabitants of the towns were those owning lands, — the freeholders, — who were all members of the congregation;" nor that "inhabitants" of towns "were in the nature of stockholders in a modern corporation."   To me these and some similar expressions convey ideas foreign to the homely simplicity of those early people and the nature of their affairs.   As I have said, the difference between us may be one merely of nomenclature; but my way of putting the matter is this, — and of course I prefer it to Mr. Adams's way : —

My idea of a seventeenth-century Massachusetts town is that it was almost exclusively an agricultural community, having little or nothing to do with manufactures except of the simplest kind, or trade, or with anything in which "stock" could be taken.   Beyond assurance of their own lands and of their interest in common lands, the just levy and economical expenditure of communal taxes, the education of their children and the care of their souls, their interests, wants, and desires were few and of the simplest kind, and will not bear being raised by the imagination ;

That the " inhabitant " included all male adults, who, either by general laws or town regulations, were permitted permanently to reside within the town limits, irrespective of their ownership of lands ;

That the whole body of people within the town consisted, first, of those who had been admitted freemen of the colony; second, of those who by original voluntary association or by subsequent vote, express or implied, had become permanent residents ; third, of that miscellaneous class of people, who, as servants and laborers, were mainly adjuncts to families and had little stake in society; and finally, of all other persons, as women and children, not usually reckoned as members of the body politic of a town ;

That in the early years of towns, as their records indicate, the first three classes above mentioned, without strict regard to their several rights, assembled " in general meeting of the inhabitants," and there, without much formality in their proceedings, disposed of their few and simple communal affairs ; but as these became more complicated or of greater magnitude, the legal rights of these several classes were more sharply defined and strictly enforced. The freemen, legally inhabitants of the town, were the sole electors of all colonial officers, deputies to the General Court, and voters on questions of a public nature as distinct from those merely communal; and though there seems to have been no uniform rule or practice in all towns, that which appears to have been most common was for all adult inhabitants, whether freemen or landholders or otherwise, to vote on all questions of communal affairs ; and this was made law in 1641.

And with this simple array of their forces, these towns, unique in their origin, lacking essential experience of like circumstances, and without ecclesiastical interference or restraints save those imposed by the General Court, after a few years learned to manage their municipal affairs with such wisdom and success, that in the course of time they so enlarged their views, but without overstepping the bounds the law had set up, that they became a power which modified the action of the government, and in the fullness of time most effective agencies in the dismemberment of the empire, and so famous throughout the civilized world.

POLITICAL MAXIMS

An Address delivered before the Bostonian Society,
December 12, 1893

POLITICAL MAXIMS

ADDRESS BEFORE THE BOSTONIAN SOCIETY, DECEM-
BER 12, 1893

JAMES OTIS'S words arraigning the commercial
policy of Great Britain, so hostile to colonial interests,
were the first of their kind ever uttered before a judicial tribunal on this continent. They were heard far
beyond the walls of this room,[1] and to them John
Adams attributed a powerful influence in bringing
forward the controversy which resulted in the sever-
ance of the empire ; but to no single cause or agency
was that event attributable. A hundred years before
this it was said in legislative assemblies, by the farmer's fireside, in the shops of mechanics, and by those
following the plough, that " The Rights of Englishmen follow them to the end of the earth ; " and " No
Representation, No Taxation." In no place on this
continent were these words heard earlier or oftener
than in the old State House, and this, perhaps, justifies
me in making them prominent in my present address
to the Bostonian Society.

However that may be, these political maxims soon
became the shibboleth of political action in thirteen
colonies, and were powerful in bringing on and carrying through the American Revolution. They now

---

[1] Otis's argument against writs of assistance was made in 1761,
before the Superior Court then sitting in the Council Chamber of the
old State House in Boston, where the present address was delivered.

find place in Bills of Rights. They have shaped constitutions and colored history.

I shall return to them; but first I wish to say a word about the class of epigrammatic phrases to which they belong.

In every age the wise have sought to express their highest thought and deepest feeling in apothegms. Men of science have their axioms; jurists, their legal maxims respecting the rights of persons and of property; the great divines, their epigrammatic phrases of doctrine; literary masterpieces are full of epigrams; and the common people have their proverbs, their songs, and their ballads. No class is without them, and none which is not profoundly influenced by them. Better far in the van of battle than the justice of their cause are the national airs and patriotic maxims of a people.

"I knew a very wise man," said Fletcher of Saltoun, "who believed that, if a man were permitted to make all the ballads, he need not care who should make the laws of a nation." It were worth inquiry who was the "very wise man" whom Fletcher heard. Not Bacon, certainly, for he was dead long before Fletcher was born; and for the same reason, not Sir Philip Sidney, though the thought was not far from Sidney's own, when he said, "I never heard the old song of Percy and Douglas that I found not my heart moved more than with a trumpet."

But though the words which caught Fletcher's ear fell not from the living lips of Bacon, still I think that in one of the most acute of his observations he has given the reason why to song and ballad rather than to maxim or proverb should be assigned a higher place among those influences which govern mankind. For poetry, he says, " being as a plant that cometh of the lust of the earth, without a formal seed, it hath sprung up and spread abroad more than any other kind. But to ascribe unto it that which is due for the expressing of affections, passions, corruptions, and customs, we are beholden to poets more than to the philosophers' works." [1]

The song of the people is neither polished nor precise. Its power is its sincerity. Academic songs and ballads seldom go deep into the hearts of the people. To reach the popular heart, they must spring from the people, or at least voice their sentiments. Dibdin's sea-songs were worth more for manning the royal navy than Campbell's matchless lyrics.

While song is true and sincere, proverbs, maxims, and epigrams seldom express more than half-truths — or truths not always true. But their power is none the less on that account.

Bacon noticed this also ; and over against the maxims he quoted he placed opposing maxims. And Archbishop Whately, in commenting on Bacon, has given examples, such as these : " Take care of the pence and the pounds will take care of themselves ; " " Be not penny-wise and pound-foolish ; " " The more haste the worse speed ; " " Wait awhile, that we may make an end the sooner ; " " Take Time by the forelock ; " and " Time and tide for no man bide." Coleridge noticed in his day that " the rustic whistled, with equal enthusiasm, ' God Save the King ' and ' Britons never shall be slaves.' "

Perhaps no legal maxim is more dear to those of the English blood than Coke's " A man's house is his castle." It is the security of his family, and associ-

---

[1] *Advancement of Learning*, Book 2.

ated with home-bred rights and joys, — a maxim which gave occasion to what Lord Brougham regards the finest passage in Pitt's oratory : " The poorest man may in his cottage bid defiance to all the forces of the crown.   It may be frail — its roof may shake — the wind may blow through it — the storm may enter — the rain may enter — but the King of England cannot enter ! all his force dares not cross the threshold of that ruined tenement." [1]

It has been said that maxims are seldom more than half-truths ; and Dr. Johnson thought that " in all pointed sayings some degree of accuracy must be sacrificed to conciseness."

Political maxims, though generally true to the spirit of law, are often contrary to its letter, and oftener still, while true to sentiment, are false to fact ; but sentiment rather than reason rules the world.

I once heard a distinguished orator scorn and ridicule the often-quoted English constitutional maxim that " the king can do no wrong," as though it were a rule of royal morals.   It is nothing of the sort.   Its equivalent is and must be in every government.   It merely asserts that sovereignty reposes somewhere ; and, inasmuch as there is nothing higher than the king in sovereignties, or the people in democracies, the king in one case and the people in the other must be presumed to be right.   And therefore the English say, " The king can do no wrong," and we say that " The sober second thought of the people is always right."

The English people have one advantage, for if the king *should* do wrong they can decapitate him — as they once did ; and they drove another into exile : an

[1] Brougham's *Statesmen.*

awkward piece of business for us, in case our sovereign does wrong! The maxim is a wise one for both peoples.

Another English political maxim and perhaps the most potent that ever fell from English lips is this, that " Englishmen carry English rights and privileges with them to the ends of the earth." This maxim really expressed the correlation of allegiance and protection of English subjects wherever they might be; that wherever the Englishman went, he owed indefeasible allegiance to his sovereign, and might always claim his protection. In a word, once an Englishman, always and everywhere an Englishman. Wherever he goes, England requires his allegiance and may demand his services; wherever he goes, he may demand the protection of his sovereign, and fleets and armies fly to his aid. That was the theory; but our fathers found it convenient to forget half of the maxim: they claimed English protection, but forgot English allegiance! This doctrine Englishmen and their descendants in this country have sometimes claimed and sometimes denied, as was for their interest. It lay at the foundation of the right claimed by the British government to impress its subjects though found on American ships; and in 1812 it had much to do with bringing on the war. Our countervailing maxim at that time was " Free Trade and Sailors' Rights."

But at an earlier day, whenever British legislation affected the colonists unfavorably, they claimed that they possessed all the rights of Englishmen; that is, that whatever rights an Englishman living in England might possess and enjoy, an Englishman and his descendants living in America might possess and enjoy. An absurd claim. The maxim meant simply this and no more : that the King's subjects born in America, on going to England, should possess and enjoy all those rights and privileges that Englishmen born in England and living there might possess and enjoy. We have incorporated its just interpretation into our Constitution : that " The citizens of each State shall be entitled to all privileges and immunities of citizens in the several States." [1]

That is, a citizen of Massachusetts going to South Carolina, for example, shall be entitled to all the rights and privileges of a citizen of that State. It is hardly necessary to add that it does not mean that a citizen of Massachusetts going to South Carolina carries with him all or any of the privileges he enjoyed in Massachusetts, though that was at one time claimed.

But whatever its true meaning, this maxim has done more than any other to make England, next to Rome, the greatest power for civilization the world ever saw. It encouraged the spirit of colonization. For when the colonists went forth, the British Lion stalked before them, and over them floated the protecting banner of England. This nerved their hearts in distant and perilous expeditions which other people feared to make ; and it inspired them with courage and constancy which no other people exhibited. It lent keenness to the edge, and firmness to the temper of their swords. They went forth with insolence, and often acted with brutality, as well as with courage and self-reliance. They assumed that they had rights which it would be preposterous for Spaniards, Frenchmen, or Dutchmen to claim ; but they braved the perils of the sea and of savage countries, and the sun now never sets on English dominions !

[1] Art. IV. Sec. ii.

We Americans, of all people, should be the last to quarrel with the pretentious claims of this English maxim; for without its influence in arousing the spirit of adventure and sustaining the colonists amidst the perils they encountered, it is more than doubtful whether the old thirteen colonies would have been settled by Englishmen; and it is certain that the day of their becoming free and independent States would have been long postponed; for no sooner did our forefathers feel the restrictive commercial policy of England than they began to claim the rights of Englishmen. Their claim was, that whatever rights and privileges Englishmen living in England might possess and enjoy, the same rights Englishmen and their descendants living in America should possess and enjoy. This was their interpretation of this maxim in the days of John Winthrop; it was the same in the days of Samuel Adams; and by the Declaration of Independence they made it good. And to-day, all rights and privileges which we obtained by war, and incorporated in our State and national constitutions, are only the " rights and privileges which followed Englishmen to the ends of the earth."

Another maxim which did us royal service from a very early period, and contributed more than any sentiment to bring on and carry us through the war of the Revolution, was the cry which flew from one end of the continent to the other — " No Representation, No Taxation."

This is generally thought to have originated in the days of the Stamp Act; but in 1647, one hundred and eighteen years before, Edward Winslow wrote : " If the Parliament of England should impose laws upon us, having no burgesses in their House of Commons, not capable of a summons by reason of the vast distance of the ocean, being three thousand miles from London, then we should lose the liberty and freedom I conceived of English indeed." [1] And the General Court of Massachusetts, October 2, 1678, said, " The subjects of his majesty here being not represented in Parliament, so we have not looked at ourselves to be impeded in our trade " by the Navigation Acts.[2] Chalmers says this was the first announcement of the doctrine.[3]

I hardly need say to one conversant with English constitutional history that the maxim had no foundation in English law or practice; for at the date of the American Revolution not one ninth of the English people had any voice in choosing the representatives who made laws for them; nor until the Reform Bill of 1832 had such great cities as Liverpool and Manchester any direct representation in Parliament.

Though the Massachusetts people held their lands as of gavelkind in Kent, they did not accept as their virtual representative an English member returned to the House of Commons from a Kentish borough — though such a member by the English doctrine represented all England and the colonies as well.

Nevertheless, the maxim was in the spirit of the Constitution, and that was sufficient for the colonists and even for some of their friends in England.[4] Political maxims, whether true or false, either with or

[1] Palfrey, ii. 178, n.; v. 244, 270, 274.

[2] *Massachusetts Records*, v. 200.

[3] *Annals*, 439; Hutchinson, i. 322; *Memorial History of Boston*, i. 367.

[4] Campbell's *Lives of the Lord Chancellors* (Phila., 1848, edition), v. 210, 211, 220, 229, 243, 253, 429.

without limitation, have generally been construed to promote justice — not to thwart justice.[1]

The colonists claimed the rights of Englishmen, it is true; but when their Tory fellow-citizens — no matter how respectable — invoked those rights to promote ends not agreeable to public sentiment, their appeal often ended in a coat of tar and feathers; and instead of the right of free speech, they were privileged to a free ride on a rail. So when the colonists had achieved their independence, they listened with no patience to those political maxims which had been so efficient in raising the people to resist the king's armies. These maxims were a good cry against the king's government which they thought oppressive, but not against their own, though the people were in distress, as in the days of Shays's rebellion.

It remains to speak of maxims which have gained currency, entered into the national life and influenced the conduct of the people in our own times.

For a people great in many forms of literature, the English have been singularly deficient in the gift of epigrammatic expression. Few of their proverbs originated among themselves, and compared with the French they lack those pointed sayings which every one admires but which few are capable of producing.

Warburton's fine saying is one exception. In the House of Lords, on the occasion of some angry dispute which had arisen between a peer of noble family and one of a new creation, he said that "high birth was a thing which he never knew any one to disparage except those who had it not; and he never knew any one to make a boast of it who had anything else to be proud of."[2]

[1] See Burke in Brougham's *Statesmen*.   [2] Whately's *Bacon*.

There is, however, one patriotic maxim which, considering its author, the circumstances under which it was uttered, and the immediate and lasting effects it produced, is worthy of a place among the great sayings of the best ages. Indeed, neither in English nor in any other language do I know any words not purely literary or moral (and those I am about to quote are essentially both), which an Englishman might have been so proud to have uttered, as Nelson's signal from the deck of the Victory at Trafalgar, " England expects every man to do his duty." Their immediate effect is historical; nor do I think England has ever forgotten them: certainly her soldiers with Wellington in his Peninsula campaign did not; nor those who held the mangled but steadfast squares on the blood-stained heights of Waterloo, nor those others, of whom it was said: —

> " Theirs not to make reply,
> Theirs not to reason why,
> Theirs but to do and die.
> Into the Valley of Death
> Rode the Six Hundred; "

nor those who withstood the siege of Lucknow; nor those who followed Gordon into the Soudan.[1]

I would not over-estimate the effects of those words on any part of the English people; but it is noticeable that not long after their utterance there came into English literature, thought, and conduct, a seriousness, an elevation and devotion to high ideals, as exhibited by Arnold of Rugby, Newman, Maurice,

---

[1] " Where even the common soldier dares force a passage for his comrades by gathering up the bayonets of the enemy into his own breast, because *his country expected every man to do his duty*, and this not after he has been hardened by habit, but, as probably, in his first battle." Coleridge's *Friend*, Vol. II. Essay ix.

Robertson, Tennyson, and others, which have made her history for the last sixty years, upon the whole, the most illustrious in England's annals.

Our own countrymen have said memorable words, some of which at least became household words.

When Charles Cotesworth Pinckney said to Talleyrand "Millions for defense but not one cent for tribute," he spoke for the nation; and so spoke Lawrence dying on the deck of the Chesapeake, in those pathetic words, " Don't give up the ship." The most venerable and illustrious of living Americans,[1] still, to be occasionally seen in our streets, once gave as a sentiment, "Our country however bounded." A patriotic maxim, though in the heat of party politics I believe it subjected its author to some obloquy; and so did Seward's "Irrepressible conflict" and his "Law higher than the Constitution." Sumner's "Nothing is settled until it is settled rightly" is a moral rather than a political maxim; and Chase's "An indestructible union of indestructible states," though constitutionally true, lacks the ring that reaches the popular heart. Jefferson's self-evident truths formulated in the Declaration of Independence were addressed to the race and to the ages, and therefore belong rather to political philosophy than to patriotic maxims.

But we, more than other English-speaking people, have patriotic maxims which satisfy the head of the statesman and the heart of the people. What every American ought to remember, and some time will, is that one, once a citizen here, but now sleeping by the sea at Marshfield, made, — not indeed the songs of the people, but what are next best, — all our patriotic

[1] Robert C. Winthrop, who died November 16, 1894.

maxims which stir the heart and form popular sentiment; for all such in this century (save the dying
Lawrence's " Don't give up the ship ") sprang from the
lips of the great orator. John Adams had said, " Sink
or swim, survive or perish, I give my heart and my
hand to this vote;" and when the Fourth of July
bells pealed just before he died, he exclaimed, " Independence forever."   But from Webster's lips in Faneuil Hall, these words winged their way to the heart
of the nation.   Wholly his own were those other
‚words, " Our country, our whole country, and nothing
but our country;" " Liberty and Union, now and forever, one and inseparable; " " The people's government, made for the people, made by the people, and
accountable to the people."   These last express with
precision Webster's theory of the national government, and Lincoln's also, for he adopted them in his
immortal speech on the field of Gettysburg, and they
are now quoted oftener than any of his own words.
Nelson's " England expects every man to do his
duty " wrought nobly at Trafalgar, and has since inspired her sons to noble deeds; but Webster's words
— words which winged the shot that Grant fired —
wrought results vastly greater than those of the
famous sea-fight.

Great services may be forgotten, but maxims defin-
ing the patriotic relations of the people to their country, and of the government to the people, and of both
to civil liberty — maxims which sank deep into the
national heart in the day of their utterance, and since
have been a saving power — are not likely to be forgotten; nor is Daniel Webster, from whose fertile
brain and patriotic heart they all sprang.

REMARKS

AT THE DINNER OF THE SONS OF THE AMERICAN REVOLUTION

Concord, Massachusetts, April 19, 1894

REMARKS BEFORE THE SONS OF THE AMERICAN REVOLUTION

APRIL 19, 1894

It is a high honor for me, as I gratefully think, Sons of the American Revolution, though not of your number, nevertheless, to join with you as a guest in the celebration of April 19, 1775.

That was indeed a day made forever memorable by events of great import to that age and people, and as the years roll on, not unlikely to be counted among those events which will affect the political condition of no inconsiderable part of the human race.

It was neither unexpected nor unprepared for. The Provincial Congress, adjourned from Salem, met at Concord, in this venerable church edifice, October 11, 1774. As I look over the roll of its members gathered from all parts of the province, and recall the earlier and later history of some of the most distinguished of them, it was, as it appears to me, one of the ablest bodies of statesmen ever assembled on Massachusetts soil; nor am I unmindful of later representative bodies, nor even of the three great conventions assembled for the formation or amendment of the constitution of the Commonwealth. Among its members were Thomas Cushing, Samuel Adams, John Hancock, Joseph Warren, William Heath, Benjamin Lincoln — the last two afterwards major-generals in the Continental Army — Samuel Dexter the elder, John Pickering, Samuel Holten, Elbridge Gerry, Samuel Osgood, Nathaniel Peaslee Sargent, Nathaniel Gorham, Richard Devens, James Prescott, Joseph Hawley, James Warren, George Partridge, Robert Treat Paine, William Baylies, James Sullivan, Timothy Bigelow, Jedediah Foster, Joseph Henshaw, Artemas Ward, Moses Gill, Samuel Freeman, Samuel Thompson, John Fellows, and John Paterson. John Hancock was President and Benjamin Lincoln Secretary.

Such were some of the men. This was some of their work: By October 12 the Congress was fully organized, and on the 13th it addressed Governor Gage. It recognized preparations for war in "the rigorous execution of the Port Bill;" in the "acts for altering the charter and the administration of justice in the colony," manifestly designed to abridge the people of their rights; "in the number of troops in the capital, increased by daily accessions drawn from the whole continent, together with the formidable and hostile preparations you are making on Boston neck," — measures which "greatly endanger the lives, liberties, and properties, not only of our brethren in the town of Boston, but of this province in general." The Congress met the crisis with a prescience, wisdom, and practical skill to promote the popular interests and to neutralize the efforts of the loyalists, never surpassed and seldom equaled; and within sixteen days arranged to seize the revenues of the province; practically annulled the acts of 1774 subverting the charter; voted to inquire into the state of the provincial army, to appoint a Committee of Safety, to send an agent to Canada to secure its coöperation, "to provide a stock

of powder, ordnance, and ordnance stores *now;*" re-
commended "that the militia companies elect officers,
equip, and hold themselves in readiness, on the short-
est notice from the Committee of Safety, to march to
the place of rendezvous," and "for the choice of three
general officers." In a word, the Provincial Congress
had recognized the probability of war and prepared
for it six months before April 19, 1775.

But this is not all. Hancock, Adams, Gerry and
Paine, in May, 1775, fresh from their labors at Concord, were in the Continental Congress at Philadelphia, and, as the journals of that body warrant me in
saying, made possible, on a wider theatre of continental affairs, that which was done six months earlier in
this little town of Concord.

Do we claim too much, therefore, in saying that
this edifice in which the Provincial Congress sat, and
in which we are now sitting, — sacred alike to religion
and liberty, — in which the substantial foundations of
independence were laid in 1774, ought to be no less
dear to New Englanders, at least, than that hall in
Philadelphia in which Independence was declared
July 4, 1776? Citizens of Concord, this is your
shrine. It ought to be the shrine of a nation. Invoke
for it Divine protection from lightning and tempest;
provide for it protection from fire and the wasting
tooth of time!

Of the events of April 19, 1775, I need say but
little. They have passed into history. Every year
they are recounted in our public journals. They are
household words.

My purpose is not to rehearse them, but to ask
what these events meant for the colonists at the time;
what they have since meant, and what they may mean

for future ages. On the first question I have some direct authentic intelligence from an actor in those scenes.

When the action at Lexington on the morning of the 19th was known at Danvers, the minute men there, under the lead of Captain Gideon Foster, made that memorable march — or run, rather — of sixteen miles in four hours, and struck Percy's flying column at West Cambridge. Brave but incautious in flanking the red-coats, they were flanked themselves and badly pinched, leaving seven dead, two wounded, and one missing. Among those who escaped was Levi Preston, afterwards known as Captain Levi Preston.

When I was about twenty-one and Captain Preston about ninety-one, I "interviewed" him as to what he did and thought sixty-seven years before, on April 19, 1775; and now, fifty-two years later, I make my report — a little belated perhaps, but not too late I trust for the morning papers!

At that time, of course, I knew all about the American Revolution — far more than I do now! And if I now know anything truly, it is chiefly owing to what I have since forgotten of the histories of that event then popular.

With an assurance passing even that of the modern interviewer — if that were possible — I began: "Captain Preston, why did you go to the Concord Fight, the 19th of April, 1775?" The old man, bowed beneath the weight of years, raised himself upright, and turning to me said: "Why did I go?" "Yes," I replied; "my histories tell me that you men of the Revolution took up arms against 'intolerable oppressions.'" "What were they? Oppressions? I did n't feel them." "What, were you not oppressed by the

Stamp Act?" "I never saw one of those stamps, and always understood that Governor Bernard put them all in Castle William. I am certain I never paid a penny for one of them." "Well, what then about the tea-tax?" "Tea-tax! I never drank a drop of the stuff; the boys threw it all overboard." "Then I suppose you had been reading Harrington or Sidney and Locke about the eternal principles of liberty." "Never heard of 'em. We read only the Bible, the Catechism, Watts's Psalms and Hymns, and the Almanack." "Well, then, what was the matter? and what did you mean in going to the fight?" "Young man, what we meant in going for those red-coats was this: we always had governed ourselves, and we always meant to. They did n't mean we should."

And that, gentlemen, is the ultimate philosophy of the American Revolution. It correctly assigns its underlying cause, it explains and accounts for the action of the patriotic party. Doubtless there were subsidiary causes affecting localities and interests, especially on the sea-coast and in larger commercial towns; but the yeomanry of the interior felt none of those grievances. And yet, from Maine to Georgia, they were among the first to resist the British pretensions. Thomas Paine once said something like this: "The British ministry were too jealous of the colonists to govern them justly, too ignorant to govern them well, and too far away to govern them at all." That puts the matter very neatly; but Levi Preston, the Danvers yeoman, put it far better; for no other words known to me ever expressed the actual condition of affairs with more historic truth or more tersely. For the attitude of the colonists was not that of slaves seeking liberty, but of freemen — freemen for five generations — resisting political servitude. And as Mr. Webster (who must often have conversed with his father on the subject) once said, with his usual historical accuracy and with a felicity all his own: "*While actual suffering was yet afar off . . . they went to war against a preamble. They fought seven years against a declaration.*" The preamble was that of the Stamp Act: "Whereas it is necessary to raise a revenue from the colonies for their defense." The declaration was, "that the power of Parliament over the colonies extends to all cases whatever."

Yes, the men at the North Bridge knew well enough what it meant to them, but not quite so well what it means to us; the men of '61 explained that quite fully; but neither the men of '61 knew nor do we who survive know just what it may mean to future ages. Few events in the world's history have been of more tremendous consequences than those of the 19th of April, 1775; and nothing but a completed cycle in the world's history will reveal their full significance.

It was no new thing to overthrow dynasties or to disrupt empires. It was no new thing to make conquests or to repel invasions. But the battle-fields on which the condition of any considerable part of the human race has been permanently changed are few; and fewer still those on which has been instituted a new principle of government apparently destined to affect the whole human race. Thermopylæ saved for a time the civilization of Greece, but it did not advance the civilization of the world. Waterloo merely restored the old status of Europe. The wars of the great English Revolution did not bring into the Brit-

ish constitution true representative government —
that came two centuries later with the Reform Bill of
1832.   But the Concord fight, as Levi Preston substantially said, preserved, if it did not inaugurate,
what Webster called " a government of the people,
for the people, and accountable to the people."

The 19th of April, 1775, was indeed notable in the
progress of national autonomy and representative government.   Other days come and go.   The sun rises
and hastens to its setting.   But on the 19th of April
no second morn will rise.   Its sun once risen never
set.   It still rides high and clear.   Its prescribed
arc is not through the visible heavens, but over the
ages !

A mile away from us is the North Bridge.   We
are familiar with the scene and the incidents which
make it memorable.   We see Major Buttrick with
his little band of farmers moving down to dislodge
Captain Laurie's company.   We see Isaac Davis and
Abner Hosmer fall.   We hear Major Butterick exclaim, " Fire, fellow soldiers, for God's sake, fire ! "
That was the fight at Concord Bridge.   That was the
" shot heard round the world," the shot that will re-
sound through the ages, forever vibrate in the air,
forever quicken the pulses of the human race.

PALFREY'S PEOPLE OF NEW ENGLAND

REPRINTED FROM "THE NATION" OF JULY 10, 1890

PALFREY'S PEOPLE OF NEW ENGLAND

Dr. Palfrey's diligence has not added much that
is essential to what was known about the period
covered by his fifth volume. The field had been too
thoroughly reaped for profitable gleaning, and his
views on American history too often expressed to warrant expectations of novel treatment. It is a compact and convenient résumé of the history of the
" Great Awakening," the " French Wars," and of the
events which led to the outbreak at Lexington in
1775. And it is something more : it completes Dr.
Palfrey's " History of New England," one of the most
considerable historical works coming from any American. Few historians have shown greater industry
in gathering original materials, or a firmer grasp of
complicated masses of facts, or greater skill in arran-
ging them in perspicuous order and presenting them
in a narrative always clear and often felicitous.

Dr. Palfrey's scheme of a history of New England
was full of difficulties. The people of the New England colonies were of the same race, it is true, and
doubtless of a similar way of thinking on political and
theological questions ; but from the outset diversities
of opinion or interest, or both, led them to seek different localities in which to develop their several autonomies. Nevertheless, from the coming of the Pilgrims to the withdrawal of Washington's army from

Boston in 1776, the watersheds of New England's history inclined towards Boston Bay, and in Massachusetts was the main stream to which all other streams were affluent.   But Dr. Palfrey's purpose was wider than is implied by his title: not merely to write a history of the several colonies as organized political bodies, but " the history of the people of New England," and, as we learn from the preface of his last volume, to show that " the work which in five generations was done in New England for the continent and the world, was done by Englishmen of Puritan training," and that, " as far as human judgment may trust itself, no other class of men contemporary with them was equal to the achievement."

This makes Dr. Palfrey's " History of New England " quite another matter.   It no longer primarily concerns the foundation and erection of States, but the original and developing character of the people, and the ideas, principles, and conduct of those who did what no five generations of their contemporaries had done, nor as Dr. Palfrey thinks could have done. Assured of his purpose to set this forth, his reader reviews his entire history with new interest; and if not a descendant of the New England Puritans, then with pardonable scrutiny of the facts, and of Dr. Palfrey's qualifications for pronouncing a judgment so affrontive.   Even those who may be supposed to accept it most complacently are aware that though history is not science, nevertheless, the writer of it is amenable to the laws of scientific investigation.   If his insight is at fault, or his methods uncritical, or his statements of facts one-sided, or he is blinded by prejudice, his work will not be accepted as final.

For writing this history Dr. Palfrey possessed

many qualifications, but his defects were serious. Without originality or special historical insight, he accepted the conventional theory of New England civilization, and did not go very far beneath the surface, or deal satisfactorily with facts which did not agree with his preconceived notions. The history of the New England colonies rests on patents, charters, or royal commissions; and for the interpretation of these, legal training or natural legal insight, such as Belknap, Trumbull, Ramsay, and Deane possessed, is indispensable. Dr. Palfrey lacked both, and his constitutional discussions do not command respect. His imagination formed no pictures of domestic or social life, and we turn his pages in vain for the causes which in five generations changed Englishmen to Yankees, or to learn how, for example, living amid scenes of danger, they lost their inheritance of British pluck, and at the same time managed to preserve their moral courage and stamina unimpaired while acquiring wealth by slave-trading, piracy thinly disguised as privateering, and smuggling.

He says of the Puritans that "the rank, the wealth, the chivalry, the genius, the learning, the accomplishments, the social refinements and elegances of the time were largely represented in their ranks. . . . The Earls of Leicester, Bedford, Huntington, and Warwick, Sir Nicholas Bacon, his greater son, Walsingham, Burleigh, Mildmay, Sadler, Knollys, were specimens of a host of eminent men more or less friendly to or tolerant of Puritanism." The wealth of England, he adds, was on the side of the Puritans, and so were many of the landed aristocracy, many of high rank in the army and navy; and if few of the Elizabethan dramatists or writers of lighter literature are found among them, they may justly claim such names as Selden, Lightfoot, Gale, and Owen, and such poets as Spenser, Milton, and Marvell. Nor were they wanting in the amenities and graces of social life; and he records with satisfaction that Colonel Hutchinson could dance and fence, loved music and played the viol, shot guns and bows, and delighted in painting, graving, and the liberal arts. He completes what he has to say about the Puritan by adding that he was "a Scripturist," "a strict moralist," and "in politics, the liberal of his day."

The reader acquainted with the character of the New England Puritans is ready to ask what all this has to do with them. If this was intended as a description of them, and there is no other, nothing could be more misleading, or could more strikingly mark the uncritical methods of the historian. Puritans of this stamp were not the founders of New England, and they dropped out of English affairs even, with the coming of Cromwell and his Ironsides. A few of them came over, but not to stay. Neither the society in which they found themselves, nor the work for them to do, was to their mind.

Doubtless Puritanism divided English society by a vertical line, on both sides of which were men of all classes and conditions. So far Dr. Palfrey is accurate. But there was difference in Puritans. Those who came to New England formed a horizontal stratum, not a vertical section, of English society. They were selected Puritans: above them, the nobility and the gentry; below them, the peasantry and the rabble. Among them were two or three families of rank, and a few conventional gentlemen, who either died early or returned to England. No poets came; none ad-

dicted to art, science, or literature, save theological;
none distinguished in statesmanship or arms, and but
few who led the social life of Lincolnshire or of Suffolk. Some of their leaders were men of affairs and
acquainted with law; a larger number were Calvinistic clergymen, and a half dozen had some pretensions
to gentility; but mainly they were yeomen, trades-
people, mechanics, and servants.

Dr. Palfrey says that "the spirit of Puritanism was
as old as the truth and manliness of England." This
is quite true. Dr. Storrs has just told us that Moses,
and several of the patriarchs, and Christ, and many
notable pagans were Puritans. This is also true.
But such truths do not describe the character or the
work of those who came to New England. We may
imagine, if we will, the statesmen, poets, and divines
whom Dr. Palfrey has mentioned, engaged in ordain-
ing party fences, the ringing of swine, or in an expedition against the Pequots and burning them when
found, or in trying Mrs. Hutchinson for heresy, or inspecting Mary Dyer's monstrous birth for evidence
of a special providence, or we may imagine Colonel
Hutchinson and his family dancing and playing cards
about Boston Bay; but such imaginings are not the
history of the Puritan New England. Puritanism
there was "the truth and manliness of England"
specially vitalized and intensified by the Five Points
of Calvinism enforced by the Synod of Dort. There
were "State Puritans" and "Doctrinal Puritans" in
old England, but only the latter found their way to
New England. When Calvinism came into England,
Arminianism came also; and between these two grew
up a deadly hostility which did much to form the New
England Puritans for their work, civil as well as

ecclesiastical. King James, a renegade from Calvinism, allied himself to the Arminians; and so did
Laud and his party who hounded the non-conforming
clergy, — a strange conjunction of liberalism in creed
with absolutism in politics, which cost Charles I. his
head, and, with other causes, George III. his colonies.
All this and more Dr. Palfrey knew, but it was not
an agreeable phase of his subject, and he left it alone.
Nor is it altogether grateful to learn, not from Dr.
Palfrey's history, for he is silent on this also, that
the New England Puritans in their acceptance of the
Resolutions of the Synod of Dort, deliberately rejected the richest legacy of Greece to the modern
world, — the validity and finality of human reason
when at variance with authority, even the highest.
Neither is it grateful to learn that it is with Hooker,
in defense of reason and law as its most valid expression, that the modern world, including the last two
generations of the Puritans, is in accord, rather than
with Calvin and the first two generations, who rejected
the Common Law of their race for the Mosaic Code
of the Hebrews.

The New England Puritans were narrow and in-
tolerant, not because the age was narrow and intoler-
ant; they were so from choice. They discussed the
matter, and knew the difference between tolerance and
illiberality quite as well as we do. Their testimony
on this point is clear and explicit. They acted as
sincere believers always act when great interests are
at stake. They believed that conformity led to eternal death. Therefore they crushed it out as our
fathers crushed out the Tories, and as we crushed out
the Copperheads. Conscious of their mission, they
made no apology for their principles; but they wished

to be understood. It was their singleness of purpose, their absolute sincerity of belief, their utter conviction that happiness here and hereafter depended upon the acceptance of the Calvinistic scheme, which gave the New England Puritans their power and success where others failed. Dr. Palfrey's misapprehension of this vital quality of New England Puritanism pervades his whole work, and no part of it more than the fifth volume. He treats "The Great Awakening" with entire candor, but as he would treat a modern revival of religion. He sees in it no connection with primitive Puritanism, or permanent influence upon other events of that day or of later days. He has noted in the second generation a declension from the high political spirit of the emigrants, apparent in the rise of parties at the revocation of the first Massachusetts charter and during Dudley's administration, and he attributes this to the influx of commercial adventurers and the increase of wealth and luxury; but he fails to notice that this declension was rather in their theological belief, as is evident from the fact that the Mathers, Danforth, and others, the champions of civil and ecclesiastical liberty, and who as such merit and receive his commendation, were "faithful among the faithless found" in asserting and maintaining, with pathetic earnestness, the old Calvinistic doctrines.

There can be no doubt about the declension. It was manifest among the godly in the acceptance of the halfway covenant and in some departures from discipline. Ratcliff, the Church of England chaplain of Andros, had preached in the Old South, and not without hearers; King's Chapel, Christ Church, and Trinity marked the growth of Episcopacy; Harvard

College, having repudiated the Mathers, relegated
herself to the mild doctrines of the " Dudleian Lectures," whose founder scrupled not at " Episcopal
ordination ; " and even more alarming to those of the
ancient faith was the circulation of a book inculcating
whispered belief in the salvation of all. To arrest
" the great and visible decay of piety," a synod was
called in 1725 ; but the Episcopal clergy of Boston,
through the Bishop of London, invoked the royal in-
terdiction. There was mourning in Zion, nor comfort, until Edwards, at Northampton, seizing live coals
from the altar of Calvinism,[1] touched the hearts of his
own people. Then came Tennent and Davenport in
New England, and Whitefield from Georgia to Maine,
preaching predestination, election, free grace, and the
wrath to come upon the ungodly. The effects were
instantaneous. By estimation there were forty thousand converts in New England alone. Old profes-
sors were quickened to new life ; Calvinism had free
course. And to Dr. Palfrey this was the end of it.

But it did not end thus. One of its later effects
was manifest in the expedition against Louisburg in
1745 — more like a crusade than a military movement
— when the undisciplined yeomanry of eastern New
England, inspired by the preaching of Whitefield,
who inscribed their banner with " Nil desperandum
sub duce Christo," attacked the French Catholics behind the bastions of Louisburg with the zeal of the
Christians against the infidels in the Holy Land.
Another effect of " The Great Awakening " was this :
it was the " relay " of the electric current of Calvinism which, beginning with Winthrop, unloosed the
bands of the English hierarchy, and coming down to

[1] Doyle's *English in America*, i. 132.

the days of Samuel Adams unloosed the bands of the British empire. There was still another effect. The Puritanism of New England far more than that of old England, owing in part to local causes, was not merely a creed, but a habit of mind which became hereditary as character, and has survived to the present day. This was so caused by the recurrence in the middle of the last century of influences like that of the Synod of Dort in the previous century. And there was still another effect. Calvinism in New England, differing from Puritanism in old England, was much more than a creed. The creed has changed, but character remains ; and the constancy, zeal, and singleness of purpose, and intolerance already spoken of — in a word, the Calvinistic spirit — of the remote ancestor reappears even in those whose measure of liberality is the intensity of their dissent from opponents, or who limit the universality of salvation to such as accept the doctrine. Character thus formed was the greatest legacy of the New England Puritans to their descendants, for by that they have prevailed. Of this transforming and sustaining power of Calvinistic Puritanism Dr. Palfrey gives us no hint. As he frankly informs us, with Geneva he had no sympathy. It may be so with us, but the facts remain.

More than half of Dr. Palfrey's fifth volume is given to the causes and events which led to the American Revolution. It affords little evidence of insight, and is disfigured by singular misstatements of essential facts. No doubt the causes which led to forcible resistance, whether originating in Great Britain or in the colonies, were earlier and more effectively operative in New England than in the other colonies. But it is nowhere noticed by Dr. Palfrey as extraordinary

that, on the arrival of the news of the passage of the
Stamp Act, months before it was to take effect, and
therefore not as against " intolerable oppression," as
he says, the people from Maine to Georgia declared
their determination to resist it by violence to persons
and property which there was no effort to prevent or
arrest.   It is obvious, therefore, that there must have
been other causes operative anterior to that event, and
not confined to commercial centres quick to discern
whatever was likely to interfere with their interests,
but pervading agricultural communities remote from
centres of business or intelligence.   The only absolutely sincere and universally operative cause of the
Revolution was the desire and determination of the
majority of the colonists to be free ; a desire common
to all branches of the Anglo-Saxon race wherever
found ; a desire quickened in the American branch by
remoteness from the home government, and a growing
consciousness of ability to set up and maintain one
for themselves.   With this desire and determination
they left their English home ; and if these motives
were sometimes in abeyance, they were never given up
until they became accomplished facts.   Against this
view of the case are their profuse and not altogether
sincere professions of allegiance.   They were, indeed,
sincere on one condition : that they should have their
own way, which was generally the case down to the
close of the war in 1763.   When the Revolution came
it was inevitable, and it was conducted as rightly as
revolutions ever are.   The exigencies of the cause
required and justified the "thorough" measures of
the Whigs and the application of Samuel Adams's
theory of politics : " Put your enemy in the wrong and
keep him there ! "   To conduct a revolution on such

grounds is doubtless good practical politics and even good statesmanship. But to write history in that spirit gives no promise of its continuance. Another interesting fact not adverted to by Dr. Palfrey, notwithstanding his frequent reference to events passing in England, was the contemporaneous English Revolution, going forward almost with equal step, and with the same general purpose of enlarging popular liberty against prerogative, which reached results more surprising, if possible, than those which followed the American Revolution. In both countries the revolution was brought about by agencies acting efficiently in the British Parliament as in the colonial assemblies.

Still more extraordinary is it that Dr. Palfrey nowhere thinks it necessary to state that the American Revolution — as was the case with the contemporaneous English Revolution — was the result of party action, not of unanimous popular action. He has, indeed, something to say about government officials, placemen, and commercial adventurers opposing what he would have us think was the grand movement of an entire people towards their objective point, — colonial independence. This view of the Revolution may have arisen from Dr. Palfrey's theory respecting the New England settlers and their descendants. In his judgment the work was mainly theirs, and one which no other contemporary generations of men could have done. At times they may have been a little too strenuous, a little inclined to magnify small causes of discontent with the mother country or her representatives; but even in these respects it was an excess of a noble spirit of liberty without taint of self-interest, or an unwillingness to share common burdens with

others, or to submit to regulations necessary and reasonable for the commerce and government of an
empire of which they were parts. On the other hand,
they were loyal and dutiful subjects, glorying in the
name of Britons, and " without the most distant
thought of independence."   But when, after the close
of the French war, the British government unconsti-
tutionally undertook to tax them, then, and for the
first time, as one man, on axiomatic principles of English liberty enunciated by Hampden, Sidney, and
Locke, they resisted the king and Parliament, and
took the field for a seven years' war.

This is the old, conventional theory of the origin
of the American Revolution. But, by the estimate of
John Adams, two fifths — some others say three fifths
— of the colonists, including a large proportion of the
cultured classes, were Tories, who, by an organized
system of terrorism not easy to be understood in these
days, were obliged to flee the country or to fall in
with measures of the Whigs. Free speech was not
allowed, nor would silent adherence to their convictions answer. They must speak — speak loudly, and
only in one way. They must act — act promptly in
accordance with the most vehemently expressed sentiment. Now it agrees neither with reason nor with
the facts to represent this party, as Dr. Palfrey does,
as made up of British placemen, colonial office-holders,
mercantile sojourners, and a few men [1] like Hutchinson, Oliver, Samuel Quincy, Jonathan Sewall, Daniel
Leonard, Timothy Ruggles, and the greater part of
the Episcopal clergy, who malignantly sought the

---

[1] It would seem that he never read Sabine's *American Loyalists*, and
counted their number or estimated their character and standing in
society.

destruction of their native land, which they had done much to improve, and in which were their dearest interests. Yet such is the general impression one gets from his history.

The degree of Dr. Palfrey's partisanship would be incredible without proof, but a few examples must serve. The Seven Years' War had added more than £300,000,000 to the British debt; and " was it not equitable," Dr. Palfrey represents the British government as asking, " that the North American colonists, as subjects of Great Britain, should pay their proportion of it? " especially since the argument might be plausibly maintained that part of it had been incurred in their defense. Dr. Palfrey ought to have known — and with the statutes before him it would seem that he must have known — that the British government never asked, nor, so far as appears, ever contemplated asking, the colonists to do any such thing.[1] They were asked to pay one third of the estimated expense of their future defense. The preamble of the first revenue act of 1764 and that of the Stamp Act set forth the purpose to raise money "towards defraying the expenses of defending, protecting, and securing the colonies and plantations." Such was the purpose, — not to pay the British debt or any part of it; and neither in the Parliamentary debates nor elsewhere is there any warrant for Dr. Palfrey's amazing statement. Of like nature is his assertion that the duties collected from the Sugar Act, after certain deductions, were to be remitted to the royal Exchequer in hard money, thereby draining the colonies of their specie. Not a penny was to go abroad. The sums collected were to be paid into the

[1] *Massachusetts Historical Collections*, vi. 194; ix. 270.

receipt of his Majesty's Exchequer by certificates to be entered apart from all other moneys, and applied from time to time by Parliament to defraying the expenses above mentioned.

Of willful perversion Dr. Palfrey was utterly incapable. On the contrary, no historian ever wished to be more accurate. He had his theory of New England history, and according to that the prevailing party at every stage of it were right in their principles, purposes, and mainly in their measures ; and the other party were entirely and malignantly wrong, with nothing to excuse or palliate their conduct. The history of New England neither requires nor will it bear such treatment. It will bear telling in its entirety from 1620 to 1787. It has its seamy side, as has the history of every period, however glorious ; and this it is neither wise nor necessary to conceal as Dr. Palfrey occasionally does ; nor to place it in a wrong light, as he frequently does ; nor to apologize for it, as he invariably does, — sometimes on grounds of necessity, which has always been made to condone some of the most flagrant acts of political and ecclesiastical tyranny recorded in history.

Dr. Palfrey's insight into the essential character of men is no more trustworthy than his insight as to the causes and relations of events. Nor is he impartial. He conceals the well-known blotch on the character of Samuel Adams, and dwells upon charges, now known to be false, against the character of Hutchinson. He performed a great service in writing the history of the New England colonies, so that it need not be rewritten ; but the history of "the people of New England" requires an historian of a different order.

McMASTER'S HISTORY

OF THE PEOPLE OF THE UNITED STATES

From the "Andover Review" of June, 1886

McMASTER'S HISTORY OF THE PEO-
PLE OF THE UNITED STATES

MR. JOHN BACH McMASTER has undertaken to
write the history of the people of the United States,
from the Revolution to the Civil War, in five volumes, two of which, bringing the narrative down into
Jefferson's administration, have already appeared.
The first, published in 1883, was favorably received
by critics as well as by the public; and the second,
which has recently appeared, shows no loss of vigor
in its execution or of interest in its materials. A
new history of the United States should be its own
excuse for being. Mr. McMaster's work is undoubtedly a positive contribution to history, and by its
excellences no less than by its defects will provoke
criticism. This should be so; for one of the promises of a better literature is our discontent with what
we already have.

It need not be said of the first edition of a work
dealing with a great variety of facts, that errors have
crept into it, or that some things essential to completeness have been overlooked, or that some unwarranted conclusions have been drawn from authorities
cited in their support. Such errors and defects are
inevitable.

Mr. McMaster possesses manifest qualifications for
writing history. To say of an historian that he is
honest, that he collects his materials industriously

and allows them to stand for what they are worth, without foisting upon them a partisan or sectarian theory, ought to sound as strange as when said of a judicial magistrate. But it does not; and when such things can be truly said of a writer of history, it is very high praise. Mr. McMaster's industry is marvelous, even to those familiar with similar researches. He overlooks some things, but he conceals nothing. We may conjecture the direction of his sympathies in respect to the great political parties which were forming during the early stages of his history, but there is no lack of candor in dealing with them, and he dares to look even Washington in the face. This has not always been so. Charles Thomson, the patriotic secretary of the Old Congress, wrote its history, which he intended to publish; but his courage failed at the pinch, and he burnt it. We might guess his reasons, even if he had not given them, when we read the " Diary of John Adams."

Mr. McMaster entitles his work " A History of the People of the United States," and thereby indicates an intention which is more fully avowed in his introductory chapter. He says that in the course of his narrative "much, indeed, must be written of wars, conspiracies, and rebellions; of presidents, of congresses, of embassies, of treaties, of the ambition of political leaders in the senate-house, and of the rise of great parties in the nation. Yet the history of the people shall be the chief theme."

He makes no claim to originality in drawing this distinction between the history of the people and of the nation to which they belong. In 1879 John Richard Green, whose early death was a loss to letters, published a " Short History of the English People," in which he proposed "to pass lightly and briefly over the details of foreign wars and diplomacies, the personal adventures of kings and nobles, the pomp of courts, or the intrigues of favorites, and to dwell at length on the incidents of that constitutional and social advance in which we read the history of the nation itself." To Mr. Green's authority for this theory of what makes the history of the English people Mr. McMaster has now added his own for a similar theory of the history of the people of the United States. But Mr. Green's ideas upon English history appear to be questioned by high authority, presently to be adverted to; and it is proposed to offer in this paper some special considerations which make them less applicable to the history of the United States.

The success of Mr. Green's history was immediate and brilliant, — only equaled by that of Macaulay's historical essays and of his "History of England." But this success was due, in part at least, to Mr. Green's rare historical insight, to his condensation and artistic grouping of materials, and to his singularly pure and attractive style. His theory also gained adherents as a protest against that class of historical compositions in which wars, the doings of courts and parliaments, and foreign relations were treated as the staple of history, while the progress of literature, and of science, of art, and of manners was relegated in brief summaries — as notably by Hume — to the end of a chapter. Hildreth, whose history is one of the best, rigorously excluded from it everything like a theory of politics, and, to make amends, published an excellent one as a separate treatise, and cynically commended it to the attention of "such critics as have complained that his history of the United States had no ' philosophy ' in it."

But Mr. Green's scheme of history seems to be challenged by Professor Seeley in his " Expansion of England," who regards the progress of a people in literature, art, and manners as properly belonging to the history of the " general progress that the human race everywhere alike, and therefore also in England, may chance to be making; " and that such matters would be more fittingly treated, as they have been, in the history of literature in England.

On the other hand, he considers " that history has to do with the state; that it investigates the growth and changes of a certain corporate society, which acts through certain functionaries and certain assemblies. By the nature of the state every person who lives in a certain territory is usually a member of it, but history is not concerned with individuals, except in their capacity of members of a state. That a man in England makes a scientific discovery or paints a picture is not in itself an event in the history of England. Individuals are important in history in proportion not to their intrinsic merit, but to their relation to the state. Socrates was a much greater man than Cleon, but Cleon has a much greater space in Thucydides. Newton was a greater man than Harley, yet it is Harley, not Newton, who fixes the attention of the historian of the reign of Queen Anne."

These extracts indicate that Mr. Green and Professor Seeley were not in accord respecting the scope and proper limitations of the history of England; and yet neither could push his views to extremes. Although Mr. Green passes lightly and briefly over foreign wars and the intrigues of courts, they form no inconsiderable part of his history when comprised in a single volume, and a still greater part when, in a new edition, that volume is expanded into four. And, on the other hand, Professor Seeley would often find himself in the presence of unorganized forces, not belonging to the state and having no direct relation to it, yet visibly affecting it, and therefore to be taken into historical account.

But even if Mr. Green's theory of the history of England is correct, it does not follow that it is applicable to that of the United States; for there is a wide difference between the two nations, and an appreciation of this difference is essential to the verity of our history. Louis XIV., without exaggeration, might exclaim, " I am the State ; " and there was a time in England when the phrase " King, Lords, and Commons " expressed the existence of a deep gulf between these factors in the Constitution and the electors of the Commons. They constituted only one sixth of the people, and did not include the citizens of such great towns as Liverpool, Manchester, and Birmingham. And there was a still deeper gulf between these electors and the great body of unrepresented people. Nor was there on one side of this chasm knowledge, wisdom, and virtue, and on the other weakness, ignorance, and vice. For neither literature nor religion, save so far as it was political, had recognized relations to the state, or direct influence in the management of its affairs.

But Mr. McMaster finds no such state of affairs here. From the day when Englishmen first appeared on this continent in organized societies, the people and the state have been interchangeable terms ; and everything included in one is also included in the other. Nor will the history of either permit the exclusion of wars, conspiracies, or rebellions, or of according to them less than their just prominence among those causes which have made the United States what they are to-day. What things constitute the proper subject of history, and their relative importance in its narrative, is determinable only by the completeness and verity of history.

The history of the United States is without pageantry or splendor, but it is unique; and upon a due appreciation of its character, and a conformity to the requirements of a truthful setting forth of it, will chiefly depend its usefulness not only to us, but to foreign nations, which seem to be sensible to the value of the facts which lie behind it, if not to the felicity of their literary expression.

This history may be briefly outlined. The English colonies in North America, with some political and religious diversities, began their organic life on this soil under substantially the same conditions, which continued down to the Revolution. Whether they were crown-provinces, or had obtained charters from the king, or from the proprietaries, or had organized under their patents, they had moulded these various powers into constitutions of government which, in 1775, gave a higher sanction to armed resistance to royal authority than any wrongs they had suffered, or any wrongs they feared. A strange, unique history! Thirteen incorporated land companies — for such was their legal character — developed, with only a nominal adherence to their acts of incorporation, into thirteen independent, constitutional governments. This is what they had accomplished at the close of the Revolution: not union, then, or nationality. These, in all but the name, belong to our own day; and, like the first, are the results of civil war.

When we look at these colonies as organized societies we find, as we find nowhere else, that the people and the state were identical. The state was the people " as a mode of action." In other lands a king, or a king's mistress, or a cabal, made wars, invaded personal and public rights, and ruined finances; but if an American colony was turbulent or disobedient, it was the turbulence and disobedience of the people; if wars were waged, or embassies dispatched, it was by their order; if schools, colleges, or churches were set up and maintained, it was because the people willed it; and if, at one time, the covenant was held in its rigor, and at a later time, in a modified form, it was the voice of the people speaking through the General Court, or a synod, that so ordained.

Contrast this state of affairs with what prevailed even in England, in which alone, of the European nations, popular ideas had made any considerable progress. On the side of the political organization called the state were arrayed many prerogatives no longer based on reason; the power of making war and peace irrespective of popular sentiment, and all those agencies which were clothed with the insignia of nationality. Apart from and over against the state, but having certain relations to it, were the people, among whom might be found art, science, literature, and all those social and moral forces which do not depend upon the state for their efficiency. Where such distinctions exist between the people and their government, a history of the English people may be something apart from the history of England; but the essential correlation of the people and the government

for the United States — in fact, their identity — makes
the history of the people, so far as it implies a distinction, a political and historical solecism.

Apparently Mr. McMaster intended such a distinction, to judge by the title of his history, and from the
fact that in the history itself, he has passed over in
silence, or relegated to a subordinate place, those matters which do not have a direct relation to what is
called the progress of society, using the term compre-
hensively.

Mr. McMaster's history opens in the midst of a sad,
shameful period of our national life, if we accept the
pictures he paints of it; and that they are drawn with
a general fidelity to truth there can be no doubt. But
it is equally true that the people suffer undeservedly
in reputation by this division of their history in the
middle of an important epoch, the whole of which is
essential to a right understanding of its parts. The
treaty of peace in 1783, with which Mr. McMaster's
history opens, is an apparent, instead of a real, land-
mark in our history. Essentially, it was a political
recognition of a fact accomplished by the capitulation
of Cornwallis nearly two years before. By beginning
his history at the time which he has selected, the people are not only denied the period of their glory, but
also of the presentation of those circumstances which
extenuate their shame. On the 19th of April, 1775,
the war for independence opened with spirit, and it
was carried on with courage and self-devotion. For
undisciplined soldiers, the troops generally fought
fairly well; and the officers were patriotic, if not particularly well educated for the profession of arms.
Congress and the colonial assemblies exerted themselves with vigor, and the people did not lag behind.

High-water mark of patriotism was reached in those efforts, public and private, which were crowned by the surrender of Burgoyne's army in October, 1777. With this event the people hoped the war would end; but it turned out otherwise, and the disasters at Brandywine, in September, and at Germantown, in October of the same year, fell with disheartening effect upon the country. This soon began to appear. The strength of the army gradually fell off from 46,901 in 1776 to 13,832 in 1781, the last year of the war; and the actual payments on military account, during the same period, dwindled from $21,000,000 to $2,000,000.[1] The people were becoming tired of the war, with its merciless drain upon their resources; and when the French army, with its ample military chest, took the field, there was danger lest the further prosecution of the contest would depend upon French men and French money. Jobbery and self-seeking were as rife as in the last years of the late Civil War. The unpaid soldiers were mutinous, and traitors near Washington's person corruptly revealed his plans to Clinton almost as soon as they were formed. Congress was torn with dissensions, and its proceedings were marked by incapacity and indecision. And the colonial assemblies were no better. In the dire extremity of the army, — its ranks depleted, its military chest empty, the soldiers destitute of food and clothing, requisitions were treated with indifference and almost contempt. This was the beginning of a state of affairs which continued some years after the time at which Mr. McMaster opens his history of the

---

[1] These and similar figures in this paper express facts only in a general way, and for any more exact purpose are to be received with caution, although found in respectable authorities.

people. Few more humiliating stories than those he relates can be found in the annals of the Anglo-Saxon race ; the treatment of the old soldiers ; the barbarities practiced on the refugee loyalists ; the continual disregard of congressional requisitions for the support of the government ; the Newburgh Address ; the violent resistance to the administration of justice ; the hostile legislation between the colonies ; the proposed issue of irredeemable paper-money for the purpose, openly avowed, of defrauding creditors. These, and other similar acts, threatened political and social anarchy. Nevertheless, the people did not fall into anarchy. On the contrary, government performed its functions, and steadily moved forward in the development of more complete and efficient forms. And if the history of the people in its entirety from 1774 to 1789 be taken into account, as in fairness it ought to be, though sorely tried, they were patient, courageous, prodigal of themselves and of their money, and worthy of the highest encomiums. Their history is the history of a period. Men who signed the Address to the King in 1774 also signed the Constitution of the United States in 1787 ; and during this time — less than half that assigned to a generation — what labors and sufferings did they not endure, what depths of humiliation did they not sound, what heights of glory did they not tread, — these men, less than three millions, who, in resistance to parliamentary taxation, put, it has been asserted, nearly three hundred thousand troops into the field, raised and paid out from the general treasury above a hundred millions of dollars, proclaimed and secured independence, changed their colonial governments without passing through a period of anarchy, quelled intestine commotions, entered into union, and established a national government which secured their prosperity and happiness. What people, in a time so brief, ever achieved so much? Nevertheless, they were very human. Sometimes they faltered; sometimes they lost heart, and even their heads; but they recovered both in season to prevent irretrievable disaster, and finally accomplished their great purpose. Now anything less than this history in its entirety, however faithful it may be in details, is injurious to their just fame, and loses its value for example or warning. Their mistakes and weaknesses and vacillation undoubtedly form a part of their history; and so do those great achievements and characteristics by which they finally triumphed. The remnant that were wise, constant, and virtuous were the people, — the Washingtons, Greenes, and Sumters, not the Arnolds, Conways, and Parsonses. In determining the character of the people of the Revolution, as a whole, it is not a question of majority. The men are to be weighed, not counted. On the side where the ultimate *force majeure* was found, there the people were to be found, — whether in the majority or in the minority no matter; and if the outcome of their endeavor was success, then were the people intelligent and wise; and if it was beneficent, then were they virtuous. The period from 1774 to 1789 was a period of rebellion, revolution, and reconstruction. But it will never be understood so long as it is regarded as an exceptional epoch in our history; for from the first day that organized English colonies were planted on American soil they began to rebel, to make revolutions, and to form constitutions. This they continued to do in clear political sequence, with scarcely a break, down to the day when they found themselves under a

stable government of their own. This is true of all
the colonies, and the essential political history of each
is the history of every other. The history of their
governments and of their peoples is one and inseparable; and their several peoples were one people, — an
organism with functions of scarcely distinguishable
honor or usefulness. There were no rich, no poor; no
high, no low; no wise, no ignorant; no virtuous, no
vicious, in the European sense of these terms.

It is doubtful, therefore, whether this history can
be adequately told in a series of monographs, or if
the history of the people be severed from that of the
political constitutions which expressed the popular
sentiment. But if this is attempted, the series certainly should include one on the people themselves;
for few subjects are more interesting or instructive
than the changes in the character of the people of the
United States between the landing at Jamestown and
the period which closes Mr. McMaster's second volume. For such a history we could well spare, or pass
lightly over, some other matters. History ought to be
made interesting, if verity in the general effect can be
preserved. But many entertaining subjects are of secondary importance. We need not be told — certainly
not with much detail — that in a new country, remote
from great centres of wealth and civilization, roads
were bad, bridges few or none, hotels execrable, books
rare, and newspapers lacking their modern features.
Such a condition of things marks only a stage of material progress, — not of civilization. Refined and cultivated communities have often found themselves surrounded by similar circumstances in the past, and so
will others in the future. The essential character of
the people is vastly more important.

At the time Mr. McMaster's history opens, Englishmen and their descendants, with slight admixture
of other blood, had lived for a hundred and fifty years
on this soil, under climate and influences widely differing from those to which their race for a thousand
years had been accustomed. What changes had these
new conditions produced in the physical, intellectual,
or moral character of these Anglo-Americans? On
its native soil the race had wrought great things and
acquired a great character. Less by military genius
than by courage and indomitable pluck, it had waged
successful wars. Rapacious in conquest and greedy of
the commercial results of colonization, yet it was the
most equitable of nations in dealing with its dependencies, save Ireland, and most benign in forming
governments for them. Nor was this greatness of
the past alone; for, recently, under the inspiration
of Pitt's genius, its spirit, bursting insular bounds,
had shone with unsurpassed splendor. There was no
continent and no clime that did not witness it. In
Europe, on the field of Rosbach, it had upheld the
hands of Frederick the Great, as he repelled the last
assault on continental Protestantism. At Plassy it
had opened a new empire in India. On the sea it had
humbled the power of Spain; and on the Plains of
Abraham it had destroyed the empire of France in
America.

No people in modern times had reached such heights
of national glory. Nor were their moral victories less
splendid. The nameless horrors of prisons were abolished; the slave-trade was destroyed; the penal code
mitigated; a reform bill passed, and moral instruction
carried to the cottages of the lowly, — achievements
which conferred lustre on such names as Howard,

Clarkson, Wilberforce, Burke, Romilly, and Hannah More.

With such affiliations, with such inheritances, with such stimulating examples in the elder branch of the race, how did the younger branch bear itself in its western home? From their first coming to these shores to the fall of the French empire in America their work, though difficult, had been simple : to subdue a wilderness and its savage inhabitants ; to develop self-government under the conditions imposed by their charters ; and to promote religion, education, and social progress. But after the fall of the French power a new, complicated, and difficult problem confronted them : to subvert the disastrous commercial policy of the empire, peaceably if possible, but to subvert it at all hazards ; to disrupt an empire when the necessity became inevitable ; to declare and maintain independence ; to change colonial governments into independent states, without intervening anarchy ; to form and establish union under a frame of government which should recognize the autonomy of states, while it embraced them all under a federal jurisdiction.

No people had ever undertaken a more difficult work, or accomplished it more successfully. England, in the days of Cromwell, attempted a permanent change of her government, and failed conspicuously. Later, France also failed in a similar endeavor prosecuted by methods at which mankind stood aghast.

But the American people have succeeded where those of England and of France miscarried. Chance and circumstances doubtless had something to do with this difference in results, but it was mainly owing to difference in character. The Anglo-American had acquired an element of character which did not belong to his British progenitor. Whatever he may have lost, he had gained the power of organization; and without this power he must have failed. This requires explanation. To the typical Englishman, the unit of force was the individual man; to the typical American, it was an organization. The force which reformed English prisons was John Howard; the force which reformed American prisons was the Prison Discipline Society. And something like this difference in modes of action has characterized the two branches of the race in those great movements which constitute the glory and the hope of the age.

This change in methods of action began in necessity. The first comers recognized it at once, and, with that practical sagacity which has always characterized them, they proceeded to organize themselves into a state-militant as a protection against an insidious foe; into a church-militant to deal summarily with intruding heretics; into town governments for the conduct of communal affairs; into school districts to carry education to every man's door; into watch-and-ward divisions for protection against fires and midnight marauders. And these people have lived and breathed and had their being in organizations ever since, and with manifest advantages, especially at the outset; for not only was every man utilized, leaving none superfluous or idle, but utilized for every conceivable exigency of the state, of which he became a part in a manner before unknown. And the value of this pervasive system of organization was even more manifest, when, in the fullness of time, barely two millions and · a half of people were arrayed in resistance to the most powerful empire of the world. Never did any race exhibit such power of organization, or put it to such efficient use, as did the colonists during the American Revolution. Town governments, committees of safety, committees of correspondence, inter-colonial associations, extemporized provincial congresses, and even organized mobs, kept well in hand by Samuel Adams and Isaac Sears to strike in exigencies where legal methods were inefficient, not only successfully resisted the power of Great Britain, but subverted the royal provincial governments, without violence, by provincial congresses which took their place *ad interim.*

We can seldom trace a national habit to its origin, but in this instance we may. It was due to the colonial charters; for the acceptance of a charter was in itself an act of organization, and the corporate existence in conformity to its provisions compelled the immediate organization of all those institutions, or their equivalents, such as legislatures, courts, towns, military companies, and the like, which on English soil, in the course of ages, had grown up without organization. A new necessity formed a new habit. And the habit once formed, the people organized themselves in all possible relations to the colonial state, and finally to all religious, social, and moral enterprises. Happily for them, also, the acceptance of charters changed their natural relations to the parent country into organic political relations to the crown which engaged the power of the state for their protection from domestic anarchy and foreign foes. The lack of this advantage, which can hardly be overestimated, is manifest in the unhappy condition of those colonies — of which Rhode Island is an example — which were without charters, or acquired them too late. This was not fully understood by either party at the time; but we now see that when Charles I. signed a colonial charter, he signed an instrument which, in the hands of the colonists, became an incipient declaration of independence to disturb all his successors ; and the fact that the English colonies were lands held of the crown, or were corporations within the realm, for extra-territorial purposes, and as such creating certain reciprocal rights and duties, is the master-key which unlocks their political history from Jamestown to Lexington.

This acquired faculty of organization still abides, and is used for the accomplishment of every conceivable purpose, and perhaps threatens to impair the force of individual action in great enterprises. But it ought not to be overlooked in the history of the people of the United States; for the people owe to it their independence. It is their greatest contribution to the science of practical politics, and its use is becoming common and efficient in other lands.[1]

But it is in the state that our history mainly centres, and there it must be sought; for by the government

---

[1] De Tocqueville opens the XIIth chapter of his first volume of *Democracy in America* with these words : " In no country in the world has the principle of association been more successfully used, or applied to a greater multitude of objects, than in America; " but he states the fact as he found it when he wrote, without tracing its historical origin. In chapter V. of his second volume, he recurs to the subject and asks, " Is this the result of accident ? or is there in reality any necessary connection between the principles of association and that of equality ? " Apparently he thought there was. But association in America is an historical fact which antedates by sixty years the operation of politico-philosophical causes. The first act of social existence in the dominating colony of New England was an act of association which made necessary all successive steps in that direction. Equality was scarcely a genetic force in a close corporation of landholders into which the prime condition of entrance was membership in the established colonial church. Of the general correctness of De Tocqueville's view, however, there can be little doubt.

have been accomplished those ends which most powerfully affected not only the material prosperity of the
people, but also their national character. It was by a
foreign treaty that the people gained a recognized
position among the nations. By the same treaty their
rights in the fisheries were restored, and thus was
formed a nursery of hardy seamen who, when free
play was given to their spirit, challenged England's
assumed sovereignty of the seas. And it was the same
treaty which opened the Mississippi to the turbulent
commerce which poured down from its tributaries.
The Ordinance of 1787 — which Mr. McMaster has
passed over without endeavoring to unravel its intri-
cate history, and with only slight recognition of its
character — excluded slavery from the Northwest, and
made it the home of freemen who now have grown to
prosperous millions. It was by treaty that Louisiana was purchased in 1803, including territory which
more than doubled the area of the Union, and saved
to Anglo-American laws, customs, and manners the
vast regions beyond the Great River. It was through
the Assumption Act and the Funding System that
Hamilton "touched the dead corpse of the Public
Credit, and it sprung upon its feet," — acts whose
moral significance is found in the fact that the public
credit has ever since been without stain, that specie
payment was resumed, and that justice was done to
the veterans of the Civil War.

Such are some of the themes — " of congresses, of
embassies, of treaties " — which enter into the real
history of the people of the United States, and constitute its chief value for the citizen as well as for the
student. They ought not to be crowded into a corner.

On the other hand, it is noticeable that from the

peace of 1783 to the close of Washington's administration such matters as are embraced in the phrase
" the progress of society " were almost of necessity in
abeyance. For during this period the States were perfecting the machinery of their several governments,
and the general government was determining its own
powers, and adjusting its relations to the States. The
people were chiefly occupied "with wars, conspiracies,
rebellions ; with presidents, with congresses, with embassies, and with treaties," which Mr. McMaster regards as of secondary importance.

But though they were chiefly so concerned, nevertheless molecular action was going on which affected
their moral and intellectual character; it was due,
however, neither to the state nor to popular action, but
to forces entirely overlooked by Mr. McMaster, or so
treated by him as to afford no indication of their
power. For when George Whitefield, John Wesley,
Francis Asbury, John Murray, Elhanan Winchester,
and Joseph Priestley died, the people of the United
States were something quite different from what they
would have been had these Englishmen never lived
and labored on American soil. Asbury's influence,
doubtless, was the most widely and most powerfully
felt ; and it is, perhaps, no exaggeration to say that he
saved the West and the Southwest to civilization. For
as the hardy but illiterate people who from the hills
of Virginia and the Carolinas scaled the Alleghanies,
and from their western slopes descended into the valley of the Mississippi, it was Asbury and the three
thousand Methodist preachers ordained by him who
met and organized them into religious societies, so that
within twenty years from the peace of 1783 these
trans-Alleghanean communities were nearly as well

supplied with religious institutions as the older States from which they had emigrated.

The labors of Murray and Winchester, the apostles of Universalism, also, were too considerable to be passed silently by in the history of the people of the United States, and the same may be said of the rehabilitation of Episcopacy by Madison, Seabury, Parker, Bass, and White.

Of Priestley's scientific and political influence we are told something, but nothing of his theological opinions which a little later convulsed New England churches, and gained adherents from whom came the greater part of our imaginative literature even to the present day.

No reasonable exception can be taken to Mr. McMaster's low estimate of colonial imaginative literature, and he doubtless places a just value — which is high — upon the theological speculations of those days, which for acuteness and depth were not surpassed by any similar work emanating from the British islands. But the historian should not undervalue the political pamphlets of Otis, Hutchinson, the Adamses, Jay, Dickinson, and Livingston, for they have not been surpassed either in the discussion of great principles or in their application to practical affairs. The legal erudition of those times, also, is almost phenomenal, when it is considered that from a people without training in legal principles and with a profound distrust of lawyers there sprang almost at a bound, when needed, men such as Gridley, Prat, Adams, Parsons, Jay, Dulaney, Wythe, and Marshall, either of whom, with a little special training, would have filled with credit the place of Mansfield, of Camden, or of Eldon.

The causes of the literary poverty of men of such large and varied general ability opens up an interesting field of speculation, but not to be entered on at this time.

It is easier to raise questions respecting the history of the people of the United States than it is to answer them. Nevertheless, such questions are legitimate. For example, Mr. McMaster tells us that "in the Southern States education was almost wholly neglected, but nowhere to such an extent as in South Carolina." And yet, from Virginia and the Carolinas emigrated to Kentucky, Tennessee, and Mississippi a race of men like Daniel Boone, Andrew Jackson, George Rogers Clarke, and John Sevier, who not only wrote good hands (as their early autograph letters, preserved in collections, show), but who seemed to be fairly educated for civil affairs, and able to carry forward in their new homes a civilization differing in some respects from that of the East, but in no respect inferior to that of the communities they left behind them. These were not the sons of wealthy planters, educated at Eton, at Winchester, or Harrow, or even at William and Mary ; or of parents able to provide for them private tutors. The educational history of these emigrants is an interesting subject for investigation.

The modification of the character of the descendants of Englishmen on this soil, already spoken of, was brought about mainly by their situation. But during the last quarter of the eighteenth century there had come into their life a new force, — faith in the power of ideas. Down to that time Anglo-Americans, like their progenitors, were men severely practical and averse to general propositions. Their faith in the power of creeds and dogmas, religious and political, was steadfast. They believed in heavy battalions and serried ranks, but with them faith in the power of ideas was not even a conception. Their legislation related to affairs, not to systems; and the doctrinaire was not known within their borders. But for the last century it has been different, and this difference is due to Jefferson. Where Jefferson got his idealism is a mystery; for though he has many disciples, he had no known master. It is usual to attribute it to the influence of French writers — Rousseau especially; but the vitality and permanence of this element in his character suggest an original rather than an acquired force. About Jefferson as the head of a party, as an administrator, and even as a man, opinions may differ; but there can be little doubt that he was the first statesman who had faith in the sufficiency of ideas not merely as tests of the validity of political institutions, but as a power to subvert arbitrary government and overthrow errors, however strongly intrenched in ancient wrong. In this respect perhaps he stands first among thinkers, and certainly among the greatest of those who have profoundly and beneficently modified the character of an entire people. His influence seems destined to affect the thought of mankind.

De Tocqueville has noticed this change. "The Americans," he says, "are much more addicted to the use of general ideas than the English, and entertain a much greater relish for them: this appears very singular at first, when it is remembered that the two nations have the same origin, that they lived for centuries under the same laws, and that they incessantly interchange their opinions and their manners. . . . They have no philosophical school of their own, . . .

yet they have a philosophical method common to the whole people." The way may have been prepared for this change, as he suggests, by their democratic habits, but Jefferson was the founder of the school of political idealists. He struck the key-note, first heard in his "Summary View," in 1774, and with a louder strain sent it round the world in the great Declaration. If one would see the change produced by Jefferson, let him read the Declaration of Rights by the Congress of 1774, and then the Declaration of Independence of 1776. One is a specification as cold as an indictment to be tried by a petit jury; the other, a trumpet call to the race and to the ages. It was the comprehensiveness of Jefferson's immortal Declaration which made it powerful in one generation to sever the bands of an empire, and in another to break the shackles of four millions of slaves, and in the present — but who shall forecast the future of Ireland or limit the potency of Jefferson's words? To redress the balance between England and her colonies he invoked the power of ideas. He thus added to the armory of a struggling people a new weapon, — now the dynamics of nationalities, — restless, resistless, unassailable by fleets or armies!

This force, which Jefferson set in motion, sometimes took a direction which he did not contemplate and of which he would not have approved. The real inspiration of the young statesmen who forced the War of 1812 was less the local cry of "free trade and sailors' rights" than an aspiration towards nationality, caught not from Jefferson, indeed, — for the father of state rights was not a nationalist, — but for which they were indebted, nevertheless, to Jefferson's idealism: an aspiration to which Webster gave utterance at

Bunker Hill in words never forgotten, "Our country, our whole country, and nothing but our country;" and again, even more effectively, in the Senate Chamber, in those other words, "the Union, one and inseparable," taken up by the people and realized after four years of civil war.

The advent of such a force into the life of a people is rare, and when apprehended in its full significance it is one of the most impressive events in their history; and its recognition is a test of historic insight. It is America's contribution to political philosophy; and if it be thought to belong to politics rather than to history, it is, nevertheless, an event inseparably connected with the history of the people of the United States, and is fast becoming a part of the history of the human race. As the race moves down through the ages, it has a life and progress which includes the life and progress of every nationality. Into this mighty stream are affluents which bear on their surface traces of the soil and vegetation of their sources, and these mark the differences between nations.

Mr. McMaster's book is a valuable contribution to our history, and will be the cause of work better than its own. His industrious collection of materials and his effective arrangement and courageous presentation of them cannot fail to stimulate other workers in the same field. But he does not always discriminate as to the value of authorities, and his history suffers somewhat in consequence. Observations in science, unless made under conditions which insure accuracy, are of little value; and this is beginning to be recognized in respect to history. No conclusions should be drawn from the unsupported testimony of such travelers as Anburey or Brissot; and sectarian

and party prejudices often render worthless the works
of native historians.

With these observations we take leave of Mr. Mc-
Master's history. Where we have received so much
and of so great value, it is ungracious to ask for more
or for something different ; but our just claims upon
Mr. McMaster are limited only by his ability. His
series of historical monographs is accepted with gratitude ; but if he has

> " . . . . left half-told
> The story "

which he is able to tell in full, — and certain vital
signs leave little doubt on that point, — he must for-
give us if we are not entirely satisfied with what he
has already done.

JOSIAH QUINCY, THE GREAT MAYOR

An Address before the Massachusetts Society for
promoting Good Citizenship, at the Old South
Meeting House, Boston, February 25, 1889

JOSIAH QUINCY, THE GREAT MAYOR

In front of the City Hall in Boston are two statues in bronze — one of Benjamin Franklin and the other of Josiah Quincy. The artist has represented Franklin in his old age and the culminated splendor of his fame, revisiting, as he had often expressed a desire to do, the city of his birth, and standing in reverential attitude, with uncovered head, before the spot hallowed by memories of the old Boston Latin School, in which he received the rudiments of his education. No better site could have been chosen. With equal felicity of position Josiah Quincy, in the prime of manhood, stands on the opposite side of the inclosure, before the most august symbol of the city which he had done so much to build up and adorn. As works of art these statues provoked the vituperative eloquence of Boston's most gifted orator, and I hear that they divide the opinions of experts. However this may be, the characters they commemorate gain in respect with the passing years and the spread of letters.

In some circumstances of their lives Benjamin Franklin and Josiah Quincy resembled each other; in others, they were strongly contrasted. Natives of the same town, each represented the class from which he sprung, and each had no inconsiderable influence in shaping the institutions of Philadelphia and of

Boston, in which they severally resided. Franklin
was of the people, without fortune or interest or
social position; but by self-culture and industrious
use of his powers and opportunities, he became distinguished at home and abroad, and here, if nowhere
else, is known as "the Great Bostonian." Josiah
Quincy, on the other hand, was of "good family" —
a phrase which denoted the highest distinction of
rank accorded in the Boston of those days. His fortune, "counseling ignoble ease and peaceful sloth,"
was ample; but closing his ears to the sirens, he bound
himself to laborious days, and, having acquired reputation in national affairs, so successfully promoted the
development of municipal institutions that he is now
best known as "the Great Mayor."

The life of Franklin, often written, has been read
in many lands, and thousands, following his precepts
and example, have lived successful lives. Josiah
Quincy's life by his son, a model of literary skill and,
as a filial biography, unsurpassed if ever equaled, is
less known than it ought to be; for in the field of
civic affairs, everywhere now assuming importance, I
know of no more instructive or exemplary life ever
lived in America. That phase of it — its instructive
and exemplary quality — is my theme this evening.

He was born here in Boston, on the easterly side of
Washington Street, a few doors southerly from Milk
Street, February 4, 1772; was graduated at Harvard
College in 1790; admitted to the bar in 1793; and
married in 1797. In May, 1804, he was elected to
the State Senate, and in October of the same year, at
the age of thirty-three, a representative to Congress,
where he sat until March 4, 1813. Declining further

service in that body, with the exception of several terms in the General Court and the session of the Constitutional Convention of 1820, he was in private life, giving much attention to the cultivation of his ancestral acres at Quincy, until his appointment in 1821 as judge of the Municipal Court of Boston, over which he presided for two years. From May, 1823, to January, 1829, he was mayor of Boston. Failing of reëlection, he was chosen president of Harvard College in 1829, and held that office for sixteen years, residing at Cambridge. After his resignation of the presidency in 1845, he returned to Boston, resuming his summer residence at Quincy, and there, in his house overlooking the sea, he died, July 1, 1864, at the great age of ninety-two years, four months, and twenty-seven days.

Few of our public men have lived so long or through so many extraordinary events. His life began little less than a year before Samuel Adams in Faneuil Hall reported the "Rights of the Colonists," in one of the most important state papers of the Revolutionary period; and it ended little less than a year before Lee surrendered his army at Appomattox Court House. At the first period the Revolution, which severed an empire and made thirteen subject colonies independent States, had become inevitable; at the second, the last slave shackle in Anglo-Saxon lands had been broken, and the decree of God was on the wing which reunited the great Republic as one, free and inseparable. What momentous events intervened! The first shot at Lexington and the bloody carnage at Bunker Hill; the Declaration of Independence and Cornwallis's surrender at Yorktown; the Treaty of Peace, in 1783, and the framing of the

Constitution of the United States, in 1787; the acquisition of Louisiana, including territory west of the
Mississippi, more than doubling the area of the Republic; and the War of 1812, which first aroused the
spirit of nationality in the people, and on the sea
compelled the respect of the world; the adoption of
an economic system developing antagonism between
the manufacturing North and the cotton-growing
South, at one time seriously threatening the Union,
and the beginning of hostility to slavery which finally
led to its extinction by civil war.

At the beginning of the Revolution Josiah Quincy
was too young to have intelligently observed what
was passing about Boston between 1774 and 1776, if,
during these years, there had not been found a more
safe retreat for him at Norwich, Connecticut; but
from the adoption of the Constitution nothing of public interest escaped his notice.

There was, however, one interesting event of which
he may have had a vague recollection. It was the
"tea party" of December 16, 1773. In the afternoon of that day, his father, standing here in the Old
South where I now stand, and speaking to those who
sat where you now sit, said in words which have become historical: "It is not, Mr. Moderator, the spirit
which vapors within these walls that must stand us in
stead. The exertions of this day call forth events
which will make a very different spirit necessary for
our salvation" — words true now, and as applicable
to affairs in this city to-day as they were more than a
century ago when they reëchoed from these walls. In
the evening of that afternoon the infantile ears of his
son must have heard, though they heeded not, the
tramp of men hurrying past his father's door to gather

in this place; and they must have heard the war-whoop which came up out of the darkness of the street and was responded to by shouts from these dimly lighted galleries. Then Griffin's Wharf; then the Boston Port Bill; then Lexington and Bunker Hill; then the Siege of Boston and the Declaration of Independence — events which he could have known only as we know them.

Though Josiah Quincy doubtless knew Samuel Adams, it does not appear that he sought his society. Samuel Adams was much the older, and they were of different political parties. But with John Hancock, who married Dorothy Quincy, his father's cousin, he was better acquainted, and once at least was his guest in the old Hancock House, now unfortunately no longer standing. Honor to the man, the President of this Society, who, with a just sense of the value of patriotic associations to good citizenship, did so much to save the Old South!

He knew Washington also, and so did Mrs. Quincy. Their estimates of the personality of that great man were widely different, she regarding him as "more than a hero — a superior being, as far above the common race of mankind in majesty and grace of personal bearing as in moral grandeur;" and he, forsooth, as not unlike "the gentlemen who used to come to Boston in those days to attend the General Court from Hampden or Franklin County, in the western part of the State — a little stiff in his person, not a little formal in his manner, and not particularly at ease in the presence of strangers." In this difference of estimate we see one touch of nature which makes all married couples kin.

I have given you a mere outline of Mr. Quincy's life. It was long, useful, honorable. In whatever field of labor he entered he soon became distinguished; but when, in May, 1823, in the second year of the city, Josiah Quincy became its mayor, he found the place suited more than any other, I think, to his talents and his moral qualities; and in the six years that he served the city he did the work which gave him his highest fame, and in the retrospect of a long and varied career the most satisfaction.

His new office certainly was less conspicuous as a theatre of action than the floor of the House when filled by Randolph of Roanoke, Clay, Calhoun, Webster, and Macon; and the proceedings of the city government attracted less attention, if any, in Europe or in this country, than national affairs from the Embargo of 1807 to the Peace of 1815. And when, in 1823, Josiah Quincy, in the prime of life and in the fullness of his great powers, reëngaged in public affairs as the chief magistrate of a small city, it is not unlikely that his old associates at Washington, whom he had led in attack, and some of whom had felt the vigor of his onset, regarded the change of position as a descent. Even in this day of grace the mayoralty of a great city, which with its grand possibilities to all sincere men might well seem the summit of a career, is too often looked upon as a stepping-stone.

On the other hand, when, in 1829, he became president of the oldest and most conspicuous college in the land, and not unknown in Europe, it was doubtless thought that Mr. Quincy at length had reached a position more worthy of his great abilities and of his rich and varied culture. But it is a fair question whether during the eight years he was in Congress, where, encountering Henry Clay without discomfiture, he delivered a series of speeches, in the judgment of Webster the best of that period, or during the sixteen years when he was president of Harvard College and rescued it from financial peril, reformed its administration, and placed it on a firm basis, he did a work so peculiarly his own, or one so far beyond the powers of other men, or by which he desired or deserved to be remembered, as that of the six years when he was mayor of Boston.

Mr. Quincy, voluntarily retiring from Congress on March 4, 1813, never officially reëngaged in national affairs, to the regret of his friends and, as his son suggests, possibly to his own in later years. I think we need not share that feeling. Doubtless with opportunity he would have acquired great distinction, and possibly be more widely known to-day. We now see, however, that John Quincy Adams accomplished everything in diplomacy or in national administration that Mr. Quincy could have done, nor could Mr. Webster's senatorial career have been surpassed. But what other American known to history could have equaled Mr. Quincy's work in municipal affairs; or who will presume to determine its relative importance to that of either of his great compeers?

I have no desire to magnify the subject assigned to me. Certainly I have none to overestimate the relative value of different periods of service in Mr. Quincy's life, and still less to underrate the service of those who, from John Phillips to the present hour, have filled the mayor's chair with honor. Boston has been fortunate in the selection of her chief magistrates; but by any standard and by any comparison Mr. Quincy's work as mayor was a great work of enduring value, and his place is high up among able and useful men of his age and country.

I think we may safely go farther, and say that in the department of American municipal affairs no one of his countrymen ever had a wider, more profound, more permanent, or more beneficent influence than had Josiah Quincy as mayor of Boston. This was due in part, no doubt, to the fact that Boston was one of the earliest incorporated cities in the country, and perhaps the first to bring all departments of its government into that harmonious adjustment which made it a pattern for other cities in the United States, and, in certain particulars, for some in Europe. It is equally true that Josiah Quincy, like all men essentially great, recognized the advantages of his position and made the most of them ; and so far as he made Boston what it was, and as widely and permanently as it has influenced the institutions of other cities, so wide and permanent ought to be his just fame. Such was his opportunity. Then came his hour ; and I think he made it an epoch in the history of municipal government.

Who and what then was Josiah Quincy; how did he equip himself for his work; for what do his life, his character, and his services stand to us ?

Here was a man in rare combination of birth, talents, personal accomplishments, and estate — the most enviable man of his day in America. That was his good fortune. It is our fortune, if we so will, that there was nothing in any of the essential circumstances of his life, or his character, or conduct, which we cannot imitate, adopt, and follow. And it is just this imitable and exemplary quality which makes him,

on the whole, the best model hitherto appearing in
our American life upon which to form ourselves.
The consummate genius of Henry Clay, who first
aroused the spirit of nationality in the people, or
of Webster, who moulded the Constitution to it, or
of Lincoln, who called a million of armed men to
its defense, so far transcends the limits of ordinary
rational aspiration as to make imitation ridiculous.
Had Mr. Quincy belonged to that class of men, in
despair we might turn off the lights and, in the seclusion of our homes, giving rein to imagination, vainly
identify ourselves with those rare spirits who have
appeared to dazzle, to delight, and to elude us. Happily for us, in what he did for good government, or in
what his example may inspire us to do for good government, he was of a different order, though I think
we shall quite as soon see another Henry Clay, or
Daniel Webster, or possibly Abraham Lincoln, as
another Josiah Quincy. Each in some particulars
surpassed him. But in the genius of character — in
the combination of intellectual and moral qualities —
he has had no superior in our American life. And
it is character which finally prevails; which moulds
institutions and forms a people for greatness; which
gathers to itself and expresses what is best and most
permanent in race qualities. It is the dominating
and permanent influence on society. The stream finds
its path, not by the lights which glitter along its
course, nor by sun, moon, or stars above, but by its
headlands and firm-set shores. Our Puritans prevailed, not because of the intellectual greatness of
one, but because many were great in character; and
so it must ever be. Great as were Mr. Quincy's abilities, his preëminence was in character. And it is

this which draws us to the Old South to-night; not to search his life for entertaining anecdotes — of which there are many — or points effective in biographical description. With set purpose I shall pass over everything, however attractive, which is not profitable for doctrine, for reproof, for correction, or for instruction in the righteousness of citizenship. I wish to discern in his life and character and services, if I may, whatever will instruct and inspire us to the formation of like character, to undertake similar services so far as our circumstances allow, and to act with the same fidelity to duty. Failing in this, I fail utterly.

Mr. Quincy did not, like Franklin, raise himself from poverty to affluence and power; but he was exposed to perils which Franklin escaped — perils which most of us escape; perils of social position as the only son of an eminent revolutionary patriot enrolled by great services and early death among the martyrs; of his singularly attractive personality — a fatal gift to one of less austere self-control; of his fortune, permitting a life of elegant leisure elevated by no sincere purpose; of an hereditary domain crowned by an historic mansion hospitable to illustrious visitors from other lands, as well as his own, including three Presidents of the United States — a social distinction satisfying to a moral sense less robust, less exacting than his own. How many have been wrecked by perils which Josiah Quincy avoided; how few have acknowledged the obligations he assumed; how many have laid down the burdens he carried nearly a hundred years; how many, withholding, or in disgust withdrawing, themselves from public affairs for which they are eminently fitted by education, fortune, and

social position, have yielded to the seductions of pleasures, not always innocent, and lived their lives and
exhausted their gifts with no results of value to themselves or to others!

Franklin and Quincy were both great men; and it
is not their least — perhaps it is their highest — claim
to grateful remembrance that each, pushing aside the
obstacles and escaping the perils which beset him,
made the most of his powers and opportunities.
Higher honor no man ever gained than this; than
this of no man God requires more. Seldom has the
same town produced two such men, each recognized
as the best type of some characteristic trait of its
people — Franklin of their thrift, the result of right
conduct; Josiah Quincy of their fitness for citizenship, which for two hundred years, in peace and in war,
had made Boston a most conspicuous and influential
municipality; himself to become more widely known
as the rights and duties of citizenship are accorded
their just place in the education and life of the people, as they must inevitably be with the development
of republican government.

Mr. Quincy's talents were great, so great that more
safely than most men he could have dispensed with
laborious preparation for his public work; but, save
John Adams and his son, John Quincy, I know no
one of our countrymen who so assiduously prepared
for it. From early manhood he fitted himself for
citizenship with very clear notions of its value and
just demands; and he cultivated his powers by an
exhaustive study of every question likely to engage
them.

Although completely equipped for office, Josiah
Quincy, so far as I can discover, never sought it; nor,

what is quite as much to his credit considering his
easy fortune, did he ever refuse it. I think we may
safely say that he never accepted office for its honors
or its emoluments, nor declined it to escape its labors,
its responsibilities, or even its obloquy.   When he
accepted the mayoralty it was not that he might make
himself famous, but, as he hoped, that he might
make the city eminent for good order, for honest
government, and for the prosperity of its people —
make it

> "Athens the eye of Greece, mother of arts
> And eloquence, native to famous wits
> Or hospitable ; "

nor did it change his determination or his conduct by
a hair's breadth when he foresaw, as he did from the
beginning, that after such services the people would
reject him.

He succeeded John Phillips as mayor, in May, 1823,
and held the office six years. The history of his administration being in some sort a " Tract for the Times,"
I desire to preface it by recalling to your recollection
the state of municipal affairs in Boston in 1821, at the
time the people were discussing their fundamental
government — whether it should remain, as for two
hundred years it had been, essentially democratic, or
be changed more completely to a representative government.   An interesting question not only in Boston
but elsewhere ; for, about the time when Mr. Quincy
was giving attention to the subject, Guizot, who had
been of the ministry of Louis XVIII., in which he
took an active part in the establishment of representative government in France, was preparing a course
of lectures, afterwards expanded and published, in

1852, as " The History of the Origin of Representative
Government in Europe." Guizot believed in representative government, and yet when he published that
work he had witnessed the bad fortune of the experi-
ment in France in 1820, the severer test of it in 1830,
and its disastrous failure when Louis Napoleon seized
the government in 1851. Nevertheless his faith en-
dured, and in the wreck of hopes and reasonable expectations, with sublime serenity he said that "among
the infinite illusions of human vanity we must number those of misfortune ; whether as peoples or individuals, in public or in private life, we delight to
persuade ourselves that our trials are unprecedented,
and that we have to endure evils and surmount obstacles previously unheard of. How deceitful is this
consolation of pride and suffering ! God has made
the condition of men, of all men, more severe than
they are willing to believe ; and he causes them at all
times to purchase at a dearer price than they had anticipated the success of their labors and the progress
of their destiny. Let us accept this stern law without
a murmur ; let us courageously pay the price which
God puts upon success, instead of basely renouncing
success itself."

It heightens our respect for Mr. Quincy that, though
he was opposed to a city charter and resisted it by
speech and pen as long as there was any chance of
defeating it, yet, when it was adopted, with sincerity
and untiring labor he devoted his powers and his time
to make it successful.

Like some other able men of his day, he believed
the pure democracy of the town meeting more suited
to the character of the people of New England and
less liable to corruption and abuse than a more com-

pact government, which, with all its checks and balances, checks after the collision and balances after the
load is overturned quite as often as before — a system
which breeds confidential clerks and swells the population of Montreal — a sort of " Waterbury watch "
affair, out of which you get no more time than you
put into it!

After nearly seventy years of representative city
government it is premature to say what form it will
ultimately take ; whether it will return to the old
democratic simplicity, if some practicable scheme can
be devised, or still further simplify representation by
abolishing all intermediaries, such as the Board of
Aldermen and Common Council, and, intrusting everything to the Mayor, with such heads of departments
as he may choose, hold him responsible for good government. This has one advantage of a monarchy. If
the people dislike the monarch they can decapitate
him, as they often have done ; with representative
bodies this is not quite so convenient, though often
quite as desirable and necessary !

It took six thousand years to ascertain whether,
by just law, the sun should revolve around the earth
as a centre, or the earth around the sun. Copernicus
settled that question ; and we await the advent of an
equal genius to adjust the revolution of political bodies agreeably to the divine order. In the mean time
we must wait, but not idly. As we ourselves have to
do, so did Mr. Quincy take things as he found them
— not altogether as he would have chosen. When he
came to the government he found matters much as
they are now. Then there were proportionally as many
who pleaded, as we do, in excuse for declining participation in public affairs, that their opinions, tastes,

and what seemed to them right modes of action, were
so different from those of a large part of the people
and so unlikely to result in success that it was hardly
worth while to waste their energies in the vain endeavor to secure good government; that matters were in
a bad way doubtless, but that they could better bear
the ills of bad government than afford the time required for their correction; that a few right-minded
people were of small account among so many wrong-
minded, and at worst that they were as well off as
others. Mr. Quincy had quite as good reason as we
have for impatience, discouragement, and disgust with
popular ignorance, unreasonableness, and caprice, with
the greed of the selfish and the indifference of well-
to-do people.

The change from the old town government to a city
government, requiring a surrender of methods dear
to the people by immemorial usage and the adoption of new methods necessarily abridging many of
their former liberties, caused discontent, which increased rather than diminished after their first·year's
experience of the new system. For two hundred
years the town government had performed its functions, upon the whole, with results satisfactory to
the people. It was their own — to them a great
merit; for in it they made their power felt without
much dilution by passing through a representative
medium. It was economical — another merit; for
the people were economical. They treated the unfortunate and vicious classes with slight regard to
health, comfort, or their possible restoration to better
conditions. Streets were narrow, ill paved, unswept,
and drainage disgracefully inadequate; but wide
streets, well paved, well lighted, and well drained

were costly luxuries, to be had only by taxation.
They had rebelled against British taxation, and quar-
reled with the domestic article. They disliked the
thing, by whatever name. Consequently their legislation was from hand to mouth, with little regard to
system or prevision of remote consequences, good or
bad.

This was a serious embarrassment to Mr. Quincy,
whose broad and forecasting mind projected measures
requiring time for their perfection and for yielding
their best results. Of course the people were not un-
aware of the impracticability of 7,000 voters assem-
bling in one place, usually Faneuil Hall, to choose
town officers, levy taxes, and determine with due
deliberation the various and complicated legislative
and executive affairs for a population of 40,000 ; and,
as we shall see, they had delegated some of the more
important functions to executive boards. Nevertheless, five times between 1784 and 1821 they had refused a charter, and finally accepted it only by a
majority of 1,500 of the 5,000 voters who took the
trouble to express their wishes at the polls.

The government had changed, but the people remained the same. Old habits were strong. They
missed their March meeting — a sort of festival day
on which they had assembled in Faneuil Hall, chosen
town officers, and done their town business, as had
their fathers for two hundred years, and outside exchanged friendly greetings and the news, and now and
then made sharp bargains. For the young were frolic
and sport and gingerbread and fire-crackers, dear to
boys. How different from all this were cold, isolated
ward rooms, with no debates and no James Otis, or
Samuel Adams, or Harrison Gray Otis, the most bril-

liant of orators until Wendell Phillips arose in Faneuil Hall to electrify the peninsula and recall the austere virtues of the Puritans.

Nor was sentimental attachment wanting. The town meeting had endeared itself to the people in affording opportunities for resisting every form of royal predominance, civil or ecclesiastical, which interfered with their rights, real or imaginary, and by its agency in bringing on and carrying forward the Revolution. Some of the older men had seen how effectively, how wisely, Samuel Adams had handled it, and generally, though not always, how unselfishly. It had been the palladium of their liberties, and they were sorry to give it up.

Now these principles, reasons, and prejudices, although shared by Josiah Quincy, were a serious hindrance to his government, into which they were carried by the people, and made themselves more and more manifest as the stringency of new rules interfered with old customs and interests. There was laudation of old ways and much carping at the new, chiefly because they were new.

From a very early day many legislative and executive powers of the town government had been given over to Selectmen, Overseers of the Poor, Board of Health, Firewards, and Assessors ; and it came to pass that the first three of these boards constituted a Finance Committee, which determined appropriations, assessment of taxes, and expenditures. Although they owed their election and nominally their powers to the people, practically they were self-perpetuating oligarchies, which claimed to carry their functions into the new city government in 1822, and were only suppressed by the tact and persistence of Mr. Quincy in asserting the just authority of the new government under the charter.

When Mr. Quincy became mayor the new government had been running a year. The first mayor, an able and worthy gentleman, does not appear to have given much attention to municipal affairs; and other public burdens, with failing health, prevented his grappling with troublesome questions. He left them with Mr. Quincy. The charter, as drafted by the late Chief Justice Shaw, was a model. But paper government was one thing, and a working government was quite another thing — a machine needing adjustment. This was no easy matter. An indolent, easy-going mayor, to whom conscience was of less account than comfort, caring less to have matters run correctly than smoothly, and more solicitous respecting his reëlection than for the public interests, would have got on with a tithe of the trouble which Mr. Quincy took to himself.

In everything relating to the construction or working of the charter and to the management of city affairs, he had a way of his own. He studied subjects until he knew them better than any other man. Of this, I dare say, he was conscious, and perhaps he was opinionated. Nevertheless, he was a just man, judicially just, determined, inflexible, steadfast. Nothing escaped his eye, and in labor he was untiring.

Here was the right man for the place, yet very much in the way, — in the way of all wrong-headed people; of those whose private interests conflicted with the public interests; of all who had jobs; of all who wished to be left alone in pursuit of their selfish courses or passions, regardless of the general weal.

In giving an account of the new mayor's work I

cannot go very fully into details; but in general
terms, and with due regard to facts, I think I may
say that there was no one of our public institutions,
nor anything in the mode of conducting them, which
gave rank to Boston among cities quite out of proportion to its territory or population, and made it a
model for other cities, which either did not originate
in the inventive mind of Josiah Quincy, or owe to his
shaping hand completer development and more beneficent action.   His work covered public morals, health,
education, convenience, and comfort; streets, sewers,
and water ; penal, reformatory, and industrial institutions; markets, police, fire department, and an incipient public garden.   With efficient coadjutors and,
in a general sense, the public support, yet he was the
greatest factor in every work.   He inspired, he led.
Before his time mayors were often merely presiding
officers, — ornamental figure-heads.   Executive powers had fallen into the hands of boards.   Lack of
unity and efficiency followed.   Mr. Quincy determined to be mayor.   Therefore he gathered up all the
powers which the charter, in express terms or by fair
construction, gave him, and he used them with results
before unknown ; not to engross power, but, as he
said, " to produce and fix in the minds of all influential classes of citizens a strong conviction of the advantages of having an active and willingly responsible
executive, by an actual experience of the benefits of
such an administration of their affairs ; and also
of their right and duty of holding the mayor responsible in character and office for the state of the police
and finances of the city."

Such were Mr. Quincy's views respecting good government.   To bring it about taxed his powers to the

utmost. He succeeded, and his success was the best
solution of the problem of city government hitherto
presented. The sequel is worth noting. After he
left the mayoralty, in 1829, there set in a departure
from his views, which finally became wide. Old jealousies between the different departments of government revived. The legislative branch claimed a share
in the powers of the executive department, and both
in those of the mayor. The General Court yielded to
the clamor for popular rights; and after a time we
came to have a government which, lacking unity of
power and consequent responsibility, did not govern.
Matters finally came to such a pass that, in 1885, the
Legislature again intervened and remodeled the charter so as to act more nearly in the spirit in which Mr.
Quincy administered it sixty years before.

When Mr. Quincy had established the government
on a good basis, he instituted a series of reforms,
more than a score in number, which gave to Boston a
high rank among municipalities, and made it in many
respects a model city; a model of institutions for the
criminal, the improvident, and the unfortunate; of
well-paved, clean-kept, and well-lighted streets; of
sewerage and systematic removal of public and private offal; of administrative measures concerning
public health, education, police, and markets; of the
preservation of natural scenery, such as the islands in
the harbor, and for the inauguration of a park system,
now unfolding itself with promise to public health
and morals and the sense of beauty.

Without order of time, and grouping some related
measures, I now specify a few of Mr. Quincy's services. If to-day, or at any time before to-day, Boston

has or has had the reputation of being one of the cleanest and most healthy of large cities, it is due mainly to Josiah Quincy. He took the matter in hand soon after his inauguration — and there was need. Conflicting boards claimed sole authority to clean the streets and remove offal. Consequently the work was not well done. The powers inefficiently exercised by these boards were transferred by legislative authority and municipal consent to the mayor and aldermen, who got to work with such effect that "for the first time, on any scale destined for universal application, the broom was used upon the streets; every street, alley, court, and household yard, however distant and however obscure, was thoroughly cleansed." The death rate was lessened and the comfort of the people increased.

With like vigor, and with similar discouragements, Mr. Quincy overhauled criminal and pauper institutions. There was an almshouse in the heart of the city. Its inmates, allowed to wander through the streets, some intoxicated, some begging, had become a public nuisance. For nearly a hundred years their care had been intrusted to the overseers of the poor, excellent gentlemen, with old-time notions of their powers as well as of the management of paupers. With this board he had a contest. He won; and, as a result, there were set up on spacious grounds at South Boston, amidst healthful influences, a House of Correction, a House of Industry, and a House for the Reformation of Juvenile Offenders. This change, salutary to their inmates, promoted the security and comfort of dwellers in the city proper. Several of these institutions have since been removed to Deer Island. The House for Juvenile Offenders, which originated with Mr. Quincy, attracted the attention of De Tocqueville, sent by the French government in 1832 to inquire into the penitentiary system of the United States.

Before Mr. Quincy's time some of the leading religious societies had derived considerable revenue from the sale of burial rights in tombs beneath their church edifices. Respectable medical practitioners said there was no harm in this; but Mr. Quincy effectually opposed its continuance on the score of public health, and this led to the establishment of extra-mural cemeteries, now so common, of which Mt. Auburn was the first.

Public morals, no less than public health, engaged his attention. There was a district of the city, now quite respectable, then congested with jail-birds, thieves, miscreants, and the most abandoned of both sexes, who haunted houses of ill-fame, and, issuing therefrom, committed all sorts of crimes, including murder, and in their Boston Alsatia defied the police. Mr. Quincy took them in hand, and shortly the worst offenders were in the House of Correction at South Boston. The district was restored to good order and respectability, and the city became more secure.

Mr. Quincy's work appears at its best only in the fullest details, though time does not allow their recital. Nothing within municipal authority escaped his attention; there was no department which, after his six years of service, did not show the effect of masterly organization and administration. There are two subjects, however, which even in a cursory survey of Mr. Quincy's labors ought not to be overlooked.

Every one knows, generally at least, that Boston owes to Josiah Quincy what is now best known as

Quincy Market; but unless he has studied the subject, no one knows the change effected in that section of the city, or the labor by which private interests were satisfied and the people induced to engage in an expensive work which resulted in the erection of " a granite market house, two stories high, 435 feet long, 50 feet wide, and covering 27,000 feet of land, including every essential accommodation, at the cost of $150,000. Six new streets were opened and a seventh greatly enlarged, including 167,000 square feet of land, and flats, docks, and wharf rights were obtained to the extent of 142,000 square feet; and all this was accomplished in the centre of a populous city, not only without tax, debt, or burdens upon its pecuniary resources, notwithstanding that in the course of its operations funds to the amount of upwards of $1,100,000 had been employed, but with large permanent addition to its real and productive property."

It is perhaps less well known that Mr. Quincy extinguished private rights to lands at the foot of the Common, since become part of the Public Garden, which secured what was then one of the most repulsive, now one of the most beautiful, spots in the world, and made practicable the policy of the State, in laying out and filling up the Back Bay and opening public squares, for which the people were not then prepared.

It has been often said by some who were citizens of Boston during Mr. Quincy's administration that the trait of his character which most strongly impressed them, as exhibited on many occasions, was courage, and that he might well be best remembered still as

" the Fearless Magistrate." There was one occasion on which he gave an example of moral courage which even in this sketch ought not to be passed over. It was in respect to the fire department. This organization held an important relation to the property and the lives of the people. Numbering twelve hundred young men, bound together by common associations and common dangers, impatient of new ways and jealous of any infringement on their customary privileges, they were a power at the polls quite out of proportion to their numbers — a power which they were not slow to exert on occasion. Mr. Quincy's efforts in reducing the department to stricter discipline, and even more, his insistence upon the use of hose instead of buckets and cisterns instead of pumps, and his bringing from Philadelphia and New York new and improved fire engines, had caused ill feeling which showed itself in insubordination and acts of violence. This state of things prepared the way for an outbreak in the last year of Mr. Quincy's administration on the appointment of a chief engineer not to the firemen's liking. Mr. Quincy's resoluteness in meeting this exigency, and the promptitude and efficiency with which he filled the places of those who expected to force the mayor's position by tendering their resignation, showed the people how fearlessly he could discharge his duty even at the cost of his reëlection, as he foresaw might be and was the case.

In estimating " the Great Mayor," it is not enough to look merely at the amount and variety of his services. Though his intellect was of a high order, his influence was largely in character, devotion to his work, untiring industry, sincerity, decision of manner tempered by exactest courtesy, cordiality, helpfulness, physical and moral intrepidity. Some of us saw him in his old age, the most venerable figure in our streets; others, at the college before time had bowed his form; but the memory of few now present reaches back to the days when, in the prime of his long life — with his high-bred face no more noticeable man in America [1] — often before the sun was up, he rode his daily round of inspecting the city; or when, in a riot, he put himself at the head of the truckmen, hastily extemporized as an auxiliary police force, and moved down upon the mob. In every relation of life, public or private, his character, bearing, and personality gave assurance of a man. Such qualities impressed institutions as well as society.

To found a city, or to establish institutions and indelibly stamp them by character and services, has ever been held a great achievement. When Themistocles, the Athenian, would boast, he said that he "could make a small town a great city." Mr. Quincy never boasted, though he was not unconscious that he had great powers, or that he had wrought into the fabric and texture of the city what would survive the fashions of municipal government. Since his time changes have taken place, and others will doubtless follow; but neither the work nor the fame of Josiah Quincy can ever perish. They are on the rock. His

---

[1] The likeness facing the title-page is from a portrait painted by Stuart when Mr. Quincy was mayor, and is one of the four of him in oil which remain. But in none of them can we see him as he appeared on taking his degree, in peach-colored coat, white satin small-clothes with silk stockings, and powdered hair; nor in the splendid uniform of the "Huzzars." Page painted him in his robes as president of the university, and Story made a statue which is regarded as one of his best works. There are also portrait busts of him by Greenough and Crawford.

mayoralty was great in economic and material results
— promoted cleanliness, order, comfort; but was even
, greater, I think, in its successful endeavor after public virtue, purity, and social right.

In the lowest and least complete estimate of his
services Mr. Quincy earned the respect of his con-
stituents and the benediction of later generations; but
the former rejected him and we are in danger of for-
getting him. This ought not so to be, more for our
own sake than for his. After he had filled the office
of mayor for six years with assiduity and success
unparalleled, the people, in spite of these services and
partly because of them, refused to reëlect him.

What then? Did all his great services go for
nothing? Was self-respect clouded or honor lost?
The citadel of self-respect is unassailable from without, nor is honor the gift of the people. They can
neither bestow it nor withhold it. It inheres in conduct and in character, is not gained save by honest
endeavor, nor lost save by misconduct. It was Washington's in the successes of Trenton and Princeton,
and no less his in the defeats of Brandywine and Germantown; his when Gates and Conway, Mifflin and
Samuel Adams, I am sorry to say, would have deposed
him; and his, no less and no more, when kings and
princes and people in remote lands and later ages pronounced him greatest among men. No — nothing is
so honorable as honor unjustly withheld, no praise so
acclaiming as the silence of lips that should speak,
no victory so victorious as defeat in just cause. For
when men were silent and their eyes averted, as Josiah
Quincy stepped down from the mayor's chair in 1829,
public health and security spake; and so did beneficent institutions; and so spake the new Faneuil Hall

Market, and spacious warehouses, and broad, well-paved streets; yea and the very stones of those streets, and the virtuous poor who owed to him comforts before denied, and youth reclaimed from vicious ways, and just men and women looked on him with kindly eyes, and with according voices proclaimed honor to whom honor unjustly withheld was due; and he has taken his place among those dear to God, who serve their fellow-men without expectation of reward.

But what is all this to men of limited capacities and commonplace opportunities — to us members of the Society for Promoting Good Citizenship, who have neither high aspirations nor special fitness for public affairs? Rightly considered, it is everything; it is incitement, endeavor, success, or consolation. I have said that among great men Mr. Quincy was exceptionally rare in this: that his character, his conduct, and his services are imitable. There is no one in this audience, however low in fortune or social position, none however high, that may not wisely form himself on Josiah Quincy's character and imitate his conduct; and if we lack his opportunities, at least we may remember that before he was the great Mayor he was the great Citizen; and before he was the great Citizen he was a good citizen — as any one of us may be!

His political ethics were simple, easily adopted, and of universal concern. He believed in the duties of the citizen; that peril to the republic or to the city or to civilization is less from the intrusion of the lower classes into public affairs than from the withdrawal of the wealthy, educated, and refined class; less from the spoliations of the proletariat than from the indifference of the wealthy and educated; and he regarded as less obnoxious to just censure him who takes on the duties of the citizen for private ends than one who abstains for merely personal convenience.

I do not think Mr. Quincy found all his work congenial. That such a man — a man who understood and enjoyed the best of the world's literature, who loved agriculture and the society of refined men and women — should busy himself, forsooth, with drains and cesspools; with back yards and crowded tenements; with criminals, and the poor, and the squalid, and the sick, — this certainly could not have been altogether attractive to Mr. Quincy, a born aristocrat, who could run his lineage back to the rolls of Battle Abbey without encountering the gallows or losing himself in a felon's cell; a man who made no profession of democracy; who would have weighed votes rather than have counted them; who preferred the judgments of experts to the unformed opinions of the crowd; who sought the society of gentlemen rather than that of 'longshoremen. Nevertheless, where he was called, there he was to be found!

Though not a believer in the democracy of party, it is by no means certain that he would have approved of recent legislative acts which seem to regard the Great and General Court, rather than the people, as the true fountain of municipal government under the constitution. I doubt if he ever contemplated, as a practical relief from bad government, any departure from that faith on which our political system rests — faith in the ability and the desire of the people to govern themselves wisely, honestly, efficiently.

I think Mr. Quincy saw, what all of us must see, that the people, acting without some unifying principle and purpose, are as the sand clouds of the desert, driven blindly and blinding; but when, as in the late Civil War, they are animated and guided by beneficent purpose, though like the sea sometimes turbulent, they are wiser even in their anger than any man however wise or any number of men less than the whole.

Nothing concerns the people so much as government. It is the test of public morals, as the regulation of life is the test of private morals. Deprecate it as we may, quarrel with it if we will, nevertheless the world's judgment of us as a people by the practical results of our government, whether national, state, or municipal, is fair, and from that judgment there is no appeal. Mr. Quincy, therefore, made it a constant purpose of his life to present good government to the people as the highest end of civil society; to endue them with a unifying sense of its value, and to inspire them with the desire and determination of making themselves fit to take it up, carry it forward, and transmit it to their successors. He would spare no expense to educate them; would withhold no warning voice calling them to duty or impressing them with the conviction that expedients must be temporary and in the long run unsuccessful, and that, after all makeshifts have failed, none but the people will, or can, correct what is wrong or secure what is desirable in their government.

Josiah Quincy was not of the people, but with the people and for the people — always! If he never indulged in the illusions of hope respecting the perfectibility of popular government, he never indulged in the illusions of despair. His participation in government, as a private citizen or as a public officer, was part of his religion; not a new religion, but older than Sinai, and finding one sanction, at least, in the necessities of civilization. It needs disciples and, it may be, its martyrs.

Thus lived and died and was buried the first citizen of no mean city. Some of his fellow-citizens equaled him in genius, some in learning, and some in fidelity to duty; but in the combination of these qualities he had no superior and few equals. Mr. Quincy's death, though on account of his great age not unexpected, produced deep feeling among all classes of his fellow-citizens, and was followed by expressions of grief from every part of the country, and even from foreign lands. When he died a conspicuous personality was withdrawn from human view; but his life and character and influence remain. They have passed into the life of the city for which he did so much; a character which, as it becomes better known, may we not hope, will be accepted as the type for those who owe it to their ancestry to be great in affairs, capable of self-government, free, patriotic, and beneficent in all public relations. In honorable place among those who have founded cities, reformed institutions, and served God by unselfishly serving their fellow-men, is the name of Josiah Quincy, " the Great Mayor."

DANIEL WEBSTER AS AN ORATOR

Remarks at the Dinner of the Alumni of Dartmouth College, June 28, 1882

Of the three papers on Daniel Webster which follow, only the last was ever published ; the other two were printed from the reporter's notes in a few copies which the author sent to personal friends. Each paper contains matter not found in the others, but also something common to all. These repetitions were natural under the circumstances, and the editor has decided not to avoid them.

DANIEL WEBSTER AS AN ORATOR

You have alluded to the fact, Mr. President, that there are some interesting memorials of Daniel Webster under my care in the Boston Public Library. This is quite true. There is a volume made up in part of the reporter's shorthand notes of the second speech in Reply to Hayne, with additions and corrections in the hand of Mr. Webster. There is also the vase presented to him by citizens of Boston, in recognition of his services, especially in that session of Congress made memorable by the great Reply; and what has a double interest to us considering the subject and the author, is the original manuscript of Rufus Choate's masterly Discourse on Daniel Webster, delivered here in 1853.

These memorials are greatly valued by the city in which Mr. Webster resided, and are specially interesting to the alumni of this college, upon which he conferred distinction as a graduate, and in whose service he delivered one of his most remarkable legal arguments.

We have reason to be proud of Mr. Webster's relation to the college; for his place among great men as well as among the greatest of orators is well assured.

After all fair deductions are made, his oratory, in its mass and quality, stands upon the whole as the most considerable product of its kind in the age in which he lived, and challenges comparison with that of any age. His work as an orator is still vital. It lives and speaks not merely as literature, but with the original vigor and freshness of the spoken word in laws enacted through his powerful advocacy; in the institutions which he moulded into permanent form; and in the Constitution of the United States, which owes much to his eloquence for its just interpretation, and its very life to that sentiment of nationality which he awoke in the hearts of the people.

Mr. Webster, in learning and special culture, was surpassed by many; some have been his equals in logical power; but in sustained, rich, and effective oratory, of great compass and variety, he is without peer among his countrymen, and is to be counted with the immortal few gathered from all the ages. As a public man he at once attracted attention. Lowndes said of him, "The North has not his equal nor the South his superior." His personal history became well known. Competent critics have estimated his abilities as lawyer, statesman, and diplomatist; and his power as an orator has been defined with a precision and felicity which leave nothing to be desired.

Parker, Brownson, Hillard, Everett, Choate, Curtis, Winthrop, Evarts, after such as these had spoken what remained to be said? So we thought yesterday, sir. [Senator Bayard.] To-day we learn once more that to genius old themes are always new. But he who adds a leaf to the chaplet of Webster weaves laurels for his own brow.

How clearly has the orator of the day seen, and how clearly has he made us to see, that the words of the dead statesman are still vital, — still the best thought and the best word; and that he who would equip himself for the coming contest must draw his weapons from the armory of Webster. They are all there:

> " Illic arma ; currus illic ; illic arcus Ulyssis !
> Sed ubi Ulysses ? "

I shall not dwell on the characteristics of his oratory — its swift marshaling of forces, its steadiness along the line, its honest Saxon cheer of onset, its vigor of attack and overwhelming weight of column, its knightliness of battle, its clemency in victory, its reserves never in action — all this is familiar.

The only view of Mr. Webster as an orator which has not lost something of its freshness from frequency of presentation, and which if adequately presented would assist in determining his place among the great masters of spoken eloquence, is that which takes in at a single glance the combination in his oratory of immediate effectiveness, breadth, and the permanent value of what survives as literature. Others have moved audiences as powerfully. Some have spoken words equally rich as literature ; and the speech of a few has passed into national life. Mr. Webster's eloquence was masterly in all these particulars ; and in this combination of great qualities was unequaled.

Any critical estimate of Mr. Webster's productions must fairly include some reference to the age and country in which he lived, the education within his reach, and the circumstances which environed him.

He has been compared with the great orator of antiquity. But had Webster been born in an age and country in which life itself was a liberal education ; in a country where every object on which the eye rested was a work of art or a source of inspiration ; in an age when language had reached perfection as an instrument of expression ; and especially had he made oratory the exclusive purpose of his life, prosecuted under famous masters of the art, — such a comparison would be fairer.

He has been compared with the great orators of England — with Chatham, Fox, and Burke — all men of genius thoroughly equipped for oratory by education and training, and mainly indebted to this for any special superiority to Mr. Webster. Equal to any one of these in intellectual force, as richly endowed as any of them with individualized gifts of eloquence, as an orator he wrought results, immediate and permanent, which compare favorably with those produced by every one of these orators.

Erskine said that the speeches of Burke, which all the world read with wonder and delight in the morning, had cleared the benches of the Commons the night before; and I have heard it said of Mr. Webster, that he lacked that power of popular oratory which takes audiences off their feet; and that those who, drawn by his immense reputation, went to hear him, came away disappointed. He was not a popular orator after the fashion of Henry Clay. Doubtless he lacked those peculiar graces of speech and manner which made the commonest efforts of Everett and Choate so attractive.

Few persons now living have heard Webster at his best, or before he had reached that time of life which marks decline in certain powers of the popular orator. The tradition of those who heard him when he was a young man following the circuit of the New Hampshire courts, and the testimony of the few survivors of those audiences which hung on his lips at Plymouth Rock and Bunker Hill, is that he never lapsed into dulness, but that his eloquence was always rich, flow-

ing, and captivating. What that eloquence was in
his prime, those of us can understand who heard him
say, in 1843, at Bunker Hill: "It is not from my
lips, it is not from any human lips, that that strain of
eloquence is this day to flow, most competent to move
and excite the vast multitudes around. *The powerful speaker stands motionless before us!* "

More fortunate still were those Sons of New Hampshire who heard him, an old man, say at Boston: "I
see that the emperor of Russia demands of Turkey
that the noble Kossuth and his companions shall be
given up to be dealt with at pleasure. And I see
that this demand is in derision of the law of nations.
Gentlemen, there is something on earth greater than
arbitrary and despotic power. The lightning has its
power, and the whirlwind has its power, and the earthquake has its power; but there is something among
men more capable of shaking despotic thrones than
lightning, whirlwind, and earthquake; that is, the
excited and aroused indignation of the whole civilized
world!" The orator was transfigured by his eloquence. His words became the elemental forces they
represent, and all that vast audience sat in awed ex-
pectancy of some audible expression of the excited
and aroused indignation of the whole civilized world!

Oratory fulfills its functions when its immediate
purposes are accomplished. It aims to convince and
persuade. That done, its work is done. But eloquence sometimes passes into household words or
survives as literature. Sometimes, though rarely, it
becomes embodied in deeds which endure forever.
Mr. Webster possessed these varied powers of eloquence in a combination not often found, and in a degree which leaves him without a peer. In the forty

years of his public life, more uniformly than any other orator he gained his cause; and his causes were large, affecting laws, policy, institutions, government, and the permanent sentiments of an entire people. But apart from its immediate effects his eloquence lives imperishably in the results achieved by it, as well as in the body of literature he created.

The verity and significance of these statements appear, when we look at the work of some accounted the world's most famous orators, with whom Mr. Webster is often mentioned.

The great Athenian orator pronounced the most elaborate compositions which ever fell from human lips. As such they defy all comparison. But what was their permanent or even their immediate effectiveness? They precipitated the crushing power of Philip on the orator's country which he lacked the courage to defend, and he died by suicidal hands amid ruins which his eloquence could neither avert nor postpone.

The history of Cicero as an orator is still more deplorable. If we may trust Mommsen, the latest and best critic of Roman history, the genius of that great orator displayed itself without sincerity in costly rhetoric, on affairs having no sequence of value to Rome.

Chatham is a great name, and he was one of the greatest orators, if we may accept his traditionary fame. But what did his eloquence accomplish? The great commoner, from high place in government and in the possession of vast resources and almost unlimited power, wrought mightily for the glory of England. His eloquence contributed to the repeal of the Stamp Act, but was powerless to change the policy of the government.

Great words were those — "I rejoice that America has resisted." They electrify us to-day, as they echo from the walls of St. Stephen; but they accomplished nothing, they prevented nothing. With vehement, splendid declamation he inveighed against the use of Indian auxiliaries in Burgoyne's army; — only to denounce, not to prevent; only to call out the damaging reply that he denounced a policy inaugurated by himself. His mighty eloquence was unprevailing eloquence. Neither alone nor with the auxiliar oratory of his great allies could he stay the madness of the king. Their eloquence availed nothing then; it has availed nothing since! Burke's genius was amazing, but it was not that of an orator.

Lord Brougham said that Charles James Fox was one of "the greatest statesmen, and if not the greatest orator, certainly the most accomplished debater that ever appeared upon the theatre of human affairs in any age of the world;" and another, scarcely less competent as a critic, has added: "He has left no memorial of any good he wrought by his eloquence, his Libel Bill being the only good law he ever introduced."

Let me not be misunderstood. I am not unmindful of the inadequacy of this test. I know that the words of famous orators are privileged with immortality. Like the songs of great poets, like heroic deeds on lost fields, like the Parthenon in ruins, they are the imperishable treasure of the race. But if just fame is theirs without permanent success, what measure of fame is his who achieved the success he merited! Happily for the people, Mr. Webster lived in times which closed to him those subjects which so largely formed the themes of famous orators. There was no venal government to denounce, no tyrant to

objurgate, no people to excite to deeds of valor.
Had his prime corresponded with our Revolutionary
struggle, what invective — surpassing that of Adams
and Otis — would he have hurled against the royal
tyrant; and who can doubt that his battle cry in the
hour of disaster would have rung like that heard in
Roncesvalles!

On this point we are not left to conjecture. His
supposititious speech of John Adams on the Resolution for Independence — as nearly impromptu as such
things ever are — attests the vigor of his patriotic imagination as well as the promptitude of its resources.

But he lived in peaceful times. And when his
day offered no fit occasion for the spirit that burned
within him, he made at Plymouth Rock and at Bunker Hill occasions for its utterance. When common
forms of oratory were found inadequate to arouse and
instruct patriotic national sentiment, he formed and
carried to its highest development a new kind of popular oratory which in his mouth became a trumpet that reached the ear of twenty millions of people.

Observe some few of the occasions made memorable by Mr. Webster's eloquence, and some examples
of its transforming power. Neither Plymouth Rock
nor Bunker Hill; neither the commerce of our inland
seas or navigable rivers; neither the constitution under which we live, nor those institutions of learning
and charity which serve to make life a beneficent gift
of God, are what they would have been had Webster
never lived and spoken. Lived and spoken; for it
was by eloquence that Mr. Webster accomplished
what neither learning nor logic could effect. Webster's eloquence overthrew the masterly judgment
of the Superior Court of New Hampshire before the

Supreme Court of the United States in the Dartmouth College case, — overthrew it instantly and forever. This more than any other of his arguments throbbed with his own heart-beats. It reached the hearts and flooded the eyes of venerable magistrates. Pinkney, who questioned Webster's law in the case, thought that the court was carried less by sound argument than by force of oratory. If so, the fact adds testimony to the imperial power of Webster's eloquence — powerful even to the saving of life — thy life, O mother beloved, now immortal!

This was not the eloquence of an hour. No. We hear it to-day, in this great presence, happy in the assured prosperity of her we love — vital as on that first day ; and not we only, but every college and literary institution in the country hears it, and will hear it as long as colleges and literary institutions exist. That was eloquence indeed ; argument made constitution ; godlike eloquence which spake and it was done.

In 1820, Mr. Webster brought into relief, clear as never before, the story of the Pilgrims. The descendants of those first comers had been wont, at stated times, to gather at the Landing, and there recount with filial piety the story of the sufferings, the constancy, and the faith of those whose plantation had become a state. Webster found there the Pilgrims' rock ; he made it the shrine of a nation ! On that memorable twenty-second of December, Webster's words of faith, liberty, law, and religion became audible to twenty millions of people; and they will be heard as long as the ocean's voice resounds along that shore. This was the first of that remarkable series of patriotic orations addressed to local audiences, but so spoken that a nation heard.

Mr. Webster invaded all provinces of oratory, and from all returned victorious. If calm, unimpassioned reasoning, with no highly raised passages, powerfully addressed to the understanding, has a place in oratory, then the argument of Daniel Webster, which reversed the judgments of the illustrious judicial tribunals of New York, and pronounced the commerce of navigable streams and inland seas a unit, subject to the exclusive control of the general government, is entitled to high rank. It overthrew the laws of a great State, which for thirty years had stood upon the statute book, affirmed by judges as eminent as any in the country. A gloss of the Constitution of the United States by Daniel Webster became an integral part thereof, affecting vast interests, and for time measured only by the duration of the government. Of what other orator can such words be spoken; and what place among orators is his of whom they can be justly said?

At Bunker Hill, in 1825, Mr. Webster took up the great work of his life — to arouse and nationalize the patriotic sentiment of the country. For this work he was raised up; to this he gave his life; from his boyhood it haunted him like a passion. He pursued it with a zeal and constancy not always understood even by his friends. Foreigners wonder at our estimate of Webster. What marvel when we ourselves have so lately, and at so great cost, through fire and blood, come to understand the mystery of that saving faith of which he was the great proclaimer and only prophet.

On that memorable occasion he announced his creed : "Our country, our whole country, and nothing but our country." These words were not addressed to the descendants of the few New England troops, who on the heights of Bunker Hill and on its declivities joined unequal battle with the veteran soldiers of England. No. These words — such words as no other man had ever spoken — were heard by thousands to whom Bunker Hill was unknown in its great lesson of patriotism. They became household words beyond the Mississippi and by the shores of the Great Lakes. They were caught up and recited in every schoolhouse in the land ; and at the country's call were repeated in deeds of immortal valor on a hundred fields!

These two orations served to make possible a nationality springing from aroused and enlightened public sentiment. The Great Reply, with a sweep of logic as unerring as the planetary movements, and with an eloquence as thorough-bred as the muse of Milton, made nationality a fact which four years of civil war could not obliterate. It was his " omnific word " heard

" Far into chaos "

which commanded the pillars of the Constitution to stand. These words, so spoken, made the day and the speaker immortal. Nothing can touch him!

In estimating Mr. Webster's rank as an orator we should not forget — for it is his distinction — that nearly all the great triumphs with which his name is associated were his personal triumphs. The abolition of the slave trade and of slavery, the Reform Bill, the repeal of the Corn Laws, and other similar modern reforms have been effected by various influences, such as the press, groups of orators and writers, social and political organizations — sometimes with the whole civilized world in the lists — all striving to

the same end.   But in Webster's victories he stands
for all these forces, and he stands alone.

> " Alone his task was wrought,
> Alone his battle fought."

He led no party. Neither the power of the government nor the prestige of administration was with him ;
nothing but his cause and the might of his imperial
eloquence.   Forty years of victorious eloquence, with
never a defeat ; for the country always, and never for
self ; conquests for the country, and still held by the
country — all this is historical.

Mr. Webster in his oratory has delineated the
characters of some of the chief actors in the most
significant events in our history.   Adams, Jefferson,
Hamilton, Madison, Jay — what portraits are these !
And that great central figure !   Who had conceived
the character of Washington in its just proportion, or
what creative hand in art had made him, in form and
feature, to live on the canvas, as his character appears
in the discriminating eloquence of Webster?

Friends, you who love learning and its institutions ;
you who mark with just pride that great volume of
commerce which pours its lifeblood, unchecked, along
our great rivers and inland seas ; you who believe in
that

> " . . . true liberty
> . . . which always with right reason dwells,
> . . . and from her hath no dividual being ; "

you who believe in the stability, permanence, and
value of the Constitution of the country, resting on
enlightened, patriotic sentiment, name him who, of
that crown reserved for the world's most prevailing
orator, is worthiest in your suffrages.

REMARKS AT THE DINNER OF THE

ALUMNI OF DARTMOUTH COLLEGE

At Concord, N. H., June 17, 1886

ON THE

OCCASION OF THE DEDICATION OF A STATUE OF DANIEL WEBSTER

REMARKS

THE Seventeenth of June, already crowded with histories, gains one more title to respect by the events of this day now drawing to a close. Annually with the rising of its sun immortal memories awake: memories of 1775, when in their "agony of glory" the yeomanry of New England twice repulsed the veteran troops of Great Britain on Bunker Hill, and by a defeat which was victory made inevitable an independent empire; memories of the same heights when Lafayette, in 1825, surrounded by surviving heroes of the Revolution, laid the corner-stone of a superstructure which began an era of monumental art in America, and Daniel Webster added lustre to the commemorative eloquence inaugurated by him at Plymouth Rock.

Nor do the transactions in which we have this day participated lack happy associations with those historic events; for here, at the capital, in the presence of sons whose sires were at Bunker Hill in 1775, and who were themselves by the side of the Great Orator on the same spot fifty years later, his townsman, the orator of the day, in words worthy of the occasion, has made memorable the day which witnesses the unveiling of the first commemorative statue, and that of her greatest son, ever set up on New Hampshire soil. The day will stand apart by itself; for though other notable days will come, on precisely such a day as this no second morn will ever rise.

To-day a duty has been performed. In the presence of the highest authorities of the State, with civic procession and military display, the reproach of many has been taken away by the vicarious munificence of one.

Although the erection of a statue of Daniel Webster in this city is of peculiar interest to the people of New Hampshire, yet from other sections of the country have come those who desire to honor the memory of him who knew no section, — nothing less than the whole country; — him who expounded and defended its Constitution; who assisted in making and interpreting its laws; who conducted its diplomacy at a critical period, and always so spoke as to command the ear of his countrymen — those who followed the plow, or turned the spindle, or went down to the sea in ships, or studied the eloquence of the best ages.

The orator of the day has sketched the life, character, and services of Daniel Webster. He has vindicated him whose political opinions divided parties, and whose principles and everything save his patriotism and his ability had been called in question. But were it otherwise, we have come hither with no such purpose; nor do we wish to reconsider our estimate of him. To us he stands high, clear, and unassailable in his great offices, and unapproachable in the greatness of his public services. Let those who will, accuse us of undue devotion to his memory. We make no reply,

"Namque erit ille nobis semper deus."

The dedication of the statue of Daniel Webster is completed; but we, sons of Dartmouth, and most of us sons of New Hampshire, have come together by ourselves that we may indulge sentiments suggested by our relations to the State and to the college, and through these to Mr. Webster. For whatever he may be to others, to us he is something more and something different. Others speak of him as the wise statesman and consummate orator; but in this gathering we think of him as a son of New Hampshire and as our brother of Dartmouth College. And here, in the reflection of his greatness, and as heirs of his affection for the State of his birth and for the college where he was educated, we go from the graves of our ancestors to the neighboring graves of his ancestors, and tenderly brushing the moss and lichens from both, thank God we are sons of New Hampshire. Once more, as when at Hanover, we sit in the seats where he sat, or roam the woods where he roamed, or ply our boats on the bosom of the Connecticut where he plied his boat, and again thank God that we are also sons of Dartmouth.

He loved the place of his birth and the place where he was educated. We love the same places; and it may be that none can enter the circle of those affections save by the unpurchasable right of inheritance. Be it so. We to-day are once more children by the graves of our forefathers, and youth in the places sacred to learning; and these shall be the themes of our discourse.

But [1] I am sure, Mr. President, that the alumni of Dartmouth College desire, first of all, to express to

---

[1] All which precedes this point was omitted in the delivery of the Remarks.

his Excellency the Governor and to the honorable Council of the State of New Hampshire their grateful sense of the privilege of participating in the dedication of a statue of Daniel Webster on his native soil; and to add that they regard the selection of the president of the college for the part in these interesting ceremonies, which he has performed with distinguished success, as a manifestation of good-will by the State to the college, which is appreciated by all its friends.

The relations of the college to the State are peculiar. As a corporation it is older than the State; for the charter of the college, which is still the basis and measure of its rights, and irrevocable except for cause, came from George the Third, when New Hampshire was a royal province, without charter, and governed under the king's commission, which was revocable at his pleasure.

To-day we witness an extraordinary proceeding. The State accepts as a gift from an estimable and loyal citizen, and with the according voices of thousands of other citizens, also loyal, sets up in a conspicuous place, before the most august symbol of its authority, a statue of Daniel Webster, — to whom more than to any other man is due that construction of the Constitution of the United States which overthrew a legislative act of the sovereign State of New Hampshire, reversed the solemn decision of its highest judicial tribunal, and erected within its jurisdiction an *imperium in imperio* which will endure as long as the Constitution endures.

And it is well. For the State and the college have been mutually helpful. The State has been the benefactor of the college; and if not munificent when compared with more opulent States, yet liberal in a degree honorable to a government which derived its revenues from a people without profitable industries until the stimulus of foreign capital had aroused the slumbering giant of the Merrimac; and whose agricultural interests rapidly declined when canals and railroads opened the markets of the East to the disastrous competition of the more fertile West.

But now a new era has begun. Necessity has developed a new industry. Thrift and the near approach of hunger have stimulated the conversion of pure air and mountain scenery into merchantable commodities, happily indispensable to the sweltering corn-growers and pork-packers of the malarial prairies. A retributive corner has been made, — reasonably permanent, if we may rely upon the providentially slow growth of mountains, and remunerative, we hope, " beyond the dreams of avarice."

These inspiring facts open a vista. In the distance the college is seen reveling in opulence !

If the State has been liberal according to her means, the college has recognized her reciprocal obligations, and met them with promptitude and efficiency. Erase from the State's roll of honor, of which she is justly proud, the names of those sons of Dartmouth who have gained distinction in science, in jurisprudence, and in public affairs, and the place of New Hampshire would be less conspicuous than it now is among her sister States. Give back to unlettered drudgery those undistinguished sons of Dartmouth, who, with minds quickened by liberal studies, have followed their professions on hillsides or in sequestered valleys, — narrow but necessary fields of labor, — and there would be a manifest decline of intelligence, good judgment, and moral sense in those communities.

I do not propose to dwell on those special relations of Daniel Webster to the college, to which I have adverted; but in the general relations of debt and credit between the college and the people of the State Daniel Webster was included. Born remote from the centres of civilization and culture, and without the means of access to them, there was danger, and in his case, from temperament, special danger, lest he would grow up in obscurity and add one more to the large number of richly endowed but imperfectly educated men of which New Hampshire was full, who gave to the wilderness powers which might have made them conspicuous on any theatre of action. More than most men of anything like his intellectual force, Daniel Webster needed the stimulus of education and the prospect of a career. This needed help was just what the college gave. She opened the mine, she laid bare the ore, — abundant, massive, pure, — and set it free, as currency bearing the royal stamp of genius, to enrich the wisdom of the people and the English speech of the world. This was his chief debt to the college.

Apart from Webster's natural endowments no one was more " heinously unprovided," as he said, with education or pecuniary means, " to break into college." Luckily it was not far to seek; otherwise he might never have found it. But he sought it and entered. When there, unlike Bacon and Milton at English Cambridge, he made no complaint of the education it afforded. It was the best he was prepared to receive, and both parties were satisfied. She gave him all she had to give, and with all her requirements he cheerfully complied. Both were young together; both were poor; and both struggling to gain a foothold on bare creation. It is idle, but we may guess, if we will, how much and in what respects Webster might have been greater had he, after the preparatory training of such schools as Eton or Winchester, been educated at Oxford or Cambridge, with their splendid libraries, their exact scholarship, their impressive antiquity, and the stimulating influence of the long lines of their illustrious graduates.

Such were the relations to the college of Daniel Webster as an undergraduate. He was greatly in her debt. But there came a time when all this was changed, — in an hour when her need was sore and pressing and his help was seasonable and adequate; an hour when he paid the unforgotten debt of his youth ; when he secured immortality for her, and laid the foundations of his own.

But, gentlemen, I must not forget, even in this presence, that there are other claims than ours to Daniel Webster. He was a son of New Hampshire and he was the foremost man of his country. Of all the great Americans of this century, perhaps of any century, he was the most genuinely and thoroughly American ; of all, most undoubtedly a product of our soil, climate, institutions, and modes of life. He owed much to the State of his birth ; but he owed nothing to any other State. He owed much to his New Hampshire ancestors; but to them, and to them alone, he was indebted for his rich inheritance. In him there was no intermixture of nationalities, no crossing of plebeian with patrician blood. His pedigree was of New Hampshire and as pure as the air he breathed. Unlike Morris, Gallatin, and Hamilton, he was born on our soil. His forefathers were also born on it, unlike the ancestors of some of those who in Revolutionary days rendered illustrious services to the country. For a hundred and fifty years they had lived in New Hampshire. Into them had entered the cold blasts from the polar circle and the fierce heats which seemed to have strayed from the tropics. Every drop of their blood, every fibre of their flesh, every bone and sinew, had become Americanized. For five generations, not from the safe retreats of garrisoned settlements, but on the skirmish line of civilization, they had waged strenuous war with barbarism and changed the wilderness into habitable abodes of men.

To all these transforming influences Daniel Webster was fortunately heir. We of New Hampshire think that he was also fortunate in the place of his birth. The glory of a state, sir, is in its men, — not in its broad acres; not in its fertile soil; not in its rich mines; but in its men. That is a great state which produces great men; and virile were the loins that begat the Websters, the Starks, the Langdons, the Bartletts, the Smiths, the Bells, the Pierces, the Woodburys, the Casses, the — but I need a day for the rest.

Without doubt Daniel Webster was fortunate in the place of his birth, — in sight of the majestic mountains; not far from the beautiful river: the mountains in their grandeur, the type of his character; the river in its reserved strength, no unfit emblem of his life. In this pure air, full of light reflected from the purple hills, — himself made thoughtful by the nearness of dark forests and the sound of distant waterfalls, feeding his imagination with traditions of Rogers, Putnam, and Stark, the old French war rangers, and of Cilley, Scammell, and Poor, his father's compatriots in arms during the war of the Revolution, — Daniel

Webster gathered his scanty education. A genuine
son of New Hampshire. Here he was born. Here he
" mewed his mighty youth." Here he clothed himself
with glorious manhood. He owed little to other forms
of civilization. His mind, his character, and his personality, — his thoughts, and his style of their expression, were of New Hampshire. His latest political
and constitutional principles bore the impress of his
earliest. When he left his native State he was a complete man. He gained little or nothing that was essential by association with communities more cultured
than those he left behind him. These were of the
sea ; those were of the mountains. Not always in
accord with the dominant political party of his native
State, he was more nearly so than with the extreme
Federalists of New England.

Thus he was born, so was he reared, and such he
remained, — a true and loyal son of New Hampshire.
She claims him as her own. With all his great qualities she claims him ; she claims him with all his faults.
He had faults ; but she forgave them in that hour
when he defended the Constitution ; she forgot them,
— forgot them all and forever, — when she beheld the
Union made one and inseparable by the inspiration of
his prevailing eloquence.

Her son, this complete man, bone of her bone and
flesh of her flesh, she gave to the country. Few States
ever had such a son to offer. Fortunate the country
which receives such a gift ! Costly as it was, it was
given without reserve and for all the ages. New
Hampshire neither is able, nor desires, to recall it.
She cannot reclaim his wisdom imbedded in the Constitution. She would not unloose the golden cord of
patriotism with which he bound the States in perpetual
union.

More than threescore years and ten have passed
since Daniel Webster, in the prime of his manhood and
in the fullness of his great powers, went forth from
New Hampshire to the service of his country.   What
those services were is known of all men.   To-day he
returns ; once more his foot is on his native soil, in
sight of the majestic mountains he loved so well, not
far from the river on whose banks he was born.
Shouts from the hillsides, answering shouts from the
valleys, welcome his return.   Sir, I cannot think him
dead.   Not in the flesh indeed does he stand before
us.   No longer do those dark eyes flash upon us
their inward light, and the voice which once rang like
a trumpet is now silent.   And yet, in a sense more
true than his own pathetic words, he still lives.   To-
day we have erected a statue of Daniel Webster, —
of Daniel Webster dead.   Webster dead !   Who
closed the eyes of that great intelligence ?   Who saw
the train go forth bearing that majestic soul to the
tomb ?   Who wrapped in cerements and closed the
marble doors on those thoughts that breathed and
those words that burned ?

Alas ! in the blindness of our grief we thought that
it was so, and spake of him as of one that was dead.
But time and great events, and men's second thoughts
and more charitable judgments, and loving hearts that
quicken at the sound of his name, — all proclaim him
living.   And yet we have erected a statue of Daniel
Webster, and it is well ; for monuments to great
actions and statues of men truly great are not dead
things ; nor are they to the dead, but to the living.
The deeds they emblazon are immortal deeds, not tran-
sitory ; deeds which light the centuries, not the hours,
in their pathway to glorious actions.   They illustrate

what they teach; they are what they commemorate. If yonder statue is not Daniel Webster in the flesh, it is Daniel Webster transfigured with the immortality of genius; with passionate patriotism which never grows cold; with love of home and kindred which feels no touch of earthly years; with

> " . . . truths that wake
> To perish never."

And through the years that are to come, to all who may enter yonder legislative hall, and to the long procession of men who shall walk these streets, those lips will still have language; will still defend the Constitution; will still inspire sentiments of nationality. Nor can I think that it ever will be otherwise; for the inspiration of great endeavor is its immortality; the potency of great achievement is its indestructibleness. The past assures the future. The discourses at Plymouth Rock and at Bunker Hill were not for an hour; nor was the Great Reply. In the days of their utterance they were resplendent, unprecedented eloquence; but they spake truest when they became wisdom to Lincoln and valor to Grant; they rang loudest when heard along the front of battle, and inspired deeds of immortal heroism on a hundred fields. No, the statue is not to the dead orator, but to the living, who speaks to us, and will speak to those who come after us, as he spake to those, his associates, the venerable men happily with us to-day, who

> " . . . followed him, honored him,
> Lived in his mild, magnificent eye,
> Learned his great language, caught his clear accents,
> Made him their pattern to live and to die."

A GLANCE AT DANIEL WEBSTER

Reprinted from "The Century Magazine"
of September, 1893

A GLANCE AT DANIEL WEBSTER

"A FEW flashes of rhetoric, a few happy epigrams, a few labored speeches which now seem cold, lifeless, and commonplace," says Lecky, the historian, "are all that remain of the eloquence of the Pitts, of Fox, of Sheridan, or of Plunket " — and he says this of the Pitts, among the greatest of English orators ; of Sheridan, the most brilliant ; of Fox, whom Lord Brougham, himself a great orator, pronounced " if not the greatest orator, certainly the most accomplished debater, that ever appeared upon the theatre of affairs in any age of the world."   Is Daniel Webster's name now to be added to those on whose speeches the shadow of oblivion has fallen ?   James Otis, Jr., and Patrick Henry, as orators once famous, now live only in tradition.   Clay's and Webster's speeches, it is true, have been preserved ; but who now reads Clay's, and how long will Webster's continue to be read ?

Webster's talents were undeniably of the first order : but it is said that he lacked genius ; that his limitations were serious ; that Hamilton was the greater statesman, Marshall the greater jurist, and Clay the unequaled parliamentarian ; that he originated no public policy, nor greatly improved an old one ; that his ethical sense, neither strong nor acute, was quickened to no beneficent purpose like that of

Wilberforce or of Garrison ; that he had no love for
the people, nor they for him, and that they will finally
forget him.

Doubtless much of this is true.   Nevertheless,
Daniel Webster is not likely to be forgotten, nor will
his words cease to be read.   For he wasted no time
on party politics, or on small questions, or on issues
now dead ; but always in the courts, or in the Senate,
or before the people, applied his matchless powers to
subjects of great moment and popular interest, sure
to remain vital, and, like the seasons, ever returning.
In these respects he stands alone among the statesmen of his day ; and therefore, if they would, the
people can never forget him.   Nor can statesmen,
jurists, or scholars ; because, about government, laws,
and public policy he said the most authoritative word,
save John Marshall's, and said it in a way not easily
bettered.

Marshall and Webster were of like principles and
purpose, and, working together for the just interpretation of the Constitution in its relations to the
States, for forty years they affected the institutions
of the country more profoundly and more permanently
than any other two men of their day.   Marshall's
tribunal was supreme ; but the people were sometimes
restive under its decisions, two of which were openly
defied by sovereign States, and were never enforced.
In its last analysis the efficient authority of the
Supreme Court was public sentiment.   Therefore, to
make the general government truly national and
efficient in all its departments, it was necessary to
raise the people to a conception of nationality, and
to inspire that conception with patriotic sentiment.
This was Webster's great work.   In this way he

coöperated with Marshall. Webster had the wider field, more varied opportunities, larger audiences, and a farther-reaching voice. To this work he gave his life, and his work was crowned only when the great Reply to Hayne bore fruit in the deeds of Lincoln and Grant. This the people now understand, and they have given to Webster their respect and their admiration, but not yet, I think, a place in their hearts — the true Valhalla. It may be that they have something to forget and something to remember before they learn to regard, as they regard Clay and Lincoln, this man who, though he professed no love for the people whom he served as few men have, loved kindred and friends, and the homes of his ancestors, and the graves of their dead, with a pathetic tenderness which has suffused the eyes of thousands. It may be that he must wait for men's second thoughts, their more charitable judgment, and the next ages.

A famous anti-slavery orator once publicly thanked God that Daniel Webster was not born in Massachusetts; and this was received with acclaiming shouts by the audience. Nor did they appear to notice any incongruity when the orator proceeded to objurgate Webster, just as though he had been born in Boston, and were a recreant descendant of Thomas Dudley. This is the common mistake — to judge Webster as a Puritan in origin, descent, inherited principles, education, and consequent responsibilities. He was no Puritan, nor did he ever pretend to be one. The Massachusetts Puritans, who came to Boston Bay in 1630, were east of England people. Daniel Webster's ancestors were from the north of England, and, coming six years later, entered New Hampshire by the Piscataqua, and for generations were dispersed along the skirmish line of civilization, remote from the Puritans of the Bay, and shared neither in their glory nor in their shame.

In Webster was no admixture of nationality, no crossing of plebeian with patrician blood. He was a genuine son of the soil, though not, like Burns, of a soil alive with a hundred generations of the dead, nor of a soil like that about Boston, every sod of which was quickened with associations touching the hearts and moulding the characters of those born on it; but of a soil on which his father's footfall was the first of civilized man ever heard in that silent wilderness. He was a rustic, yet with marks of gentle blood in his shapely hands and feet, his well-proportioned limbs, and his high-bred face of no known type, unlike even his own brother, who was of Grecian form and face. We know that soil and climate affect character; but it is not easy to accept, save as a poetic theory, the "pathetic fallacy" with which Wordsworth imbued his generation and our own, that Nature has conscious relations with

> " Her foster-child, her inmate, Man,"

and forms his principles and regulates his methods of action agreeably to her own. But Daniel Webster was very like Nature. Like her, he was unethical; like her, he was not revolutionary; and like her, he applied his powers along the lines of normal development.

Of the Puritans neither by birth nor by circumstances, he possessed few of their virtues and none of their defects, and least of all their indomitable provinciality of thought and conduct. In this he stands quite alone among the public men of his day in New England. His spirit of nationality appeared so early

in life that it indicated character rather than education. And the depth of the sentiment appears from
this, that though born a Federalist, and from early
manhood associated professionally and socially with
some of the very able men prominent in the " Essex
Junto " and in the Hartford Convention, he neither
accepted their principles nor imitated their conduct,
At no time was he a Southern man or a Northern
man, but to the end of his life a National Federalist
after the fashion of Washington.

This also is noticeable, that although Webster was
educated at a small college in the backwoods, where
rhetoric was in its worst estate, and at a time when
our native literature was to the last degree conventional and vapid, he soon shook himself clear of his
surroundings, and, without instructor or example,
formed a style which for all the varied forms in which
he expressed himself — either in the forum, or in the
Senate, or in diplomacy, or before the people, or in
familiar letters — still remains the best model.

Mr. Webster's fame as an orator is secure, and his
services to the country are acknowledged ; but in his
last days he suffered some obloquy by reason of his
speech of the 7th of March, 1850, — a speech which,
whatever else may be said of it, was exactly on the
line of his life-work for union and nationality, which
he took up before he left college, and pursued with
assiduity and constancy for more than half a century.
Nor do the recorded lives of statesmen give many
examples, if one other, of a great and beneficent purpose conceived so early in life, pursued so vigorously,
or crowned with so great success. He had coadjutors,
but in clearness and consistency of purpose he stood
alone. He seized every occasion — often made occa-

sion — to unfold his constitutional views, and to commend them to the people.

Both as statesman and as orator Webster owed
much to his historical sense. He was not original,
constructive, or aggressive; but he had what, as I
think, Hamilton did not have, nor Clay, — a clear
historical perception of the essential character of our
English race, always moving on the line of its normal
development, rather than by revolution, toward nationality, in which, though monarchy may have been
its form, popular government has been its objective
purpose. Webster's historical sense gave precision
and consistency to his course as a statesman and to
his speech as an orator. Every step he made was a
step forward. Circumstances beyond his control, like
the change in the tariff policy and the anti-slavery
movement, with which, as a Nationalist, he probably
had little sympathy, forced him into positions which
he would not have chosen. But no statesman ever had
fewer occasions for that immunity which the people
so often and so readily accorded to Jefferson, to Clay,
to Jackson, and to Abraham Lincoln. They made
many mistakes, including Webster's, and were for-
given; Webster made one, and was lost — for a time.

Webster's historical sense appears in his orations.
In what similar collection can be found so large a
body of thought on various subjects, covering forty
years of public life, so consistent, so evenly and so
constantly working to one great purpose, expressed
with equal cogency, propriety, and eloquence? Certainly, neither in Fox's nor in Burke's, nor in any
other known to me. Goldwin Smith has said that
" in political oratory it would be hard to find anything superior to the Reply to Hayne; in forensic

oratory it would be hard to find anything superior to
his speech on the murder of White; among show
speeches it would be hard to find anything superior
to the Plymouth oration." This Plymouth oration,
the earliest and best by Webster, in which he formed
and carried to its highest development a new kind of
popular oratory, illustrates the historic sense of which
I have spoken. After all that has been written, it
remains by far the clearest and most precise view of
those causes which, beginning with the Reformation,
and acting on the English people, in the fullness of
time led to the colonization of America, and to the
setting up here of those institutions which best exemplify the sterling qualities of our English race. The
key-note of this address sounds through all his
speeches. He struck it loudly, and the nation heard;
he struck it truly, and it dominates all later speech.

With no American orator save Hamilton — and
with him only at the bar or in the affairs of state —
need Webster be compared. Hamilton's speeches
have not been preserved, and his fame as an orator
rests mainly upon tradition. To Burke's genius for
discursive speculation or to his copiousness of felicitous, light-diffusing phrase, Webster made no pretension, nor, on the other hand, did he ever lose sight of
his purpose in prolix or irrelevant generalities, or im-
peril his cause by lack of measure, judgment, or self-
control. He was the better orator. He gained his
causes. He seldom attempted Burke's highest flights,
but when he did he came safely down. Webster's
oratory was symmetrical and harmonious, working
evenly, by just degrees, and inevitably, to his one constant purpose of convincing and persuading those who
heard him. Loyal to his art, he was never seduced

by desire of popular applause or by a wish to please the schools.

Lord Chatham is accounted the most consummate of English orators. In my youth I greatly admired that passage in his speech on the address to the king in 1777, in which, referring to Lord Suffolk, who had defended the employment of the Indians in the war against the colonies, he exclaimed : " From the tapestry that adorns these walls, the immortal ancestor of this noble lord frowns with indignation at the disgrace of his country." It is a very striking passage ; but I once heard Webster say grander words. It was on the 17th of June, 1843, when I was one of that vast throng, gathered at Bunker Hill, which saw Webster raise his outstretched arm up to the newly completed monument, and heard him say : " It is not from my lips — it could not be from any human lips — that that stream of eloquence is this day to flow, most competent to move and excite this vast multitude around me. *The powerful speaker stands motionless before us.*" I felt the thrill which ran through that vast audience, and I saw their uplifted eyes and blanched cheeks, and joined in that responsive shout which told, as no words could tell, that we had heard one of the most perfect passages in all oratory. Such sentences fairly contrast these great orators. Webster could never have laid himself open to Lord Suffolk's crushing reply, that Chatham rashly condemned a policy inaugurated by himself only a few years before. Nor could Lecky have said of Webster, as he has said of Chatham, that he was often florid and meretricious, theatrical and affected, far from pure in taste, and, indeed, too much of a mountebank. But Chatham's eccentricities were those of genius. Burke

had them, and Sheridan had them. If Webster
lacked genius, he was at least free from its eccentricities. He was perfectly sane in his oratory, and, it
may be, the greatest perfectly sane orator who ever
spoke English.

Webster could also be dull — in his later years,
very dull. Those who heard him in his prime are
quite angry when one doubts whether he ever could
have been as popular an orator as Everett or Choate
or Phillips. Few now live who heard him in those
early days, when he was at his ·best. I, who heard
him often between 1840 and 1850, never heard him
at his best but once, and then only for a few minutes.
The circumstances were these : —

At the festival of the Sons of New Hampshire,
gathered in the hall of the Fitchburg Railroad in
1849, Mr. Webster presided with admirable grace,
and spoke of his native State as her sons would like
to hear her spoken of. His speech, though interesting, was not particularly striking until, passing from
our own affairs to those of Hungary, then in her
struggle for liberty, he said : " I see that the Emperor
of Russia demands of Turkey that the noble Kossuth
and his companions shall be given up to be dealt with
at his pleasure. And I see that this demand is made
in derision of the established laws of nations. Gentlemen, there is something on earth greater than arbitrary or despotic power. The lightning has its power,
and the whirlwind has its power, and the earthquake
has its power; but there is something among men
more capable of shaking despotic power than the
lightning, the whirlwind, or the earthquake, and that
is the excited and aroused indignation of the whole
civilized world."

Before we were aware of what was coming his majestic form began to tower, and his eyes to kindle, and his voice soon caught the key-note of the vast building, till in an illusion of the senses the lightning flashed, and the whirlwind shook the place where we were sitting, and the firm foundation rocked as with an earthquake. But it was an illusion of the sort produced only by famous orators like those

> " Whose resistless eloquence . . .
> Shook the arsenal, and fulmined over Greece."

I once saw Mr. Webster when he was forty and I was eleven. The best likeness of him at that time, it seems to me, is the bust by Powers. I saw him often between 1840 and 1850, and the best likeness of him at that time, I should say, is the one now printed for the first time in this magazine.[1]

[1] *The Century Magazine*, for September, 1893.

LANDSCAPE IN LIFE AND IN POETRY

REPRINTED FROM THE "DARTMOUTH LITERARY MONTHLY"
FOR OCTOBER, 1886

LANDSCAPE IN LIFE AND IN POETRY

THIS essay to mark the stages by which familiarity with landscape is developed in our lives and exhibited in our poetry was suggested by a sentence on which my eye chanced to fall in Clarence Stedman's "Poets of America."

I had already read Stedman's book with some care, but without particularly noticing the passage to which I refer, and which I shall presently quote. His book requires and repays attentive reading. Taken on the run or opened at random, one may find some things which give pause to assent and others that provoke contradiction; but if one will begin at the beginning and follow Stedman to his close, if he will imitate his cautious estimate of included facts and use his own critical insight, and, especially, if he will follow Stedman's example and be chary of hasty generalization, he will be in the way to a fair judgment of American poetry. And if it differs materially from Stedman's, which is not likely, at least it will be with respect for the breadth of his view, his sagacity, his candor, and his charming style. Perhaps he will not be troubled, as I was not, by some things which when considered out of relation seem to be discrepancies; perhaps he will not notice them, as I did not. On reflection, Stedman's method appears to be the only practicable one which leads to satisfactory results. Of some literatures peremptory judgments are permissible. One may say, for example, with Milman, that in invention, life, and distinctness of conception, and pure, translucent language, Greek poetry stands alone ; and of Latin poetry, that in lofty sentiment, majestic, if elaborate verse, in vigor in condensing and expressing moral truth, it surpasses all poetry. And so the poetry of Italy, of Germany, of France, and of England may each be characterized in a phrase. But any such judgment of American poetry must be recalled for reversal or modification.

Should it be said, for instance, as it often has been, at home and abroad, that our poetry is without originality, and is merely a pale reflection of English thought, feeling, and presentation ; that the thin song of our mythical lark is only a faint echo of the full-throated songster which rises from English meadows three thousand miles away, — the judgment would be both unfair and erroneous, as Stedman shows, in failing to take account of that which differentiates our poetry, in form, in proportion, and in a certain purity of tone and local color, from English song. On the other hand, even with such changes from the English standard as have been made in it, and for the better, the result would hardly warrant the assertion that we have developed an original literature. Now the value of Stedman's book is this : it helps us to see just what the outcome of our poetry is thus far ; just where it falls short, and what of promise there is in its future.

Nevertheless, I have a little quarrel with him ; at least I hope I have. In fact I must have, to get on. No wind, no race ! I am in the case of a parson who has meditated his discourse to a certain text, and too late discovers a doubtful exegesis. Stedman's sentence is this: "Fellowship with the spirit of American landscape and the recognition of its beauty and majesty were the earliest, as they are the most constant, traits of American verse." Now if by the earliest poets Stedman means the group of which Bryant was the first, as seems probable enough, looking at the general tenor of his book, then there is no dispute, and I must hunt for another text; but if, as I hope, *pro hac vice*, he had in mind the whole poetic band, which, headed by Anne Bradstreet and Michael Wigglesworth, has come, hand in hand, chanting down through the American ages, then I look no further, but proceed.

Leaving Stedman for a moment, I quote from Emerson's "Nature:" "To speak truly, few adult persons can see nature. Most persons do not see the sun. At least they have only a very superficial seeing. The sun illuminates only the eye of the man, but shines into the eye and the heart of the child." He had just said, "Nature never becomes a toy to a wise spirit. The flowers, the animals, the mountains, reflected the wisdom of his best hour, as much as they had delighted the simplicity of his childhood."

Without stopping to consider how these seemingly contradictory passages may be reconciled, I quote them to call attention to the different methods of Emerson and Stedman, both poets and critics, — and to their methods alone; for no one more sincerely than Stedman himself would deprecate a general comparison. The difference is this: Stedman gives reasons, but seldom judgments, leaving them to be inferred from his whole work. Emerson, on the contrary, seldom indulges us with his reasons, but pronounces judgments peremptorily for one party to-day, for the other to-morrow; but we wait in vain for the reconciling judgment which marshals the facts and declares the general law.

I also marvel that one with Emerson's acuteness should fail to notice that conscious intelligence, whether of mind or soul, is the recognition of nature which he was endeavoring to explain and promote. Without doubt, to the open-eyed wonder-faculty of children and primitive races, and possibly even to the higher order of animals, the sun, the moon, and the stars, the sea, the prairies, and the mountains, together with the more striking phenomena of nature, as thunder and lightning, the succession of the seasons, and of night and day, are mysterious both to sense and soul; and so is a fire-cracker, a gimcrack, or a bit of colored ribbon!

" The Ode on Immortality is the high-water mark which the intellect has reached in this age," wrote Emerson in 1856. That he had studied Wordsworth and Coleridge is evident from the sentences quoted above, and other passages in " Nature." But I am not sure, though Sir Henry Taylor thought otherwise, that Wordsworth, in making use of the reminiscences of a preëxistent state, which many of us vaguely have, did not preserve throughout his highest imaginings the distinction between " the glory and the dream," and any rational theory of the development of human faculties.[1]

---

[1] Matthew Arnold, in his preface to Wordsworth's poems, says, " The instinct of delight in Nature and her beauty had no doubt extraordinary strength in Wordsworth himself as a child. But to say that universally this instinct is mighty in childhood, and tends to die away afterwards, is to say what is extremely doubtful. In many people, perhaps with the majority of educated people, the love of nature is nearly imperceptible at ten years old, but strong and operative at thirty."

No doubt with years the instincts become more intelligent; but it seems to me that in the development of the understanding of nature, either in races or in individuals, the first stage is essentially non-intelligent,. or, at best, semi-intelligent, feeling — strongest when nerves are unworn and vitality exuberant.

The next stage — hardly reaching intelligent conception of the relations of man to the external world — is that in which to all persons not color blind or afflicted with similar congenital defect, arises the perception of certain harmonies of proportion, of light, of shade, and of color in a landscape, accompanied, it may be, even with vague notions of correspondence between natural objects and human emotions. There are those — the majority of mankind — who "enjoy fine natural scenery."

But this is not that true "fellowship with the spirit of American landscape" which Stedman had in mind. That, while it does not demand the classification of the botanist, implies the development by use of those faculties upon which we rely for discrimination of differences, and for the recognition of the relation of cause and effect, and of that artistic sense found, if found at all, in the soul alone, but receiving its inspiration and its impulse from the external world. At this stage we may truly fellowship with the spirit of the landscape. But of such there are comparatively few (Mr. Arnold notwithstanding), even among those who deem themselves, and are deemed by others, cultured people. These elect persons may be called happy.

But happy indeed are those who, while they accept the philosophical distinction between soul and substance, recognizing the former alone as sentient, can yet pass into that ideal world which discovers a relationship, not vague or fanciful, but clear and real, between all created things and the human soul, and assumes the recognition of this relationship by the world of nature itself.

I now desire to trace the progress from that stage in which we are merely susceptible to fine scenery, to that in which the poet and his reader live in familiar association with nature, and, ideally, nature lives with them.

Much that passes for nature study has little claim to be called such; and the distinction between that which is real and that which is merely formal is vital not only to self-culture, but likewise to literature. Consider this, that many persons, besides an intimate acquaintance with Thomson, Wordsworth, Bryant, and Tennyson, may have a just sense of their peculiar excellences, and yet lack appreciation of nature, or a disposition to fellowship with her, or to bring the poetry they so much admire to the crucial test by confronting it with nature — that very nature of which it claims to be the interpreter.

How many of us, for example, judging solely from the descriptions themselves in " Evangeline," can say whether Longfellow ever saw the little village of Grand Pré, —

"In the Acadian land, on the shores of the Basin of Minas ; "

or the country at the foot of the Ozarks, which Gabriel entered, where —

". . . are the wondrous beautiful prairies,
Billowy bays of grass ever rolling in shadow and sunshine,
Bright with luxuriant clusters of roses and purple amorphas " ?

In one of his earlier poems he wrote : —

" When winter winds are piercing shrill,
And through the white-thorn blows the gale ; "

but in his collected poems he changed white-thorn to
hawthorn. What effect has this substitution on the
verisimilitude of the description or on the associations
suggested ? or would it make any difference in either
to the reader were he informed that neither white-
thorn nor red-thorn nor hawthorn ever grew where the
scene of the poem is laid ? Or if it be said, as fairly
enough it might be, that the fidelity to nature of Longfellow's descriptions can hardly be determined from
isolated passages, then let the question be changed to
this : How many of us who value Longfellow's poetry,
which never attempts heights inaccessible, but keeps
within easy range of common hopes, joys, and sorrows,
and delights us with descriptions of nature, can say
whether, judging from the whole body of his poetical
work, he wrote with his eye on the scene, or from general recollection of landscape, or from books; and
that, in one case, we have assurance of its continuance,
and in the other, an apprehension lest his poetry, notwithstanding great and manifold excellences, will
gradually fade away?

The test might be repeated indefinitely, but one
more example will suffice. Southey, though he possessed many admirable powers, can hardly be said to
live in his poetry, much of which was descriptive.
Passing over that part of it which lies in the realm of
fancy, and therefore not subject to verification, though
none the less amenable to the law of verisimilitude, as
Leigh Hunt has shown in respect to Ariosto and his
winged horses, can we lay finger on this and that passage in his poetry which deals with familiar aspects
of nature, and say that it lacks verity ; or, taking his

one descriptive poem, the "Falls of Lodore," which
survives, mark the vital signs by which it does survive?

This may be a small matter, but not so thought one
of the masters of objective poetry. Scott's descriptions possess the excellences so conspicuously wanting
in Southey's. Southey wrote in and from his library;
Scott, on the contrary, composed *sub Jove*, sometimes
afoot, like Wordsworth, but often in the saddle.
"Oh! man, I had many a grand gallop among the
braes when I was thinking of Marmion." Lockhart,
to whom this was said, tells us that Scott ascertained,
in his own person, that a good horseman, well mounted,
might gallop from the shores of Loch Vennachar to
the rock of Stirling within the space allotted Fitz-
James in "The Lady of the Lake." In the same
poem Scott wrote of Ellen : —

> " . . . she stooped, and, looking round,
>   Plucked a blue harebell from the ground."

Was it in reference to these or to some similar lines
that Scott, being in doubt whether the flower grew in
that particular spot, galloped a dozen miles to verify
the fact?

These and many other examples which are found
in Lockhart disclose one secret of Scott's vitality as
a poet, and indicate the degree of his "fellowship with
the spirit of the landscape."

For evidence of such conscientious study of nature,
we shall look in vain in the writings of our earliest
poets or in those of more than a score of our latest.
And to the group of which Bryant was the earliest,
and many think the best, nature was familiar in her
elemental forces and grander aspects rather than in
those minute details which concern the days more than

the seasons. So far from fellowship with nature were our earlier poets, that the lack of it was one cause, perhaps the chief cause, of the sterility of their poetry and of the literary spirit of our people.

To put this matter, which is of vital importance to the poet, and to his readers as well, on a more substantial basis, I will refer to some facts within my own observation.

When I was in college we thought that Willis, then in vogue, was one of the best of our poets. His poems had been recently reprinted, and were generally read. I recollect with what enthusiasm I learned, and often repeated, the poem he called " Contemplation," which opened in this way : —

> " They are all up — the innumerable stars —
> And hold their place in heaven. My eyes have been
> Searching the pearly depths through which they spring,
> Like beautiful creations, till I feel
> As if it were a new and perfect world,
> Waiting in silence for the word of God
> To breathe it into motion."

I thought it very fine ; nor was I alone in this. The delusion was quite general, at least among my friends. How long it continued I do not recollect ; but it was in a measure dispelled, after the coming to Hanover of a few copies of Tennyson and Motherwell — the latter probably somewhat over-estimated — just then republished in America. Their poetry opened a new world into which we entered, and there found Wordsworth and Bryant. Nor was it long before we learned that the power they had over us lay in the power which nature had over them.

This was much, though perhaps nothing extraordinary as a fact in our education. But that which even to this day seems remarkable is, that the change in us

was not radical.   It was essentially literary, — not a
new birth, or even a stage of development.   It was
the perception, in their poetry, *as literature*, of a certain freshness and vital power not found in the poetry
we had previously admired ; not any wider or closer
acquaintance with nature.   Delightedly we read about,
and in our mind's eye even saw

> " A host of golden daffodils
>   Beside the lake, beneath the trees,
>   Fluttering and dancing in the breeze,"

but without the slightest impulse to find daffodils, or
anything like them, around Hanover.   We read with
zest and, I think, with true literary appreciation, the
" Lines composed a few miles above Tintern Abbey,"
marveling, however, that Wordsworth should think
the place of writing worth noting so particularly, and
heard the

> " . . . waters rolling from the mountain springs
>   With a sweet inland murmur."

In fancy we

> " . . . turned to thee,
>   O sylvan Wye, thou wanderer through the woods,"

but we did not beat up the haunts of our New Hampshire Wye, and our Yarrow remained " Yarrow Un-
visited."   No doubt some of us looked for the descendant of Bryant's " Waterfowl," but only that we

> " Might mark his distant flight to do him wrong ! "

Nevertheless it was a delightful world, though unseen
save through the poet's eyes.   Delightful, but unfruit-
ful.   Just when or how we came out of it into a world
where we truly fellowshiped with nature, I would tell
if I knew.   For he who does know, and will point out
a practicable path by which our people may come into
that intimate association with nature which makes it a

productive power, and at the same time preserve that literary culture which is essential to the best literary art, will do them a service second only to that which Bacon rendered to mankind. For if I have any conviction deeper and more constant than another respecting the causes of our literary sterility, it is this: that poets and people are "moving about in worlds not realized," feeding on the husks of literature, without understanding that books are valuable chiefly as the repositories of thought wider and more profound than our own, and vital only when verified by ourselves; or that nature becomes the power of God in man only when presented so as to bring into their true relations the soul that is Nature and the soul that is Man.

To bring this to pass with ourselves may be more difficult than for a people that were young when the world was young. It may be that we must submit to the primitive conditions of literary success. If an apprenticeship to Nature is indispensable, it may be that as Garcia required of his pupils a year's practice of the scale, so of us, before entering upon an art which is the highest and most difficult, may be required a description of the simplest flower that grows. It seems to me, that on the recognition of the foregoing conditions and conformity to their requirements — of which I see signs — depends the future of our imaginative literature, and something more! There is promise of better things to come, and already something of performance. Who but one that had slept with his face to the stars could have written this?

"I see before me now a traveling army halting;
Below, a fertile valley, spread with barns and the orchards of summer;
Behind, the terraced sides of a mountain, abrupt in places, rising high,

Broken with rocks, with clinging cedars, with tall shapes dingily
  seen ;
The numerous camp-fires scattered near and far, some away up on the
  mountain ;
The shadowy forms of men and horses, looming, large-sized, flicker-
  ing,
And over all, the sky — the sky ! far, far out of reach, studded with
  the eternal stars."

I lived four years at Hanover, blind, absolutely blind, to scenery as fair in its way as my eyes ever rested on in any land, — and so did others, — even after we had become keenly alive to the literary value of poetry, which drew its inspiration, its vitality, and its truth directly from nature.

I believe, therefore, that the love of nature, intelligent, not born of mere wonder, as in children and in primitive races, objective, as implying familiarity with her forms and manifestations, and subjective, as finding her responsive, in her moods and symbols, to spiritual aspirations, is relatively a late development even in those races and individuals in which it is ever developed. Is it the basis of Teutonic literature? The Greeks do not appear to have possessed it. Their abounding vitality informed nature with their own personality. They gave much to her, but seemed incapable of receiving anything from her. They lived with nature under the open sky ; were acquainted with earth, and sea, and mountains ; with stars, and planets, and the sun. The Teuton, on the other hand, knew nature in her haunts. If English literature owes its fancy to Celtic blood and association, its characteristic life comes from the soil, and is fresh with the breath of the morning, and the fragrance of wild flowers, and the songs of many birds, and the idyllic sweetness of green fields.

Lest what I have said of myself, and of those with whom I associated in college days, should be laid to the account of exceptional causes, I now refer to later and wider observations.

Returning to Hanover on the centennial of 1868, I found many I had known as undergraduates; and if, amidst congratulations, inquiries, and replies, there was any remark so general that it seemed to be universal, it was this, in substance: "The old place is just the same. But what a beautiful place! what scenery! When here I did n't think much about it — in fact, nothing!" And to verify this new discovery, we must needs go to the heights which looked down into the valley to the southeast, as peaceful in its beauty as the benediction of God; or that to the southwest, with Ascutney in the distance, recalling reminiscences of those October mornings when the Python, the mist-serpent of the river, lay along the Connecticut until Apollo slew him, and Earth by night renewed — him the deathless!

In assigning the development of an intelligent appreciation of landscape to a late period of education, under the circumstances above related, it may be said that I generalize from too narrow a basis of observation; that the facts amount to no more than this: that young men, withdrawn by necessary seclusion from fellowship with nature, are insensible to her essential qualities, though possibly alive to her power in literature. There may be some truth in the observation, but I have reasons for the broader generalization.

Twenty-five years ago I passed the month of August at a place of resort among the mountains. The company gathered there was somewhat miscellaneous, made up chiefly of the middle, mercantile class, born and reared in rural New England, and *habitués* of the place summer after summer. Nearly every fair afternoon, in parties of a dozen, we made excursions in an open mountain wagon, among the hills, through woods, or along reaches of valley, which presented a quickly shifting panorama of infinite variety, seldom repeating itself in the changing lights, shadows, and cloud forms. Our driver was a middle-aged country-man, by whose side was my seat. As we rode along, suddenly would come an explosion of exclamations when a turn in the road brought into view some scene of peculiar beauty. I need not describe, if I could, the extravagance of gesture or speech by which each expressed delight. The driver was quick to catch the view, and from the light in his eyes I saw that he, too, was touched by the beauty of the scene. " Do you," I asked, "care for that which seems to please the people behind us?" "Well, 'Squire," he replied, after a moment's hesitation, "I was born in a little house over the hills there, and there I have lived, boy and man, more than thirty years. For three summers I have driven this team, and for most part the same folks. When I first began to take 'em out [with a slight gesture over his shoulder], and see 'em act so, I thought they was the biggest set of fools I ever see ; but by'me by I begun to look myself, and now [with a suppressed gulp] I guess — I'm — about as big a fool as any of 'em ! "

Now here was a genuine man, a son of the soil, who, with average poetic sensibilities, had all his life dwelt among some of the fairest scenes of earth, and had but lately come to his own. Nor was there any-thing peculiar in his case. No. There are thousands and tens of thousands, some, like him, unlettered, and others, fascinated by the gewgaws of literature, but all blind, and waiting alike for the dispersion of mists which darken their eyes to what nature would gladly reveal to those who will truly "fellowship with the spirit of the landscape."

To bring this about should be the aim of self-culture and the prime design of general education; and its accomplishment will be the first stage in the development of an original literature!

But nature has not yet closed her account with us. Thus far she has revealed herself in answer to our questionings, sometimes in the awe-inspiring majesty of her elemental forces, sometimes in the idyllic sweetness of green fields and verdure which embowers hamlets and dim-discovered spires, and sometimes by touching chords which respond to suggestions of some mysterious relationship between us and herself.

We know how much modern poetry, especially that of Wordsworth, owes to an impassioned love of nature, and to the assumption which attributes sensation to inanimate objects; and how great our loss would be if the results were eliminated from poetic literature. But I am less concerned respecting the bounds to poetic license, than the just limitations, as matter of self-culture, to our " fellowship with the spirit of the landscape." How far may we profitably adopt the theory, which must at least be regarded as ideal, that represents nature as desirous of understanding us, and of coming into intelligent sympathy with us, as we are with her? Of course such an assumption lacks any basis realizable to the senses, nor is it otherwise susceptible of verification. Nevertheless, there is an ideal view of nature in which it is not altogether

fantastical to suppose that she is conscious of herself
and of certain spiritual relations to us; and there are
those who recognize the moral harmony of the universe only in the belief that not only everything that
breathes, but also everything that has organized life,
and even things as remote from apparent design as
those which go to form what we call natural scenery, or

> " . . . something far more deeply interfused,
> Whose dwelling is the light of setting suns,
> And the round ocean and the living air,
> And the blue sky, and in the mind of man,"

have, in common with ourselves, been formed by the
same power, and subject to the same influences, are
thus brought into relation not only to the common
source of being, but also, through that common relationship, into certain undefined but not wholly un-
intelligent relations to each other.

Now, however baseless this notion may be in philosophy, it is conceivable at least in poetry and may
be recognized in our intercourse with nature. It is
the highest in that fellowship with the spirit of the
landscape, of which the lowest is mere wonder; and
so rich and satisfactory beyond all antecedent conception are the results, that happy is he who can truly
say, *Respexit tamen, et longo post tempore venit.*

But this view has not escaped challenge even in
respect to poetry. Henry Taylor, the author of
"Philip van Artevelde," cautions his readers against
a too ready acceptance of Wordsworth's *poetic* theory
of nature. He says: "The vivacity with which he
[Wordsworth] is accustomed to apprehend this power
of inanimate nature over the human mind has indeed
led him in some cases, we venture to think, too far

. . . in his poetical licenses, or in that particular poetic license by which sensation is attributed to inanimate objects, — the particular feeling which they excite in the spectator being ascribed to themselves as if they were sentient beings. Thus we find in the 'Intimations of Immortality,' —

> 'The moon doth with delight
> Look round her when the heavens are bare.'

And in the same ode, —

> ' Ye fountains, meadows, hills, and groves,
> Think not of any severing of our loves.' "

That Wordsworth was the founder of this modern school of poetic nature-sentiency there can be no doubt. But if one will think of it a little, he will perceive that the interpretation of the interrelations between man and nature, as presented by Wordsworth and his followers, does not materially differ as a *poetical idea* from that which, three thousand years ago, possessed the souls and guided the pens of the Hebrew poets, that wonderful race which anticipated the highest reach of modern spiritualized thought, and that the vital power of the best modern poetry, as well as of theirs, is derived from the interfusion, by the imagination, of the soul that is in man and the soul that is in nature.

While our race ancestors were in their lowest estate of intelligence, before the Frank had crossed the Rhine or the wolf had suckled Romulus and Remus, — while the Greeks, at their best, were without spirituality, — the Hebrew, rising to the conception of the unity of all created things, and of their spiritual relations to each other and to their common Creator, could say more loftily than Wordsworth, more loftily than Milton, —

" When Israel went out of Egypt . . . the sea saw it and fled; Jordan was driven back. The mountains skipped like rams. . . . What *ailed* thee, O thou sea, that thou fleddest ? Thou Jordan, that thou wast driven back ? Ye mountains, that ye skipped like rams ? "

Again : —

" Mountains and hills, fruitful trees and cedars . . . kings of the earth, and all people, praise ye the Lord."

And again : —

" Sing, O ye heavens . . . shout, ye lower parts of the earth ; break forth into singing, ye mountains, O forest, and every tree therein."

But the most daring and the most successful flight of the imagination in all literature, as it seems to me, was reached by the psalmist : —

" Lift up your heads, O ye gates ; even lift them up, ye everlasting doors ; and the King of glory shall come in ! "

If those who were privileged with access to the Divine Mind might, unblamed, use language which implies, in an ideal sense at least, that intelligent sympathy pervades all the works of His hand; that not nature alone, not the growing trees, not the running rivers, not the heavens whose clouds take on forms of life, but that the lifeless marble and the insensate brazen doors could recognize the approaching God, — then perhaps we need not scruple with Henry Taylor to assume the sentiency of nature, either as an element of poetry, or as an aid to a truer "fellowship with the spirit of the landscape."

THE SCOPE OF A COLLEGE LIBRARY

ADDRESS AT THE DEDICATION OF WILSON HALL, DART-
MOUTH COLLEGE LIBRARY, JUNE 24, 1885

ADDRESS

A YEAR ago the corner-stone of the library building was laid with appropriate observances. That
event was an epoch in the history of the college. It
was the beginning of a work long contemplated and
often deferred. To-day we celebrate its completion
and dedicate Wilson Hall to its intended uses.

Our thanks are due to the architect whose skill has
given us acceptable results for library economy, and a
structure of just proportions to which time will add
new graces; to the master-builders whose fidelity in
construction will be apparent with the passing years;
and to the committee to whose foresight and superin-
tending care the enterprise owes its success. And,
above all, in the spirit of those who founded this institution, would we devoutly recognize the divine favor
manifested to us in this as in all generations.

Although I wish the privilege had fallen to another,
yet most gratefully do I participate in the dedication
of the new edifice. It is now five and forty years
since I first came to this seat of learning; nor have
I ever forgotten — I never can forget — how much I
owe to what I found here, — able, judicious, and faithful instructors; beloved associates whose lives have
fulfilled the promise of their robust youth; books,

abundant compared with those before within my
reach; and the memories of those great men who had
walked these grounds, and amidst the pure and serene
influences of this place had laid the foundations of
character and usefulness.   Five and forty years later
I stand here again.   But my eyes seek in vain for
the venerable forms which I once knew.   Beloved
associates of my youth are here no longer.   Much is
changed, but much remains.   The venerable halls remain; the skies are the same; still flows the beautiful river, — still stretches the glorious landscape away
into the purple distance.

Among the privileges of my college days I gratefully remember the libraries, which were ample for
our purposes.   We could not indeed have verified
Gibbon's authorities, nor have explored any subject
exhaustively in original sources.   But the books we
needed were to be found either in the society libraries,
the college library, or that of the Northern Academy.
It was in my college days that this latter institution
was evolved, I always thought, from the active brain
of its amiable projector, the late Dr. William Cogs-
well.   It was unobtrusively located in a lower room
of Reed Hall   The name sounded well, and our pride
in it considerably exceeded our knowledge of it; for
then, as ever, *Omne ignotum pro magnifico*.   With
those who had antiquarian leanings its prestige was
angmented by the possession of two editions of John
Eliot's translation of the Bible into the Indian
tongue; but neither this admirable version nor the
academy's kindred treasures were much sought for by
the ingenuous youth of my time.

When some one defended the law on the ground
that it was open to all, " so is the London Tavern,"

growled Dr. Johnson, " — to those who can pay the reckoning." On the same terms the college library was open to us. But I fancy the accomplished librarian found his duties neither arduous nor largely remunerative.

In the society libraries, however, were famous browsing pastures stretching away from the heathery Grampians to the honeyed Hymettus. Free even to license, the privilege was seldom abused, and is of such value that it should be accorded, when practicable, even at the risk of some inconvenience. Of like value was that other privilege of carrying away to our country homes, or to the rural districts where we taught school, a trunkful of literature for the long winter evenings. To this day I hear the stage-driver's good-natured but highly objurgatory epithets lavished on those book-laden trunks, as he hoisted them to the rack ; and the no less significant exclamations of the youth who at the end of the route assisted their progress to the schoolmaster's chamber. After a half century of such usage, no one could reasonably expect to find many of those identical volumes on the shelves. Those who read them are gone. The past itself is gone, but its memories and its influences endure. I wish to pay a tribute of sincere respect to those peripatetic volumes. They did a useful work. They entered into the rural life of northern New England and aroused new thoughts and new purposes. They stimulated a desire for a broader education in some whose names had not otherwise honored our rolls; and in others who wandered from their native hills and became pioneers of civilization by the great lakes and beyond the Mississippi. Those were days of toil and privation, of spare and homely diet, of coarse and scanty raiment; but they covered no inconsiderable portion of that period which measures the intellectual movement of our New England society. We gratefully remember the good they brought to us, but we cannot wish their return.

At the time of which I speak, the libraries of the United Fraternity and of the Social Friends contained in the aggregate about fifteen thousand volumes. As I recall these collections, they fairly represented the tastes, judgments, and needs of those to whom they were mainly indebted for their existence. Each class, divided equally between the two societies, made a donation to the respective libraries in its sophomore year; that is, in that year they raised the funds with which they purchased books. These books were held for special class use until near the time of graduation and then were given to the society libraries. In my own class I was one of the committee of the Socials for that business. Two of us were selected to go to the great city, in the summer vacation, and make purchases; and from memoranda made at the time, I know that the hours spent in making our selections from the bewildering riches of Little & Brown's shelves were considered "a hard day's work." Few titles of our purchase I now remember; but in history we ranged from the Chronicles of Froissart and Monstrelet to the Memoirs of Vidocq; and I hope that my associate, who still lives, read the former with as much avidity as I devoured the latter.

Returning to these scenes of student life after the lapse of many years, one perceives that a new order has begun. The grand old hall remains as it was on that first day when its faultless proportions fronted the western sky. Would that its perishable materials might be transmuted into the imperishable marble, not only as a memorial of the great men who have lived under its roof-tree, but also of the forgotten architect who builded better than he knew.

" Tempora mutantur, nos et mutamur in illis."

We hail the new order. Not far from the site to which tradition assigns the house of the founder and first president, rises a new structure. Its exterior is pleasing and satisfies, I am told, the severe judgment of experts. For myself I will say, that having seen in many lands edifices with which it may fairly be compared, I think the architect should be willing to have his name inscribed on its least perishable part, to take its chance against the assaults of time, which envies all continuance save its own.

We are assured that Wilson Hall is fire-proof. That is a great satisfaction; for what sad associations those words suggest. Do we, envying the old world its possessions of art and literature, year after year, bring them to these shores; and then, reminded by their presence of our poverty in original power, do we consume them from the face of the earth? These may be harsh self-accusations; but those which are just — indifference and neglect — are hardly less to our discredit. With something of dismay I hear of the coming among us of the first folio of Shakespeare, or of one of the incunabula, or of the priceless treasures from Nineveh, Greece, or Italy, lest within a few years we learn, as so often has been the case, that they no longer exist save as smoke and ashes. Gentlemen of the Board of Trustees, perhaps the destruction of nothing which you possess would cause a moment's pain to those who are not the immediate friends of the college; but the knowledge that you have a safe

repository for what is worth preserving will enrich
you a hundredfold, and in time attract to Wilson
Hall treasures the loss of which would fill the world
with regret.

The arrangements made for the preservation and
use of books seem to possess every advantage which
may reasonably be expected; for a library is no exception to the general law, — that the acceptance of
any architectural scheme involves a compromise.
Something desirable must be left out, and something
inconvenient must be admitted.   The central stack,
which you have adopted, finds favor as the most economical arrangement for the storing of a large library.
To this you have wisely added ample accommodations
for special collections as well as for the convenience
of students.

In devising the plan of the library building, you
have contemplated its indefinite extension to meet the
growth of the collections.   It is well.   With the years
will come friends who will add to your funds for the
purchase of books, and others who, from the abundance of their own stores, will supply the deficiencies
of yours.   Time and friendship and filial love will create a great library here, for which you have a costly
and well-appointed building.

Too long have I delayed the expressions of your
gratitude to the memory of him whose generosity
makes us all debtors.   Alas, that our words cannot
reach the ear of our benefactor; that he cannot behold the result of his beneficence ; that he cannot see
in your faces, as I do, the grateful sentiments which
overflow your hearts!   But from all that I learn of his
character he would have found less satisfaction, were
he now present, in any words we might utter, than in

the consciousness of having promoted sound learning; and less desire that his name should endure for ages on yonder hall, that from that hall should proceed the influence of good literature enduring with the ages, widening with the ages, and moulding the characters of all who came within its reach.

George Francis Wilson was not a son of the college, but his name will ever stand high among its benefactors as the Founder of Wilson Hall.

The old order closes; the new begins.

" Magnus ab integro sæclorum nascitur ordo."

Yesterday, the library was made up of unrelated collections, each having a certain value for college or university education. To-day, these collections become a unit, an organism, The Library.[1] It is no longer

[1] The flitting of the library, between the fourteenth and seventeenth days of June inclusive, from the old quarters to the new, was accomplished by an act of filial piety which deserves commendation. I learn the facts from an estimable lady who witnessed it, and her account in substance is as follows: It was deemed eminently important that the library should be transferred to Wilson Hall before Commencement. But unavoidable delays had prevented the book-shelves from being in readiness till, by reason of the annual examinations, there were practically but four days left in which to make the transfer. The president accordingly announced to the assembled students the difficulty, expressed the belief that it could be overcome by a united effort, and called for volunteers. In response to the call the whole body of students rose to their feet. A day was then announced for each class; the monitors were requested to divide them into squads of twelve, assigning two hours of continuous work to each band, and reporting to the individuals and to the librarian. The college carpenter was directed to prepare a number of hand-barrows, holding as many volumes as two men could conveniently carry. The Librarian distributed his assistants at each end of the route, to direct the removal and the reception of the books. The volumes were rapidly dusted as they were taken from the shelves, placed in the hand-barrows or trays, and for four days these trays were plying between the buildings like shuttles, six at a time, from morning till night. A plentiful supply of lemonade in both buildings relieved the thirst of hot June days;

in lodgings nor living at sufferance among its friends. It has a home of its own, — can invite company, interchange civilities, and recognize the comity which exists between the guilds of literature. Its situation is favorable. It is surrounded by attractive scenery. Every circumstance of its life conduces to growth and longevity. Our hopes for it are high and our demands upon it will be rigorous. Let us attempt to forecast its future.

With few exceptions the increase of the library will be determined by general rather than by special considerations. The treasures of the Vatican flowed to Rome because Rome was the centre of religious thought and ecclesiastical purpose. The collections of the Bibliothèque Nationale and of the British Museum found their way to those centres of cosmopolitan art, science, and literature, because there they were needed. This accords with beneficent law. An accumulation of books brought together without due relation may gratify ostentation but subserves no useful purpose. A library, whether public or private, should be a growth, and every addition to it should represent an intelligent demand and supply present or prospective needs. Let us notice a few of these departments that ought to be made complete, either from inherent propriety or in recognition of some distinctive character acquired by the college and likely to be retained.

Whatever else the library may lack, apart from what is essential to college work, it should not lack anything which relates to the history of the institution.

the work was carried on with abundant singing and merriment; and at the end of the four days about sixty thousand of the sixty-five thousand volumes, which compose the library, had been transferred.

The college has an honorable history which ought to be known here. In some room, set apart for the purpose, should be found the memorials of the college from its earliest days ; the biographies of its founders and patrons, of its officers and students; pictorial illustrations of its buildings and of the surrounding scenery ; every work written by its graduates ; and, finally, whatever relates to the beginning and progress of an institution which has profoundly influenced the civil and ecclesiastical history of New England. In neglected garrets are manuscripts of great value for that purpose. Let us rescue these from decay and bring them hither. Before me lies a mass of such papers written by, or to, our founder, Dr. Eleazar Wheelock. From these I have learned something of the labors, trials, and privations of those who first came to this wilderness, and something of their devotion to a great purpose. I have brought these papers with me as a contribution to the college history, hoping they may interest others as they have interested me. I present them to the library.

In the annals of the college are to be found examples of devotion to her interests which should inspire all her children. When her great son was called to defend her life threatened by parricidal hands, with that thoroughness and precision which marked all his professional and public work he examined the law and the evidence of the cause which demanded his advocacy. And so did Mason, Smith, and Hopkinson, who had no personal relations to the college. But Mr. Webster was her son. He studied her history until those first days lived again. His imagination transformed the soulless body corporate — the fiction of the king's prerogative — into a living per-

sonality, the object of his filial devotion, the beloved
mother whose protection called forth all his prowess
and enkindled in his bosom a quenchless love. So
will it ever be with those who become intimately acquainted with her history; for by an unchanging law
the sentiments and affections of individuals, no less
than of nations, are moulded into an ideal personality.
Such was Pallas-Athene to art-loving Greeks; such to
the all-conquering Romans the Capitoline Jove.

Let us gather, then, the memorials of the college
into one repository sacred as the abode of the dear
and venerable mother. No one will enter it without
reverence nor leave it without new devotion. Its
threshold will welcome the returning son however
humble; and its lintel will be lifted up that the most
exalted may enter. Nor will the place be sacred to
those alone, the graduates of the college, beneath
whose revisiting footsteps the very sods become quickened. For when our great brother rescued his *alma
mater* from the conflict of parties and bore her on
his shoulders to the citadel of the Constitution, he
opened wide its doors to every sister college in the
land; and as chance or rational curiosity leads the
feet of their sons to this place, let them not seek in
vain for every memorial of the great conflict or of the
great victory. Let this room, therefore, contain every
pamphlet called forth by the heated controversy: the
hostile legislation in its authentic records; the correspondence which relates to the contest; the later discussions and decisions, in legal or legislative forums,
to which it has given rise; and finally, all those
authorities by which counsel or magistrate, in state or
national tribunal, sought to secure or avert the final
judgment of the court. The question involved in this

celebrated case was one of constitutional rather than of technical law; and it was decided on principles within the comprehension of non-professional intelligence. With its related history it might well be made the subject of an annual essay, the preparation of which would tend to stimulate habits of original research and enkindle the devotion of undergraduates. To such a proposed collection of authorities I desire to make a contribution. In his great argument reported in the Dartmouth College Case, a copy of which you have fittingly placed under the corner-stone of Wilson Hall, Daniel Webster cited as authority the first volume of Blackstone's " Commentaries." The identical volume which he held in his hand for that purpose, I now hold in mine. It belongs to a set not without interest as the first American edition of that celebrated work. Daniel Webster, whose autograph signature is found upon the fly-leaf, gave it to his brother, Ezekiel Webster, also a son of the college, whose handwriting is to be seen on a small slip of paper obviously used to mark a page for reference.

Having brought together the memorials of the college for preservation in its library, the growth of the collection may be allowed to express the views of those who contribute to its funds, and of inquirers in different fields of investigation. How widely in recent years the old fields have been extended and what new fields have been opened, is well known. The product of each clamors for recognition; but the relative importance of the several departments of literature and the draft which each should make on your resources may be wisely left to the decision of well-known laws.

In all departments of research the results within the last fifty years are amazing. No mind, however capacious, can grasp them in detail; nor will the most far-reaching presume to limit their progress. But it will not escape observation that these results are in a great measure due to more scientific methods of research made possible by the existence of great collections and great libraries.

Within recent years constitutional history has been explored in original sources, and its field has been widened so as to include all those nationalities which in any degree have participated in the general movement of organized governments in the direction of popular rights regulated by fundamental laws. This is largely due to the original authorities gathered into great libraries and made accessible to students. Such collections not only answer inquiries, but they stimulate inquirers; and, as I shall endeavor to show in the sequel, they are likely to have a profound influence on the coming literature of America. And as I deem this a subject of present importance, I pass, by easy transition, from the history of the college which interests us here, to the history of our country which interests us everywhere, and make it prominent in this address, with the hope that I may successfully urge the equipment of your library for its most exhaustive study.

The formation of a written constitution as the fundamental law of the United States, in 1787, was, without doubt, an epoch in the history of constitutional government; but it was not the origin of that form of government. It was preceded by the constitutions of several of the States, and notably by that of Massachusetts, in 1780, from which some features of the Federal Constitution were copied. Nor was the Massachusetts instrument essentially more than the

charter of William and Mary changed and enlarged
to conform to the circumstances of the independent
State which, in revolutionary times, had grown out
of a subject province of England. Provincial charters, again, were based upon those which were drafted
for the colonies in the days of Charles I., upon the
general principles of the unwritten constitution of our
British ancestors. Thus we can trace constitutional
government back to our English home, and perhaps
even to the forests of Germany. In the colonial
period the government of our ancestors was founded
on royal charters; but these were then to be interpreted, as they are now to be read, in the light of the
public law of Europe and of the municipal law of
England. When the colonists threw off their allegiance to the crown they still remained subject to the
public law of Europe; and they found it convenient
to adhere to the general principles of the municipal
law of England. Magna Charta and the Petition of
Right they undoubtedly brought with them in the
period of the great emigration; and if it is less clear
that the Habeas Corpus and the Bill of Rights, later
enactments of the British Parliament, passed *proprio
vigore* beyond the seas, our ancestors laid claim to
them, if not by virtue of their relations to the mother
country, at least as analogues of rights which had
grown up on American soil. Consequently the public
law of Europe and the municipal law of England as
they were interpreted in the seventeenth century, together with the great declaratory acts and the constitutional history of England, are still vital to us, and
so will remain as long as we are interested in constitutional government. They form the basis of our
political system, and will acquire new importance as

we approach that period in our national life when a
denser population and more complicated interests will
require a readjustment of the rights of persons and
the powers of government. These subjects and the
questions to which they give rise, including those
institutions which indicate our common origin with
Englishmen, or differentiate the administrative system of both from that of continental Europe, have
received much attention on both sides of the Atlantic.
I need only refer to the writings of Hallam, May,
Stubbs, Freeman, Lecky, and Hall, in England, of De
Tocqueville and Von Holst, on the Continent, and to
the political and historical publications issued from
the Johns Hopkins University in this country. Interesting and valuable as the results of these studies are,
they are more interesting and valuable as indicating
the application of scientific methods of investigation
to historical and constitutional questions. Such has
been the advance in this direction that Hallam's judgments on controverted constitutional points are no
longer accepted as final. The time is at hand when
students of our history will insist upon access to original sources of information. Too long have we been
obliged to accept the inflamed arguments of the advocate. We wish to recur to the facts on which the
arguments are based. We shall no longer remain
satisfied with the method of historical composition of
which Hume affords a conspicuous example; we prefer that of which Freeman is an acknowledged master.
Nor is the time unfavorable. Our colonial history
has been enriched by materials unknown to the earlier writers, and foreign archives lately closed or only
partially accessible are now wide open to the student.
A spirit of candor prevails, and there are indications

that much of our history will be rewritten with an eye closer to essential facts, and with an insight which discerns the truth through the mists of undiscriminating patriotism, partisan spirit, and sectarian zeal. The college should be able to encourage these more rational methods of historical study by pointing to an alcove in Wilson Hall containing those original authorities which incite the desire for research and afford means for its gratification.

If the past history of our college indicates the field of its future usefulness, we shall be warranted in making the amplest provision for the study of constitutional history. It may not have taken the lead in the cultivation of *belles lettres*, nor did the muse

> "That has her haunt in dale, or piny mountain,
> Or forest by slow stream, or pebbly spring,"

choose here her dwelling place. We have not filled this northern air with song. But in public and municipal law, in statesmanship and in administration, the graduates of this college have a most honorable record. Webster, Woodbury, Bartlett, Chase, Fletcher, Parker, Choate, Perley — what names are these ; what men were those, all within the first century of Dartmouth ! Here they laid the foundation of character. Here they began the superstructures. Faithful to the curriculum which assumes that discipline, rather than promiscuous reading, is the chief purpose of college life, they applied themselves to prescribed lines of work, and yet found leisure to explore the constitutional history of their country. Nor is there better reading for the prospective citizen — public or private — than the history of the race which more than any other has developed constitutional government. That history should be known both in its great epochs and

in the causes, immediate or remote, which led to them.
I think, however, that it is less generally known than
ancient history or that of continental Europe. Neither
our own history nor that of England seems to attract
the attention of young men. With some opportunities for learning the facts, I do not think that Hume,
Hallam, Sparks, Hildreth, or Bancroft, is so much
read as Prescott, Motley, or Parkman, all of whom
have chosen foreign fields. Macaulay and Froude,
engaged on any subject, attract by brilliancy of treatment. One reason for this lack of interest in our
race history may be that it neither stirs the blood nor
excites the imagination. As a whole, it lacks the
heroic element which fascinates. In episodes it does
not lack. Richard before Acre, or in great battle
with Saladin for the Sepulchre, Henry V. at Agin-
court and Nelson in the Bay of Aboukir, are examples
of heroism; and so is Wolfe before Quebec. Wellington's campaigns in the Pyrenees afford instances of
English valor; and the mangled, but unbroken, squares
at Waterloo, of English constancy. Marlborough's
battles in the War of the Spanish Succession were
"famous victories." But these heroic achievements
were on foreign soil. They touched neither the roof-
trees nor the hearth-stones of our English race. They
count for little either in the world's progress or in
our own.

But with what breathless attention do we read of
the Three Hundred who saved the civilization of
Greece; or of their varying fortunes when Rome and
Carthage contended for the domination of the world;
or of the fall of the Western Empire when art,
science, and literature, frightened from their haunts
by barbaric hordes, groped in darkness for a thou-

sand years; or of the last of his hundred battles when
the Great Captain staked his empire on the final
charge of the Old Guard, and lost. Those were great
events — those battles of heroes and demi-gods. They
affected the fortunes of nations and of races. Their
narration entrances us. But unless we misread the
destiny of our English race to impress the world with
its laws, language, and civilization, I ask your judgment whether Magna Charta, the Petition of Right,
the Bill of Rights, the Habeas Corpus, and the Declaration of Independence, as a series of events affecting the rights of man and leading up to constitutional
government, have been exceeded in importance by
any events, or by any series of events, the work of
human hands, in recorded history? They were at
least of transcendent importance, since to us, and to
fifty millions of our fellow-citizens, they are the bul-
warks of liberty.

The importance of these events does not diminish
as they come nearer to our own times. Through the
ages great words have been spoken. Scholars still
delight in the ideal republic of Plato. In almost
every department of polite learning Aristotle still
instructs. Bacon gave new rules to induction, and
Newton announced the subjection of the planets to
law. But it was reserved for Jefferson first to speak
the word which caught the ear of humanity, — the
word which men, from the beginning, with up-turned,
despairing faces, had been listening to hear: that they
were created equal; that they were endowed with
rights inalienable; that life, and liberty, and the pursuit of happiness were theirs, — words, the grandest,
the most momentous, that ever fell from human lips.
But whence came those words which startled the dull

ear of the eighteenth century? Shall we find them
in the *Contrat Social*, or did they fall from the lips
of Wythe, Lee, or Henry, in the Virginia Assembly?
Were they merely the felicitous phrasing of the sentiments promulgated by Otis, or either Adams; or were
they the concentrated expression of a thousand years
of English thought and purpose on both sides of the
Atlantic? Students should find in Wilson Hall the
answer to these questions; asked not in the spirit of
"notes and queries," but with something of the awe
with which we question the destiny of man. For
whether true or false, words have seldom been followed by such tremendous consequences. In the
generation of their utterance they nerved the hearts
of those who trod the blood-stained snows of Jersey
and stormed the redoubts at Yorktown. In the revolution which overthrew the oldest dynasty of Europe
and deluged France with blood, their appalling analogues were "Liberty, Equality, Fraternity." In our
own day they inspired Garrison, Sumner, and Lincoln,
whose shibboleth they were, in the conflict which broke
the last slave-shackle in Anglo-Saxon lands. Nor is
their force yet spent. They are as vital as when
uttered in Independence Hall, or proclaimed at the
head of the army. They are the life of those political and social portents in our sky which threaten the
peace of the generation of young men who leave these
seats to-morrow.

Jefferson's words are connected in clear sequence
with every important event in the constitutional history of our English race on both sides of the Atlantic;
and by that history, so far as it records the essential
qualities of the race, their truth and applicability to
practical government are to be determined. The

popular belief seems to be that the truth of the Great
Declaration is a domestic discovery, and that on
American soil it finds its sole expression in government. This is not altogether so. The facts are more
nearly these : that the American Revolution was a
movement of the Anglo-Saxon race, to which race
our Revolutionary ancestors mainly belonged, in the
direction of natural liberty regulated by law ; that
it acquired new impetus in the reign of James I., and
continued after the great Puritan emigration to these
shores, on both sides of the Atlantic, with nearly
equal momentum ; and that every advance on either
side had its equivalent on the other, until, in both
countries, civil and ecclesiastical liberty were firmly
established. If this seems a paradox, let me indulge
in paradoxes on vital themes, if thereby may be
stimulated a purpose to place in Wilson Hall the
means of their disproof or verification. A brief explanation, however, is required. England in the days
of Elizabeth lived under a sovereign who, with great
personal popularity and inherited prerogatives, was
nearly absolute ; but her successor, lacking popularity,
found it impossible to repel assaults on his royal privileges ; and these assaults, continued with uninter-
mitted diligence for more than two centuries, have so
reduced the authority of the crown that now it is
less than that which the people of the United States
have voluntarily conferred upon their chief magistrate.
A similar change has taken place in the distribution
of the legislative powers. The veto of the crown is
merely nominal, and the coördinate functions of legislation have been engrossed by the two Houses of Parliament.

At first they were exercised preponderatingly by

the Lords; but to-day we notice the singular fact, that while our conservative Senate seems to be strengthening its legislative power and influence, in England the power of the House of Lords has steadily declined until the authority of the government is centred, directly or indirectly, in the Commons as the immediate representatives of the people. It is also noticeable that while the people of the United States have limited their immediate power by written constitutions, the people of England not thus trammeled, have through their representatives, practically unrestricted authority in all legislative affairs. I venture to predict that this phase of constitutional government will, in the near future, challenge scrutiny on both sides of the water, and lead to results not now to be contemplated with equanimity.

We rejoice in the prosperity of our race. In the home which it has occupied for a thousand years it has founded an empire the most powerful of modern times. It has colonized a continent here in the west, our home, which sets no bounds to its aspirations. From its prolific loins have gone forth the subjects of a new empire in the far off southern ocean which will dominate that section of the world. It is an aggressive race. It evidently contemplates as its mission the freedom of man and the establishment of constitutional governments. The parent stock shows no loss of vitality; the transplanted stock, no degeneracy. We have lost neither the instincts nor the traditions of our race ; and when the time comes, as it inevitably will come, that its seat of empire is transferred to the west, we shall take up its work and carry it forward.

In preparation for this work let us study before all other history that of the Anglo-Saxon race, since in that race is found the germ of our present liberty and the promise of our future literature. Its history on either continent is our history. In its great achievements for liberty we find the safeguards of our own; in its mistakes, our warnings. Its later as well as its earlier history is still vital. It should be found in Wilson Hall in close proximity to our own. Both should be studied in their most authentic form. To that end, we need the British statutes from Magna Charta to our own times; the Parliamentary Journals of both houses; the collection of Debates; the publications of the Record Commissioners; the compilations of parliamentary history and the volumes of treaties. By the side of these sources of the constitutional history of England, and to be studied with them, should be found the corresponding series of our colonial papers, as well as those of the state and general governments. The presence of such a collection of original authorities as I have indicated would excite curiosity and lead to their study. Correct habits of investigating political and social questions would be the result, and a sound basis laid for those constitutional judgments which every citizen ought to form. In English history as well as in our own, materials are sometimes overlooked through indolence,[1] but are oftener perverted by prejudice. If one would learn how frequently, let him examine controverted questions in the original authorities, and then compare his results with those reached by any partisan historian, no matter how great his reputation may be. After some experience of this method of investigation, I

---

[1] No one would charge either Robertson or Hallam with indolence; but Arnold (*Lectures on Modern History*, 70) has pointed out a serious error into which both have fallen by trusting second-hand authority instead of exploring original sources.

must say that I would not trust the narrative, still less the opinions of any one, however learned, respecting the causes which led to the American Revolution, who had not studied the statutes, journals, and parliamentary proceedings of Great Britain, so far as they relate to American affairs, and the similar authorities of our colonial governments, from the accession of Charles I.

The value of this method of studying history is so obvious that authority for its use is superfluous ; and yet is so commonly disregarded that I will add authority to reason. Sir Henry Taylor, who has done excellent work in more than one department of letters, says : " Summary histories, such as those of Hume and Gibbon, though not to be altogether dispensed with, should hardly be read in abundance. They are useful as giving a framework of general knowledge, into which particular knowledge may be fitted. . . . Lord Stafford's dispatches and the Clarendon state papers will be studied with more profit to a statesman than any history of the reign of Charles I. ; and it is the materials for histories rather than histories themselves which, being judiciously selected, should be presented to the perusal of the pupil." [1]

Dr. Thomas Arnold also says : " Another class of documents, certainly of no less importance [than treaties], yet much less frequently referred to by popular historians, consists of statutes, ordinances, proclamations, acts, or by whatever various names the laws of each particular period happen to be designated. That the Statute Book has not been more frequently referred to by writers on English history has always seemed to me matter of surprise." [2]

[1] *The Statesman*, 3.
[2] *Lectures on Modern History*, 71.

It has been my purpose thus far to insist that any library connected with an educational institution should bring within reach of its students everything which illustrates its history, and everything, near or remote, which throws light upon the political or constitutional history of their own country. Further than that I do not presume to go. At that point I recognize the fact that a library has purposes of its own apart from those entertained by the institution with which it is connected. It is an educational institution ; it is a university in itself.

By not sufficiently attending to this fact erroneous notions as to the functions of a college library have prevailed in very respectable quarters. It has been said that the question is not whether in the great centres of art, science, and literature, should be formed collections, museums, and libraries capable of answering, so far as such collections can answer, every question which arises in any department of human thought, and of affording in the most effective way every aid desired by those who repair to them ; but whether, in an institution designed to meet a local necessity of education, and neither a centre of general culture, nor likely to become such, there should be gathered and maintained at great cost and at the expense of other departments of undeniable usefulness, a great library to which no one outside the institution will ever resort, and no one within it can possibly use to advantage. For, so proceeds the argument, the books required by any student in his college course are few, and mainly such as relate to the class work in hand ; and it is unwise to offer inducements to miscellaneous reading, since it is noticeable that those students who give to prescribed studies only such attention as will secure to them their degrees, and devote the greater part of their time to general reading, are, as graduates, less well fitted to enter upon professional studies or to engage in their life work than those who adhere more strictly to the curriculum. This implies an utter misconception of the uses of a great library whether connected with a college or standing apart from it. Even in the more limited conception of a college library, I am not the advocate of a policy which would have restricted Daniel Webster's constitutional studies while an undergraduate to the traditional cotton pocket-handkerchief. Arnold's advice to the Oxford students is more sensible : "I cannot indeed too earnestly advise every one who is resident in the university to seize, this golden time for his own reading, whilst he has on the one hand the riches of our libraries at his command, and before the pressure of actual life has come upon him, when the acquisition of knowledge is mostly out of the question, and we must be content to live upon what we have already gained." [1]

But were it a practical matter requiring immediate settlement, I should relegate this subject to those who determine the character of the instruction imparted here, and regulate the growth of the library. For my own part I look upon great libraries from a professional standpoint. I believe in them as workshops, and as legitimate equally for the undergraduate as for the professional man of letters or of science. Of course each must select his proper bench and use his proper tools. A college library will be essentially a growth representing the necessities of successive classes, enlarged by the advance of science. Nor will the increase of the new invalidate the usefulness of

---

[1] *Lectures on Modern History*, 69.

the old. Its literature at least remains. Milton lived
when the old astronomy was giving place to the new,
and was perfectly aware of the fact; but in constructing the ordonnance of his great epic he chose to see
what the Chaldean shepherds saw, instead of that
which

> "Through optic glass the Tuscan artist viewed
> At ev'ning from the top of Fésole
> Or in Valdarno."

Besides the literary interest attaching to beliefs
which for centuries have held dominion over the
minds of men, it is to be remembered that the errors
of a discarded system are indissolubly associated with
the truths of the new. No library, however extensive,
contains much that is without value; for what is regarded as worthless may possibly be of account in
the history of literature.

I think, too, that I can see another benefit resulting
from the gathering of large collections of books at the
different seats of education. The material progress of
our race on this continent is without parallel. With
a great past we are assured of a great future. This
all the world sees and admits. It also concedes to us
many kinds of greatness; but it does not concede a
great literature. Sometimes this thought makes us
unhappy, because we know that the final judgments
of literature are cosmopolitan, and from them lies no
appeal. Let us examine this matter with candor and
good temper. It is said that we are sprung from a
stock which has produced one of the richest known
literatures, — that we are generally educated, of great
capacity for affairs, of remarkable inventive faculty,
evincing vigorous thought in jurisprudence, statesmanship, and theology, and that we have done some good

work in various departments of science; but that we have produced no literature of the first or even of the second class. It concedes to us several respectable poets, historians, novelists, and *belles lettres* scholars; but with exasperating insistence adds that, with few exceptions, their work lacks original power, shows foreign culture, and might as well have been written in Europe as in America; that as a whole our literature is neither copious nor rich, but on the contrary thin and poor; that it does not taste of the soil, and is essentially a pale reflection of English thought and feeling. This, though a foreign judgment, does not differ essentially from that which may be gathered from American sources.

The usual reply is to reiterate the well-known names which for the last forty years, with few additions, have adorned our bead-roll of literary fame with the further observation that we have had other work to do than writing novels and poems. I do not propose to reopen the question on the old ground. Unless we can come to clearer notions as to the cause of our sterility in imaginative literature, and can find a remedy for it, the matter is hardly worth discussion. I suppose no intelligent American regards the outcome of our literary endeavor with entire complacency. But if the causes of our literary poverty are not permanent; if new influences are at work, promising and already producing better results, the case is not hopeless. For my own part I believe it to be full of encouragement. Let us review the circumstances which thus far have affected us unfavorably.

In the preface to his " History of New England," Dr. Palfrey estimated in 1858 that one third of the people then in the United States were descended from the twenty thousand Englishmen who came to New England between 1620 and 1640. Owing to obvious causes the bulk of the imaginative literature of America has been produced by the descendants of those emigrants. Who and what, then, were these twenty. thousand Englishmen, the first comers to this New England soil? William Stoughton, the stout old Puritan who fiercely antagonized the witches in 1692, said : " God sifted a whole Nation that he might send choice Grain over into this Wilderness." [1] Nothing can be more true or more germane to our subject. God sifted out all the poets and romancers, and all those who were chiefly men of letters. Neither Jonson, nor Massinger, nor Ford; neither the blood of Shakespeare, nor of Marlowe, nor of Spenser, nor of Sidney ; neither the Puritan Milton, nor the Puritan Marvel ; neither Francis Bacon, nor Thomas Browne, nor Robert Burton, nor Jeremy Taylor ; nor any one of less grim purpose than that which made Cromwell's Ironsides invincible, and brought Charles to the block, could bear the strong winnowing of God. Those thought worthy were compatriots of Pym and Hampden, of Ireton and Vane ; co-religionists of those who for non-conformity had been tried as by fire. Of such were the first emigrants ; men to subdue a wilderness ; to found an empire ; to set up altars to religion ; to war strenuously for civil liberty ; but not the people Apollo would have chosen to build a seat for the Muses. They were the men for their work ; but God had not called them to write poetry, and the law of heredity has been manifested in their descendants. That there was no deterioration of mental fibre in the generations of the eighteenth century

---

[1] *Election Sermon*, 1668, p. 19.

is clear from the vigor of their religious thought, of which Edwards, Mayhew, Chauncy, and Hopkins are conspicuous examples; and from the depth of their political speculations, in which Otis, Hutchinson, and the Adamses were unsurpassed on either side of the ocean.[1]

Such were our literary progenitors; and such were their limitations. Besides, no people who have produced an original literature ever encountered such difficulties as beset our ancestors when they reached these New England shores. From a soil which generously responded to the labors of husbandmen, they came to a land as barren and stubborn as any on the planet within the temperate zones. From a climate singularly favorable to animal and vegetable life, where out-door existence was practicable the year round, they found themselves in one where the extremity of heat was no less severe than the extremity of cold, and six months' seclusion from the weather was necessary for comfortable existence. These first comers have recorded that the productive power of the soil was substantially exhausted, even with the fertilizers within their reach, after four years of cultivation; and for subsistence they were obliged to betake themselves to the sea, or forsake the coast for the more fertile intervales of the interior, where they were exposed to Indian hostilities. Had the consequences

[1] Dr. Palfrey, while he contends that there was no degeneration in the first indigenous generations of New Englanders, admits that "the presence of historical objects, and that habitual contact with transmitted thoughts and feelings which local associations keep alive, provide a stimulating education for the mind, which it cannot forego without some disadvantage. The consummate flowers and fruits of a high civilization seem to require to be nurtured by roots that for a long time have been penetrating into a native soil." — *History of New England*, iii. 68.

of this state of affairs been less serious, their story would be ludicrous. The first party of Puritans came to Massachusetts under Endicott in 1628. The next year Higginson brought over a reinforcement. To encourage those in England who were meditating emigration, he wrote an account of things as he found them. He said that the land about Massachusetts Bay " is as fat black earth as can be seen anywhere." Heaven help them ; they had mistaken marsh mud for loam! They thought that English kine would thrive on foul meadow grass! In praise of the climate, Higginson wrote that " a sup of New England's air is better than a draught of old England's· ale." Good, simple soul! He died within a year of a hectic fever and was buried under six feet of Salem gravel. When it was too late the sad truth stared them in the face. Starvation threatened them and death made constant inroads upon their number. So pitiable was their condition, so slender were their chances even of ultimate success, that the wisest of their English friends advised them to abandon houses and lands and seek elsewhere a more hospitable clime and a more fertile soil. They remained, but at fearful cost.

Nor was their situation in other respects favorable to the production of an original literature, or for the preservation of that which they brought with them. The natural gravity of these sifted Puritans was made even more sombre by their position. They were far from their old home, still the object of their yearning affections though filled with those who sought their civil and ecclesiastical subjection. Behind them were a thousand leagues of stormy ocean. Before them was the dark illimitable forest, which resounded with midnight cries of savage beasts and of no less savage men. Well might they hang their harps upon the willows. The wonder is, not that literature languished, but that civilization did not die out.

Literature is a growth. Into it enter the soil, climate, and conditions upon which imagination and fancy depend. But our English race had no youth on this soil. Its infancy was in the forests of Germany. Its youth was in the heart of "merrie England." In the prime of its manhood, when all its faculties were strained to their utmost by a conflict with civil and ecclesiastical tyranny, it left its pleasant homes for a wilderness where no English spring smiled between the frown of winter and the too fervid glances of summer; where no autumnal gloaming fed the imagination; where neither the lark in the meadow nor the linnet in the copse inspired kindred song.

With some mitigation of material severities, this state of things continued for two hundred years with its depressing influence upon imaginative literature. Add this also that, from the restoration of Charles II. to the peace of 1783, the colonists were in constant conflict with those who sought to subvert their civil and ecclesiastical privileges. This resistance engrossed their faculties of mind and soul. In such a situation it would have been criminal, as they thought, to abandon civil and religious liberty for the cultivation of literature. The necessary results followed. At the end of the long contest they established liberty, made excellent laws and constitutions, but wrote indifferent poetry.

During the Revolutionary war, the colonies suffered another loss which has not been sufficiently noticed in its effect upon literature. At the opening of that conflict there lived in the colonies a class of cultivated men, mainly of the old families, who had been on the soil from the first emigration. They formed and led the social life of their times, and from them might reasonably have been expected a literature which, having its roots in the soil, is nourished by culture and social amenities. In several departments of letters they had done work to be judged respectable by any standard. But the exigencies of the Revolution demanded their expatriation. This measure was, no doubt, dictated by prudence; but the loss of these people was felt in the literature which followed their departure.[1]

Candor requires a fair consideration of the facts that have been alluded to. The Puritans, with all their great qualities, were not a literary people, in the ordinary sense of that phrase. As well might the world have expected a " Paradise Lost " from John Locke, or a " Midsummer Night's Dream " from Robert Boyle, as from those who inaugurated and for two centuries maintained the Puritan hierarchy on New England soil. But now, relieved, though but recently, from the pressure of old necessities, our branch of the race may be expected slowly to advance on the line of its original genius and produce a literature worthy of the name. Already have we entered upon a new order. The material prosperity of the people is assured. They are no longer environed by narrowing circumstances. Civil and religious liberty are free from harassing anxiety; and within this generation the people have come to feel that they are now a

---

[1] In consequence of the Revolution, 20,000 Tories went to Nova Scotia. See, too, Dawson's *Handbook for the Dominion of Canada*, 106.

nation. The descendants of Englishmen have become indigenous here. Into them have entered the summer's heat and winter's cold. The American has acquired a character of his own and is fast losing his provincialism. He has thoughts and feelings which he does not owe to his insular progenitors. To the original vigor of the stock have been added qualities due to the commingling of nationalities ; and now for the first time in our history I think we may look for a literature of our own. If its sun has not risen, its dawn appears, and there are stars above the horizon. A literature of our own. Let us consider what that implies. We know that the elemental forces are the same from age to age, and that the phenomena of life, in their ceaseless round, reappear to successive generations of men. And we see, even in the least productive periods, a few gifted above their fellows who read these mysteries of nature and of life, and reveal them anew by the utterance of song ; but these utterances are far from constituting a national literature. That only comes when the people themselves form the constituency of their bards and prophets, who under the conditions of art give expression to the thoughts and sentiments of a nation. This period, sooner or later, comes to every great people. And when from the force of commingling thought and passion the upheaval takes place, the great masters of literature, like mountain peaks, appear and their voice is heard

> " Not from one lone cloud,
> But every mountain now hath found a tongue."

If we ask what form our literature will take, and what are likely to be the most potent forces in its production, we must consider that no part of our civilization is indigenous. Neither the political nor the social system of which we are parts; neither the religion we profess nor the fundamental laws we obey; neither the literature we read nor the amenities of civilization which make life tolerable, had their origin on our soil. They are exotics. The youth of the race and its creative period have passed. We can never return to the days in which primal instincts found expression in the songs and fairy tales of the people; never again shall we

> " Have sight of Proteus rising from the sea,
>   Or hear old Triton blow his wreathed horn ; "

nor can we expect a recurrence of those influences which produced the Elizabethan dramatists.

Our coming literature therefore will, I think, be in nature of a renaissance modified by new conditions of soil, climate, and scenery, but finding its stimulating force in literature itself. It will be not unlike the renaissance in Italy when the exhumed art of antiquity acting on national aptitudes produced results of great power and originality, although the suggestion of the elder art; when

> " the glory that was Greece "

became

> " . . . the grandeur that was Rome."

By the law of heredity the basis of American literature must be the literature of England, into which long since entered the rich fancy of the Irish Celt and the picturesqueness of his Scotch kindred. If it shall lack the luxuriance of British literature, it will not be choked by its weeds. Already soil and climate have developed in us a finer sense of form and color than our English brethren possess.

The exciting force of our literary renaissance will be literature — mainly our British literature — gath-

ered into great libraries, and thence distilled into the
hearts and brains of our people ; for literature is the
only form of art in its finest models with which our
people can live in that familiar association which
makes it a productive force. We are remote from
the masterpieces of plastic and pictorial art. The
genius of the Middle Ages enshrined in the great
cathedrals of Europe will never inspire us ; nor will
the art treasures of the Vatican, or of the Capitol,
or of the national galleries of Europe, until great
political and social convulsions have disrupted governments and society in that hemisphere. But the literary art of the world may be ours. Let us gather it
then into Wilson Hall, where, stimulating those who
come hither, descendants of a master race in literature, it may have some influence in the production of
a literature worthy of those ancestors. For literature
is a power for civilization. More completely than
either of the sister arts it gathers together and expresses in permanent form the thoughts and feelings
of mankind. It has the world for its province and
the race for its audience. Other forms of art seek
locality and provoke the assaults of Time. Few of
the race ever beheld the glories of either Temple ; but
the songs of the Hebrew poets still touch the heart of
humanity. Karnac and Memphis are in ruins ; but
the wisdom of the Egyptians has gone forth into all
lands, and that which was of value in her literature
survives and will write the epitaph of the Pyramids.
The Parthenon slowly yields to the destroyer. Memorials of buried Troy once more see the light of day,
and once more will go down to darkness, but the song
of Homer rises, and ever will rise, over the world as
clear and as strong as when it flowed from lips

touched with immortality. In literature is the con-
servation of force, — the force that is in the thinking
brain and the feeling heart of a nation. It never dies.
Its form may perish, but its soul transmigrates into
other forms.

A great library — " the assembled soul of all that
men held wise " — is the sum of all literature. It is
more, for neither its mass nor its power is to be measured by counting its volumes. It is an organism in
which every part augments the vigor of every other
part and of the whole. It has absorbed famous collections around which cluster the memories of illustrious men who through their aid have enriched literature or extended the domain of science.

My daily life is passed in a great library. I seldom
cross its threshold without feeling that I am in the
presence of a conscious personality. I am persuaded
that it has purposes of its own ; that it allures the
young to healthful pleasures — itself being pleased ;
that it counsels wisely those who would avoid life's
devious paths ; that it sympathizes with the patient
seekers after wisdom ; that it knows the song the
sirens sang and tales stranger than those of the Ara-
bian Nights. It is wiser than all the living by the
wisdom of all that are dead ; and never satisfied with
the wisdom and the beauty of the past, it seeks the
wisdom and beauty that now are, — for " day unto
day uttereth speech and night unto night showeth
knowledge ; " and though the heavens are old and the
clouds are old, in the passing hour are cloud-forms
and sky-tints before unseen, and with each descending
sun new stars will rise upon the world.

Such is a great library ; and such, as the years roll
on, will be gathered here in Wilson Hall.

THE OLD AND THE NEW ORDER IN NEW ENGLAND LIFE AND LETTERS

ADDRESS AT THE DEDICATION OF THE BROOKS LIBRARY
BUILDING, AT BRATTLEBOROUGH, VERMONT,
JANUARY 25, 1887

ADDRESS

AT THE DEDICATION OF THE BROOKS LIBRARY BUILDING

THE last of what I intended to say to you this evening was written the night before Mr. Brooks died.[1] Could I have foreseen the circumstances of this occasion, my address would have been different; but, with the omission of a few words, and with a few which I have added, I must ask you to accept it as it was prepared.

I met Mr. Brooks in his early manhood, and have never seen him since. He called on me a few weeks ago, while I was away ; and I looked forward to this hour when we should renew the acquaintance of our youth ; but it was otherwise ordered.

And now that this hour has come, it quickens memories of days long ago, and of other friends, few of whom remain. It is more than forty years since here at Brattleborough, before the County Common School Association, I presumed to speak for popular education ; and here to-day once more I attempt to speak on the same subject, but not to the same audience. Gone are the old familiar faces ; and if any hear me now who heard me then, they were young when I was young.

[1] George J. Brooks, the donor of the Library Building, died suddenly on Thursday, December 23, 1880, a few days before the time originally fixed for its dedication.

To-day one more is added to free public libraries, — no new thing now, indeed, with us, or in Europe, or in that great empire which rises in Australasian seas. Nevertheless, the dedication of a free library is an event of more than local interest, since it is one, though only one, of those events which indicate the passing away of an old order of things and the coming in of a new order; and it is the going out of the old, with the loss which has ensued, and the coming in of the new, with the gain we expect from it, of which I am to speak to-night. And as your fathers and mothers were my friends, and some of you were my pupils, I am sure you will allow me to preface what I have to say with some grateful reminiscences of my Brattleborough life.

It was in the spring of 1844, a few months before graduating at Dartmouth College, that I came to this village as teacher of the Central School, and here I remained until late in 1846.

For one whose principal object in teaching was to replenish an empty purse and at the same time to review college classics and read books introductory to the study of law, no place could have been more eligible. To be sure, a salary of four hundred a year was hardly alluring, even in those days; but with respectable table-board at nine shillings a week, and free lodgings over the bank as its custodian, the days went on, though not riotously. My duties were compact; the school was in perfect discipline, and its spirit for study was high. I had only to go forward in paths well trodden by my predecessor, that admirable teacher, Moses Woolson. Thus passed — agreeably I am sure, and I hope not unprofitably — three years of my life, in which I had, I suppose, my share of a teacher's perplexities, which are forgotten now, since memory holds only the glory of the dream.

There may have been another place on this planet more desirable as a residence than Brattleborough in 1844, but I never chanced to know such. Situated in full view of the mountains, watered by fine streams, with pure air, and scenery at points exceptionally charming, for a hundred years it had been the abode of men eminent at the bar or on the bench or in the pulpit or in affairs, and of some not unknown in literature; and always of a people intelligent, refined, and rich in all amenities. It was the centre of an active but not noisy trade. Manufactures flourished without polluting the air or the waters. Thrift, which brought competence but no overshadowing fortunes, was everywhere apparent. Its leading citizens in business or in the professions were qualified to fill, as some went forth to fill, more conspicuous places and to deal with larger affairs, — men and women whose society was education, and to imitate whom was conduct and manners and exemplary life. I hardly need add that institutions of religion, of education, of public and social affairs, guided, as they had been established, by intelligence and moral sense, moved harmoniously in their beneficent courses.

So ran the stream of every-day life at Brattleborough in 1844. It was its golden age; and if, like the golden age everywhere, it had its shadows, sometimes its very gold was gilded, — for in the summer came visitors, some of whom were people of distinction, and as such welcome, and doubly welcome, I fancy, and doubly distinguished in our eyes, by their unstinted admiration of our village. Their advent filled the hotels, it quickened trade, and gladdened

the hearts of ingenuous youth who gathered wild-
flowers and berries in remote pastures. Better than
all, their presence added to that indefinable but not
less real wealth which comes from association with
those who had written for the instruction of the people and for their delight, and to the awakening of
expectations concerning the literature of America.
The value of such association to those in the formative period of life is not likely to be overestimated;
to them a complete man or woman is the centre of a
glory which, if it dazzles, also inspires. Of the nota-
bles here before my day I knew only by hearsay, but
some of the later comers I recollect; and though I
had no personal relations with any of them, it was a
great thing, as I still think, to witness daily the conduct and manners and to hear the speech of those
whose works were the outcome of our national life.
Among them were Catherine E. Beecher and Harriet
Beecher Stowe; the former, as a great teacher and
writer of useful books, stood higher in public estimation than the latter, for " Uncle Tom's Cabin " was
then unwritten. And so was the " Philosophy of
Shakespeare's Plays Unfolded ; " nevertheless, when
Delia Bacon walked our streets, she drew attention as
a remarkable woman. Heralded as a true poet by
" Voices of the Night " and by " Ballads and other
Poems," Henry Wadsworth Longfellow occasionally
came among us. But William Henry Channing, the
great preacher, was the most impressive personality.
After forty years I still see the light in his eyes; his
wonderful voice thrills me yet, and to this day I
ponder his ethical utterances. I once saw William
Morris Hunt. It must have been when he came here
to take leave of his relatives just before going to

Düsseldorf; but I met him with no thought that in after years I should know him as one of our most eminent artists. Thomas Wentworth Higginson, a more frequent visitor both in summer and in winter, was much in our social life, and even then gave promise since redeemed by the production of some of our most attractive literature.

Of course, none of my pupils were in any way distinguished, though many showed character; and one now is among the foremost of our pulpit orators, and another second to none of American sculptors. But those

> " Whose flower of happiness was crost
> In its first bud, — the early, loved and lost," —

alas, what hearts were broken, what hopes perished !

Such thoughts crowd upon me as I return to Brattleborough after a long absence ; but I have not uttered them to those who might once have listened with pleasure, — their ears are cold in death, — nor to provoke to filial reverence children worthy of such parents. No; my purpose is quite different. I wish you to see a typical New England town as it was and as it lived its life a generation ago, in contrast with similar communities to-day ; and then to consider with what loss and under what conditions and by what new instrumentalities we must carry forward society in the future. I think it will appear that the characteristic life of our New England towns under the old régime was less in the completeness and efficiency of their local institutions than in the strongly individualized personality of their representative men and women ; and that under the new régime the order and effectiveness of these influences are changed, — that henceforth persons will be of less account, and institutions of more account; or rather, as I hope, that the influence of men and women on society, instead of being lost or impaired, will be felt no less powerfully than heretofore through institutions made efficient by their intervention.

And though it is this change, with the new obligation it implies, that immediately interests us, and to which we must adjust ourselves, yet we shall more clearly understand its nature if we regard it as due not solely to local causes, but as connected with causes which, beginning hundreds of years ago, have at length transformed government, science, literature, and even theology, so that they are quite different from what they were some forty years ago, — a change which divides the old régime from the new, under both of which some of us have lived, and in it have witnessed perhaps the most momentous revolution of the ages.

If life elsewhere was more splendid than in our New England towns as they were forty years ago, nowhere was it more desirable. To what elements, to what marshaling and conduct of their forces, and to what conditions did they owe their characteristic life and its rich results? Mainly, no doubt, to original qualities in the stock, — its industry, steadfastness, intelligence, and ingrained moral sense, — and something to the circumstances of its expatriation from England; but much also to the structure of society which the first emigrants brought with them.

What, then, was the structure of English society at the time of the great emigration in 1630, and how far did it reproduce itself on American soil? The Puritans, better than most people, will bear the white light of truth. They do not need the glamour of romance, which they would have contemned as much as we ought. Englishmen, everywhere and always strenuous asserters of liberty, especially their own, have inconsiderately been credited with an equal passion for equality. Such, I think, has never been the case, not even with their descendants in America, until within the last fifty years.

On its native soil the race ranged itself in civil and ecclesiastical orders which no revolutions have effectually shaken; and as Coleridge said, in his day " the rustic whistled with equal enthusiasm ' God save the king,' and ' Britons never shall be slaves.' " This race tendency, specially marked in Virginia, with its large landed proprietors, its law of entail and of primogeniture, survived Jefferson's counterblast in the Declaration of Independence, and even the abolition of those laws brought about mainly through his influence.

This observance of rank and this facility of advancement through rank and family prestige have been united in England, quite as often as in this country, with a sense of fair play which recognizes the possessor of brains, however poor in estate or low in the social scale, provided, as Burke said of himself, he shows his passport at every stage.

The first comers to New England, chiefly middle-class Englishmen, brought with them the social distinctions of English society so far as represented in their own number. These distinctions were manifest all through their history, and have been finally suppressed only in recent times. Till then one who had a grandfather was facilitated in his political aspirations by that fact; but now it is quite otherwise. The American Revolution made no change; that was a political, not a social revolt. The laws admitting non-church-members to the franchise, and those of a later period which abolished primogeniture and divided property among all the children of an intestate, probably had more influence in equalizing the condition of people in Massachusetts than in Virginia, where landed estates, ample when divided, maintained several aristocratic families sprung from one. But in Massachusetts the ruling force after the Revolution, perhaps even more than before, was personal and family prestige, augmented in men distinguished in the war, or who traced their lineage to those conspicuous in colonial or provincial governments.

The result, as every one knows who has lived under the old order, and as no one else can fully realize, was that the substantial governing force in society formed an aristocracy of old families, including the parson, the squire, a few landed proprietors, and the village merchant. There were party divisions, of course; but whichever party prevailed at the polls, its aristocratic element controlled the government. So sudden and so recent was the transition from the old order to the new, that there are living all over New England those who can name the last old-régime governor, mayor, or selectmen, and the first of each, after the people came to the front and assumed the government; and yet the people then hardly understood, and it is doubtful whether they fully understand now, the nature and consequences of the revolution they have inaugurated.

This change was more marked and more momentous in New England than elsewhere, because it was simultaneous with a disturbance of economic conditions; and when it took place a vital force went out of society, the loss of which is felt to-day, and will be felt until it shall be reincorporated, as doubtless it can, into the mass of those forces by which society henceforth is to be sustained and carried forward. The loss was serious; for never was there a better aristocracy or one more competent to govern. An aristocracy it is true, but one which represented intelligence, industry, and moral sense ; devoted to the public weal and to the interests of society; and the outcome of whose endeavors is manifest when the old New England towns, thus governed, are contrasted with modern factory villages, — with their crudeness, their vulgarity, their disintegration and lack of governance. I mean no invidious distinction between the old and the new. I note the decadence of personal and family influence, and its consequences, as part of a larger fact, — its decadence everywhere, — and would direct attention thus early to the need of making good this loss by setting up in these towns other agencies, among which I include public libraries, and by recalling to an active participation in the conduct of these new instrumentalities those who have retired from public affairs.

Were this revolution confined to New England, it might be accounted for by the decline of agriculture, and the flocking to the cities of young men who formerly remained in the country towns, and were their best society, their strength, and their prosperity. But there must have been other causes; for the same revolution is now going on in old England as in New England, and with scarcely less rapidity in the rich agricultural West. Everywhere is the same disposition to give up the simple, wholesome life of the country for the excitements, the occasional prizes, and the more frequent disappointments of the cities.

Deplore this as we may, we cannot return to old

ways or old measures. Arrest the movement; let
agriculture become as remunerative here as in the
West; call back to the country towns from the great
cities the most enterprising of those who have gone
thither; reproduce every circumstance and condition
which existed forty years ago in these towns, even to
the resurrection from their graves, in the prime of
life and in the fullness of their strength, of the same
men and women who built up the admirable structures
of New England towns; they would be as powerless
to reconstruct society in them on the old basis as we
are. They could not do it here; they could not do it
in the fertile West.

No. The old New England towns, as they existed
forty years ago, have gone forever. They may return
in some new world, as a stage of its development; but
in this, never, — we shall repose in the Garden of
Eden as soon! Well, then, if the old have gone, we
must build anew; for whether New England is to continue New England or is to become New Ireland, so
long as her mountains stand, and her rivers run, and
human nature is the same, she will still remain the
abode of wise and prosperous people. Her past assures her future.

But we must understand the extent and significance
of the revolution now beginning to be felt as never
before, and of which the decadence of New England
towns and the change of society in them are only incidents, — a revolution which everywhere has turned
the currents of society into new channels, modified
the thoughts and purposes of people on a great variety
of subjects, impaired the force of influences and motives once powerful, and the nature of which — what
it promises or what it portends — excites solicitude

among those who wish well to society, and hope among those who do not!

Call this change the elevation of the masses, or their emancipation from political and ecclesiastical leadership, or the advent of democracy, — whatever it is, whether we regard it with hope or with foreboding, we ought to know what it has effected thus far — for the end is not yet — and what it promises or threatens in the future.

It is something practical, and will lead to practical results. Three hundred years ago, the proposition by Copernicus of a theory which relegated the earth from its usurped centre of the universe to a secondary place among the planets, though the largest astronomical fact of the ages, could be accepted or let alone without apparent consequences. Ships sailed the seas as before. The husbandman rose with the sun, and went to his bed with its setting; he sowed his seed, and ploughed, and reaped, and gathered the fruits of his toil, as his fathers had done from the beginning. Poets still used the old imagery, —

> " 'T was Jupiter who brought whate'er was good,
> And Venus who brought everything that 's fair," —

and no perceptible change appeared in literature. When the Reformation came, though it was of more ecclesiastical significance, the unthinking cared little whether the vicegerency of God had been committed to Leo X. or to Henry VIII.

But now everybody thinks, after a fashion, and the advent of democracy is quite another affair. It means business, and will neither let alone nor be let alone. Yet by what slow and uncertain steps the people moved to their objective point, and how recently they have known just what they mean! The democratic

spirit, at first ecclesiastical rather than political or social, manifested itself with the Reformation, and has
been growing ever since. In the mean time Bacon
gave his "Great Instauration" to the world, and
Harvey demonstrated the circulation of the blood, and
one or two kings lost their heads, and more, their
crowns, the meaning of which was clear enough; but
few people at the end of three hundred years seemed
to understand the meaning of democracy. Jefferson
stood alone. When our forefathers came to New England, democracy was hardly a cardinal principle of
their institutions. They rejected the divine right of
kings, and more strenuously that of episcopal ordination, as opposed to their own rights; but their notions
of the rights of men, certainly of other men, were
vague. In the leading New England colony, for the
first sixty years only members of the established
church could vote; and for the next hundred and fifty
years the dominant church, supported by town taxes,
was an oligarchy, equally powerful, even when opposed, in secular as in ecclesiastical affairs. It is
only within the memory of some now living that the
people have insisted on a really democratic system;
for long after it became nominally democratic, the
practice was oligarchical.

But it is different now. Those who once governed
are in the back seats; the people are in the front, and
the government is in their hands. What will they do
with it? Civilization is in their hands; what will
they do with that? The answer may be uncertain;
but there is one thing about which there is no doubt,
— a new order has come, and come to stay!

Doubtless the old political and ecclesiastical leaders
were wise, God-fearing men and women, and compare

favorably with those who have ousted them from place and power. Nevertheless, as an order, they have gone, and forever.

Thus far I have spoken chiefly of the decadence of towns, the shifting of political forces from the few to the many, and the loss — I hope it is only in abeyance — of personal prestige as a force in society. But I think we should take a wider view, and one that covers a longer period, not merely from historical curiosity, but to gain clearer notions of facts and tendencies, that we may understand their significance and adjust ourselves to them without loss of time. We may note specific changes, each distinct in itself, but all parts of a general change, more apparent when traced in particular instances.

Some of us recollect, for example, when the great East India merchants, and after them the great manufacturers, dominated New England not so much by their wealth as by their aristocratic pretension. Now, as such, they are without prestige, though no doubt powerful in the possession of vast capital; and the great monopolist of our day, the result of exceptional and temporary causes, must go, — go soon!

Under the old régime the man behind an institution was more than the institution itself, or at least was its most powerful agent. Edwards, Chauncy, Hopkins, Dwight, Emmons, Woods, and Channing, when they no longer catechised the children and performed general police duty as guardians of morals and manners, impressed themselves on creeds which the people accepted. To-day children in the Sunday school, greatly to their loss, are less under the immediate influence of the clergy; and with here and there an exception, the pulpit speaks the sentiments, not of the church

alone, but of the pews as well, or it is silenced.   The
schoolmaster, who once dominated the school and the
school committee and the school district, especially if
he " boarded round," is now strait-jacketed by a system and a curriculum, like a horse in a treadmill.
Some of us recollect when " Father Ritchie " personi-
fied the " Richmond Enquirer," and when people
asked, What does Greeley say ? or Bennett? or Ray-
mond ? — not the " Tribune," the " Herald," or the
" Times."   But who cares now for editorial opinion,
save as it represents a constituency ?   The great personal editors made public sentiment ; the modern impersonal journal expresses it, for now people have
come to entertain opinions of their own and indulge
in aspirations.

It is so elsewhere.   In its palmy days the " London
Times " was influential in forming public opinion, and
in respect to the conduct of affairs, because it represented the ranks which then governed England, — the
aristocratic sentiment gathered at the club, in the
drawing-room, at the dinner-table of a minister, or
from local magnates in the counties.   Then public sentiment was that of the few, not that of the many ; now
the editorial " we," if a power, expresses the average
opinion of the great middle-class of English society,
and must soon take account of the proletariat classes.

Journalism has become impersonal ; and so has
literature.   Shakespeare, of whom we know so little,
must have been well known at Stratford and at the
" Globe."   No doubt he discussed bucolics with
farmers on the Avon ; and at the theatre, play-
wrights, actors, supernumeraries, hangers - on, wits
about town, and link-boys hung on his lips, observed
his ways, and were under the influence of his per-

sonal charm; otherwise we should lack Jonson's loving account of him. Much — and just what we would like to know — each took and gave, in which the tapster had his share, when Ben and his roisterers made a night of it at the "Mermaid." We learn from Drummond of Hawthornden, how Ben could talk when he would! Bacon and Milton, as studious men, no doubt secluded themselves from the Bohemians; but each impressed the people of his time. And we shall never know how much Queen Anne's literature owes to the good things said by Dryden to the Steeles, the Addisons, the Wycherleys, and the Congreves, as they thronged about his chair at " Will's," — perhaps more than to his poems and dramas. At "The Club," Johnson, Burke, and Reynolds came to close quarters. There was no flinching, no withholding their best thoughts for publication; and, as we see in Boswell, each was better than his books, and how much the books of each gained from the conversation of all! To Burke, Fox was indebted for his political philosophy; and in Burke, who owed to others less than most men, we see here and there one of Johnson's thoughts.

Literature grows thin and colorless when it is distilled from books. Its true inspiration is in men and in nature. Leigh Hunt's regret that he had not hunted up Coleridge at Highgate when he might, and drawn from his inexhaustible thought and imagination, was rational, though too late.

No doubt literary people — and for that matter all sorts of people — have their clubs nowadays, and mix in society as formerly, yet with a difference. They sally forth to get, not to give. Fancy one of them scattering costly seed to fall perchance into an-

other man's ground, there to spring up and bear fruit
to be gathered into *his* garner! "I really believe,"
says the Autocrat of the Breakfast Table, "some
people save their best thoughts, as being too precious
for conversation. What do you think an admiring
friend said the other day to one that was talking good
things, — good enough to print? 'Why,' said he,
'you are wasting merchantable literature, a cash article, at the rate, as nearly as I can tell, of fifty dollars
an hour.'" Literary people to-day are delightful in
society, and say their good things as formerly; but
each is labeled "All rights reserved," as the unscrupulous appropriator of a seeming waif finds, for
the lawful proprietor was quoting from the proof-
sheets of his next volume or magazine article! On
our part we are as curious as people ever were to know
our literary magnates. We get one of them into a
corner; we fancy we are studying him; we go away
delighted: but the chances are that he was studying
us, and that we shall behold our distorted lineaments
in his next novel. Tiger-hunting no doubt is an exciting sport; but it makes some difference, I am told,
whether you hunt the tiger or the tiger hunts you!

Now, I need not say to one sixty years old, how different all this was when boys and girls formed themselves on the parson, the squire, the schoolmaster, the
schoolmistress, "the fine old gentleman," or "the lady
of the old school," — of which no town had more admirable examples than Brattleborough, — each a glass
of fashion or a mould of form. Then the man of
learning or travel or of special gifts held all in trust
for the society in which he lived.

I think we now recognize the great change which
has taken place in all departments of thought and

action, with the loss which has followed the elimination of personal influence, though only partial, as a power in education, manners, and conduct, and begin to be solicitous in respect to consequences as well as to the means by which the loss can be repaired.

What is the real state of the case? Whence comes this new sense of power in the people? Have they discarded old beliefs and old leaders, and determined to set up for themselves on new lines; or is it merely a general movement of society in which the people, in their haste to get on, have outrun their slower guides? Coleridge expresses the old notion, and his aversion to the new which was beginning to appear in his time. "Statesmen should know," he says, "that a learned class is an essential element of a state, at least of a Christian state. But you work for general illumination. You begin with the attempt to popularize learning and philosophy; but you will end with the plebification of knowledge. A true philosophy in the learned class is essential to a true religious feeling in all classes."

We owe a great deal to Coleridge. His poetry is of the best; his critical system we accept; and we find much to our purpose in his ethical philosophy. But he believed that the diffusion of knowledge weakened knowledge, just as he regarded the cosmopolitan spirit as incompatible with patriotism; nor did he think that the people, unaided by a select class of learned men, could save learning or religion or the state.[1]

Against all this the people seem to be in revolt, and we must side with the people. In all matters, theological, political, or educational, they will think and act for themselves; that is what the new order of

---

[1] *The Friend*, Essay ix.

things means. They may make sorry work of it for a time; and looking at results thus far, they might be better off were their thinking done for them as formerly. But this is a shallow view of the matter. We must accept the fact that knowledge, both secular and ecclesiastical, is being popularized, and have faith that society will get on, nevertheless, and find the new order not only tolerable but conformable to the divine will, and therefore to its highest interests. In the change from the old to the new there may be temporary loss and confusion. This is to be expected. Just now we are like sheep without a shepherd. Who leads one party as Jackson did, or the other party as Clay did? Where is the great leader of a denomination like the elder Beecher, or Ware, or Woods, or Channing? Whose literary canons are accepted as final? We find nowhere, I suspect, the wise dominating personal influences once found in every community. Bosses are obstreperous; but they are neither the people nor of the people, and will subside. In this transition state, with the old house pulled down about our ears before the new is ready to receive us, things are uncomfortable enough. But this is quite in the ordinary course of things. No farmer who all his life has handled hoes and scythes and rakes ever takes kindly to the machines which displace the old-fashioned implements; but his boys do.

And I wonder if one who "parsed" and "ciphered" and picked up his knowledge in the fashion of the old district school, and with excellent results, ever saw the children in a graded school come out in platoons, discharge their volleys, and fall back with the precision of military drill, without misgivings as to the development of individual character.

Our fears are often more serious than their realization. We ought to take some pains, therefore, to
learn the direction of the stream by which we stand
shivering. We call the new order the advent of
democracy. That does not help but rather frightens
us, unless we come to a clearer understanding of
democracy. If we mean the party which calls itself
by that name, then with all good Republicans I be-
wail the future of our country. If, on the contrary,
we mean the party with the other name, then I join
all good Democrats in deprecating its return to power.
I mean something which the leaders of both parties
hate with equal cordiality. Whatever form democracy may ultimately take, I think it does not now
mean socialism, nor communism, nor, least of all,
anarchy. So far we may trust the immutable principles of human nature. No power less than that
which ordained natural laws can overturn them, or
essentially modify principles coeval with the race.
Nor, on the other hand, can the natural development
of human rights be arrested.

I think we may say that democracy will not be
content with the mere right to acquire and hold property free from the exactions of privileged classes,
nor to exercise the franchise and be eligible to office,
nor to be equal before any law less comprehensive
and beneficial than the moral law. First of all, it
will demand liberty, and next equality, subject only
to unalterable limitations. It will recognize private
property rightfully acquired, but will claim public
property as a trust sacredly to be administered for
the benefit of all; and will regard as public property
all which has accrued to the state or to society by the
procession of time, or from the labors of statesmen

and philanthropists, or from the genius of inventors, or from the skill of artists, or from the songs of poets, or from the prayers of saints, or from the faith of martyrs, together with all those select and benign influences which have come into the life of man, hitherto engrossed by the well-born, the fortunate, and the righteous, but henceforth to be entered into and enjoyed equally by those who are poor or unfortunate or sinful, and by each to the fullest extent of his necessities or his desires, limited only by the equal rights of others.

It is opposed to the law of the strongest, — if there is such a law, — and to the law of the fittest, — if by fittest is meant one more capable than another to monopolize and enjoy in a high degree those things which all may enjoy in some degree.

If libraries, galleries, and museums are of value to the cultured by reason of their culture, then they must be multiplied and so administered as to conduce to the culture and consequent enjoyment of the unfortunate, hitherto little considered. If they are a solace to the refined, they ought also to minister to the coarse and the unlettered. While we live under the law of Christ we should strive for its fulfillment. It is all sufficing for society as well as for individuals; nor can we ever safely forget that the lamp of Christendom, unfed by the oil that is the Light of the world, will pale and flicker and go out, and there will be darkness over all the land! And though there are difficulties in applying this law, or in enforcing the inalienable rights of man as formulated by Jefferson, nevertheless we will remember that the advance of the church has always been along the line of highest endeavor; nor do I think it extravagant to say that the better condition of mankind, so far as it has been brought about by the modification of political institutions and of the modes of administration, is due, more than to any other human cause, to the "glittering generalities" of Jefferson. Therefore we will set up high ideals; therefore we will attempt the impossible, for only thus shall we achieve the highest attainable.

If, now, we recognize in the new order some loss of those influences by which society was sustained and carried forward, and if we have adequate notions as to the just rights and demands of democracy, then we must attend to the instrumentalities by which we hope to supply the place of those which have passed away, and consider how, under new conditions, we may carry forward civilization which, as never before, is to be of and for the people. New England once taught the old democracy that resistance to tyrants is obedience to God. That was the work of her Otises, her Adamses, and their compatriots. Once more she must lead in a revolution more momentous than the first. Decaying towns, abandoned churches, and dilapidated schoolhouses reproach the civilization which cost our fathers dear. This reproach must be taken away. Cultured men and women, affronted by the rudeness of the lower classes, have retired from the contest with disgust. They must return to duty. The army of God, now broken and dispersed, must close ranks and rally around a common standard. Not against each other, but against a common foe, let the temper of sword and shield be tested. You know what people are thinking about; and you know it is not the Trinity, nor a mode of baptism, nor the probation of a future life. No; it is questions more

fundamental than these. And next to these fundamental questions is the question how to save New
England to Christianity and to civilization.

Five-and-forty years ago, when it was found that
the old district schools in this village were yielding
unsatisfactory results, by the advice of some of your
leading men, and aided by legislative action sought
for the purpose, your fathers set up for the first time
in this State a graded school, which, successful here,
was the pioneer of those now existing in all your
larger villages.

With equal wisdom George J. Brooks — so lately
one of your esteemed citizens, now among your honored dead — considered the requirements of the new
order of things, and with munificent liberality has
given you an institution which connects itself with
your churches and your schools, and which, wisely
administered, will be a power for civilization scarcely
less influential.

Its adjustment so as to work harmoniously and
efficiently with existing institutions may be slow.
Some mistakes will be inevitable; but they should
be few. Everybody knows that organizations exist
throughout the country for promoting common-school
education and for the encouragement of teachers;
but I think it is less generally known that in Great
Britain and in the United States there are similar organizations designed to promote the establishment and
conduct of libraries, — mainly, of free public libraries.
Our own is called the American Library Association,
which maintains a journal, now entering upon its
twelfth year, in which are to be found the papers and
discussions of experts on every conceivable question of
library economy and administration, elicited during

the annual three days' sessions, constituting a body of literature which cannot prudently be overlooked by those concerned in the management of libraries.

The new order is fairly inaugurated. But in taking leave of the old order and entering upon the new under such auspicious circumstances, I am not willing to be understood as saying, since I am far from thinking, that the time ever will be when the personal influence of noble men and women will fail —

" To give us manners, virtue, freedom, power,"

or that it will be of small account in the upbuilding and maintenance of that state of society in which alone life is worth living. What I wish to say is that with the advance of general education the influence of exceptionally cultured persons, apart from the people and above them, will probably not be so much felt as heretofore, except in giving direction and efficiency to organized forces, like churches, schools, and libraries. Brattleborough has entered upon the new order. Her free public library receives cordial greetings from sister libraries as one more of those institutions which bring on the beneficent ages. Always known as one of the most beautiful of the river towns, and as the abode of intelligent and refined people, so she will continue to be known in the larger life upon which she enters to-day. She has lost one of her most esteemed citizens, — him whom she respected for his public spirit, his pure character, and his daily life, — him for whom she mourns as one that is dead. But what continuance of character and of example will be his! What ages will partake of his liberality; what succession of children will cherish his memory; what generations of men and women will owe to him higher, richer, happier lives!

I have mentioned some indications of a revolution now in progress, thus far proceeding by constitutional methods and without shock to well-regulated sensibilities, which has already shifted the power of government from the few to the many, shaken the partition walls which divide sects, popularized science, art, and literature, impaired personal and social prestige, and led to popular organization of forces once wielded by individuals, — a revolution which, though pending for centuries, was dimly seen in its approach and imperfectly apprehended in its results or in its tendency, — a revolution which, as I have said, may prove to be the most momentous in recorded history.

This revolution is contemporaneous with causes in operation which have diminished the agricultural prosperity, reduced the population, and clouded the future of our New England towns.

What then? Is it expected that free public libraries will rectify whatever is amiss in society or arrest the operation of economic laws? Certainly not. But may we not reasonably hope that they will take the place, in part at least, of forces fallen into decadence; that their establishment will be in conformity with a manifest intent of the people to organize themselves into all those forms of instrumentality which may promote intelligence, virtue, liberty, and equality; that the successful organization of the people for the maintenance of free public libraries will lead to their organization in all departments of human interest, and demonstrate that the whole people, thus organized, are wiser than any fraction of the people, however wise or cultured or virtuously disposed; and that, in making science and literature free and accessible, one step has been taken towards equalizing the conditions which enable all to enter into and enjoy those privileges to which all are entitled, and which, when entered into and enjoyed, become a force for the development of the industrial, intellectual, and moral resources of the community?

New England holds the graves of the ancestors of no inconsiderable part of the people of the United States; and never can her prosperity be a matter of indifference to their posterity, even in remote generations. They will come hither on pious pilgrimages; nor to them will her hills and mountains, her pure air and beautiful rivers, be less attractive by the presence of free schools, free churches, and free public libraries.

I have, I trust, no disposition to magnify the importance of free public libraries; but there are some facts, in my judgment, which have not been duly considered, and to which I shall presently advert, tending to show that the power of literature for the development of exact and productive thought, and for inspiring sentiments which go to the making of a great people, has not had a fair trial in New England.

At the dedication of the new library building at Dartmouth College the other day, I gave some reasons for believing that great libraries at the centres of art, science, and literature will, under the conditions of our American life, probably be powerful incentives and agencies of our progress in those departments of thought and achievement; and I now ask your attention to the fact that the present activity, in which our best critics discern a literary revival, is coincident with the diffusion of literature within the last forty years *among the people*, and that with its wider diffusion by the means of public libraries in all our towns we may reasonably expect even more gratifying results. This calls for a brief review of the literary history of New England. And if you listen to it without surprise, it must be because you are better informed as to the facts than I was when I began to look into them. The New England born have from the beginning been an educated people ; and it has been generally supposed that their literary culture was up to the level of their general ability and intellectual training. I think the fact is otherwise. Neither Pilgrims nor Puritans were literary people, nor with a few exceptions were they highly educated people. They were mainly English farmers living remote from literary centres, and having neither means nor disposition to go beyond the English parochial education of those days. At their emigration they were led by some very able and learned men, — graduates of Cambridge and Oxford, — whose studies were chiefly Biblical and polemical, and whose culture had been classical rather than English. There is no evidence that they quaffed at Chaucer's pure well, or had the slightest acquaintance with the dramatists of the Elizabethan period. Nor would this have been likely with men who regarded much of that literature as licentious, some of it even as blasphemous, — to say nothing of Shakespeare's floutings of the Puritans and Brownists, — and all of it as idle for clergymen absorbed in the great Puritan Reformation, or in deadly conflict with Laud and the High Commission, — idle for those ejected from their livings or fleeing from the processes of the Star Chamber, with no place to lay their heads. That was no time for such men to lend their ears — even if they had not, like Prynne, left them in the pillory — to Marlowe, Shakespeare, Jonson, or Beaumont and Fletcher. This likelihood is made certainty by the absence in their writings of quotations from these authors, or of allusion to them.[1] They are not known to have had a single copy of either in their new homes, and how deeply they had quaffed at their stimulating fountains while in the old home may be guessed if we read the Bay Psalm Book version of these Oxford and Cambridge graduates by which they displaced the comparatively sublime and poetical renderings of Sternhold and Hopkins.

So was it with the first emigrants ; with their children of the first and second generations, it was worse.[2] We have their poetry, and from the lists of their books which have been preserved we know what they read, — Latin poets, polemical divinity, history, public law, commentaries, and concordances. Before 1700 there was not in Massachusetts, so far as is known, a copy of Shakespeare's or of Milton's[3] poems ; and as late as 1723, whatever may have been in private hands, Harvard College Library lacked Addison, Atterbury, Bolingbroke, Dryden, Gay, Locke, Pope, Prior, Steele, Swift, and Young.[4]

As we approach the American Revolution, we find a better state of things ; but even then, as the gravity

[1] The earliest quotation from Shakespeare found in the series of Massachusetts Election Sermons is by Zabdiel Adams in 1782 ; and that is a misquotation.

[2] J. W. Dean says of Michael Wigglesworth's library, " Of classical literature there is little, and of English *belles-lettres* nothing. But what will excite most surprise is the dearth of poetry." — *Memoir of Wigglesworth*, 2d ed., 130.

[3] Doyle's *English in America*, ii. 488.

[4] Palfrey's *History*, iv. 384 n. ; v. 318 n. ; *Memorial History of Boston*, i. 455.

of their situation would lead us to expect, scholars were devoted to ecclesiasticism, politics, and constitutional law rather than to literature.[1] They had Shakespeare and Milton; but so little in popular demand were these writers that the first was not reprinted in New England until 1802–1804, nor do I find the second until 1796, though it was found twenty years earlier in Philadelphia.[2]

The splendid outburst of English song in the first quarter of this century found no echo among our New England hills. Exceptional communities, like that of Brattleborough, doubtless there were; but the average literary taste was not high for a people educated and trained to habits of close thinking on some subjects. Joel Barlow, Timothy Dwight, and Mercy Warren[3] adequately expressed the poetic feeling of New England, — and in such poetry! The literature of England, as a whole, was a sealed book to them. They were an English speaking people in the nineteenth century without Richardson, Fielding, Smollett, Frances Burney, William Godwin, or Jane Austen, or the poets later than Cowper. Of French and German literature they knew nothing until long afterwards.

But let those who can speak from observation compare the literary furnishing of a New England village about 1830 with that of the same village in 1850. At the former period there were in many country villages small collections of books, without literary value; but in the homes of prosperous yeomen, mechanics, and tradesmen there was little native fiction,

[1] Brougham's *Colonial Policy*, i. 64.

[2] Mr. James M. Hubbard, formerly of the Boston Public Library, reminds me that several plays, among them "*Hamlet*" and "*Twelfth Night*," were printed in Boston in 1794.

[3] Tudor's *Life of Otis*, 23.

save "Eliza Wharton" and "Alonzo and Melissa;" and few English reprints, save "Robinson Crusoe," "Charlotte Temple," the "Scottish Chiefs," and "Thaddeus of Warsaw;" while their poetry, if any they had, was Young's "Night Thoughts," Thomson's "Seasons," Pope's "Essay on Man," Cowper's "Task," and, occasionally to be seen, "Paradise Lost." This was excellent reading, of course; but they had nothing of Coleridge, Wordsworth, Shelley, Keats, or, save surreptitiously, Byron,— those whose song enriched English literature, and stimulated the thought of their English brethren to a degree and in a direction before unknown.[1]

This dearth of literature was less extraordinary than the limited range of their thought outside of theology, politics, and economical affairs, in which, it is but just to say, they have seldom been surpassed or equaled, — certainly not by the present generation. The fact is that down to that time they had lived under exceptional conditions. Remote from those influences which on their native soil had developed the songs, the folk-lore, and the fairy tales of the common people, remote also from the literature of the race, and engaged in conflicts which engrossed all their faculties, they were obliged to await more favorable conditions for taking up and carrying forward its literature. The result of this state of things could hardly fail to appear in the culture and literary product of New England life; and it is no marvel that the people did not keep pace with their kindred in the old home who at the same period were producing a literature in all departments which compares favorably with that of any age.

[1] Henry Adams's *History of the United States*, i. ch. 3.

A change in the people — for I am not speaking of literary centres or of exceptionally favored individuals, nor do I wish to be misunderstood on this point — was apparent as early as 1850, and has become more marked with each succeeding year. Now books are everywhere; no cottage so poor as to lack them; thought is free, discursive, and beginning to be productive. There is movement in the tree-tops. The sun is up : it shines on the prairies; it gilds the great mountains, and rises where our sun descends, on the shores of the Pacific. The heavens are flooded with light. A new world of thought is opened, and the land is stimulated to its investigation.

This change must be accounted for. No doubt the causes are many; but it is noticeable that it began to appear simultaneously with the extraordinary activity, forty years ago, of the great publishing houses of Boston, New York, and Philadelphia in their reprints of the best English authors and reviews, in which, almost as soon as our kindred in rural England, we read the brilliant essays of Macaulay, Carlyle, Jeffrey, Brougham, and Mackintosh. Now I hope you will believe that this revival of the literary spirit among a people who claim Shakespeare and Milton as theirs is due in part at least, though only in part, to the dissemination of good literature. The abundance of books stimulated the multiplication of libraries; libraries, the increase of books; and both, of reading; but all to what good end ? It is a fair question; indeed, it is a wise one. In considering the value of books as a productive force in the creation of a genuine literature sprung from the soil, — and none other can be genuine, — I am, I suppose, committed to a favorable opinion of them, since it is with them especially that my life is occupied; but I hope that I am not unmindful of the danger of their indiscriminate use, or of a too slavish reliance upon them for inspiration, for substance, or for form of literature. Victor Hugo asks : " What has the human race been since the beginning of time ? A reader. For a long time he has spelled; he spells yet; soon he will read. . . . Henceforth all human advancement will be accomplished by swelling the legions of those who read. . . . The human race is at last on the point of spreading the book wide open." In this newly acquired faculty of reading, and in legions of readers, and in books wide open, Victor Hugo discerns the hope of the world; and at these Coleridge stands aghast. We will endeavor to be more rational than either.

After all that can be said in favor of disseminating good literature among the people, why not leave it, as most other things are left, to the operation of economic laws ? If the people want books, they will have them; if not, why force them to read ? In the first place, the reasonable desires of many people are in excess of their means ; and in the next place, books aggregated and easily accessible have a power denied to them when dispersed. A library well selected and wisely administered is an organism with a life and purpose of its own. Such an organism rises here under the potent wand of Mr. Brooks. To it flock the mighty spirits of the past, — spirits mighty by their knowledge and by their wisdom, poets mighty by their gift of song, — and to it will flock those who in the future contribute to the instruction or delight of mankind, and here will dwell wisdom and beauty to enrich with wisdom and beauty all who shall come hither.

I have said little, nor do I intend to say more, in

respect to the obvious advantages to be derived from
free public access to a large body of excellent reading, either for instruction or amusement; nor to dwell
upon the fact that free public libraries may be justly
regarded as the complement and crowning glory of
our free common schools.   Granting all that may be
said in behalf of the dissemination and free use of
good literature, I confess that I am more solicitous
about the likelihood of its stimulating that original
thought of the people which will find its expression in
literature; and all the more solicitous am I, because,
when compared with what we have done in theology,
speculative thought, jurisprudence, constitutional politics, and science, the product of our imaginative literature is chiefly conspicuous by its absence.

What, then, may be fairly expected of free public
libraries in stimulating the production of an original
literature?   The literature of New England thus far
presents three phases, two of which, like "the new
moon with the old moon in her arms," are contemporaneous, while the third is like that orb risen just
above the horizon.   The first, not copious but rich in
quality, expresses the homely genuine thought and
feeling of New England people, — the outcome of
secluded life among her hills and valleys; the second,
the result of the high culture of exceptional, not representative, men and women, though pure in color,
excellent in form, and of high literary merit, expresses
little save the sentiment of its authors; while the
third, richer than either with the thought of the people stimulated by literature disseminated among them,
and now united with the lately inspired feeling of nationality, gives promise of a genuine native literature.
In the creation of this literature springing from the

people — and none other is worthy of the name — I think our public libraries are to have an important influence.

If literature is to have the stimulating and productive energy in the future which I have claimed for it during the last forty years, augmented by its concentration here in a living organism, let us consider with what purpose we ought to repair to it, and what and how we ought to read. This library is primarily a literary institution, designed, as are all such institutions, to endue the people with learning and wisdom and the sense of beauty, that they may become a fountain from which shall flow learning and wisdom and beauty in unending succession.

No literature other than what is the sincere expression of genuine thoughts and feelings which the race recognize as their own is likely to have continuance or essential power. Form, expression, and graces of style change and fall away ; substance alone endures.

Under the circumstances which produced much of our own literature serious defects could hardly have been avoided. Let us recall the worst that has been said of it; since for our purposes the worst, in its uncompromising form, is better than that balanced judgment wherein truth is found. It has been said, then, that our literature as a whole is not the outcome of earnest literary life, that it expresses no deeply seated national sentiment, that it has been inspired by no great occasions moving the national heart, that it came in answer to no call, but is the result of a "Go to, let us make a literature;" and that its garb, in the absence of a national costume, is a copy of foreign fashion-plates, — a study of old clothes! [1]

[1] See W. J. Stillman in *Atlantic Monthly*, November, 1891, 689, 691.

The grain of truth in this sweeping judgment is no doubt this, — that our literature lacks sincerity; and if so, then it is you and I and such as we who must bring about a different state of things. A genuine literature expresses the genuine feelings of the people from whom it springs. It is sincere; it has a purpose, and it is subject to verification.

We have, or are soon to have, a library ample for all reasonable uses. To the wisdom of the past it will add the wisdom of the present. What should we learn from it? Perhaps, in this day of unrest, of unsettled opinions and uncertain looking forward into the future, we desire most of all to know how life, with its problems which perplex us or strike us in a certain way, has struck another wiser than we are. If he has written a sincere book, we should be in a fair way to know. It may be history, epic, drama, poetry, or song; no matter which, provided the thought and its expression be sincere. Sincerity in a book or work of art is no less admirable than in a living soul, and it is no less rare, — absolute sincerity, no concealment of essential thought, no posing for effect, no words for rhetoric. Therefore for my own welfare I shall read only sincere books; and so ought those from whom may be expected the future literature of America; and so ought those whose lives will go to form the national life and character, out of which that literature — if we are to have one worthy of the name — must spring. My "Hundred Best Books," other things being equal, would be the hundred most sincere books.

Now that the people are the governing force, and are more and more shaping public sentiment on a great variety of subjects, they should not only be sincere, but well and accurately informed. Our education, politics, and literature within the last generation have been somewhat sentimental and sensational, and with this result, — that our best thoughts and our best books are lacking in accuracy; and accuracy, it must not be forgotten, is required of a song as much as of the multiplication table. There are books — such as Homer, for example — which tell us in the most splendid poetry, but none the less accurately because in poetry, how people lived and what they thought and how they felt three hundred or three thousand years ago; and there are others, well enough as poetry, which place such matters in a false or inaccurate light, and should therefore be avoided. A little exercise of the critical faculty and of common sense will enable us to say what books are sincere and accurate. So I would select for my reading accurate books, as accurate and as sincere as a dictionary. I know some very wise people who use books as they use dictionaries, and why not? Your library, in multifariousness and completeness of knowledge, will be not unlike a dictionary; and that is one advantage which a public library has over a private collection. From sheer necessity we must select from the great mass of books those most to our purpose. Why not select such parts of each? We go to a dictionary with set and definite purpose to find accurate, sincere answers in respect to some particular word, — not ten words or twenty words, at the same time. What would be more rational than to use other books — as histories, poems, or songs — in the same way? There is high authority for something like this. I once saw a course of study drawn up by Rufus Choate for a law student. It contained few entire books, but parts

of some volumes, and even a single chapter of others.
I am sure that I shall not be understood as recom-
mending reading without a well-considered plan. I
am far from that, and so was Mr. Choate. Formerly
at the Dane Law School at Cambridge a course of
legal study embraced a long list of books; now it is
a list of topics to be studied in all the sources of information.[1] Indeed, this method of reading, so far
from being desultory, is particular and close, and
valuable in its results; and quite as much so in the
previous preparation it implies by way of self-examination. No one, unless he is indolent, goes to a dictionary until he has exhausted the resources of his
own memory; and so no one should read a book without first asking, What do I desire to know on a given
subject, and what do I already know? There is no
book to which this may not be applied; nor is there
any way save by this directness of aim and sureness
of purpose by which we can come into direct com-
munication with the great souls among the dead.

I think this must be the true use of books, because
it brings to pass the purpose of their writers, — of
those sincere writers who have something to say. It
also brings to pass another thing of scarcely less
value. It teaches facility of access to them. One
would hardly say that it costs as much to get at the
thoughts of a great mind as it did to produce them;
but it would not be altogether absurd to say something like that. How many lives have been given to
the study of Homer; what generations of men have
been sounding the depth of Shakespeare's thought,
and how many ages will pass before the depth will
be reached! No one ever partially penetrated the

[1] H. B. Adams's *Life and Writings of Jared Sparks*, ii. 304.

recesses of Shakespeare's mind without acquiring something of his penetration; no one ever ascended the height which Milton trod without becoming suffused with the glory which rested upon his head.

If one object of reading is to bring ourselves into relations with minds broader and richer than our own, another is to bring ourselves into harmony with mankind, or at least our countrymen, with whom we have agreed to live and to work for the perfection and defense of democratic institutions, and to refute Coleridge by showing that democracy can think, — think broadly, deeply, and wisely; that it can feel and aspire, delight in visions of glory, see all that poets have seen, and imagine and express all that artists have conceived or wrought by form or color.

To this end I would read those books which are not only sincere and accurate, but those which treat subjects with breadth of view. At best our thoughts are cramped, narrow, and prejudiced, and we should court familiarity with opposite qualities and tendencies.

I have selected from the many desirable qualities of books those which appertain to greatness of character, without which we cannot become a people great in affairs, nor learned in the sciences, nor cultured in the arts; but with these qualities, united to the genius of the English race, and to what our Celtic brethren contribute to the common stock, a free, equal, educated, and cultured people, we may revive the glories of the best ages.

The people have come to the front; and who are the people? Certainly not alone the ignorant, the debased, and the spoilers. They include all the wise, the cultured, and the righteous as well. The real democracy, thus made up, must prove its right to stay

at the front.   Not less than kings and hierarchies
and aristocracies in the past, we in the present are on
trial.   If we allow any great interest of humanity to
fail, — if in our hands religion, science, art, or literature fall into decadence, — we must give way to those
who can save them ; because human nature is stronger
than democracy, and so is religion, and so are those
indestructible, unconquerable principles by which the
race aspires and achieves.

But there will be no failure, though not unlikely
there will be some confusion until democracy — its
old leaders gone — learns to lead itself.   To this end
literature must be popularized.   What has been written for the few must be rewritten for the many; it
must be disseminated.   Mr. Brooks has done his part;
we must do ours.

These are my last words.   They were written at
the midnight hour and laid aside for the morning;
and when the morning came Mr. Brooks was dead.
Imperfect and inadequate as they are, I cannot
change them.   They and the subject of them are now
before another tribunal.   That which concerns us
remains, with day of grace.   When the shadow of the
great mystery falls upon us, as it has fallen upon our
friend, may there rise up as great a cloud of witnesses
who will say of us, as we say of him, " He has done
his part " !

IMAGINATIVE LITERATURE IN PUB-
LIC LIBRARIES

ADDRESS AT THE DEDICATION OF THE WOODS MEMORIAL LIBRARY
BUILDING, BARRE, MASSACHUSETTS, DECEMBER 30, 1887

ADDRESS

AT THE DEDICATION OF THE WOODS LIBRARY, BARRE

His Excellency has said that he came up here from the capital to-day at some personal inconvenience, by which he means, as I conjecture, that he is busy just now in writing the message which he will deliver to the General Court next Wednesday, when he enters upon his second term of office as Governor of the Commonwealth. We all read His Excellency's inaugural address last year, and remember the commendations it received from all parties; and so we have high expectations regarding what he may say next week. But when we consider that about the only things the Congress of the United States and the legislature of Massachusetts do not attend to, are precisely those matters which the President and the governor, each in his jurisdiction, seriously urges upon their attention, it raises a question whether the governor could not use his time more profitably to the people, if, instead of bestowing it on a message, he devoted that portion of it which a message costs to making throughout the Commonwealth just such practical, common-sense talks as he has given us to-day, to which everybody eagerly listened and will doubtless give heed; and if so, Barre, already one of the most beautiful of towns, will become still more interesting and better qualified to take up and carry forward the civilization she has received from wise and cultured ancestors.

We have heard with instruction and pleasure the most excellent address of Judge Aldrich, in which he has treated such topics as the occasion suggests, with a fullness and precision which leave nothing to be added. I see no reason, therefore, why I should go over the same ground. Let me, rather, take up the pregnant suggestion which fell from the lips of the president of your Association in his opening address. He said in substance that there are scattered throughout the country perhaps hundreds of people, natives of Barre, who in their distant homes still hold the place of their birth in affectionate remembrance. This is as it should be; for, next to God and our parents, we are most indebted to the place where we were born for that which goes to make up ourselves, and which, of however little account it may be to others, is everything to us, and on no account to be exchanged with another, however gifted in mind, in person, or in fortune. For had the eyes of those who are Barre-born first opened to the light of heaven in some other place; had they elsewhere first beheld the phenomena of nature, either in their ceaseless round or in those sudden and occasional manifestations which impress us deeply in tender years, — they would have been in some respects different from what they now are; and something less, unless you have proved more insensible than I believe you have been, to the influences of hills and valleys not often surpassed in their beauty; or to air than which none is purer; or to skies than which none are fairer.

Yes; all these influences have entered into the life

and character — into body, soul, and mind — of all born here, moulding, transforming, and building up what we call character, not only in individuals, but in society as well, — that which marks the New Englander wherever he goes, and has given a name to New England towns in all generations.

Now, unless I misconceive, or greatly overestimate the nature and power of this influence of locality upon us in the formative period of life, you natives of Barre are greatly indebted to the place of your birth. To other towns, to which some of you have gone in quest of fortune, you may be indebted for fortune, for honors, public or social; but to Barre you are indebted for no inconsiderable part of those qualities which, if you lacked, you would willingly purchase at great price.

One of those whose good fortune it was to have been born here in Barre; one who acquired here those qualities of which I have spoken, and who, carrying them with him into a wider field of action, in due time became a member of a great commercial house known in two hemispheres for the prompt discharge of all its obligations and for fair dealing with all its customers, to-day returns bearing gifts. Partaking the honorable sentiments of his house, and moved by a sense of the obligations to which I have referred, this gentleman has, in my judgment, taken a most excellent way of recognizing his duty to the place where he was born and in which he was favored by those influences which did so much to form his character and guide his life. He has established a free public library for his native town. Let us consider what that imports.

Had Mr. Woods so chosen, instead of establishing a library, he might have created a fund the income of

which should be devoted for all time to the purchase
of books to be distributed among such families, or individuals, as found it impracticable or inconvenient
to purchase books for themselves. In some respects
such a plan would be quite as economical and would
result in a dissemination of literature quite as wide as
could be obtained through the instrumentality of a
library. But it would not be a public library, which
possesses manifest advantages over such a plan ; and
the advantage would be even greater, were Mr.
Woods's fund ample to furnish, for all time, the books
needed for the nicest research or to gratify the most
cultured taste in any department in learning.

What is a public library? It is an organization the
power and influence of which far transcend the power
and influence of all the separate volumes which compose it, just as the power and influence of a Christian
church, for example, are more than the pious and devoted lives of its members. It has organized life. It
has corporate existence. It lives and breathes ; has
sentiency and purposes. It may be immortal, and
each year added to its life adds to its power. Mr.
Woods may feel well assured that, so long as governments endure and municipal bodies perform their
functions, from yonder library, established by his
beneficence, will proceed influences which will promote
the welfare of the whole community of which Barre
is made up, arouse the aspirations of individuals, and
afford them the means for attaining higher, richer, and
happier lives ; and all this, not for one generation
alone, but for unending generations. Such is the enviable power of wealth when used with intelligence
and sanctified by right disposition.

And now a few words in regard to its administration. I hope that everywhere in our country, and so here, will be recognized this fact — that all our institutions, in order to bring about these most valuable results in moulding the character and habits of the people, must substantially represent the public sense of the communities in which they are established. Better far to endure the consequence of some mistakes than have it otherwise. Like our schools, our churches, our politics, and our social life, so our libraries should find their countenance and support in the life of the people. They must be trusted, and we must speedily get rid of the notion that they cannot carry on the government. Within a few years the people have come to the front, and they have come to stay and to govern. And in the long run they will govern wisely; but by the people, I mean the whole people; not alone those who are ignorant, debased, or vicious; but also the wise, the prosperous, and the well-disposed.

There is another subject on which I wish to say something. The orator of the day has spoken of the reading of fiction, a habit now so much in vogue; and I wish that I may speak with discrimination and precision, so as to convey my exact ideas on that subject. I have great faith in imaginative literature, when properly chosen, to refine and elevate. I do not, I trust, undervalue science, history, or philosophy; but, owing to the circumstances of the planting of New England, and the subsequent life therein, its people are fairly " up," as we may say, in those departments of human thought. But there is a vast realm which lies just below the range of those feelings by which we may commune with God, and just above the world of sense, — I mean the world of the imagination, — into which, as a people, we have never very fully entered, either by our literature or by our daily life. The result has been that our notions in respect to the beautiful, either in art or in literature, are very crude, and our attempts to realize them very unsatisfactory. Now, our progress in this ought to keep pace with our undeniable progress in the practical arts, in science, in invention, and in the application of politics to affairs. Is there any good reason why it should not? We are sprung from a race which has wrought great things, — nor is there any greater in the realm of the imagination; a race which calls Chaucer and Spenser and Shakespeare and Milton its own. And if we are in danger of falling behind our kindred in the old home; and, especially, if we are in danger of falling into materialism and of thinking too exclusively, "What shall we eat, or what shall we drink, or wherewithal shall we be clothed," then it is time to call a halt in this headlong race for material things, and give more attention to those matters which serve to bring on the life which lives by the spirit. And we shall do this, unless we are willing to see the glories of our ancestors and of our kindred beyond the sea fade and go out on New England soil.

Were it in my power, therefore, I would institute such a system of education, both public and private, as would develop and bring into their legitimate use those powers which serve to raise us above, so far above, the material world that we may understand and enjoy the world of the imagination. And in such a system a free public library would hold an important place. Within its walls ought to be found, not only alcoves for history and science and philosophy; not only for forms of the literature in which Shakespeare and Milton reign supreme, but also for the great romancers and novelists, who have explored the recesses of human nature, made us familiar with life, and added to the sum of human happiness by leading us into the fields of imagination. I would, therefore, have libraries so administered, and their funds so applied, that while they contribute to the dissemination of knowledge, they should at the same time open the fountains of imaginative literature which seem to be in some danger of drying up among us.

I am the more concerned about this when I consider that imaginative literature is the only province of art into which the circumstances of life on this side of the Atlantic permit us to enter and to live in that full and free intercourse which makes it a productive power. The sea rolls between us and those great masterpieces of plastic and pictorial art which are the delight of all who behold them and the despair of all who attempt to reproduce their essential qualities. But though none of us shall ever behold the glories of the Temple, and but few the remains of the Parthenon or the great cathedrals or galleries of Europe, which have done so much to keep alive the spirit of art among the people of the old world, yet we, as well as they, may hear, if we will, the songs of the Hebrew poet and the sublime epic of Homer and the tragedies of the great dramatists. Let us gather them, then, into yonder hall, with the best which the world has since produced of imaginative literature, so that all who enter it in this or in succeeding ages may come in contact with the richest thought and the most refined and elevated feeling of those great men who, in all ages, have lived in the spirit and wrought by its power.

Ladies and gentlemen, Mr. Woods has conferred a great benefit on your town. This he has done in discharge of the debt he incurred by being born in a place singularly favored by nature, and reared in a community of noble men and women who have given it an enviable fame. See to it that in the discharge of a like obligation, you so preserve and administer the trust committed to you, that the generations to come shall rise up and bless your names as well as his.